THE FOSSIL 2

JOSHUA T. CALVERT

THE FOSSIL 2

Joshua T. Calvert

FOREWORD

No book is created without valuable assistance. My special thanks this time go to my colleague Ralph Edenhofer, who, as a particle physicist and engineer (yes, there really is such a thing) helped me with one or two scientific questions and never grew tired of commenting on my sometimes-confused ideas. Thanks also to my colleague Drew Sparks, who contributed his input during a brief story crisis. Thanks (again) to Viktoria M. Keller, my tireless test reader, who bravely struggles through each of my raw, draft texts, searching diligently for gaps in logic and boring passages— all within just days, dedicating her time exclusive of every- thing else. I can count myself lucky to have such people at my side.

I hope you enjoy the read!

Joshua T. Calvert   Kuala Lumpur, November 2019

1

FILIO AMOROSA, 2042

Filio stood in the ruined chamber, completely alone. The paramedics and doctors had disappeared through the only entrance and had left her with the half-destroyed glass box, and the bodies of Gould and the man in the black suit.

In her hand, she held the tiny globe she had recovered from the room below the glass chamber. It had simply floated in the air as if it had been waiting for Filio to fall through a hole in the floor—a hole she hadn't even seen. She wasted no time in imagining why this had happened, or how it could have been at all possible. It seemed to her as if she were dreaming—confused, yet strangely congruent, and with the vague surety lurking in the background that everything would soon turn out to be just that—merely a dream.

She heard screams in the distance, angry shouts and noise that she could not make any sense of. But she didn't hear any more gunshots.

Next to her, she saw the battered armored door that lay to the left of the hole in the glass box. She turned to one side and looked down at the man in the black suit. The handle of the knife with which Pano had killed him protruded from his left eye. Aside from that and the blood that covered the left side of his face, the stranger seemed strangely untouched. His facial features seemed almost relaxed and his suit practically unscathed.

A cold shiver ran down her back as she shifted her gaze to Peter Gould, who leaned against the wall, his body twisted, a broken gaze on his face. A quiet filled her head, as if, without meaning to, she had simply erased everything that was happening around her. As if, under a bell jar in which time stood still, she stared, one after the other, at the two corpses and the bodies of the slain security men. Her eyes finally remained fixed upon the dark blood in the glass box. As if magnetically drawn to it, she eyed the pool of blood and began to breathe more and more heavily.

The knowledge that one of humanity's most incredible discoveries—a being of such power and wisdom who had survived millions of years—might have been shot dead, stunned her. If she had correctly put the pieces together, Karlhammer and his Human Foundation owed the constant stream of miracles they had developed in the fight against poverty, disease, and climate change to Xinth, who had shared his knowledge with them. Although she did not know much, there was one thing she knew for sure— humanity still needed the help of this alien being.

With a curse on her lips, the bell she had been under shattered, and all the noises rushed in upon her again like a raging storm. Despite its violence, she rose in defiance once she recalled what Karlhammer had promised her and what Xinth had shown her—she had to go to Mars. Nothing had changed, and the Human Foundation had found a way to get her there in the next few weeks. But this would only be possible if this facility were not infiltrated or destroyed. Her purpose was clear.

"I am Filio Amorosa," she growled as she rolled up her blood-stained sleeves and staggered into the narrow hallway. "I've dealt with worse problems."

Once back in the cavern with its many work areas, she took brief stock. Some of the partitions had been destroyed, the bodies of red-uniformed men scattered in the ruins. In some areas, men and women were arguing with each other while others were cowering under their tables, sobbing. Four security guards squatted near the center and supplied one another with bandages. Sounds of wailing and cries of pain came from all directions.

She suddenly swerved into the first work area, a detached quadrangle containing four long workbenches, on which some boards had apparently been manufactured with the help of robotic arms. Under the workbench to the far left, four figures in red jumpsuits were crouching, arms slung around their knees and looking anxiously at her.

"Get up," she said. When no one moved, she repeated louder, "GET UP!"

They hesitated briefly, looking at each other, and then crawled from under the table. Without her having to say anything, they lined up in front of her and looked at her expectantly, even as they gazed wide-eyed at her blood-smeared clothes.

Maybe I'm scaring them. Good, Filio thought. "Does anyone have a radio?" she asked aloud.

"Uh... yeah, we all have one," said a young man with frizzy hair, pointing to a small bracelet on his wrist.

"Good. Signal that there is no longer any immediate danger, and... is there a kind of Control Center or something like that around here?"

"Yes, there's a Control Center!" said a young woman,

whose sweaty blonde curls were plastered around her face. She pointed vaguely to the east.

"Good. Also send a message that the center should be staffed again immediately, if it isn't already. The evacuation must be aborted," Filio commanded, pointing to the woman who nodded obediently and began to speak to her wrist.

Turning to the man, she continued, "Collect all the weapons that are lying around, even those in Xinth's chamber. I don't want anyone to hurt themselves or panic and get any stupid ideas. Bring them all here and put them on one of the workbenches. We might need them later. Understood?"

The man nodded and she motioned him and the other two away. "Get going!"

Once they had left the work area at a jog, the blonde nodded, and Filio exited as well, rushing back into the central aisle between the individual areas. She hurried over to the four mercenaries, who were looting through a first aid kit.

She cleared her throat "What's his condition?" she asked as she pointed to the man who lay stretched out on the ground and was being treated by the others. Apparently, they were not quite sure what to do.

One of them, a man with gray temples and knotted muscles that stretched under his shirt, looked up at her, his brow furrowed.

"And just who might you be?"

"The one in charge here right now," she said curtly, silencing him with a gesture when he was about to respond. "I'm also a doctor, and this man here has been shot clean through the shoulder," she said, pointing at the wounded man. "I can see from here that the bullet missed his coronary arteries, so he can be transported. Two of you should get him to the infirmary as soon as possible."

The other two first looked at the gray-haired man, but he was still gazing at Filio, so she motioned to them. "Get going, or do you want your comrade to bleed to death?"

After one more brief hesitation, two of them picked up the wounded man and carried him away, while the gray-haired one stood up in front of her. "Who are you?"

"Dr. Amorosa," she replied. Then she shook her head and said, "But we'll have time to get better acquainted later. We have more pressing problems."

"I don't know you."

"I don't care. As you have certainly noticed, we have a security problem that we need to fix as quickly as possible, and I just happen to know how we can do that. I also know that we need to restore some order to the chaos here and, as I've just seen, you're not quite there yet. You're welcome to disagree, of course. If you know what you're doing, Karl-hammer will certainly promote you once he's recovered. If not..."

The mercenary seemed to want to respond in anger, but his mouth opened only briefly, then closed again, leaving only a grim expression. They would probably never become friends, but that was of no concern to her.

"So, now that we've sorted that out, let's just do what needs to get done. Are you familiar with the jamming system?"

"I know that one exists."

"Good. Do you know where the engineers and mainte-nance people are who are responsible for it?" she asked.

The mercenary pointed to one of the many work areas. A crane hovered above it.

"Tell them that one of the jamming transmitters has

been dug up and destroyed. It must be the one that is in a direct line between the entrance where the two agents and the soldier were brought in, and McMurdo. The most important thing right now is to get that gap in the jamming field closed. Understood?"

"Understood," said the mercenary. He straightened his armored vest, which sat skin-tight over his muscle shirt, then lifted his rifle from the ground and ran toward the closed-off engineering area he had just pointed to.

"Hey, soldier," she shouted after him. He paused to turn to her.

"Yeah?"

"Your name?"

"Treuwald."

"Thank you, Treuwald." She nodded at him one last time and ran into the eastern corridor, where she nearly collided with a dark-haired woman who had just stumbled out of a nearby door.

"Oops," she said. Both women were able to extend their arms and soften the impact at the last moment.

"Which way to the Control Center?" Filio asked.

The woman frowned briefly before pointing down the corridor. "Third door on the left."

"Thanks." Without another word, she continued down the hallway under the warm glow of the ceiling lights and counted the doors. She stopped in front of the third door and knocked on the cold armored metal.

Nothing happened.

"Is anyone in there?" she shouted, but no one answered.

"Are you looking for someone?" asked a voice from the right, and Filio looked into the face of a young man in a black jumpsuit. He appeared a little hurried as he swiped a keycard through the slot next to the door.

"Yes, this room," she said, pulling the door open and entering before he protested.

"Wait!" he shouted, but she was already standing in the rectangular, unadorned room. Display foils lined the walls, and it contained several desks. There were a dozen feedback chairs that could operate AR devices. Men and women in black overalls were sitting on six of them. They were gesturing frantically.

"You're not allowed to be in here," said the man who had involuntarily opened the door for her.

"Yes, I am. I'm in charge of the Mars mission, and Karl-hammer is on his way to the infirmary."

"What?"

"Karlhammer won't be making any announcements anytime soon, but your colleagues there should already know that," she said, pointing to the occupied feedback chairs. "There's a lot to do if we don't want The Enemy to be able to smuggle in any more agents. And we don't want that, do we?"

"The Enemy?" the young man asked, his eyes widening as if he had just seen the Devil himself. "He was here?"

"Yes. He tried to kill Xinth, and he may have succeeded."

"Xinth? Oh my God." The whole world seemed to be collapsing before the man's eyes, and she had to take care not to make things sound too serious if she wanted to avoid him running away screaming.

"We'll manage it. Now listen..." Filio looked at his name-plate, which identified him as Jonathan Bateman. "Bateman. We must act quickly and decisively, right now. We can get the job done if we work together. Are we going to get it done?"

The young operator nodded, his lips trembling. His eyes were still wide, but he seemed to be slowly calming down.

"Very well, Bateman," she said, pointing to one of the free chairs. "Get started. Can you hear me when you're plugged in?"

"Uh-huh." Bateman nodded eagerly and threw himself into one of the vacant seats, then snatched a set of data glasses from a bracket in front of it and shoved it onto his head.

"What all can you control from here?" she asked, looking at the display foils that covered all the walls. All sorts of camera images, diagrams, and number sequences were flying back and forth, so fast that one could only take it all in with data glasses.

"Practically everything," Bateman replied, seeming much more focused now that he wore the glasses. "Cameras, climate, and atmospheric control, all the electronic devices used by the workforce. Choose something."

"How many staff are there?"

"Eight hundred."

"Eight hundred?" she blurted in surprise. "How big is the facility?"

"A hundred and forty thousand square meters, including all rooms on all levels."

"Good grief," she exhaled, trying to imagine these incredible numbers in the form of actual rooms. She could not do it. Filio shook her head, as if clearing it, and put a hand on Bateman's shoulder. "How many entrances to the pyramid are there?"

"Two that we know of."

"That you know of?"

Bateman shrugged. "Karlhammer was never sure if Xinth ever really told us everything. From the very beginning, he only took us into his confidence a little at a time."

"Okay then, radio the security staff. They'll have a super-visor who is still alive, won't they?

"Yes, Captain Brown. He's in charge of two hundred people."

"Good. Tell him to post a third of his people at each of the entrances. The last third will be split up and posted at the most sensitive points—the infirmary and the Control Center."

"And Level Zero," Bateman suggested.

"Level Zero?"

"Where the Mars Project is located."

The Mars Project, Filio thought. It was tough for her to resist the urge to pump him for more information about that level. She had to remind herself that there were more important things right now.

"Good, then include Level Zero."

Bateman began gesticulating, making pulling and swiping movements with his slender fingers.

"Also send a team to accompany Treuwald, one of Captain Brown's men. He is on his way outside with techni-cians to repair a faulty jamming transmitter. Since it's a transmitter, I assume you can't see which one is defective from here."

Bateman shook his head.

"Very well. Next, we need a team to identify and report who's dead. They should all be collected and placed in a central area. You know better than I where that should be. All medical staff who are not already in the infirmary should go there. There must surely be some staff members that have been specially trained for disasters such as a fire, right? Well, contact them. They should make sure that all the injured are taken to the infir-mary. Staff with first-aid training should also go with them."

"Understood," Bateman said, his gestures becoming a little more emphatic.

"Do we have contact with the outside?"

"Yes, via satellite."

"Has a request for reinforcements already gone out?" she asked.

"Yes, the evacuation order automatically informed headquarters."

"Well, tell them that we need as much firepower as possible. I guess you have more of these mercenaries on the payroll, right?"

"That's correct. But it will take time. The largest contingents are in South Africa and Indonesia."

"How long?"

"Hard to say. For the mobile intervention forces, at least fifteen hours."

"That's a long time," she said, rubbing her forehead with a cold hand. "But that will have to do. The engineers should find a way to barricade the entrances as soon as the team is back from the jamming device. Next, we need to ensure an adequate supply of food and potable water. Captain Brown is to oversee distribution."

Filio looked at the young man and sighed. "Can you connect me to the entire base via a loudspeaker system so that I can be heard everywhere?"

"Yes, that's not a problem," Bateman said absently, continuing his gesturing without pause. "You can speak."

"This is Filio Amorosa speaking. I am currently in the Control Center. The evacuation order has been canceled. An intruder tried to kill the Builder. The intruder was eliminated, but Luther Karlhammer and the Builder are in the infirmary, and the physicians are currently fighting for both their lives. Your safety is not in any acute danger at the present time.

"As to matters of security, you are all to follow and comply with any announcements made by Captain Brown and his staff. Efforts are being made to provide you with medical care. Remain calm and professional."

Filio paused a moment in consideration. What she would say next was a risk, but she had to improvise.

"You are the best of the best—that is why you have been selected for this project. Mr. Karlhammer expects you to demonstrate this professionalism, even now. Our mission down here is not yet over, and we will not let The Enemy hinder us in achieving our goals and ideals. You will receive your orders from the Control Center. Remain in contact with at least one other person at all times and follow all announcements quickly. Amorosa out."

She tapped Bateman, who then ended the connection. "What do you think?" she asked the operator thoughtfully.

"I think it's a stroke of luck that you're here. Whoever Gould's deputy is, he's either had a panic attack or has fallen victim to The Enemy," Bateman said, without pausing his gestures. It seemed to her almost as if she were talking to a robot.

"You don't know who's the number two here?"

"No. It is not as if organization charts were sent out whenever anyone took up their duties. The whole thing is so secret that we all had to provide thousands of signatures, and every long-distance call with family is monitored. Besides, Mr. Karlhammer is not exactly known for delegating authority to anyone at all, unless absolutely necessary."

"Since we're talking about Karlhammer... he told me to

look at some of the records he said he intercepted from the *Mars One* mission."

Bateman's head slowly turned toward her and, with one hand, he raised his glasses high enough so that he could look at her. She didn't fail to notice that his fingers were shaking slightly.

When their eyes met, the young man winced. "I don't know—"

"Sure, you don't know anything," Filio said, raising her voice in accusation. "Can we please do without the charade? I need to know what happened there. Besides, I would hardly know they existed if Karlhammer hadn't said anything to me, would I? Think about it!"

Just as Bateman was about to open mouth again, she pointed a finger at him. "I spoke with Xinth... just before he became unconscious, and what he showed me has to be compared with the data we have from *Mars One*. So, show it to me!"

There was a knock on the door before the operator could respond, and she looked at him inquiringly. He made a gesture, and a razor-sharp camera image appeared on a rectangular area of the display wall showing a tired Pano Hofer standing at the door and staring impatiently into the camera.

"That's Capitano Hofer," she said. "Let him in and show me the damned data."

I have to know, she thought again and again, and this one sentence repeated like a mantra in her mind.

MARS

"Hey Javier," Filio called to her comrade while he was struggling with the maintenance panel. Its red color stood in clear contrast to the white cylinder of the kilopower nuclear reactor that rose in front of the Spanish astronaut like a small advertising column. It was already being covered by the first drifts of sand.

"Huh?"

"How long do you still need?" Filio asked. She looked over to their rover. Its roof of solar cells gleamed in the sunshine, giving the false impression that the atmosphere outside their suits could actually be warm.

"You don't really want to put pressure on me while I'm messing around with a nuclear reactor, do you?" Javier asked over the radio. He removed the faceplate and began making inputs on the small display located behind it.

"Oh, that's just a harmless, little mini-reactor," she responded cheerfully, just as she was interrupted by another signal.

"Hey, Timothy here. The sandstorm to the east has died

down a lot more quickly than expected. We should be getting some half-way decent weather in the next hour."

"Understood, command," Filio said per protocol, watching as Javier shut the panel.

"Everything here is also running on schedule," said Javier. "I think we can easily reduce the inspection intervals a bit."

"No, we will keep to protocol," she insisted. "As soon as we let one thing slip, we'll start letting others slip as well, and that never ends well."

"Whatever you say. Are we driving back?"

Instead of responding, Filio waved him toward the rover, which she had already reached, and hoisted the cockpit door. Once they had taken their seats and had shut out the howling of the cold wind, they set off in a westerly direction.

"Take a look at EDI's navigation data. Make sure that the storm is not still causing interference in the network," Javier said. He sat at the wheel and steered a path over Mars's stony surface toward the base camp, which was located about two miles away from the basalt cave. From time to time, larger boulders blocked their way, requiring him to drive around them and slowing their progress.

"Hmm, it seems that EDI is receiving a signal from the east."

"One of us?" the Spaniard asked.

"I don't think so. It's forty kilometers away," she replied. "Command, Rover One here. Do you see the signal that EDI is indicating?"

"Timothy here. Yes, we see it, too, and have already tried to contact Mission Control, but we can't establish a connection. The atmospheric interference caused by the storm is apparently still too strong."

"Could that be from any of our people?"

"Negative. You are the last ones still out. The rest have already returned to base."

"Maybe a satellite that's crashed?" Javier suggested. "Or perhaps one of our reconnaissance drones has fallen?"

"The signal doesn't match the drone transponder codes, but I can't rule it out," Timothy replied, his voice fluctuating briefly from a bout of static noise.

"Should we take a look?" Filio suggested. "Our onboard system estimates it will take about two hours of travel time to reach the place, and our batteries are fully charged, way more than enough power for this. Since the signal source is located directly under a high cliff, we are in the right place to reach it without detours."

"I'm just looking at the last satellite images. The signal can't be localized precisely to the meter since we still can't establish live contact with the orbit, but unless I'm completely mistaken, it's located near the monolith."

"You mean the rectangular boulder that fell from the cliff?"

"In theory... Yes. Since the last photo taken by the Mars Reconnaissance Orbiter dates back to 2005, it's hard to say," Timothy replied. "Be that as it may, once you've found the signal source, you can also take some snazzy photos of that monolith thing, so that we can make the eggheads at home happy."

"Understood," she responded, then terminated the connection.

Javier turned the rover, steering around a large, brown stone. They drove back east at high speed. The dust storm could be seen on the eastern horizon. It resembled a kind of dark wall—black and grainy, and flickering from the constant lightning. Fortunately, it was not one of the dreaded global superstorms that sometimes covered half the surface of Mars. During these dust storms the Red Planet's fine dust sanded everything smooth and got into even the most tightly sealed devices—thus making field operations almost impossible. Visibility was also reduced practically to zero—objects could not be identified from more than a few meters away.

The lightning was also much more severe than on Earth. In the passing storm, whose trailing end they now saw, several hundred lightning strikes could be measured simultaneously from orbit.

The ride took them past a long chain of hills. Behind them, they could still see the top of the *Mars One* in the rearview mirrors. It stood upright, as it would for take-off, half-deserted. Ever since they had moved to the module base in the volcanic caves to better protect themselves from Mars's violent radiation, it had only been used as a work and research facility.

All mission personnel meticulously participated in caring for their spacecraft because it was their only way back to Earth, which from here appeared little different from the many stars in the sky. It shone a little brighter than the others, but that was about it.

"The signal is being sent on all frequency bands," Filio explained. Each word she spoke was automatically transmitted to EDI at the base, and from there to the satellites in orbit as a backup.

"That would rather indicate a crashed satellite. The integrated recovery barques do that, don't they?" Javier asked. His broadcast voice sizzled and crackled.

"Certainly possible," Filio said, sounding relaxed. "Let's take a look. A short drive won't hurt, and maybe we can get out of preparing dinner."

"Shit, it's our turn today."

"Oh, yeah, that's right," Timothy cut in from the base. "We're all too happy to wait for you. We're not that hungry, anyway. Right, people?"

They could hear laughter and loud remarks in the background. Their voice transmissions, however, interfered with each other, causing static noise.

"How very kind of you. But we're going to examine the signal source very closely," Filio jokingly threatened, and the base transmission switched off again.

"Why do you think we're no longer receiving anything from the satellites? Now that the storm has subsided, they should be responding, shouldn't they?" Javier asked as he steered them across a field of fist-sized regolith stones, rattling the instrument panels.

"Hard to say. Maybe the higher layers of the atmosphere are still too charged?"

"Hmm. I don't know. But we also had a storm the day after our landing. There was some interference, but no loss of contact. Besides, EDI is still broadcasting, and has already fixed their positions by laser. They're still up there."

"Well, obviously one of them isn't," she replied.

"Obviously."

They continued over the red-brown plain of loose sediment, which was whirled up by the light wind. A kind of dusty haze about a half-meter high swirled eastward. It looked like dirty ground fog, and seemed to be almost sucked along by the moving storm front. From orbit, it almost looked as if the Martian surface was trailing after the storm.

They reached the cliff about two hours later. It rose about 400 meters in front of them, northeast of Olympus Mons, near where their station lay below the planet surface. It formed a kind of broken scarp above the plain. Large chunks of rock regularly fell from it and lay like gigantic menhirs at the foot of the heights.

The monolith dominated their sight. It stood there towering, its edges of perfectly uniform length. They did not need a second glance to realize that the structure was not something natural, as was assumed when the Mars Reconnaissance Orbiter transmitted images of it in 2005. At the time, the image resolution, taken from more than 200 miles in space, was too poor to provide any certainty. But this monolith was so symmetrical, and its edges so sharply outlined, that there could be no doubt of it now.

Javier parked the rover about ten meters away, and they got out slowly, almost awkwardly.

"My God," Filio radioed breathlessly. Her helmet caused her voice to echo, which was relayed in her transmission, giving it a ghostly sound.

Carefully, they approached the monolith, which was about six meters high and two meters wide. While Javier held a device forward and read the values from his helmet display, Filio took a step closer and placed a hand on the anthracite-colored surface.

"Hey, why do women always have to touch everything?" Javier asked, catching up with her.

"We don't touch everything," she disagreed. "Only interesting things. That's why so many men don't get any."

"Very funny. The thing gleams, by the way, but only a few dozen millisieverts, which isn't very different from the general radiation values out here. Holy shit, this thing is really here, isn't it?"

"Yes," Filio breathed, barely audible over the radio. "It's really here." She made some swiping movements on the smooth surface.

"No dust on the surface. Nothing."

"A nanonic surface?"

"I don't know. In any case, it must be extremely smooth if not even Martian dust sticks to it," she said, patting herself on her left arm and witnessing a small cloud rise from the layer of brown dirt on her suit. A moment later, the white area on her spacesuit became beige again as dust quickly reaccumulated.

Her head turned again to the seamless material, something that could not possibly exist here.

"I can't believe it," Javier said excitedly as they circled the object and surveyed it from all sides. "We have to get this to the lab to conduct tests."

"Uh-uh," Filio disagreed. "Mission protocols. We can't take anything with us that could pose a danger to the station."

"How could this pose any danger? It's a monolith, and a very flat one at that."

"In itself, it's a danger because it's obviously of extraterrestrial origin. And if my instruments haven't gone crazy, it's exactly minus one hundred and thirty-three degrees Celsius cold, so exactly the ambient temperature, which—"

"We don't know that, Filio," Javier interrupted, looking up to the top of the monolith over which the sun shone on them.

"Yes, that's what it says here." She held up the small display to him, although she knew what he meant. As he shook his head, she sighed. "Who else can have placed something like this here, if not extraterrestrials?"

"The Chinese, maybe? When something improbable happens, the most likely explanation is usually true. Chinese or extraterrestrials, what seems more logical to you, huh?"

"You mean, Chinese who secretly organized a mission to

Mars before we did and without the world knowing about it?" Filio turned to the rover, which stood stoically in the light wind, seemingly unimpressed by the knee-high mist of dust. The contrast between the vehicle—with its many sensor components and the countless inscriptions of different consortia, authorities, and manufacturers—and the absolutely smooth, perfectly symmetrical and uniformly colored monolith, could not have been greater. And yet they shared one essential trait—they both looked artificial. Anyone could tell at first glance that both were foreign to this place.

"Filio to Command, we have found your monolith, but... this is no boulder that just happens to be rectangular," she radioed the base.

The transmission hissed and crackled briefly, then Timothy replied, "What do you mean? What is it then?"

"I... I don't know. But it's definitely artificial."

"Can you send us a photo?"

"Yes, just a moment," she said, holding her arm a little forward. It beeped briefly, then she asked, "Did you get it?"

"Yes... Uh... Yes, Filio, we're seeing it right now. The others are all standing behind me. What the hell is that?" Timothy asked hesitantly.

"It looks like the thing from Arthur C. Clarke's books," someone else shouted into the radio.

"What are we supposed to do with it?" Javier asked.

"We have to get it to the base," Timothy said without hesitation.

"But the protocol—" Filio objected.

The pilot interrupted her. "Protocol? You've got to be joking. This thing shouldn't exist at all, and we're on a research mission," Strickland said. The voice of the mission's head of research sounded clear through the radio, which meant she had pushed Timothy away from the microphone. She sounded excited, hardly able to hide the fact that she was having trouble maintaining control of herself. "It's a sensation. My god. An artifact? What is that? Is there a seam, a button, a recess... anything?"

"Nothing we could see. Javier said that it's giving off a low amount of radioactivity," Filio replied. "I cannot allow it. The mission protocols are clearly—"

"Filio." Strickland immediately broke in and sighed as if she were not nearly 50 kilometers away but was standing right next to her. "This is something we can't ignore. The mission protocols were never formulated for this kind of scenario, the discovery of such an... artifact! We can't just leave it there."

"But we can't transport it," Javier interjected, turning to Filio. They stood there between the rover and the monolith like two tiny white toy figures.

"Please, Filio. We need to examine this more closely," said Strickland, now a little more in control of herself than before.

There was a rather long pause, during which only the slight noise of the wind could be heard, crackling over the radio.

"Very well, you're right," she finally conceded. "Bring the heavy cargo rover, the one with the crane. We still have six hours of daylight, so the solar cells will provide energy. Pack spare batteries. We don't know how heavy this thing is."

Excited chatter from the base could be heard over the radio.

"We're already on the way," Strickland shouted so loudly that Filio involuntarily turned her head to the side, before turning back and looking again at the dark monolith that cast a broad shadow over her and Javier.

"What are you?" she whispered.

Two hours later, the cargo rover reached the site. Strickland and Timothy jumped out and ran toward Filio and Javier with the typical springy gait made possible by Mars's low gravity. From orbit, it almost looked like four little white men in helium-inflated suits were running around in the middle of the red desert.

"That's—" Timothy began.

"—fantastic," Strickland said, finishing his sentence and looking silently at the monolith for a moment.

"I know that this is really amazing, maybe even disturbing." Filio pointed to the black rectangle and then to the cargo rover with its two retracted cranes. "However, we have to get this thing into the base as soon as possible before it gets dark, and our rovers don't have any more juice."

"We'll take care of it," Strickland said immediately, running back to the rover as if she were afraid that Filio might change her mind. When Timothy remained still, staring at the object without emotion, Filio grabbed him by the shoulder. "Get to it, Timothy!"

They brought the cargo rover a little closer to the object. At the same time, Javier drove the second rover west and put some distance between the two.

Filio stood a few meters away and watched Timothy activate the crane control. The two gripping arms looked extremely slender, downright fragile, but they could carry many times their own weight, just like the reinforced frame and the massive roof structure of the cargo rover, which looked like an armored caterpillar.

Four supports extended out sideways and drilled into

the regolith layer. Then the mechanical gripping arms grabbed the monolith on two sides, precisely in the middle of the object. It seemed a strangely brutal act in light of such an important discovery, as if the two were utterly incongruous. Everything about this situation was somehow unreal and downright illogical, like something needed to be drastically different to make it all seem conceivable.

When she saw that the crane was apparently struggling to move the monolith, Filio went over to the other rover. She returned with a handheld device.

"I'll scan the surface with the laser scanner," she announced over the radio, holding the scanner in front of her.

"Yes, take your time," Timothy said from the driver's cab of the cargo rover. "The thing isn't moving one millimeter. I'm already at eighty percent power."

"Very careful. Don't damage the crane," Strickland ordered. She stood to the side, a few meters away. She was motioning, pressing her palms down as if trying to calm the object.

"Hey, people. There's a seam!" Filio looked at her device and signaled Timothy to stop operating the gripping arms. Over his radio connection, she could hear the howling of the servo motors slowly abating.

"Where?"

"On the flat side. It's tiny, so we couldn't see it with the naked eye, but there's a seam."

"There is more than that," Javier said.

Filio and Strickland had to look around briefly until they spotted him on the other side of the monolith. He had just come out of a crouch and held a foldable shovel in his hand. The others came closer and looked at the small hole he had dug in the soil.

"You can retract the gripping arms," Filio radioed to Timothy.

"Why? What did you find there?"

"The monolith... It... It seems as if it continues under the surface, and sideways at that."

"That means it's not a monolith at all?"

"I don't know," Filio admitted, "but as it stands, this part that sticks out of the regolith layer isn't the whole thing. We need more equipment and more time to expose this object, and we need a muon detector. Whatever this thing is, I think it is much bigger than we thought."

2

PANO HOFER, 2042

Filio pulled the data glasses off her head and took a deep breath.

"Well?" Pano asked. He stood next to her, looking with interest at the wide display on the wall in front of them. There, the satellite image of the four astronauts in front of the monolith could be seen from a bird's eye view. The image was so close that it seemed as if the camera was hanging directly over their heads. The resolution was a little grainy but surprisingly sharp.

"It's inconceivable," Filio said, rubbing her tired eyes.

"I suppose you don't mean the monolith?"

"I see myself and know that it's an original recording, but I have no memory of being there and saying all that," she whispered absently.

"It's weird," Pano said, stretching his chin out to scratch his beard. In profile, the thick white bandage over his right ear seemed to glow beside the dark rings under his eyes. "All this satellite data and the radio recordings have been here for three years, and no one has ever known about it."

"He destroyed my life, spawned a whole generation of

treasure hunters, ninety percent of whom have thrown their lives away in search of a dream. States and organizations have plunged themselves into small wars to acquire wreckage just because they didn't know about it."

"He must have had a reason," Pano replied cautiously, throwing a sidelong glance at her that she did not seem to notice.

"Of course he had a reason," Filio growled. "His people must have hacked into the satellites before the mission to be able to control them at the touch of a button. If this had come out, the entire satellite division of the Foundation would have been finished."

"The satellites around Mars come from the Human Foundation?" Pano asked, surprised.

"Yes. In the '30s, they released a new generation of high-resolution satellite camera systems that can use the images to create complex AR holograms. Thanks to compression technology they developed for the data, the packets were small enough to send them back and forth between Mars orbit and Earth with the corresponding delay. Or should I say, that Xinth developed?"

"Since this seems to have been completely new technology, it must have been easy to install a back door." Pano nodded to himself and narrowed his eyes as he looked at the monolith's still image. "Xinth told you about the shipwreck. Maybe he told Karlhammer about it before, and he, in turn, put the signal there so you can find the monolith."

"Looks like it. Xinth obviously didn't know what exactly we would find there. Hortat's ship, yes, but not what that find would lead to."

"Do you think that the monolith is part of the ship?"

"Yes," Filio nodded, "I think that millions of years of

sediment shifts have buried the majority of the ship below the regolith layer. Anyway, it's a miracle that it's still there."

"Why?"

"Volcanoes, quakes, storms—choose anything you want. Mars, like most other rocky planets, is in constant motion. Even in a period of sixty million years, which is pretty modest by cosmic standards, I would have expected the ship to be destroyed by erosion, shifting layers of rock, or material decay. But what surprises me most is that the monolith lay exposed."

Then Filio pointed to the still image. "But I wonder what it is."

"A tail fin?"

"A spaceship doesn't have to be aerodynamic, so it doesn't need a tail fin. "

"Why don't you look at the data?" Pano asked as he tapped the data glasses in her hand with his finger.

"The data's been shredded by interference. The next intact package is several hours old. I'm going to look at the analysis data, but I need a short break," she sighed, put the data glasses on the small desk in front of her, and rubbed her throbbing temples. After a long sigh, she looked over to Pano, who was still staring at the picture, as if it revealed more to him than the naked eye could see. "How are you?"

Pano turned his gaze away from the three astronauts and the monolith and looked Filio in the eyes. He struggled to keep his concern out of his own eyes`, but it was difficult.

"She'll be okay," he finally said, more to himself than to her. It was as if he had to convince himself that he was right. "She'll be okay."

"The operation, it—"

"—it took six hours, and it will take a while for her to come out of the anesthesia. It's been now..." Pano thought briefly, "about twelve hours, and the doctor said that by then we will be able to see whether she can receive a platelet-factory implant. You're a doctor. Is it really that difficult?"

"Well, an operation always places great stress on the body's whole system," she said somewhat evasively. "If she had been sufficiently stable, they would have already inserted the implant during the operation. Enough surgeons were available. This means they preferred the safe option—to wait and see how she recovers from the first procedure. If her condition then permits, they will proceed with the platelet factory. She'll then be out of the woods in no time."

"I hope you are right." Pano searched the astronaut's face for clues but saw nothing but honesty. In any case, he doubted whether she was capable of expressing herself without being very technical or correct. She seemed to him like a woman who had no patience for beating around the bush, and that was obviously also true for how she spoke, even if she did not seem to be as brusque and gruff as Agatha.

"I hope so, too."

"Are you sure it's a good idea to stay here for now?"

"Yes, because there are no alternatives," Filio answered immediately. "There are too many people here for us to fly them out with only three helicopters. Besides, we don't know what to expect in McMurdo."

"And the jammers? Are they working again?"

"At least that's what I'm told. I'll look into that right away, but first I'm going to go through the rest of the data." Filio picked up the data glasses again and eyed them, the corners of her mouth contorted as if they disgusted her. Pano looked into her eyes. It appeared as if she were conflicted, as if curiosity and the desire to flee were locked in a struggle for supremacy.

"All right. I'll go to Agatha and Karlhammer and... to him... and see what the current status is," he proclaimed, giving the German a friendly pat on the shoulder. Although he had known her less than 24 hours, he felt that the incredible events of that day had brought them much closer than most people could achieve even in several lifetimes. It was a profoundly unrealistic feeling, but no one had ever said that emotions have to be realistic. He in particular never had.

Filio nodded and shoved the data glasses onto her head. A moment later, she was already conducting her hands fluidly in the air and operating the virtual control panels of her simulation.

Pano's gaze rested for a moment on her as he tried to imagine what was going through her head as she continued to review the data, without the slightest clue in her memory that could confirm her own presence in them. How did it feel to have to trust a satellite because you no longer believed your own brain?

He turned away at last and left the small control room where walls covered with display foils were lined with desks. A dozen other red-uniformed Human Foundation employees sat at them, working silently, absorbed in their virtual realities. It looked like a scene from a silent movie.

Pano proceeded down a corridor and reached Cavern One, the huge hall with the high ceiling, where he'd heard that Jackson had found the Builder. Later the Builder had, for some reason, been taken to his chamber and the glass box. Another corridor took him to a wide hallway that provided access to six rooms. The metal doors installed in the entrances were so different from the rock that they almost screamed their foreignness.

The first four rooms were reserved for patients of the

improvised hospital ward, the rear two were an operating room and a storage room.

Karlhammer was in the first room on the left. He was being kept in an artificial coma as far as Pano knew. In the first room on the right lay the Builder. In front of that door, just as before the South African's, two gunmen stood and stared grimly straight ahead.

"Has the doctor already been with her?" he asked one of the men. The man nodded.

"Thank you." Pano still had to get used to hearing exclusively with his impaired ear even though he was wearing his hearing aid again. The decision to sacrifice his healthy ear to shoot the man in the black suit was not difficult for him. He had not even thought about it at that moment, nor did he regret it for one second. Fortunately, he lived in a time when there were medical solutions to this problem, even though he would never be able to hear like a human being again. However, he would have time to think about that later.

He briefly knocked on the third door on the left, identified as "Room 3", and carefully pushed open the door.

Agatha was in one of four beds. The other three stood empty. The walls were covered with white panels that housed all sorts of levers and handles. A few monitors beeped behind her head at long intervals, delivering the background noise typical of hospitals—the kind that made people want to run away.

"Hey," Agatha croaked tiredly. Pano came closer in surprise.

"I didn't realize that you were awake."

"That's probably because... probably because I barely open my eyes," she said weakly. He was somewhat uncomfortable with seeing her so defenseless. She always seemed so tough and unflappable. Pano felt like he was looking at a flaw in the universe that he made real merely by noticing it.

"How do you feel?"

"As if I had shot myself in the spleen."

He smiled and gave a barely noticeable shake of the head. "Ah yes, it really is you."

"Because I'm lying here and I'm not dead, I assume you took out that guy in the black suit."

"You can bet your life on it."

"I guess I did," she said with a faint smile. He answered with a wink as he sat on the side of her bed.

"I wouldn't throw you out at the moment."

"Huh?" he asked, confused.

"Out of my bed." She lifted her left hand weakly. The back of her hand was covered with a patch from which tubes emerged that ran up to several bags of liquids hanging above her on poles. "However, it's more because of my condition, not that you should get any ideas."

"Hey, I think I saved the day, so I thought I'd at least get the princess as a reward. That's how every good fairy tale ends," he joked.

"I don't think this is a very good story," she said, slowly. "In a good story, I would still have a spleen, you would still have a good right ear, my brain would have more answers than questions and... well, a window wouldn't be bad either."

"If there is a customer satisfaction form around here, I'll make sure to write that all down," he promised, offering her a sealed cup with a straw. Carefully, he brought it to her cracked lips and stuck the straw between them. "Slowly."

Agatha greedily sucked the lukewarm water and nodded. When he took the cup away, she gratefully closed her eyes and gave a long sigh. "That's better. The doctor said that I'd have a sore throat from the intubation. I can tell you, that was an understatement. It feels like it's been treated with sandpaper."

"That's probably because of the rough words you force through your trachea all the time."

"You are literally begging for a sample," she countered, and they looked at each other quietly for a moment before they began to giggle.

After shaking lightly with laughter for just a few seconds, Agatha raised her hands defensively, which seemed to cost her a lot of strength.

"Laughter... not a good idea," she croaked hoarsely and took another sip from the cup when he held it to her lips again. "What happened? How much time has passed?"

"Twelve hours," he said without hesitation.

Agatha's eyes grew wide before weakness quickly closed them again.

"Filio Amorosa somehow took command, I think," he told her.

"The astronaut with the haunted look on her face?"

"Yes. Karlhammer is one room away. That... alien, or whatever it is, is in the room opposite. Gould, who was obviously the head of this institution, didn't make it. She just started saying what needs to be done, and people have been doing it." Pano shrugged.

"Shouldn't we get out of here?"

"Not possible. If I understood correctly, there is a miracle device in the basement that was about to be turned on until we ruined the whole thing."

"We smuggled in that killer without realizing." Agatha sighed in frustration.

"Yes. Luckily, no one seems to know about that except those who were in the Builder's chamber when that was

you first." The nurse stood with his back against the door-frame so that the doorway was free, showing the hallway outside.

"Can you walk at all?" Pano asked Agatha, looking at her anxiously.

"I think so. Someone helped me walk to and from the toilet before you came."

"Your circulation is relatively stable, but I still would suggest that you use a wheelchair." The nurse pointed behind the bed, and Pano had to bend a little to the side to see the electric wheelchair.

"She suffered a gut shot," he protested.

"Everything's been stitched, the microphage therapy is already underway, and in a few days your colleague will be ready for action again," explained Tim, rolling his eyes as Pano stared at him with his mouth open. The nurse pushed himself from the doorframe and approached Agatha and Pano, then walked around the bed and began moving the wheelchair closer to the bed.

"In a few days? It should take at least a week... and what is microphage therapy, pray tell?" Pano frowned and stood up quickly when the nurse was about to bump into him with the wheelchair.

"Help me," the nurse said to him, and together they hoisted a rather unhappy looking Agatha, dressed only in a white surgical gown, to her feet. They assisted her into the wheelchair, which had padded armrests with small control levers at their ends. Seeing her so helpless irritated Pano, so he looked intently at the nurse, who was strapping her into the wheelchair.

"So?"

"Huh?"

"Microphages? Back to work again in just a few days? How is that supposed to work?" he asked impatiently.

"It must be clear to you that most of the Human Foundation's inventions originated right here, in this place, right? Inventions that Mr. Karlhammer adapts for us humans, with Xinth's help. Microphage therapy is one of them," Tim reluctantly explained.

Taking a step back, the nurse went over and opened a wall panel, fishing out a pure white microfiber blanket. He returned with it and covered Agatha's legs, which were exposed below the edge of the gown and clad in compression stockings from knees to feet. They looked as white as marble. "Microphages are intelligent, programmable cells that are currently multiplying inside your colleague and building a new spleen for her, while others are taking care of waste products—blood, tissue fluid, etcetera. If you want to know more about it—well, I'm just a nurse here and I only understand half of it, in reality."

The young man walked around behind the wheelchair, grabbed the handles, and pushed it forward after Agatha growled in frustration—the chair's control levers apparently did not work. "Mr. Karlhammer doesn't like to wait."

3

AGATHA DEVENWORTH, 2042

Agatha hated feeling naked and vulnerable. The nurse was so impatient that the right footrest of her wheelchair almost collided with the room's door frame. If it had, she would undoubtedly have been catapulted out of her seat and would have needed another operation. She imagined herself lying helpless on the floor, pulling the hospital gown over her back, her buttocks bare. She wanted to ban the image from her head, but it persisted and was uselessly nourished by the feeling of being an old, helpless woman who was being pushed to some kind of audience. Then she remembered the restraints Tim had fastened. She'd likely be reinjured from being thrown against them, too.

At least she wasn't in pain. Whatever she'd been injected with, it worked wonders. At the same time, she disliked the idea of carrying some microorganisms inside her that had been programmed by someone to practice medicine on her all on their own.

What strange things are waiting for us here? she wondered while the nurse pushed her down the hall to the next door on the left. Pano overtook her and went ahead to hold the door open for her.

He's being as considerate as he would be to a disabled person.

"Everything okay?" he asked as she rolled past him.

"No," she said truthfully, then struggled to put a smile on her face as she admonished herself not to be so surly with him. He had saved her life, and he wasn't such a bad guy.

The room they entered was no more spacious than her own, and seemed even narrower. On the right wall, a long glass tube stood on massive feet. Its upper half had been flipped open. A thin haze swirled inside it, making it difficult for her to make out the white stretcher within. Oversized boxes were affixed to the head and foot of the tube, and large displays were attached to the sides facing her. All kinds of buttons were flashing on them.

On the left side of the room, Luther Karlhammer lay on a hospital bed that was exactly like hers. He was covered up to his hips and his torso was bare. For his age—he had surpassed his sixties—he was astonishingly well-toned, although his skin seemed a little pale.

Two physicians in white coats, AR glasses flipped up across their foreheads, stood behind his bed. They cleared their throats and nodded in Agatha's direction as she was rolled in. She frowned when she saw the astronaut Filio Amorosa standing there, too. The scientist appeared wrung out, and the bags under her eyes looked heavy enough to injure her back. Her whole figure seemed bent as if she had just taken a yoke from her shoulders and hadn't yet taken time to stretch her back.

But not her eyes, Agatha admonished herself. *They are still flashing as actively and relentlessly as ever before.*

"Ah," Karlhammer said, smiling weakly after turning his head to look at her. From the middle of his forehead, a kind of white cloth sprang, bloated like a balloon, and stretched around his skull, covering the entire top of his head. Along the sides and back of his head, all hair had been shaved from his scalp. It made her almost feel nauseous when she realized what the white cap was there for. "There you are."

"My missing spleen wouldn't let me come any sooner," Agatha said, shrugging her shoulders, which pulled unpleasantly at her abdomen.

"Be glad that you don't have to lie here with an open skull," Karlhammer said, giving someone behind her a wink. Shortly afterward, Tim brought two chairs and placed them to one side of Agatha. After a brief wave from the South African, Pano and Filio sat side by side and looked at Luther curiously.

"Well, I would be even happier if you were completely healthy, but I guess it could have been worse."

"Oh yes," Karlhammer agreed, trying to nod, which he interrupted as pain distorted his face. After briefly closing his eyes, he opened them again and let out a long breath. "I'm indebted to all of you. Especially to you, Capitano." He fixed the South Tyrolean police officer with his gaze.

"How's that?" Pano asked while he pretended to fumble at his hearing aid because his once-healthy ear was hidden under a thick bandage.

Karlhammer smiled weakly. "I'm serious. You came to get answers and instead saved this entire institution from The Enemy. So, the least I owe you is answers to the questions you raised." He turned to Filio, moving his head very carefully. "We built a device in a secret test bunker under this facility using Xinth's specifications. It will take you and a crew to Mars."

"Come again?" the astronaut asked. Her eyes were wide

open, and her voice sounded almost shrill. "I don't understand."

"We don't really understand either. It's a kind of transport capsule that we've built following the Builder's instructions, without really understanding what we were doing. Xinth has refused to provide us with details as to how it works. But the fact is that it consumes a lot of energy. Our engineers had to install a total of sixty-six FHR reactors before the performance level Xinth required could be achieved."

Pano raised his hand and interpreted Karlhammer's questioning look as an invitation to speak. "FHR reactors?"

"They're small thorium nuclear reactors that are cooled with liquid salt," Filio explained impatiently, gesturing for the South African to continue. Her hands moved to clutch the small metal rail at the foot of the bed as if she needed to hold onto something to keep herself together.

"There are two seats in the capsule and no instrument fittings. We assume that this could be a kind of wormhole generator, even if the performance of the installed reactors does not seem sufficient to us. But since we've never physically observed a wormhole, we can't really say anything about it. The only thing I'm very sure about is that it will work."

"Really?" Agatha asked in surprise.

"Xinth wasn't as generous in terms of his knowledge of technology as you might think. We achieved most of our breakthroughs because he gave us some support and food for thought—the rest was actually accomplished by my employees, and to a modest extent, by me," Karlhammer explained, not without pride.

"A few suggestions for increasing efficiency here, a helpful hint there when we weren't making progress, and an astonishing level of experience in assessing public perception. However, the construction of the transport module, as we call it, was a completely different matter. It took five years to build everything in such a way so that Xinth finally approved it, and that happened just yesterday. Everything about the module virtually screams that we are dealing with a high level of technology that is so far beyond our knowledge that we would not be able to build even build a replica on our own. I brought you here so that you would be the first to go through."

Karlhammer fixed his gaze on Filio, who nodded right away. "However, you should be aware of the risk. We don't know what the module will do, and if—or how—it works. Xinth didn't want to tell us anything about that."

"I think it has something to do with the Twelve-Fold Space," Filio added, suddenly thoughtful.

"With what?" Karlhammer squinted, and looked at his doctors, who shrugged their shoulders in unison.

"The Builder... He... He showed me a kind of vision or memory before he lost consciousness. In it, I saw his fellow beings, or fellow aliens, set out from Earth. In spaceships. He said they had traveled in the Twelve-Fold Space or something like that. I didn't understand it myself, and he didn't reveal anything except the position of the ship that Hortat, The Enemy, crashed on Mars because Xinth had sabotaged it. If your design is a transport module, as he says, then it may have something to do with that."

"Maybe," Karlhammer said. He seemed to be letting what he had just heard melt on his tongue. Then he clicked it, raised a finger, and said, "As much as I would like to hear more about this vision, I have little time before these gentlemen stick me in the Auto-Med tube again," he said as he pointed to the physicians.

Agatha looked at the open glass tube and wondered whether it was one of those prototypes that the Human Foundation had announced as a medical breakthrough for this year's in-house fair in Johannesburg.

Krauthammer continued. "The Enemy will wait a while for his agent, the intruder, to return. Since we are out of the reach of mobile networks or anything else here, that respite could be quite generous, but we cannot hope for it. We do not know how far The Enemy has penetrated the governments of Earth, but the reaction that is still to come will tell us where the center of his power lies. That's why we do not have much time. I've been told that our reinforcements are on the way and we'll dig in here as best we can. However, if the U.S. military, the EU armed forces or the Chinese make their way to us, the future won't look particularly rosy and our window of opportunity will shrink to almost nothing.

"I suggest that you, Filio, get into the transport module as soon as possible and travel to Mars. You two, make your way out of here," Karlhammer said, looking at Agatha and Pano. "I'll give you two pilots who will fly you to the machine in McMurdo in one of our helicopters. You'll transfer there and fly back to America, or wherever you suspect The Enemy is."

"Suspect *where* The Enemy is?" Agatha asked, bewildered. "We've only just learned from you that it exists at all, and if I hadn't seen with my own eyes what this killer who followed us could do, I still wouldn't believe it."

"But you believe it now," Karlhammer insisted, sounding exhausted. "That's the only thing that matters. Find The Enemy and put a stop to him before it's too late and he destroys this facility. It's perhaps the most important instrument that we still have in our infinitesimally small arsenal for the survival of humanity."

"How?" Pano interjected, bending forward. He blew into his folded hands, which he held in front of his mouth as if praying. "How are we supposed to find him? If what you say is true, he has been pulling strings in the background for three years without anyone being able to discover him. And even if we track him down, he may have more killers around him who'll make life difficult for us."

"He's going to have to break cover, because we did so, albeit unwillingly. The Enemy knows now, or will know very soon, that we know he's aware of this place. So, he must act, because he can guess that we will act as well. I will connect you with Workai Dalam. He'll certainly place the not insignificant resources of the Sons of Terra at your disposal. I've also ordered the Foundation board to cooperate with you."

"Very well," Agatha said, waving aside Pano's irritated look. "We'll do it. I've seen things down here that I wouldn't have believed, no matter who told me, and I've seen how that killer led us around by the nose. Even if you hadn't asked us to do it, I'd be damned if I'd just sit back and watch what happens next. I don't like anyone messing with me."

"I can confirm that," Pano said dryly.

"Thank you," said Karlhammer. A long sigh escaped from his throat, sounding a little like a chord from a mistuned guitar. "I have already issued all the necessary instructions. My adjutant, Cho Wayan, will be right here and tell you everything else you need. He'll take over command down here and will speak for me. According to the doctors, my Auto-Med procedure for removing a blood clot will take at least ten hours. I wish all of us good luck."

"We should have started the procedure a long time ago," said one of the two large doctors, raising a critical eyebrow, leaving no doubt as to what he thought of the whole conversation.

Karlhammer made a dismissive gesture and rolled his eyes. "Yes, yes, your concerns are noted."

The doctors apparently took this as an invitation and began to fold down the sides of the hospital bed. An eye blink later, Tim also got moving and began to shoo Filio and then Pano away. Until the nurse returned to Agatha and loosened the brakes of her wheelchair, she watched Karlhammer's bed being pushed next to the tube and electrically raised, and his body being pulled into the tube on the automatic stretcher. As Tim wheeled her out of the room, she twisted her neck to see more, only able to see the lid lowering and two robotic arms inside extending from the two boxes at the tube's ends. Then she was back in the hallway, and the door fell shut behind her and the nurse. The magnetic lock engaged with a short, audible vibration.

"I'll take her from here," Pano said to the nurse, who shrugged, stepped aside, and disappeared into one of the front rooms. Filio stayed with them for a moment and seemed to want to say something, but then turned away.

Agatha loudly cleared her throat, causing Filio to stop.

"Yes?" the astronaut asked as she turned back to face her. Agatha was again struck by her delicate physique and restless eyes.

"I admire your courage," Agatha said, openly pointing a finger downward to indicate the lower level as Filio wrinkled her brow in irritation at the interruption.

"I have to go to Mars," Filio finally replied, and her entire body emphasized the words *have to* in her sentence. She seemed so tightly wound that the contracted state of her muscles alone would have sufficed to keep her upright.

"What is it that drives you so intensely?"

"I don't like being in the dark, and someone has turned off the light by which my former crew and I wanted to change the world. I don't accept that. Whatever happened out there, I'll turn on the light again and find out who it was," Filio explained.

"Then, I wish you and all of us good luck. I have a feeling that we will all still need you to do the right thing up there, Doctor," Agatha said, looking for any disturbing trait in the astronaut's face. She couldn't find one, which alarmed her even more than if she *had* found one. Typically, she found signs of character flaws or intrinsic time bombs lurking in people's personalities in pretty much everyone. But not in Filio Amorosa. That could either mean that this woman was excellent at fooling people, or that she really had nothing else in mind other than uncovering a mystery that had become her personal nemesis.

The astronaut seemed to grow uncomfortable under Agatha's searching gaze, and Filio took a deep breath before smiling and nodding. "I wish you both every success. Stop The Enemy." Addressing Pano, she added, "And thank you again."

"My pleasure," he said, and Filio turned on her heel and hurried at a jog toward the hallway from which he had also come before.

"She can't wait to get into that thing in the basement," Agatha snorted. She shook her head, which precipitated a dull feeling between her ears.

"Ten horses couldn't drag me into that thing," Pano said from his position behind her wheelchair. He began pushing her toward her room. "A technological marvel from the head of a sixty-million-year-old being who didn't think it necessary to explain how the thing works? No thanks."

"So, you'd rather leave the most secret place on earth to

track down an alien who may have infiltrated the most powerful government in the world and subjected it to its will and, uh, take it down?"

"Hmm," he said, pushing her through the door and back to her bed. "If I think about it, I'd rather lie down here with you, share breakfast in bed, and start Sunday with a bottle of beer in my hand. And before you ask... Yes, it's Sunday."

"How nice of you to remember my splendid analysis of your character at our first meeting," she said, winking at him as he helped her out of the wheelchair and into bed.

"How could I ever forget those first charming words you spoke to me? Especially now, seeing you so stunningly well-dressed. I simply lack the strength of character to resist your advances."

"I don't tolerate beer or machismo in my bed. Unfortunately, that eliminates you."

"Please! Admit it—that's precisely what turns you on," Pano teased, grinning from ear to ear.

"That's at least as much of a turn-on as my thrombosis stockings."

"That's..." He looked at her white legs and nodded appreciatively. "Those are rather remarkable specimens."

"Now, just so that we don't have to talk about my stockings anymore, I suggest that you talk to my attending physician and find out when I'll be mobile enough to get out of here. Maybe those microphages can finish their job while we're in a helicopter or a plane."

"Why are you in such a hurry? You have any idea where we can start looking?" Pano asked, sliding her legs under the blanket and pulling the covers up to Agatha's breasts.

4

FILIO AMOROSA, 2042

Filio did not waste any time. She met Karlhammer's assistant Cho Wayan at the Control Center, which she had left half an hour earlier in answer to the South African's summons.

Wayan was a slender man of average height with Southeast Asian features, possibly from Indonesia or the Philippines. His hair was short and smartly styled, and his suit immaculately pressed. She wondered if he had arrived so late because he had needed time to groom and dress.

"You're Mr. Wayan?" she asked, as she closed the armored door behind her.

"You must be Ms. Amorosa." Wayan smiled neutrally and turned in her direction, while the operators behind him gesticulated in the air and took over the entire organization of this beehive in pyramid form.

"*Doctor* Amorosa, yes," she corrected him, and wondered in the same breath why she had done so. Perhaps his groomed appearance had triggered a kind of careerist allergy in her that she had not felt for a long time. Maybe it was the years she'd spent on the high seas among treasure hunters that had made her completely forget how much she disliked people in suits.

"Please excuse me, *Doctor.*" Wayan's facial expression betrayed more amusement than honest regret. She could hardly blame him.

"I have to go to the transport module," she said. The idea that a device built by Xinth and that would take her to Mars could actually be located far below where she now stood electrified her. To her surprise, Wayan nodded immediately and his mouth morphed into a more serious expression.

"Follow me, Dr. Amorosa. Bateman, monitor things here and keep me informed should anything change. Order the pilots to Helipad Two as soon as Dr. Meinhard has given Special Agent Devenworth permission to travel."

Karlhammer's assistant turned back to Filio and pointed to the door. When she did not move, he went on before her with a smile. "You're not an especially easy sort of person, are you?"

"That probably depends on who you ask," Filio said as she followed Cho Wayan into the hallway and then through one of the giant caverns that looked like overturned ships from below. Men and women in red and black uniforms were walking around everywhere, some carrying injured people on stretchers while others were busy with repairs. Filio couldn't imagine how a single man could have done so much damage.

No, that was no man, she corrected herself, and shuddered at the memory of The Enemy's sinister agent.

"Well, if I ask Mr. Karlhammer, he will probably express a great deal of admiration for you. Otherwise, I wouldn't have been instructed to take you to the transport module," Wayan said, raising a brow in her direction. His eyes had a wakeful glow, though he seemed tired, and there appeared to be a hint of criticism in his voice.

Filio was sure that every nuance in the gestures, facial expressions, and language of this cliché of a careerist was well chosen, but she had neither the time nor the desire to decipher it all. After all, the best thing about her career as an astronaut was that she had no career to pursue. Instead, she had endured one of the most stringent selection processes in the world and then had the job. If she had needed to engage in a constant struggle at the ESA in order to climb the salary ladder, or to protect herself against competitors who were always trying to discredit her to their own advantage, she would have gone mad. In a way, she even respected Karlhammer's assistant.

"Probably," she said absently, making room for a squad of mercenaries who walked past them wearing heavy body armor and armed with assault rifles. She hoped the grim-looking group was on its way to the entrance and exit to protect them from further intruders. "I assume you don't agree with his decision?"

"It is not for me to question Mr. Karlhammer."

"Very diplomatic. Who would have expected that?" Filio said laconically. "Can you also be honest?"

"If you want me to."

"Nothing but."

"Well," Wayan threw her another sidelong glance as he turned into one of the many corridors at the end of the cavern, "I was against it."

"Why?"

"Because we had chosen an excellent man for the mission, and he must now remain behind."

Filio sighed. She had usurped someone else's position —again.

"At least you indirectly saved the life of the last astronaut whom you replaced," Wayan said as if reading her thoughts.

"If I understand Mr. Karlhammer correctly, this mission will make it possible for me to save everyone's lives," Filio said. A moment later, they stepped into a rectangular room with walls covered by glass, and proceeded through it to the left of two elevator doors. There was no control panel, but an indicator above showed that the car was on its way to them.

"Doesn't that put you under an extreme amount of pressure?" the assistant asked as they stared at the indicator.

"No," Filio said, shaking her head, "I don't have time for pressure. I know full well that I have to go to Mars, and if you knew what I have sacrificed and lived through over the last few years, you'd know that I would rather die than not have this chance to bring about the best possible outcome."

"I believe you. The question is probably more what you regard as the best possible outcome. Getting to the bottom of the failed *Mars One* mission? A souvenir for your deceased comrades? Revenge for the fact that no one wanted to believe you?"

"I am not interested in revenge any more than I am in public opinion," Filio said, tapping her foot impatiently as the elevator display moved ever closer to the small zero. "I'm interested in The Enemy, in what he has done to us... and in what he still intends to do."

"I heard that Xinth was communicating telepathically with you—" Then Wayan abruptly cut himself off and pointed to the elevator car as the doors in front of them opened. They were barely inside before he said, "Level T, authorization code Z-22-Alpha-89 Cho Wayan."

The elevator started moving, carrying them downward.

A quiet noise accompanied their descent, like a sonorous background melody that had something ominous about it.

"He did," said Filio, picking up where Wayan had interrupted himself. "Has he done that many times before?"

"Only once that I know of."

"Oh?"

"When we found Xinth, he had killed three of the earlier expedition members who had apparently tried to kill him because they were afraid of him. They thought he was some kind of monster. That was shortly after Dan Jackson disappeared, and they searched for him in here.

"Karlhammer was flown in immediately after surveillance camera footage reached him. It was he who was the first to communicate with Xinth when he walked unarmed into Cavern One to confront him. I wasn't allowed in, but I could see when the Builder grabbed Karlhammer's head. The security guards wanted to storm in to save him, but I held them back per his instructions. After a few minutes, Xinth released him, and Mr. Karlhammer told us that Jackson's consciousness had somehow merged with the Builder."

"That sounds... incredible."

"Yes, but it was a good explanation for Xinth being able to speak English immediately, as if he had always been able to," Wayan said, twisting his mouth scornfully. "Well, it seemed to be the only explanation. In any case, the Builder was very cooperative from that point on and spent a lot of time with Mr. Karlhammer. You know the outcome of that meeting."

Filio gave no response, and they continued their way down in silence. After a few minutes, the elevator braked, and the doors slid open.

In front of them was a sparsely lit corridor of bare

concrete walls, which led to a round vault door with a hand-wheel in the middle. At the same time, four square flaps opened in the ceiling above, and on the floor in front of the vault door. Self-firing systems with thick cartridge belts shot out from the recesses and pointed at them. Red lights flashed menacingly on small cameras on top of the barrels, and an ominous electronic buzz filled the room.

"Cho Wayan and Filio Amorosa," said the assistant, without moving anything, not even his little finger.

For a while nothing happened, then the self-firing systems retracted behind their flaps as suddenly as they had appeared.

"My goodness," said Filio, as she tentatively followed Wayan, who moved with surprising calm toward the armored door. It opened in front of them as if a ghostly hand were turning the wheel.

"Our people don't know exactly what they built for Xinth," the assistant remarked. "But they are relatively sure that the transport module is highly explosive. Apart from that, an act of sabotage down here, however unlikely, would be devastating. They don't want to know how many billions the Foundation has diverted to build this device and the facility—not to mention the time and personnel costs. Do you know how difficult it is to make about a thousand people disappear in such a way that no one thinks to look for them?"

"Yes," Filio replied bluntly, and Wayan looked at her briefly before pointing through the circular opening.

She stepped through and into an equally round room roughly the size of a tennis court. There was a lot of activity. Men and women in white coats walked around like bees in a hive, wearing facemasks and carrying analytical equipment. In the middle of the chamber—its all-white floors and walls reminiscent of the interior of a UFO from popular science fiction—stood a platform with two seats.

"That's it? *That's* the transport module?" she asked, stunned. The device looked as if someone had welded roller coaster seats onto a steel platform.

"I assure you, Dr. Amorosa, that the intrinsic qualities this module possesses would excite you," said someone standing at her side. Filio turned to the source of the soft voice and saw a slightly smaller man with sparse hair and a jolly man's belly standing next to her. He was holding an old-fashioned clipboard pressed in front of his chest and smiling at her.

"I'm Cassidy Morhaine, head of the experimental facility and your co-pilot. If you can call it that," he said by way of introducing himself. They shook hands.

"You?" Filio asked in surprise before regaining control.

Cassidy laughed cheerfully and pointed to his generous belly. "Not the typical look of an astronaut, huh? But we're more like planetary walkers, I think. I can walk."

"I hope you can do more than that," she said, smiling to make her words sound less harsh.

"Well, they tried to equip me with a certain amount of intelligence," Cassidy replied with a chuckle, pointing to the small, round platform in the middle of the room. At its base, several technicians clad in blue overalls and bearing tools were at work. "Shall we?"

"Gladly."

"You must have a thousand questions."

"I don't think a thousand questions would be enough to take care of all the question marks in my head," she said, causing Cassidy to laugh once again as they reached the platform. The two seats were made of a black, shimmering material that somewhat resembled a smooth microfiber.

"I have been in charge of the project from the very beginning, and I know more about this thing than anyone else on the planet." He pointed to the platform or, she thought, possibly below it. "But that doesn't mean I know very much. We built it according to Xinth's design, and discovered a new composite material that is even stronger than carbon nanotubes and can be used as a superconductor without any measurable loss. In addition, it's led to an efficiency increase in our magnetic coils of several hundred percent. An astonishing amount of field strength was created by the combination of—"

"Will it work?" she said, interrupting the scientist, who was apparently just warming up.

His smile became a bit brittle. "Well, I very much hope so. Otherwise quite a few hours of my life would have been spent in vain."

"You don't know, do you?" Filio asked, looking closely at the stocky man. His bushy brows danced comically at every word, and his full mouth seemed to be in constant motion.

"What do you mean?"

"I mean what happened up there!"

"Of course I know. There was an attempted burglary or something. We were on lockdown for a few hours after we were first supposed to be evacuated. But now the lockdown has been lifted," Cassidy said naively.

"An enemy agent entered the facility and tried to kill Xinth—he, I mean Xinth, is currently undergoing surgery, as is Karlhammer."

Her future comrade's eyes grew wider with each word she spoke, until Filio feared that they would fall out of their sockets at any moment.

Someone said, "Ahem," and she looked around. Cho Wayan had stepped up next to her and he was giving her a dark look. But his gaze wasn't quite as grim-looking as Cassidy's—the scientist was glaring furiously at Karlhammer's assistant.

"Before you say anything," Wayan said, raising his soft, uncallused hands, "I would like to point out that Mr. Karlhammer himself formulated the emergency protocols, including that vital work areas that have their own protective mechanisms are not to be informed of the cause of any emergency earlier than necessary if it could cause a panic."

"Panic? Surely you don't believe that we would have been so frightened that we would have blown ourselves up here!" the scientist barked, obviously growing increasingly agitated. To Filio, he seemed to resemble a flesh-and-blood personification of Rumpelstiltskin.

"Well, I think you both can get along without me from here on," Wayan said with a pained smile. "I'm needed in the Control Center."

Filio nodded cheerlessly and turned back to her co-pilot. "When do we start?"

"You just can't wait, huh?" Cassidy asked, looking thoughtful as he glared after Karlhammer's retreating assistant.

"No. I... the Builder... he showed me something."

"Xinth?" Cassidy set his clipboard down and grabbed her by both shoulders, turning her to him with extraordinary strength and forcing her to look him in the eye. "Is that true? What did he show you? Was it about how this apparatus works?"

"No." Filio shook her head. "He showed me that The Enemy crashed on Mars after Xinth sabotaged his ship in order to neutralize the threat he posed. I know what we have to look for."

The scientist managed to nod, looking simultaneously

perplexed and comprehending. "So, can you steer the transport module to the right place?"

"Huh? No! I didn't know until now that this transport module existed at all. All I was told was that there was a way to reach Mars."

"Oh." Cassidy let his shoulders sink in disappointment. He suddenly seemed very tired. "Then we have to keep hoping that Xinth has prepared everything as it should be. We've relied on blind trust these last few years, and after all, the thing could have turned out to be a bomb."

He did not mention that it still could be one, even though she knew from a brief, penetrating look at him that they were both thinking the same thing.

"Do you know anything else that could help us?" she asked him.

"I don't think so. I took a quick look at some of the satellite images, including all the audio recordings from the monolith's discovery, or listened to them, I should say." Cassidy made a dismissive hand gesture. "I've seen them before. It always stops as soon as they return to base—without the monolith."

"I didn't even know we were at the monolith. I always thought of it as the poorly resolved image of an almost symmetrical boulder taken by Curiosity in 2005."

"Do you think that the transport module will take us there?"

"Actually, I had hoped that you'd tell me something about how this machine works," she admitted, chewing on her lower lip as she examined the inconspicuous platform with its two seats. It was hard to imagine how they would get to Mars or anywhere else with it. "Do you think it's a wormhole generator or something like that?"

"No." Cassidy rocked back and forth with his index

finger pointed toward the platform. "A wormhole would have to be stabilized first and then maintained. If you were sitting in the middle of the emerging terminus, the forces that acted in it might tear you to pieces."

"I am aware of that point of view of our current scientific knowledge, but a technology that is so far from ours... who knows what the Builders could do that we would think of as pure magic?"

"You have a point there, of course. Despite that, I still doubt it. Still, until we know better, I'll assume that certain elementary laws apply now and always—no matter how high the level of technology might be."

"That would reduce the probability of a faster-than-light means of transport to almost zero," she said.

"Relativistic speeds would be enough for me," Cassidy muttered. "Then we could reach our destination in twenty minutes or half an hour."

It did not escape Filio's notice that his hands trembled slightly and shone with sweat as he rubbed them together in front of his chest like a baker kneading dough.

"We'll see," she said neutrally. "Xinth gave me something else. A key."

"*A key?*"

"Yes." She reached into her left jacket pocket and held out her closed fist to him. When he eyed her with a creased forehead, she turned her fist upward and opened it. In the middle of her palm lay the small black marble, which shimmered like bare obsidian. "Can you do anything with this?"

"Can I *do anything with this?*" he asked in a way she couldn't interpret. Then he reached for it, and she pulled her hand back with lightning speed.

Cassidy growled disapprovingly and told her to follow him. Together, they climbed onto the platform after the scientist shooed away a technician who had been tinkering with one of the seats. There was no sound when Filio's boots touched the sheer metal.

"There! You see? I know every detail of this thing and I'll be damned if this ball doesn't fit exactly into this recess," Cassidy said, pointing to a small box that rested on a metal strut that arose between the two seats and just below where both armrests ended. Filio had to look twice to see the indentation in the form of a tiny hemisphere. The white material made it difficult for her to recognize contours.

"May I now?" her companion asked with a challenging gleam in his eyes. When she hesitated, he said, "You'd better start trusting me. We'll be using this thing together, whether you like it or not. I live by the principle of trusting everyone until he or she convinces me otherwise. I think that is both a more comfortable and a more encouraging way to live. If you've lost your positive outlook on life somewhere along the way down to this cellar at the end of the world, I very much hope that you'll find it soon, because I'm certain we'll need it."

Filio was looked for a sign of ridicule or anything suspicious in his face. She really tried, searching for patterns in his facial expression that might remind her of someone who had once cheated her or let her down. Yet she knew he was right. She had never been such a person, albeit her betrayal of Romain and the crew of the *Ocean's Bitch* had caused her to lose precisely this positive attitude toward trust that Cassidy spoke of. She knew he was right. It was as if his words had spoken to a truth in her that she had been trying to ignore. The more she thought about it, the more she realized that she had not only rendered her old scrapper crew incapable of trust, but perhaps herself most of all.

Although everything in her wanted to refuse, she

handed the ball to Cassidy, and was almost relieved when he immediately took it. She had feared that she would change her mind and pull back at any moment. Now that the little globe was gone, it seemed as if a ton had been lifted from her, and the honest joy reflected in the scientist's eyes ignited a tiny light inside her that she just now realized how much she had missed.

"Thank you," he said simply, and was about to place the marble into the recess when Filio's jerked a hand forward and stopped him. "What?"

"Is that really a good idea? Shouldn't we first sit down... in the seats?"

"Hmm," he said, looking around the doughnut-shaped room. All eyes were on them. There were about 50 people down here. They all looked tired, as if they hadn't seen daylight for ages, which was probably the case.

"You're right, of course," Cassidy finally said, straightening up. Filio did the same, and they stepped down from the small platform that was only big enough for the two seats.

As soon as they had the cold concrete floor under their feet again, the scientist waved, beckoning to a young woman in a white coat, who looked as stiff as an eel frozen from shock.

"Begin with the preparations for the start. We're getting underway."

"Right now?" the woman asked, looking at both of them as if they had lost their minds.

"Of course, right now!" Cassidy said with animation and waved her away impatiently. Addressing Filio, he said, "After such a long time, it probably seems almost unreal to my people that we are really going to use this thing, and not just at some indefinite point in the future, but right now."

Right now, she repeated in her head, and noticed an intrusive tingling that rose from the soles of her feet all the way to her scalp. It was the same tingling that she felt at the launch of the *Mars One*, and yet now she recalled the images of the *Mars Two* exploding just before launch, which haunted her like a glimpse into hell.

"Are you okay?" Cassidy asked anxiously, and Filio had to shake her head to bring her thoughts back into the present.

"Yes. Let's get started."

MARS, 2039

"I don't think the satellites are receiving anything anymore. Whatever prevented them from sending us back any signals or connecting with the earth, this new storm is closing down everything," Javier said with a grumble as soon as they returned to the base.

"So that means we are now as blind as Mission Control?" asked Filio casually. She knew that her maintenance engineer simply wanted to change the subject and chose to grant him the short pause he apparently needed to order his thoughts.

Timothy and Strickland, on the other hand, didn't seem willing to be so gracious, or else they were oblivious to Javier's mood.

"What a damned time for this to happen! We have to get out there again!" Timothy cursed, and Strickland nodded almost frenetically.

"There is a damned object under the regolith layer, something that is larger than our base, if our scans weren't faulty!"

"*If,*" Filio said.

"You don't really think we should ignore that, do you?"

"No, I don't." She shook her head and pointed vaguely upward as she peeled out of her suit. "But we won't be going anywhere in that storm out there."

"Wind speeds are barely forty kilometers an hour. It's more of a lukewarm breeze," Timothy interrupted, making a scornful hand gesture that catapulted his left glove against one of the lockers.

"And how do you want to solve the problem of the lack of sunlight? Are you going to stroll over there?" Javier asked, grumbling again. His rolling 'r' seemed downright menacing, even though he was a pretty gentle guy, Filio had found. During their training and preparation, they had affectionately called him their 'teddy.' However, this encounter with something wholly unforeseen and inexplicable seemed—for the first time in their experience—to have jolted him out of his usual mellow temperament.

"We could take one of the radionuclide batteries," Timothy suggested, but Javier was rolling his eyes before the pilot could even finish his sentence.

"Of course, Timothy the engineer is already fiddling with a solution. Simply connect a completely different energy source to a standard system. Voltage ratios and energy levels are not essential matters today. I'll just build a converter with Lego bricks and write 'wonder box' on it, then we can set out straight away," the Spaniard mocked, his voice dripping with sarcasm.

"Hey!" Timothy looked angry, ready to start an argument.

Filio forestalled him. "Shut up, both of you," she ordered impatiently. "We will look at the data together now and then decide how to proceed. We cannot ignore this discovery. It is perhaps the most important thing we could find here. However, that doesn't mean that we're going to act recklessly. This thing has obviously been here for a very, very long time, and will still be there if we wait a few days. The stupidest thing would be to act rashly now and make mistakes, even though we aren't under any time pressure. I understand that you're curious, I am too. But haste won't help us. Is that clear?"

"Clear," Timothy muttered, and Strickland followed suit, sighing loudly. Javier finally nodded, releasing the furrow between his eyebrows and letting his scrunched forehead relax.

"Good. We will meet in ten minutes in operations." Filio shooed her comrades away like chickens that had broken out of their coop, then sighed as she sat down on the small plastic bench in front of the lockers. They'd had it manufactured by the 3D printer after voting on the use of available resources. She had decided early on to allow voting on some matters because she'd always rejected overly strict hierarchies. In her eyes, good leadership began with an open ear, and she believed that one should not only hear what others think, but also implement what they said when it made sense.

The bench had actually contributed significantly to their comfort, since the most critical conversations often took place in the locker room next to the airlock, as they had quickly discovered. It may have been because, strictly following protocol, they only went out in pairs and therefore came back in pairs. Since their radio traffic was always recorded and stored, the locker room was the only space where they were free of listening devices. As a result, after each excursion, they could discuss everything in radio-privacy and without regard for protocol, plus feel free to raise questions. This had proven to be extremely valuable to the team.

Some of the best changes that had come about following requests sent to Mission Control in Darmstadt had been conceived in the locker room. In the meantime, that space, although it was crowded—and in fact, anything but cozy—served as a kind of relaxation oasis in the base. It was no surprise to Filio how much tension was caused just by the knowledge that someone was always listening, even when you were snoring in bed. Privacy was something so essential to a person's mental health that she would suggest rethinking permanent surveillance for the next mission.

Of course, mission planning had dictated this approach, because it served their safety if smart people at home were able to monitor the vital signs of all mission members and could also look into whether anything had happened. Just imagine that she or one of her crewmates slipped in the washing module, especially in the wet cell where the connections for the vital-sign pads had to be removed. Minutes, even seconds, could be crucial to surviving or dying here—and each and every one of them was irreplaceable out here.

Nevertheless, showering with a camera pointed at one's back was not particularly relaxing. Although only a few staff members watched them from Darmstadt, unlike the many voyeur shows on TV, it still felt like being on Big Brother and that was a very unpleasant feeling.

Filio used the precious minutes of solitude to allow herself to indulge an all-too-human habit—she bent her shoulders, sighed deeply, and buried her face in her hands. The discovery of that strange monolith had hit her more profoundly than she was prepared to admit. She was much more comfortable with facts than fiction, and the facts told her that the structure was not a natural object.

But what should she do with a fact that did not fit in with any other realities in her personal scientific cosmos? Had she really reached a point where the most improbable had come to pass and become the reality? An artifact of extraterrestrial origin, on a planet that directly neighbored Earth, and on the only planet besides Earth that humans had ever trodden—what was the probability of such an event?

The fact that she was doing everything possible to maintain calm, and not rush off heedlessly to examine the object, was not only due to the moderate dust storm, which turned out to be very convenient. She also wanted to buy some time. There was no record of such an event, and she had gained confidence regarding this mission from the fact that there were rules and behavioral instructions for every situation.

Or was the specific problem as simple as fear of what they might discover? All through her life she had drawn strength from the plans that she had directed at any obstacle in her path. This approach had taken her from the street via an orphanage to the first human-crewed spacecraft to Mars —and that wearing a star above her nametag.

But what's my plan for this thing out there? she asked herself, sighing again. She rubbed her hands over her face one last time and then got up, tied the sleeves of her jumpsuit around her hips, and made her way to the operations center.

Timothy, Strickland, Javier, Heinrich, and Dimitry were already waiting, seated in front of the long desk that was equipped with all sorts of touch elements, and below the four-meter-wide display film that covered the entire wall behind it. The mission commander, whom Filio served as deputy, had just returned from a reconnaissance mission he had undertaken with the German geophysicist into the deeper basalt tunnels. Their faces were drenched in sweat, and their stench reached as far as the door when she came through it.

Suddenly it became quiet and five swivel chairs turned to her.

"Is it true?" Dimitry Vlachenko asked immediately, looking at Filio with big eyes as if he had just seen a ghost.

"We have found an obviously unnatural object where—"

"It's a damn alien artifact," Timothy excitedly interrupted her, banging a fist into his open palm. "And that's just for starters."

Dimitry made an impatient gesture for him to keep quiet, and the pilot grumbled in frustration. Then the Russian looked back at her and motioned her to continue. "Please, Filio."

"Maybe it's extraterrestrial, maybe it's not. Javier correctly pointed out to me that this is only certain when its authenticity has been established."

Strickland and Timothy continued to look agitated, while Javier remained silent. Heinrich simply looked at her as if he had only just now realized that the film he was watching was not the one for which he had bought a ticket.

"Since the beginning of the exploration of Mars, three satellites have crashed on its surface, four landing capsules have suffered accidents, and several rovers have been rendered inoperable due to lack of battery power," she said, drawing further protests from Strickland and Timothy, whom she tried to fend off by raising both hands in appeasement.

"Did it look like a rover?" Timothy asked, snorting in frustration.

"A crashed satellite? Precisely on the spot where the monolith was photographed in 2005? Pah!" Strickland joined the wave of frustration.

"The only thing I want to say is that we don't know enough yet," Filio said loudly, continuing to talk a little more quietly once they had calmed down. "We need to collect more data."

She turned and faced her superior before continuing. "The object looks strange, and its shape is too uniform to be of natural origin. However, it is also relatively far away, and it's not going to run away. Therefore, we should proceed with caution."

"You tried to recover it?" Dimitry asked rhetorically, folding his powerful hands in front of his mouth as if he were watching a particularly suspenseful film.

"Yes, to no avail. It does not seem to be a monolith, but merely the rectangular continuation of a larger structure under the upper regolith layer."

"So, what do you suggest?" he asked, giving her exactly the look she had feared—a combination of entreaty and expectation.

The Russian commander was charismatic, a trait she envied, and he was able to delegate quickly and efficiently. That made him the better commander, as she had been told when the roles for the mission had been assigned. After many months of joint work, first on the *Mars One* and now on the surface, she had even come to agree with that assessment. It was more important to have someone with authority who knew how to choose his tool correctly than to let the best tool decide that it is, in fact, the best tool. For a hammer everything was a nail, just as for a drill everything was a wall that could tolerate one more hole. She had not agonized long, and had been forced to admit the mission hierarchy had been set up wisely. She was also pleased that Dimitry had recognized her talents from the beginning and often asked her for advice. A first officer couldn't wish for anything better.

Until today, she confessed and squared her shoulders instead of following her first impulse to let them slump.

You'll think of something, she admonished herself, *you always think of something.*

"The engineers will have to pull the chestnuts out of the fire again," she joked, gesturing to Javier, who hummed in affirmation. In fact, however, she was just trying to buy time to think.

No one else laughed or gave her so much as a tired smile, so she just started chatting. If she wasn't given time to work out something, she could only say what she was thinking at the moment.

"Well, let's gather together what we know. The object emits ionizing radiation, but to a minimal degree. Its surface is so smooth that not even the Martian dust sticks to it, and it has the same temperature as the environment. What do you remember?"

"Maybe a superconductor made of ceramics," Heinrich said, rubbing his temples. Apparently, she was not the only one who felt overwhelmed by recent events.

"Exactly," Filio agreed. "Ceramic can become superconducting starting at about minus one hundred and thirty degrees. If it is an artificial celestial object, a superconducting surface would make sense to ward off energy spikes."

"Don't superconductors consume an extremely high amount of energy? I'm just a biologist," Strickland said, "but my physics knowledge goes at least that far. This would mean that there is enough energy in the object to cool down the shell that much."

"Think of the ambient temperature. The part of the object protruding from the surface like a monolith could transfer the cold of the environment to the part below."

"Superconductors are known more for conducting electricity, not temperature," Javier countered.

"If someone can manage to create an object here that survives time and is smooth as a baby's behind down to an atomic scale, he'll also manage to distribute low temperatures," she responded.

"If it's been here for a long time. What if it's only been here a few decades?' asked Javier."

"The amount of sediment covering it would definitely speak against that," Timothy said.

"Someone with such technology can certainly dig himself in," the Spaniard insisted, his sparkling eyes challenging the pilot.

Before Timothy could respond, Dimitry loudly cleared his throat and silenced them with a glance, then turned to Filio again. "But how does the radioactive emission fit in?" Dimitry asked in irritation. "You mentioned ionizing radiation, didn't you?"

"I did—but I don't know how it fits," she admitted, shrugging her shoulders. "But that's the best I can make of it so far. Perhaps something is decaying beneath the surface? Damage? A defect? An accident? Some kind of deposit? We don't even know what the thing is, let alone who put it there."

"I like your thinking, Dima," Heinrich joined in again and nodded carefully. The ordinarily quiet German took a deep breath and delayed a moment until all eyes were on him. "If it were a spaceship, a superconductor would make sense in terms of the defensive capability you suggested. And it might be connected to the on-board network, which in turn would mean that we could alter the energy level and—"

"Alter the energy level?" Strickland cut in, confused.

"Connect a cable to it, pump in electricity," Javier summed up impatiently.

"Exactly. Perhaps we could get some process started that way—like using a defibrillator, to use a simple illustration," Heinrich said, nodding again as if he were finding the idea more and more attractive.

"Yes, we could start a destruction sequence," Strickland said. "But I don't think it's a good idea."

Dimitry looked inquiringly at Filio, who gave a barely noticeable nod in the direction of the German, and then he cleared his throat again and stood up. "That's how we will proceed. We can't dig it out with the means at our disposal anyway, and if the thing has endured so long here, a small electric shock certainly won't hurt it. After all, one of the countless lightning bolts on this stormy Red Planet will have already hit it by now."

"Unless such a lightning strike is responsible for the fact that the object is as dead as it appears," Strickland said, but Dimitry didn't seem to pay any attention to her remark.

"Filio, you and Javier gather everything you need." He turned to Strickland. "Ellen, you stay here and take over operations. Timothy, you prepare the cargo rover. I think we'll need the space. Heinrich and I will see to the suits and the oxygen. In six hours, we'll meet here again and discuss our procedure. I hope that we'll be back in contact with our satellites by then and can get a weather report—or get in contact with home. One can always dream."

After everyone else had departed without a word, disappearing through the connection module in different directions, Javier held her back with one hand on her sleeve.

"Do you really think this is a good idea?"

"No," she frankly admitted. "But it's the only idea we have."

"Is it good to start right out with the first idea?" Although they were alone on the threshold between the star-shaped connection module and—behind them—operations, where Strickland was sitting and just now putting on a pair of data glasses, he whispered and looked around carefully.

"No, but that's what Dimitry wants, and he's the boss."

"As simple as that?"

"That's how simple it is," she said, meeting his gaze with her chin stretched forward.

"I wouldn't have thought it." Javier looked at her as if he was seeing her for the first time.

"Has following his instructions hurt us so far?"

"No, but—"

"Look here. This time it's about a strange object that we hardly know anything about, and it will be difficult to gather new information about it without changing its nature. Based on the little data we have, Heinrich's idea is the best for what we can do with it. The alternative would be to leave the object alone and contact Darmstadt so that a lot of people who are even smarter than us can come up with a course of action. However, we haven't had any contact from home for some time, and we must assume that the problem is more serious than we'd like to admit. So, let's do something now.

"I would have liked to wait a few more days or weeks, but hey," she said with a pained smile, "at least we won't die of curiosity or restlessness, like Timothy or Strickland, if we take the first step."

"I hope you're right," the Spaniard muttered, scratching his unshaven chin and causing a rasping sound that Filio found unpleasant.

"I hope so, too," she admitted. "But look at it positively. It's an engineering problem, which means we're being allowed to play, and the boss just sent us to the toy department and said take anything we want. If that doesn't sound good to you, I don't know what will."

Javier scrounged up a faint smile for his face. In fact, his deer-brown eyes regained a touch of their gentle glow, one that would have caused many ladies to grow weak back on Earth.

"Well then, let's solve a problem," he finally said.

5

AGATHA DEVENWORTH, 2042

The rotors of the spacious C-2 Moonhopper helicopter thundered through the night. Agatha looked down on the pyramid through the armored window. It was lit by such faint moonlight that it seemed more like a temporary imprint on her retinas than a solid object. From up here, the gigantic dimensions of the structure created by the Builders could be seen. One could also make out that the pyramid did not have precisely uniform sides and edges. Too much sediment may have been deposited over the millions of years.

It would take the U.S. Navy fleet about five days to get within its fighter jets' range, which she and Pano hoped was enough time for the two of them to disappear. In Agatha's imagination, a host of helicopters and jets suddenly appeared, filling the airspace around them with explosions and plasma clouds, while on the ground far below them, luminous trace ammunition crisscrossed the night. They had to prevent that nightmare from becoming a reality at all costs. The stakes were simply too high.

"What do you think?" Pano asked over the radio. He sat directly opposite her as there were no other passengers in the private luxury helicopter. Its spacious cabin contained only four ridiculously large leather armchairs that could each be converted into a complete AR and VR environment. Luther Karlhammer was not regarded as someone who liked anything to waste his time. She remembered reading an interview with him in which he had personally complained to the universe for punishing people with the need to waste time on eating. He had probably never enjoyed the comfort of this flying palace, always preferring to spend his time on board in virtual conference rooms.

Humans were really a peculiar sort of creature, Agatha noted, not for the first time. "I think we'll have better success with our new mission," she sighed, looking out.

Pano followed her gaze and nodded. "We'll put this baby to sleep. We've already had jobs that were more difficult."

"Have we? Really?" she asked in surprise.

"No, but I thought that I would save the pessimism for later when the shit really hits the fan."

"I wouldn't have expected anything else from you."

Pano abruptly changed the subject. "How do you feel?"

"Oh, the Italian wants to talk about feelings. What a cliché!"

"I'm South Tyrolean," he corrected her with a grin. "We're more like Germans, just more handsome and with access to a sea where you actually like to bathe without having to make excuses for it."

"Germany has access to the sea?"

Pano looked at her with a raised eyebrow until she sighed in frustration.

"Hey, man, that was a joke," she said. "Not all Americans are as uneducated and ignorant as you might think."

"Good to know. I remember—"

"Everyone remembers such a story," she interrupted him, making a dismissive hand gesture. "Hey, I was in the U.S. and they thought we were still riding horses to work," she said in a bad imitation of a teenage voice. She continued, "In the States they thought Belgium was a province of France." Her voice returned to normal. "But that's probably only true of those who live between the Appalachians in the East and the Rockies in the West and spend their free time shooting at cuddly toys with shotguns or complaining about the Democrats."

"Well, you seem to be your old self again!" Pano said with joy, clapping his hands. "I ask about your feelings and you complain about people."

"This microphage stuff seems to work pretty well," she said after a brief pause. "I wonder how long Karlhammer has been sitting on this technology. Just two days and I can run again. Okay, I have to eat like a barbarian." Then she pointed to the large cardboard box on the armchair next to her. "But I guess things could be much worse after being shot in the spleen."

"And how are you doing otherwise? After all, an alien-possessed killer forced you to shoot yourself."

"You mean, how am I coping mentally?" Agatha asked.

"Uh... Yes. I guess so."

"That asshole wasn't the first piece of shit to try to kill me. I don't care what he did to me," she lied, looking out the window again to afford her partner no way to examine her for clues that she wasn't telling him the truth. The truth was that, in addition to the stubborn trembling in her left hand, there had also been a feeling of helplessness in her that she had not felt since her early childhood.

She wondered if she had only been able to suppress it

during her career and as a result thought she would not be capable of such a feeling again. The experience of someone forcing her own body into acting against her will, effectively locking her out of herself, was not only the most horrible thing she had ever experienced, but it had now burrowed into the back of her head as a deep-seated fear.

In her dreams, she kept seeing replays of the man in the black suit, hearing him ordering her to press the trigger. It was as if it were all happening over and over again, live and up close. She had often convinced herself that she had her life under control, including her emotions and thoughts, by learning to focus like when using a magnifying lens to burn a leaf or a sheet of paper.

The Enemy's alien contract killer had shattered her magnifying lens with his magic tricks. What else could one believe in if someone could simply ignore all fundamental scientific assumptions, or if they apparently did not apply to him?

"You like the image of yourself as a real tough gal, huh?" Pano asked as he looked at her with a mixture of admiration and concern.

Agatha wasn't sure if she should find it annoying or charming. "Yup, you're damned right," she finally replied, smiling as his eyes widened in amazement.

"You have to work on your sense of humor."

"Why? So that I can better handle your bad jokes?" she asked.

Pano replied, "That would be a start." He nodded with a grin.

"We've already talked about Director Miller," she said. "I suggest that we arrange a meeting with him and put the squeeze on him."

"I don't think it's going to be that easy," he said.

"Oh no, it's never easy, but I wasn't trained for easy."

"I'm sure you've been trained for difficult," he replied ambiguously. "But we shouldn't go breaking down doors when we can walk through them. It would be better to prod him here and there by feeding him disinformation to see how he responds. Sometimes provoking a reaction is more effective than head-on confrontation."

"Very wise. Did you learn that in the youth prison?"

"I came out on parole early, without having to jerk off my probation officer. And that means something, considering where I come from."

"It seems like a great place to be, this South Tyrol," Agatha muttered.

"That it is," said Pano, breathing a long sigh, while his eyes took on a dreamy expression. "What I wouldn't give to be there now and not know anything about this whole business."

"You'd rather be sitting in a mountain village, completely ignorant, than be one of the few people who know about the existence of aliens who ruled the Earth a long time ago?" Agatha asked incredulously.

"Yes, much rather. How does this knowledge benefit us? It's all like a science fiction film, just that we can't turn it off after the credits. The film continues, with an uncertain outcome."

"But you are having an impact on history, at least to some extent," she said.

"Yes, but the price for that is probably never being able to have a quiet night's sleep again. Whenever I gaze into the starry sky, I will no longer see the great mystery under whose vastness I feel infinitely small and insignificant. Instead, I will see Xinth and huge human-aliens. I will no longer be able to see a documentary about the pyramids without thinking of covert excavations.

"I won't be able to see a black suit without thinking about that sick killer. I won't be able to meet any government representative without thinking that he may have been infiltrated by an alien. I won't even be able to laugh at those people who toss around bizarre conspiracy theories for fear that they might actually be true. Is it all worth it?"

"I have no life outside of work," Agatha admitted with a trace of candor, pausing to think for a moment. "This whole thing makes my job even more fulfilling—sometimes in a very frightening way, I have to admit. But I hate nothing more than I hate the idea of having no control over what is happening around me. I couldn't simply live like an ignorant sheep, satisfied just eating the grass around me while wolves howl in the distance."

"What's really in our control?" Pano asked. "We're subject to the tides of the cosmos, the sunrise and the sunset. The weather, our gender, our appearance, our native talents and inclinations. Not even our thoughts or our breath are within our control. Both come and go."

"Possibly. But even if we were to live in a deterministic universe, I would still be me—a control freak, as you'd say. So, I have no trouble surrendering myself to determinism. Perhaps my path is predetermined in such a way that I control everything—or at least have the impression of doing so."

"Do you have a plan for how to control the situation we're in?" Pano asked.

Agatha searched for a hint of sarcasm in his voice but couldn't find one. She turned to look out the window, pausing in thought as the ubiquitous darkness seemed to flow past them and the bare, gray ice sheet shimmered beneath.

She turned back to face Pano. "We're flying to Australia and will report success in the investigation to the Director. Judging by his reaction, we'll be able to see whether he had counted on that or not. My country's fleet is already underway, which means that the Department of Defense has reacted, in any case.

"They would not usually do that without an order from the president when it involves an entire carrier strike group. Such a fleet movement is viewed with suspicion by the whole world. That doesn't mean the president is involved with the details. A few hints from his Joint Chiefs of Staff are usually enough to persuade him to sign orders, as long there's no fear of diplomatic complications.

"The same could apply to Miller. If he knows nothing about the whole thing and has acted only on instructions, then our suspicions are misplaced. If we tell him now that we've uncovered explosive information, he will either do everything he can to get us back as quickly as possible, or he won't assign any extra resources because he already knows about the matter and all necessary measures have been taken."

"Or," Pano said, "he'll see through this kind of thinking and act accordingly."

"Yes. There are no guarantees in this matter."

"Maybe we should get in touch with the Sons of Terra and ask for their support?"

"I don't work with terrorists," she countered immediately, shaking her head decisively.

"Terrorists who were right all along."

"Now you're about to repeat the adage that one man's

terrorist is another man's freedom fighter." Agatha rolled her eyes to make it clear to him what she thought of that.

"But that's the case here," he insisted. "They warned of danger, and no one believed them. So, they began to use force against The Enemy and his puppets."

"Do you know what terrorism is?"

"Tell me," he sighed, throwing his hands in the air. His massive soundproof headphones made him look like a frog.

"Inefficient. Terrorism is the tool of asymmetric war. Terrorists belong to a minority that does not have the material and means to engage their adversary in a conventional conflict. So, they choose a weapon that is far more powerful —fear. In the last ten years, fewer than a thousand people a year have died as a result of terrorist attacks, while millions have died from accidents, diabetes, cancer, and cardiovascular disease. Fast food is more dangerous than a terrorist if you look at the bare numbers. Nevertheless, daily political and media life revolves largely around the problem of terrorism, which has been widely proclaimed the issue of the century.

"Fear sells well, and it's a good tool to use in election campaigns. But this fear is illogical, which is why it suits us human beings so well. The probability of dying from consuming sugar in excess is thousands of times higher than being blown up by a suicide bomber or being run over by a hijacked truck. But terrorists work with powerful images that the media is only too happy to use. These pictures stick, while a sugar cube looks quite harmless, don't you think?"

"So, what are you trying to say?" Pano asked.

"The Sons of Terra spread fear, they don't work to achieve their aims efficiently. It would be much more effective to engage in covert operations and target those whom they consider to be agents of The Enemy. Instead, they carry out actions such as the high-profile destruction of the *Mars Two* spaceship on Cape Canaveral.

"They could also have simply sabotaged the supply chain beforehand. That would surely have been cheaper and would have generated less publicity, and thus less pressure to hunt them down. So why do they choose the path of public fearmongering when they are only concerned with eliminating The Enemy? In any case, that's not the way to win over ordinary people."

"Hmm..." Pano scratched his broad chin, which was darkly colored by a rough three-day beard. "You are seeing a contradiction there, I gather."

"I don't think I understand what they're doing. They seem to have clear goals that relate to a genuine threat, but one with a low public profile," Agatha said, kneading her hands as if she were working the worry stone she had left in the top drawer of her office desk. Sometimes she had spent whole nights massaging the stone and pondering a case.

"Do you think that Workai Dalam's background as a scrapper has something to do with it?"

"You can bet the bank on it," she assured him. "He was the first scrapper to find something, and apparently this something led him to found an organization that was committed to fighting an alien."

"Maybe he saw The Enemy himself down there in the depths," Pano suggested.

"Maybe."

"I think Miller is a good place to start. If that creates problems, or if we can no longer use the resources of Interpol or the CTD to track down The Enemy because the authorities have been infiltrated, we should then turn to Workai Dalam. I got his contact number from Karlhammer's assistant, Wayan." Pano pulled his hand terminal out of the pocket of his fashionable leather jacket and waved it.

"When the time comes, we will seize every opportunity that will help us catch The Enemy," she agreed, thinking of the man in the black suit and how he had scrutinized her with that penetrating look and then forced her to shoot herself.

Pano seemed to interpret her brooding facial expression correctly and did not continue the conversation.

The flight to McMurdo lasted just over an hour, which seemed to Agatha like a bad joke compared to their seemingly endless snowcat journey through the ice desert. When they reached the airspace above the base that had been abandoned on their last visit, it was no longer deserted. Two huge transport ships lay off the rocky coast, and a steady stream of small boats shuttled back and forth between them and McMurdo's quay wall.

Mountains of crates were piled up there, and the people around them looked like ants from the air. Heavy battle tanks rolled on snow chains over the unpaved tracks between the houses, followed by transport crawlers and helicopters on trailers. Agatha estimated that several thousand soldiers and hundreds of vehicles were busily preparing to set off for the pyramid.

"My God, it looks like a war zone," she commented on the unreal scenario below them, as the pilots, sunk in their AR cockpit, turned the helicopter hard east toward the landing area.

"This will be a war zone soon," Pano said with certainty, leaning far over the arm of his chair to look down and back. "Those tanks down there are mainly equipped with anti-aircraft guns, and the transport containers undoubtedly contain the latest Chinese Chin-Feng gun-batteries that can bring down your navy boys."

"Let's hope that we can quickly find a solution to our alien problem before they rehearse the end of the world. According to the Antarctic Treaty, no military equipment can be moved here, unless I'm mistaken?"

"You're not. I just hope that the Chinese don't react immediately and send a fleet here, whether out of rivalry with the Americans or even just out of curiosity, which is exactly what might have led them to take this step. A step, by the way, that will certainly be mentioned in the Security Council," Pano added, leaning back into his luxury armchair as their helicopter traced a circle and quickly lost altitude.

Shortly afterward, they set down on the tarmac directly behind the turboprop machine that had brought them from Namibia. A cold shiver ran down Agatha's back as she recalled her last encounter with the military plane and the six hours she had inexplicably lost. Now it waited with its ramp down. Four soldiers were talking with two pilots in gray overalls. The propellers were already spinning at a leisurely pace.

The noise of the rotors above them slowly subsided and then the co-pilot's announcement came through their headphones, "All clear, agents, you can get out. Have a good flight, and good hunting!"

"Thank you, Lieutenant," she radioed back, nodding her thanks to Pano as he opened the door. Before descending the stepladder, she reached for her oversized packed lunch from the neighboring chair. She secured it in one arm, climbed down, and then ran out into the biting cold. The airflow of the rotors lowered the temperature by a further ten degrees and made her think her lungs were going to freeze at any moment.

Ducking her head and using the packed lunch in her arms to hug her down jacket tightly around her, she rushed to the ramp of the C-220 Albatross at a continuous run, trying to ignore the burning feeling in her face. It felt like someone was continuously spraying ice chips at her.

"Good morning, Special Agent," said one of the two pilots dressed in lined, one-piece overalls, as he greeted her with a handshake. "I'm Major Greynert, and this is my co-pilot, Lieutenant Sue Tse." Greynert turned to shake hands with Pano.

Agatha and Pano also shook hands with the young Chinese woman.

The major turned to the four soldiers clad in winter camouflage. They all wore the Human Foundation logo on their combat suits as well as the insignia of mercenary company B12. They somehow seemed larger than was natural, so Agatha surmised they were wearing military exoskeletons under their clothes. Their sealed full-coverage helmets had round eye visors that gleamed like chrome and made them look—ironically, she noted—like aliens.

"That will be all. Take good care of our people out there."

"Aye, Major. Child's play against those navy bedwetters," a scratchy-sounding voice responded over the helmet speakers, and the four mercenaries turned as one and jogged away with long, steady strides.

"Very well then, agents, come aboard. We can get started immediately."

Agatha and Pano, shivering and flapping their arms, were all too happy to comply with the invitation and followed the two pilots into the well-lit interior of the turboprop. As the pilots moved toward the small door to the cockpit, Agatha froze.

Just before the door and to its right sat the two navy pilots who had flown them from Africa. Their hands were bound with cable ties that had been attached to overhead retaining straps for parachute lines.

"They've woken up," she said aloud, regarding the two. They seemed tired and drained, but otherwise in good health.

"Yes, Ma'am," answered Major Greynert, glancing at the prisoners. It was only now Agatha noticed that they were also gagged. "We found them in a rather confused state, but according to their medical cuffs, they're healthy."

"What do you intend to do with them?" Pano asked. The Capitano seemed far from happy about the situation facing the two pilots who had brought them here.

"Until we get to the Foundation's airport north of Melbourne, orders state that they are to be kept quiet. Once there, we'll let them back into the cockpit so that they can fly home."

"Just like that?" Pano asked suspiciously.

"Just like that," the major said, nodding. "What do you think? That we're going to murder them and hide them somewhere?" Greynert chuckled, but Pano wasn't smiling.

"Listen," the major continued, "we're not monsters. We are an ambitious foundation and have no interest in a conflict with the U.S. military."

"But you're preparing for it out there." Pano made a vague gesture toward the ramp that had just closed.

"No, we are preparing to defend our property," the major disagreed.

"There is no property ownership in Antarctica," Agatha said.

"Yes, there is. Everyone can set up research stations here. If there were no property, we would hardly have been able to buy McMurdo from the Americans, right?"

"Good point."

"Apart from that, they sent us their killer, and that's an attack in itself."

"I thought you had no interest in a conflict with the U.S. military," Pano said. He sat down on the left bench and buckled its three-point belt.

"We don't, but we'll fight if they force us into it. But we won't be the ones who start a war, so we will return the aircraft—including the pilots," Greynert said.

"That sounds like politics," the South Tyrolean sighed. He offered to help Agatha as she was trying to buckle in. She refused with a shake of her head.

"Of course it is. One of the largest donors to the Human Foundation is the Communist Party in Beijing. We will need their political, diplomatic, and military support if the U.S. Navy really attacks us down here," Greynert said, his expression going grim. "That, too, is dangerous, because China, as a new economic and military superpower, has been waiting a long time for a chance to show the world that the U.S. is no longer number one."

"That's playing with fire," Agatha said, pursing her mouth. "I hate politics."

"Well, you work for the politicos."

"I don't know if you can still say that," she disagreed, and Greynert smiled as he scrutinized her.

"I hope you're right."

"You don't trust me?"

"Karlhammer trusts you. That's good enough for me," the major said, sketching a salute. He turned on his heel and followed his co-pilot into the cockpit. The door clicked shut and they were alone with the two silent navy pilots and the increasing rumbling of the propellers.

After they started flying, it gradually grew warmer. The temperature soon reached a comfortable level, which made Agatha drowsy. Before she knew it, she had fallen asleep.

6

FILIO AMOROSA, 2042

When Cassidy said they would begin preparing for the start, Filio had assumed that it would start immediately. Contrary to the usual Hollywood clichés, launch preparations did not usually consist of a video montage of frantic technicians, racing clock hands, and time-lapse clouds that showed how long it took and how much work flowed into it. On the contrary, rocket launches were basically boring, because there was little to do. Most of the time was taken up in the long-term preparation that had led to the day of the start.

This had also been the case with the *Mars One*—the astronauts had been driven out to the rocket, entered the crew capsule, and waited three hours until 'Go' so that all systems could be checked and confirmed several times. Then came the launch and a few more hours until the rendezvous with the fuel packs and the primary space vehicle in orbit.

Filio had assumed that it would be similarly straightfor-ward with the strange transport module in the heart of the pyramid, because there were no systems to monitor. But she was obviously wrong. First she, Cassidy, and several white-clad scientists were led into a hallway that ran like a ring around the doughnut-shaped room that contained the module. The corridors had doors on the left. One was intended for them. It led to a spacious changing room, where their white and red suits were ready and waiting for Mars.

Their appearance was very different from those of the International Space Agency. Everything seemed much slimmer, and the surface was slightly rippled, like masking tape. Every available surface, even the smallest ones, bore the 'HF' logo of the Human Foundation with its blue globe in the background. The helmets were also slim, but at the same time looked more massive because the suits seemed so small.

"What kind of material is that?" she asked, while a whole swarm of helpers helped her and Cassidy into the spandex-like suits.

"These are ruthenium polymers that are highly dense, and they house intelligent microphages on the inside, which give the material a kind of memory function," explained the scientist enthusiastically. "When we got the molecular formulas we were completely ecstatic, because we were actually able to manufacture all this under guidance. However, there are only three specimens, each of which is a prototype that has devoured millions of dollars. Wearing them will afford us protection from micro impacts, tears, or other damage. That's because the material can be rearranged and sealed using microphages."

"And how is pressure regulated?"

"With pressure." Cassidy smiled broadly, and gratefully accepted his helmet from an aide. "The variable contact pressure of the suit itself ensures that pressure remains stable."

"Like MIT's early experiments with its Bio Suit," Filio replied, nodding in understanding, and then again in thanks to the technician who held out her helmet toward her. "That was back in the 1950s, wasn't it?"

"Yes, only this time it works."

Next, they went to the Mission Control room, which turned out to be surprisingly small. There were only two workstations without any displays or input devices. Two women were sitting wearing data glasses, immersed in their work.

Just when Filio wanted to ask what they were doing there, one of them raised her hand, and Filio felt Cassidy pushing her out onto the ring hallway and through the next door, where medical tests were waiting for her. They were placed in two reclining chairs and connected to cable after cable until they looked like old-fashioned distribution boxes.

As it turned out, the suits had to be correctly calibrated and compared with previous medical data so that they could provide accurate results as soon as they were on Mars. A membrane perfuser served to pump everything she needed into her bloodstream from an arsenal of drugs and vital substances, at any time, and the blood was permanently monitored over an injected probe.

"Can we control these necessary procedures via our helmets?" she asked Cassidy after the devices had been connected for more than three hours and were still calibrating.

"No, it's done automatically. Major interventions are controlled by ground personnel."

"But that doesn't make sense! There is over twenty minutes of communications delay between Earth and Mars," Filio protested.

"Those are the rules. Xinth apparently wanted it that way."

"Well then," she muttered with a dismissive wave.

It took another two hours before the two doctors finally came back in and freed them from the cables. Her feeling of pleasure, however, was premature. They had to endure close to another hour in another room while the wireless signal transmission was put through its paces under the most varied radiation and interference conditions.

Only then were they allowed to watch with data glasses while the transport module was being powered up in the Control Center. To prevent unforeseen problems in the inflow of electricity or, if necessary, to allow quick corrections, each of the 66 thorium reactors, which were located 20 meters deeper in the reactor space, was connected individually. This process alone, which was monitored and logged step by step, took another hour.

When they finally returned to the main room to sit on the seats, Filio was already dog-tired and quickly nodded off into sleep after strapping herself in with the three-point belt. When she woke up, she first thought someone had awakened her, but realized she had apparently come out of sleep all by herself.

A glance at the time display in her right armrest showed two hours gone by. "Oh man," she muttered. "This takes forever."

"You have to understand that several years and countless hours of overtime have gone into the construction of this one object. We don't have a backup or a Plan B if this goes wrong," Cassidy said, almost apologetically. He was still awake, and his eyes radiated pure confidence. "We prefer to stay on the safe side."

"I've noticed."

A young man in a white coat approached her from the left and gave her a hand terminal.

"Hmm?"

"Mr. Wayan for you, Ma'am."

"Wayan?" Astonished, she picked up the device and held it to her ear. "Hello?"

"Cho Wayan here. I would like to inform you that Mr. Karlhammer has successfully survived his second surgery and will be able to leave his hospital bed in about a week."

"Oh, that's good news. And Xinth?"

"He is also stable, but the doctors have put him into a coma until they understand his anatomy better," said Karlhammer's assistant, sounding tense. "Until they have collected more data about his physiology, they don't want to risk anything."

"I guess that's good news under the circumstances."

"Yes, I assume so."

Wayan paused, and Filio sensed that he was expecting something from her.

"Was that all?"

"No. According to our informants, the U.S. Navy Seventh Carrier Strike Group has just gotten underway and set course for the Antarctic Ocean."

"That means it's the Americans, huh? The Enemy has infiltrated the U.S. Government."

"At least that's what it looks like. Aircraft carrier groups do not operate in the Antarctic Ocean. Unless it's just an exceptional course loop, and if they maintain their current heading, they will be at McMurdo in about five days." Nothing in Wayan's voice betrayed his feelings as he spoke, but Filio imagined he was nervous.

"And you would like to point out to me once again that

we should not waste any time finding a solution before that fleet arrives, right?" she asked aloud.

"Something like that, yes."

"We are doing our best."

"Thank you. Please give me Dr. Morhaine, Okay?"

"Of course." She handed Cassidy the transparent hand terminal with a nod. "Mr. Wayan for you."

"Thank you. Hello Sir," her seat neighbor said, then began alternately nodding and shaking his head. "Yes, sir... No, sir... Uh-ha... Of course, sir... I've already thought about that... Yes... Naturally... You'll hold out... We'll find a solution... Yes... Thank you very much."

Cassidy finally returned the hand terminal to the young man and tensed up a little.

"He's given the Go," he finally announced with a smile. He adjusted his headgear and made one last check of the plugs that connected to the flat plastic backpack that contained air, water, and food supplies.

"That means we'll leave in another ten hours?" she asked dryly, and Cassidy's smile became a little more constrained.

"No, we have a countdown. Raise the volume!"

A female voice rang out through the room, which was now suddenly empty, and the person behind the voice began to count downward from 30. Filio had not noticed that the entire staff had suddenly disappeared and the main door was closed. Since there were no windows or visible openings, she suddenly felt very lonely and isolated, as if she were sitting directly on a bomb right before an atomic test.

"So, it's time to go," she breathed, putting on her helmet, which reduced the countdown to a barely audible level and gave her breathing a high-pitched echo. The helmet display indicated green for a secure seal, and she signaled Cassidy with a thumbs up. He responded to the gesture by pointing his index finger to his ear.

"Activate radio," she said, hearing her own echo as she spoke.

"Very good," the scientist said over the radio, also giving a thumbs up. Next, they manually checked the seals of their helmets to their suit collars and then leaned back.

Filio looked at the black marble, the Builder's data key, which now sat like a menacing foreign body in the middle of the white armature, and felt cold sweat begin to soak into her headgear. She held one of her gloved hands in front of her face and saw it trembling.

A conflicting mixture of emotions fought intensely for supremacy in her gut. An unfamiliar fear rose within it, one that fed on two things—the memory, still all too fresh of the *Mars Two* exploding just before the start, and the uncertainty caused by the fact that she had somehow survived the explosion of the *Mars One*, but could not remember anything about it. She didn't know what to fear more. What if the third attempt went wrong? After all, it was a prototype designed by an alien. No, not by an alien from elsewhere in the universe, but by an alien from another time on Earth.

Filio shook her head and breathed heavily. Just the implications suggested by these thoughts made her very dizzy. Until now, she had not allowed herself any rest. She had prioritized securing her survival and that of her immediate, fellow human beings. Now, however, so close to her primary goal, her knees were shaking for the first time. She was so close to finally returning to Mars, which hadn't left her with even the slightest memory of ever being there before.

Had she not remembered the flight there, she might not

have believed anyone who told her she had been a member of the first Mars mission. Now she sat here, deep underground in Antarctica, in a pyramid built tens of millions of years ago by a precursor species of humanity, and she was supposed to reach Mars in a simple seat perched on a platform. As if that didn't sound crazy enough, the machine was a device that even its engineers didn't understand.

"This is how Laika must have felt," she said over the radio, just as the countdown reached 12.

"Laika?" Cassidy asked. She could clearly hear the tension in his voice.

"The first dog in space. The Soviets shot her into orbit with *Sputnik 2*," Filio said. She must have felt just like we do now. No idea of how the capsule works and what will happen to it."

"I think you're probably right. She died didn't she?"

"Yes, the heat killed her during the flight into orbit."

"What's that you're rubbing with your fingers?"

"This?" Filio looked at the ceramic piece between her fingers. She had recovered it from the debris of the stern of *Mars One*. It was barely larger than a coin, and served as evidence of her memories. "A piece of the *Mars One*. A tiny piece of wreckage, if you will."

"Very encouraging," Cassidy muttered. "Three seconds left!"

Filio briefly considered closing her eyes, as she had done when the *Mars One* was launched, but decided against it. She was too curious about what would happen next.

The countdown voice intoned 'Zero.' Nothing happened. She waited a few seconds until she looked over to Cassidy, who answered her gaze and shrugged.

Then the background suddenly turned deep black, and Filio whipped her head around. It was black everywhere, although the same lighting conditions as before continued to exist around them. They were enclosed in a massive-looking ball that contained a space beginning with the platform under their feet and extended up to about a meter above their heads.

"What is that?" she asked, but Cassidy did not answer her, and she could not turn her gaze away from the pitch-black sphere. It looked like an oversized version of the marble in the recess between their seats.

Nothing moved. There were no vibrations, no more humming and hissing, as she had heard coming from somewhere beneath her during the countdown. It was as quiet as a graveyard, and the sphere in which they were sitting was simply there, as if it had always been there.

She looked along the immaculate surface of the sphere, looking for some deviation in the smooth blackness, but could not find any.

"Cassidy?" Finally, she managed to turn her gaze away from the sphere that locked her in and looked at her neighbor, who had his head tilted back, looking around in amazement. "Cassidy?" she repeated.

"Uh... Yes?" He turned to her with widened eyes. "This is... fascinating."

"What? What's this supposed to be?"

"I have no idea," he freely admitted, barely shaking his head. "But it seems to be a kind of energy field, not something material."

"Are you sure?"

"No."

"Hmm. Is anything being displayed on the sensors?" she asked.

"No. I also have no contact with Mission Control anymore," Cassidy said, leaning as if to make sure that his feet on the platform were still inside the sphere and had not vanished.

"So, we might still be under the pyramid?"

"To be perfectly honest," he replied, coming back into an upright position and looking directly at her, "I regard anything to be possible at the moment."

"We're certainly not on Mars where we should be," she said, frustrated, trying to breathe against her rebellious heartbeat by simulating a calm rhythm of deep inhalation and exhalation.

They kept quiet for a time that seemed to stretch like chewing gum, but nothing happened except that their suit sensors told her that the oxygen content inside the sphere was steadily decreasing.

"So, what's it like on Mars?" Cassidy asked after a while, in a chatty tone even though a slight trembling in his voice betrayed his tension.

"I don't know," she admitted, allowing her gaze to become lost staring into the impenetrable black of the sphere. "I simply don't remember."

"How was Mars in the vision?"

"Hmm?"

"In the vision that Xinth showed you!"

"Oh... Well, it was green and supported life."

"What else did you see? Come on, I can't stand just waiting in silence like this any longer," Cassidy urged her, and after looking to the side, she saw that the smile he had screwed on had disappeared.

"Well, he showed me a wrecked spaceship of elliptical shape, which had a kind of large tail fin and was anthracite in color. The wreck was relatively well-preserved and stood under a high cliff that looked quite bare and rugged," she recalled aloud, trying to remember details of the vision now that she realized that the distraction from her own worries and fears was doing her good. "If I imagine the same scene replaced by the images of the Red Planet available today, it would be a rather boring and bleak place, full of sand and stones."

"Ah, that's almost like a trip to Mars," Cassidy joked. His casual tone sounded forced but eager, so she went along and nodded. Filio imagined the scene from the vision without grass and trees as she closed her eyes and tried to envision it all in more detail in order to distract herself further.

At one point, she felt a gentle pressure on her right arm and opened her eyes. Cassidy's hand lay there and pressed it lightly.

"What's up?" she asked, looking at his face through his visor, which seemed to have turned to stone. She suddenly noticed that the area behind his head was no longer black, but shimmered gray. It was dark and bright at the same time until she saw that her helmet lamps were active and were shining on Cassidy.

"What the hell?" she muttered, looking around in slow motion. They were still on the platform, only now it looked dusty and brittle as if it had aged thousands of years in just moments. In addition, it no longer had a fluted structure. Around her were four walls in which she could see countless recesses and handholds.

"Where are we?" Cassidy asked.

Filio was unable to answer. Instead, she unbuckled herself and stood up somewhat stiffly.

Cassidy followed her example and quickly went to her side. "What's all this? I don't feel too good."

"You're feeling a bit nauseous, and you're having trouble coordinating your movements, right?" she asked.

Cassidy nodded, taken aback as if he had just confessed to something worthy of guilt.

"That's because of Mars gravity. It is only about a third of Earth's standard," she explained, draining breath from her lungs with a hiss.

"That means—"

"Yes. We are on Mars," Filio said, finishing his thought. "The temperature of minus a hundred degrees also fits," she confirmed, searching the walls for a door, which she eventually found. It formed an oversized passage set in a rectangular recess. "Where we are, exactly, is not clear to me."

"Can it be that we are in a structure that once belonged to the Builder?" Cassidy asked with eyes wide as he reached for her arm.

She looked at his hand and allowed the touch. She could hardly blame him for feeling afraid, even if she did not.

"I think that's likely," she said, looking back at the platform and the two seats, which looked much larger and more worn than those they had sat on back on Earth. "I'd bet this was a two-way transport vehicle, and we came out on the other side. These seats were definitely not made for people, but for giant beings like Xinth."

"But if this was constructed by the Builders and they have disappeared for many millions of years, then—"

"—then this means that we are very likely to be very deep below the surface," she concluded his sentence, while at the same time the cones of light cast by their helmets glided up to the ceiling. Thin grains of dust were drifting down, performing a weightless dance among the photons.

"Oh, damn."

MARS, 2039

Filio looked through the rover's windshield into the dust storm and tried to understand how Javier was able to maneuver around the smaller stones in these visibility conditions. The boulders appeared on the radar, but he had to see the smaller rocks with his own eyes to avoid accidentally damaging the underbody. She saw nothing but brown haze in front of them.

The dust on Mars was so fine and pervasive that during a storm it resembled fog, even though the wind speeds of 40 to 50 kilometers per hour were still rather tame. An abrading storm of 100 to 200 kilometers per hour, on the other hand, looked quite different and could scrape off more than just the paint from the hull if you remained in its grip for too long.

Two massive spare batteries connected to the electric motor of their vehicle were towed behind them, along with eight plastic crates containing equipment. Behind the large cylinders in which the battery modules stood in rows, the containers looked small, but they were heavy enough to make them a real problem for the rover's range, even in the one-third G that prevailed here. For this reason, they had decided to travel with both vehicles, even if they had to leave Timothy and Strickland without one.

This meant, however, that they could not count on any rescue or support from the two should an emergency arise. But there was no other solution than to take six additional batteries for the return journey, in addition to the four radionuclide batteries, which meant that they had taken all the batteries at their disposal. According to Dimitry's calculations they should be enough, and that was all that mattered now.

"It's going to be a great pleasure romping around out there," Javier complained. He reminded Filio of her Spanish grandfather, who had struck a similarly lamenting tone when she tracked him down in a nursing home in her late teens. With an oxygen tube sticking in his nose, he had told her his whole life story, covering pretty much the entire emotional spectrum from the most profound vale of tears to the heights of triumph. "That's just the way Spanish people are," he had said at the time. "We have fire! You have that, too!"

Filio had never seen him again, nor had she felt the desire to do so. She always had to remember that he was the father of her mother, who had preferred to spend her time in the train station injecting heroin instead of taking care that other junkies did not abuse her daughter. Perhaps that was why she didn't value exuberant emotions. They might have broken her otherwise.

"You can just sit back, relax, and let a real engineer take over," she suggested, grinning as he gave her a scowly side-long glance, "Mr. Maintenance Engineer. You can then do what you do best, and stare at the instrument panels over a cup of coffee and wait for any bulb to turn red so you can screw off a cover and re-solder a cable."

"I hate you," Javier said dryly, but with a chuckle.

"Thank you, that means a lot to me."

The journey dragged on for several hours, as the few meters of visibility did not allow for higher speeds. Filio felt like they were a spoon stirring a brown soup in slow-motion without any particular purpose. If she hadn't been checking the instruments, she would have thought they were driving in a circle. Everything outside the windshield looked identical. There was the same image of red Martian soil, brownish rocks and boulders that they passed from time to time, rounding them at a snail's pace. Nothing changed, neither the surroundings nor the ubiquitous wind-stirred sand that looked more like fine dust.

"There it is," she said when a massive object appeared on the radar. According to the coordinates, it could only be the monolith.

"Well, finally," Javier said with a sigh, leaning a little over the controls as if trying to see the sky.

Filio took a look at the atmospheric sensors and pointed to the simulated 3D map in the center console, which used all the on-board sensors to create a real-time representation of the environment. "It would be best to park just to the right of the object. Then we'll have shelter from the wind so we can work."

"Understood," the Spaniard confirmed, pressing a button on his control unit. "Hey guys, I'm marking a place to park, best place yourselves behind us as close as possible so that we can create a decent shelter from the wind."

"Dima here; copy," came the answer via radio. It was accompanied by static, but the words were understandable.

They'd had no contact with Strickland and Timothy for an hour, which they had expected.

When they finally came to a halt, the subliminal hum of their electric motor was replaced by the gentle noise of dust blowing against the rover. Filio pointed to the driver's door and Javier nodded before taking his helmet off the bracket above the center console and putting it on. When she did the same, and the light-emitting diodes on her collar indicated that the collar ring was correctly sealed, she raised a thumb, and he opened the driver's door. Dust blew into the cabin immediately, and she hurried to climb over to his seat and then out, closing the door again.

The monolith towered over them, not three steps away —a dark shadow untouched by the brown swathes that tugged at it.

"Holy shit," Dimitry said over the radio. He had just stepped up next to her and searched the foreign object with his helmet lamps. "I saw your recordings, but somehow I couldn't or wouldn't believe that this thing really existed."

"I know the feeling," Filio said, nodding, which—naturally—he could not see. "Even though I've already seen it with my own eyes."

"What about the structure below?"

"We dug down a little bit and saw that the whole thing seemed to continue downward. We detected some anomalies, among other things, using the rover's sonic wave sensors. The onboard computer then constructed a rough, imperfect, yet still recognizable image from the readings. Apparently, the flat rectangle in front of us is a kind of continuation of a much larger structure."

Heinrich had just arrived next to her. "How big?" he asked.

"You saw the data. Several hundred meters in diameter."

"Hmm. Then I'm curious to see what four radionuclide batteries can do," said the German geophysicist. The ubiquitous dust made the flag that was embroidered on his sleeve and also adorned her suit appear as faded and unreal as everything else.

Filio had to pull herself together to keep from continually staring into the swirling walls of particles that enveloped them just a few meters away. It seemed to her like standing under a bell jar into which someone had blown particularly dirty cigarette smoke. The menacing monolith and the gloomy twilight created by the eerie atmosphere made her imagine that something could spring out from the haze at any moment without giving her any time to react.

"We should keep visual contact with each other at all times," she suggested. Dimitry and Heinrich cast a brief glance at her before nodding in understanding. Filio could see from their tense faces that they had been thinking the same thing.

"How about someone lending a hand here?" Javier shouted. They turned around at the same time. He had just opened the side door of the first rover and pointed to the transport crates inside the hold from which they had removed the benches back at the base.

"You grab the boxes. Heinrich and I will get the RTGs out of the cargo rover," Dimitry ordered, and they split up.

It took them almost a quarter of an hour to get the six crates out, as they had to set each one down several times due to their weight. Eventually, however, they had arranged a small semicircle of the crates in front of the monolith, while Heinrich and Dimitry anchored the radionuclide batteries into the ground with retaining bolts.

The current low visibility made the roughly child-sized cylinders look like the monolith's smaller siblings. The monolith separated her and Javier from the other two team members. The isotope batteries were, in principle, rather old technology. An unstable atom, which is called a 'nuclide' due to the specific number of protons and neutrons in its atomic nucleus, disintegrates inside the battery, and the resulting radioactive heat generates electrical energy.

This principle, which had already been used during the Apollo missions in the 1970s, allowed them to obtain reliable energy for decades. It was also maintenance-free and did not incur any damage from radiation, as the solar cells would—sooner or later—on the surface of Mars. Today, of course, they were much more efficient and delivered a higher energy output, so Filio hoped that it would be enough to... yes, to achieve effectively *what?*

So, what could happen? What would happen if we flooded the Mars One *with electricity? Maybe the emergency lock would activate, and some relays would burn through,* she thought, looking at the crates that stood between her and Javier.

"We don't really have a better idea," she thought aloud.

"Huh?" Javier asked.

Filio shook her head. "Well, let's get started," she said, bending down to open the first crate.

They began to install the energy transformers and converters, connect them to each other, and lay the corresponding cables, which looked like finger-wide spaghetti. They ran between the radionuclide batteries, the small transformer boxes, and the plier-like connections that they had clamped to the right and left side of the monolith. The object was just narrow enough.

They then fixed the cables to the ground with steel bands and long bolts so that the wind, a careless team member, or rolling stones did not tear out a cable and destroy their project at the worst possible moment. The safety modules they had installed at the transition of the radionuclide batteries to the transformers were a particularly high priority, lest they accidentally damage their source of radioactive energy and impose more stress on the radiation protection of their suits than the Mars surface already did.

It took them more than an hour to double-check all the screws, clamps, bolts, and surveillance electronics, and to go through checklists that ran up and down their helmet displays until Filio finally nodded in satisfaction. It looked as if someone had looted a studio belonging to a science show for children and poured everything out here haphazardly.

"You see the order in the chaos, don't you?" Dimitry asked with some doubt, hands on hips.

"Yes, don't worry," Filio assured her mission leader. "And if something goes wrong, it'll be Heinrich's fault, because it was all his idea."

"Clearly," said the geophysicist, raising his hands in surrender. "If the engineers can't make any progress with their training in building blocks, then those who had the good ideas must be blamed."

"At least we actually create something, while you pebble physicists theorize about the composition of the Earth's crust," Filio countered, gesturing with a kind of 'voila' flourish to the work she and Javier had achieved, which admittedly didn't look very impressive.

"You can both shut up. As a physicist, I'm the only real scientist here, after all," Dimitry said with his rolling Russian accent, making a dismissive hand gesture before grinning at each of them. "So I know best who is to be praised or blamed. Apart from that, I am also the boss, so I am always right anyway."

"Wait, isn't the boss always the one who has to assume responsibility when something goes very, very wrong?" Javier asked, winking innocently with a deer-brown eye when Dimitry gazed at him.

"For that, one of you good-for-nothings would have to establish contact with the satellites," he countered, and they all chuckled. It was laughter typical of four nervous astronauts who were facing a problem they didn't understand, which they were about to solve using something they understood. That was no contradiction in terms, and one could even argue that precisely this type of approach was in line with the core idea of science—but given the scope of their discovery and the possible consequences if they failed, it was a more-than-unfavorable situation.

"Well, then." The Russian waved in Filio's direction. "Beam us up, Scotty!"

"I'm more of a Star Wars fan," she said with a weary grin.

"My condolences," her three male colleagues intoned, almost in chorus.

"What? At least four of the movies were great. As for Star Trek, I would have to think carefully about which of them, if any, were any good," she continued the friendly banter.

"I don't remember anything but Jar Jar Bing," Dimitry said, pointing to the small multifunction display on her wrist.

"*Binks,*" Filio corrected him with a snicker. *So, the nervous joking is over,* she thought, looking down at the green button that flashed intrusively on the display and almost seemed to jump out at her.

She pressed it.

The energy transfer procedure was unspectacular, and the situation only changed in that the four white-and-red-clad astronauts remained standing in front of a lot of cable spaghetti and staring silently at the monolith amidst the dust-laden wind, instead of alleviating their nervousness with small talk.

Filio took a look at the readings on her wrist display and fished the plastic-laminated tablet out of her thigh pocket. With a swiping gesture, she pulled the data onto the much larger display and held it close to her visor. She never liked to use the display projected onto her visor for looking at data analysis and complex readouts because everything overlaid her external view, which confused her.

"All values are stable so far," she announced over the radio. "Power transmission at twenty percent. Slowly increasing the intensity now."

"Okay, nice and gentle," Dimitry said almost reverently.

"How am I supposed to gently increase the intensity of the energy transmission?" she asked with a snort, rolling her eyes as she activated the next programmed phase.

"Well, just be careful!"

"Sure, Boss. I pressed the button very carefully, and now the energy is coming through very gently," she said sarcastically, staring at the monolith as if spellbound when the output of the RTGs reached 80 percent. Of course, no lightning flashed over its surface, nor did the air crackle or the ground vibrate, as might have been the case in a Hollywood movie.

But they were here to provoke a reaction, so they were also justifiably tense. They were attempting to resuscitate what they suspected to be a machine, and any competent physician would, after all, keep her eyes open to see if the patient woke up—at least in a movie. Since she was a doctor herself, she knew, of course, that this was nonsense. CPR was simply aimed at getting the heart to beat long enough for the emergency physician to arrive and perform the actual life-saving procedures. A patient suffering from cardiac arrest would certainly not suddenly open his eyes and begin breathing on his own during cardiopulmonary resuscitation.

Hopefully, this patient won't either, she thought tensely, and stared at the data on her wafer-thin tablet. "One hundred percent. Oh."

"What do you mean, *oh?*" Dimitry said in alarm. He approached her to stare at the display in front of her.

"The radionuclide batteries are losing energy faster than expected."

"How is that possible?" Heinrich wanted to know, and he approached from the other side. Javier, too, wanted to catch a glimpse of the reading and took the only remaining free space in front of her. They now formed a small circle. Their helmets were bent forward, almost touching each other.

"No idea. It almost looks like energy is being sucked out of them," Filio conjectured.

"But this is a deteriorating radioactive—" Heinrich objected.

"I'm aware of that," Filio tersely interrupted him, "but it's now deteriorating much faster and generating a lot more heat in less time. If this rate of increase continues, the batteries will be completely discharged in fifteen minutes."

"In fifteen minutes?" Dimitry asked, stunned, almost shouting.

Filio's face grimaced at the extreme volume that penetrated her ear. Too late, her helmet system counteracted the spike in volume. "That's certainly what it looks like!"

As if to provide proof, she tapped the appropriate reading with the gloved index finger of her right hand and tilted her head a little to look past Javier to the monolith. "The surface of the object has also become two degrees warmer. This could be due to natural fluctuation in the superconductor, but I don't believe in coincidences."

Javier drew back a little and they again formed a loose semicircle in front of the object.

"It actively sucks energy," Heinrich repeated, stunned. "You sure it's not a battery or sensor malfunction?"

"As far as errors in technical systems go, you can never be one hundred percent certain," Filio said, without taking her gaze from the monolith. "But this would be the first time in nearly a century of radioisotope generators that something like this has happened, so I consider that to be very unlikely."

"That means that something has actively responded to what we're doing," Dimitry concluded, looking up at the object as if he were looking at a kind of new world wonder —only on another planet. The rectangular colossus, swept by dark dust, seemed more threatening than ever, the regolith particles swirling around it like a whirlwind. If one looked up at it, it almost gave the impression you were being sucked upward.

"Or it might be an automated system," she countered. "Or it has something to do with the nature of the object itself. Oh."

"What?" Dimitry asked immediately. "Could you please stop saying 'oh' all the time? It almost makes me wet my pants because something has gone wrong."

"The batteries are now empty."

"Already?" he and Heinrich asked at the same time, while Javier continued to stare at the monolith as if his gaze was magically attracted to it.

"Already. They are empty. Completely empty. I no longer register any energy output, and the only thing that still seems to emit anything is the generator shielding," she confirmed briefly, trying to suppress the slight tremor in her voice.

Then suddenly something happened. It began with slight vibrations that started in the ground, continued up past their boots, and caused their knees to shiver as if a sudden attack of the chills was striking them.

"Oh, bljad!" Dimitry cursed in Russian, but unlike Heinrich and Javier, both of whom took a step backward, he remained by Filio's side.

The vibrations lasted a few seconds and then ceased. It became calm again.

"Are your sensors reading anything?"

"Negative," she said, scrolling through the data. "Nothing that would run through the cables or interact with the transformers and converters. As to what's going on in the object, we can see absolutely nothing."

"I think we only need our eyes for that," Dimitry said, and when she looked at him inquiringly, he pointed forward.

Filio looked at the monolith, which began to fan out in slow motion at its base just above the Martian surface, until, divided into two rectangles, it formed a kind of triangle, as if someone had placed two oversized playing cards next to each other. Carefully, she and Dimitry moved sideways to better see past the wide side in front of them and paused in amazement as they saw a round hole gaping between the separate sides of the object, in which it was dark and which apparently led into the depths.

"Son of a bitch," Heinrich muttered over the radio. He had just appeared with Javier on the other side of the opening and carefully leaned forward to make his helmet spotlights illuminate a kind of tube that led downward.

"So, now we have our reaction," Dimitry said ominously,

and for a moment, the radio fell silent. Only the barely noticeable hissing of interference broke through the oppressive quiet, and Filio imagined that the storm had just gained considerable force, lightly howling through the seams of her helmet.

7

AGATHA DEVENWORTH, 2042

Their arrival in Melbourne was so unspectacular that Agatha thought she was in the wrong movie. After flying through a powerful typhoon south of Tasmania and being violently shaken, the landing north of Melbourne's outskirts was as smooth as butter.

When the ramp opened, a team of medics in white suits was already on hand and came in to take care of the two Navy pilots and determine their flight worthiness.

Major Greynert and his co-pilot escorted Agatha and Pano out and pointed to a small G-8 business jet that was parked in a waiting position on one of the feeders. A small staircase was lowered. In front of it stood two gorillas in black suits and sunglasses, holding their hands folded in front of their stomachs.

"That's your means of transport to New York," the major roared over the noise of the still-spinning propellers, pointing to the G-8 before taking her forearm and pulling her toward him.

Agatha waited for the noise of a rushing tanker to pass.

The major pulled her even closer to him and touched her lightly on her hip.

She gave him an irritated look, not sure if he had just touched her indecently or if he only wanted to be sure she was safely out of the way of the vehicle, even though it had maintained a few meters distance from them. However, as he did not grin suggestively, as men so liked to do, nor hold on to her any longer, she decided to ignore the matter.

Pano was obviously unable to do so because he glared at the major so angrily that she feared he might have a go at the pilot.

"Is there a phone on board?" she shouted, shielding her eyes from the merciless sun of the red continent.

"Of course!" Greynert hollered as he shooed her and Pano toward the small jet. He and his co-pilot then boarded a waiting autonomous cart that took them toward the small terminal building a few hundred meters away in front of a small woodland.

The whole complex looked like a circular bald patch within a colossal eucalyptus forest, from which the most exotic bird screams and animal cries might be sounding. Agatha had often heard of Australia's incomparable biodiversity, achieved through strict protection against non-native species and of the environment in general, while the extinction of fauna was running rampant around the world.

By the time they had gone the nearly 200 meters to the G-8, her forehead was already thick with perspiration, and she was happy when she was able to strip off her down jacket and hand it to one of the two gorillas. The man, sporting a brush cut, looked at her in bafflement, but she had already climbed the five stairs and stepped through the narrow opening into the cabin before he could say anything.

An Asian pilot wearing a sleek trouser suit and flight cap

greeted her with a professional smile and shook her hand. "I am Captain Jackie Dong Won, welcome on board."

"Special Agent Devenworth. Thank you very much."

"How long will the flight last?" Pano asked as Agatha moved on, dropping into one of the six expansive, cream-colored leather seats.

"Nearly five hours," the pilot answered, still smiling. "We have immediate start clearance. Each seat has its own minibar on the side. Just pull the drawer up. Here," she opened a hatch in the armature behind her, next to the toilet door, and pulled out a satellite phone with a finger-thick antenna, "is a satellite phone. You need to hold down the asterisk and wait for the connection tone, then you can dial. If you have any questions during the flight, just press the speaker icon on your right armrest."

Dong Won turned around and was about to disappear into the cockpit when the two musclemen also came into the jet.

Agatha instantly stood up. "Captain?"

"Hmm?" The pilot turned around and popped on her rehearsed toothpaste-commercial smile.

"They aren't coming along."

"In accordance with requirements, each of Mr. Karlhammer's private planes is to be accompanied by two of his bodyguards," she explained patiently.

"How nice to have requirements, but we fly alone," Agatha insisted, ignoring the two men's narrowed eyes.

The pilot's smile remained firm as she weighed the situation.

"We can also call Mr. Karlhammer and waste time," added Agatha. "I don't think his bodyguards are necessary, especially since he is not on board."

The woman eventually nodded and told the two men to

leave the plane. They shrugged their shoulders and left. The pilot followed them to the exit and quickly tapped several times on a touchscreen next to the combination stairway and door, which then folded up and closed. The captain disappeared into the cockpit.

"This luxury is kind of disgusting," Pano said, commenting on their surroundings, and actually looking like he was feeling very uncomfortable in his skin. His hands fidgeted on the leather armrests as if they were coated with itching powder.

"How so?" Agatha asked with a hint of sarcasm. "Because, out of twelve billion people, five billion live below the poverty line, and half of the population in rich countries lives on basic state income?"

"Why does Karlhammer initiate all these projects to reduce poverty and disease when he wastes money on something like this?"

"He is a visionary and a workaholic," she said, pointing to her seat, which would have accommodated two adults of her size without any problems. "Would you fly economy, if you were in his position, and try to work there?"

"Probably not. Nevertheless, it is somehow offensive to indulge in such luxury when half of humanity is regarded as a useless surplus that has to make a monthly pilgrimage to the issuing offices and—"

"Pass me the offensively luxurious satellite phone," Agatha interrupted, and held out an open hand. The aisle between them was not unusually wide.

"Okay," Pano said, pressing the remote-control-sized phone into her hand. "What about the two steroid swallowers?"

"Unwanted eavesdroppers."

"This whole thing is really making you paranoid, isn't it?"

"Or, maybe this whole thing isn't making *you* paranoid enough," she countered as she dialed Director Miller's number.

Their plane was already rolling to the runway when the staccato dialing noises sounded in her ear.

"What an old piece of junk," she muttered, waiting for the satellites to forward their signal to headquarters in New York.

"You can try it through the normal channels and let the whole world listen in," Pano said mockingly.

Agatha snorted in response.

"Miller!" the director's voice boomed in her right ear. Apparently, he had lost none of his vigor in the meantime.

"Agatha here."

"Devenworth? Where have you been all this time? I thought you had frozen to death down there!"

"I almost did," she said, giving a thumbs-up to Pano as he looked on.

"*And?* Did you find out what happened to Jackson?"

"I'm doing quite well, thank you very much."

"Don't play the suffering little soul," Miller chided, and she couldn't resist the hint of a grin. "It doesn't become you."

"We know what happened to Jackson."

"Well? I'm eager to hear. Please do not tell me that the Human Foundation is behind it."

Agatha looked at Pano and frowned. "What's up?" he asked, his lips tonelessly shaping a question.

"Why do you say that, sir?"

"Because Washington is standing on its head right now. The Republicans around Senator Danes have been able to persuade the president to send the *USS Barack Obama* and her fleet escort to the Antarctic," Miller said, and his tone left no doubt as to what he thought of it.

"How come?" Agatha asked, feigning ignorance.

"Because contact with the plane that flew you and the Capitano to McMurdo has been broken for more than two days."

"You can't be serious! They could have sent a damned reconnaissance plane or repositioned a satellite."

"Everyone with any sense in the White House has said that, but it's obviously a purely political maneuver," he said. "Strangely enough, however, the majority of Pentagon chiefs of staff have also voted in favor of this move, which surprises me. Wait a moment," Miller said. He was temporarily muffled, and she heard him shouting at someone through the covered transmitter. There was a brief rustle. "I'm back. In any case, President Harris—"

"Elisabeth Harris is already sworn in?" asked Agatha, surprised.

"Since last week. The next time, you should download a news feed before you disappear into the depths of the South Pole."

"Clearly."

"In any case, after some back and forth she agreed, provided that the fleet does not drop anchor, but merely shows its presence. It is rumored that she is doing Senator Danes and his circle this favor, so that he has the feeling of having imposed limitations on the Human Foundation, and can thus score points with his core voters. At the same time, one can probably assume that she will receive Danes' approval for the health insurance reform." Miller paused and sneezed. "Sorry. Politics, you know. Since it's the season, my allergy is at its worst. I don't want to know what this horrible chess match is costing the taxpayer."

"Half of the people don't pay any taxes at all," Agatha said half-heartedly, pondering what he had just revealed to her. Apparently, The Enemy had infected the best contacts in the Pentagon and with certain senators. Or he had already brought the president under his influence, and she was steering the affair through the dangerous political currents of the capital just cleverly enough not to be too obvious.

"If you won't even begrudge me the old clichés, I might as well depart this cruel world here and now," Miller said in his typical snarling manner. "Where are you now?"

"We're on our way to you."

"From where? How?"

"In one of Luther Karlhammer's private jets," she answered frankly, ignoring Pano's expressions, first alarmed, then warning.

"You're kidding me, I hope," the director said.

"I wouldn't do that."

"Well, great, that's just what I needed. The White House is sending a sinfully expensive message to the Human Foundation because it may have done away with a military plane and its two pilots, and you have nothing better to do than to show up in a plane belonging to its chief. You're really not making it easy for me."

"How do you think we were able to get out of McMurdo?" Agatha asked, rolling her eyes. "The Albatross should, any moment now, be on its way to the nearest navy base that has an adequate landing field."

"Hmm. Just come back. If you are ready to be picked up somewhere, I'll send you a vehicle. No detours, understood? I want to hear your report as soon as you have American soil under your feet," Miller said, ending the connection.

"I don't think he knows anything," she said, holding the

satellite phone away from her and pressing the red 'hang up' symbol with her thumb. She then tossed it to Pano, who caught it and dropped it carelessly on his lap.

"What makes you so sure?"

"He considers the relocation of the Carrier Strike Group to be a purely political ploy."

"Maybe he said that just so you'd think so."

"No, he wouldn't have had to bring up the issue in the first place. It doesn't make sense." Agatha shook her head and raised the drawer on the aisle-side of her chair to pull out a bottle of water. She made a face when the sparkling liquid poured into her mouth and throat. Apparently, Karl-hammer had a weakness for carbonation.

"I don't think that's a particularly sound reason to exonerate him of complicity," Pano said. Through the large window beside him, they could see that they were piercing a thin layer of clouds.

"We can't definitely exclude him, but it's unlikely," she agreed.

"Let's wait a little longer with our conclusions."

"Do you know what's bothering me?"

"The fact that I look so damn good and am so charming that I constantly make you blush?"

"I'm far more fascinated by your obviously blossoming imagination than by your charm," she said, looking at her hand terminal—ostensibly to check the time, but in fact, to avoid his gaze.

"So, what's bothering you?"

"The guy in the black suit. How did he do that?"

"That thought control number?" Pano asked, raising his shoulders and hands in a typical Italian gesture as the corners of his mouth fell. "No idea."

"There has to be an explanation. Maybe some kind of

pheromone, like with ants? That stuff can completely alter the brain's metabolism. Why shouldn't it work on humans?"

"The guy was an alien. That's as good an explanation as any other."

"Did he look like an alien to you?" Agatha asked, shaking her head. "Hardly."

"Maybe they can shape-shift or something like that."

"You don't really mean that, do you?"

Pano raised both hands defensively. "Hey, we've already stood before a huge alien with bronze-colored skin."

"Touché!" Agatha sighed in frustration and pondered. "Maybe it's something like a virus that's conveyed by exhaled breath?"

"Maybe it's psi waves—"

"Man, Pano, I'm serious about this!" she told him impatiently.

"Hey, you said *Pano*." He grinned and she felt like slugging him. When he saw her angry reaction, he cleared his throat and quickly added, "A virus wouldn't have such an immediate effect. It would have to spread through the air, which can take quite a long time, and then attack and affect the body's cells. But of course I'm no biologist, nor a physician."

"True—to both parts. Perhaps we should come at this from another direction. How was The Enemy able to give such powers to someone so obviously human? And how is this infiltration, which the Sons of Terra are constantly warning about, accomplished? Does he visit politicians, company bosses and God knows who else, and then show them his alien brochure? Hardly."

"Maybe he infects them with something, brainwashes them, implants a chip... The list of possible methods is endless, and in the end, it'll probably be something we haven't thought of," Pano thought aloud as they flew through some turbulence and everything began to rattle.

"I rather believe that solutions to difficult questions are usually much simpler than the questions themselves," she said, strapping herself in.

"Why don't you just call Workai Dalam and ask him what his theory is? After all, he could be the only person on Earth who has ever seen The Enemy. He was the one who found the first traces of the *Mars One*, wasn't he?"

"Yes, but—"

"Moreover, his entire theory about The Enemy was apparently correct. It's not unreasonable to assume that he knows more than we do. No, it is even very likely that he knows much more," the South Tyrolean continued, pointing to her hand terminal, which she still held in her right hand.

"Good point." Facing her terminal, she said, "Show contact number Workai Dalam."

The number appeared on the transparent display. With her free hand, she entered it into the satellite phone that Pano had tossed onto her lap, and compared the numbers again before finally pressing the green handset button and raising the unit to her ear.

Again, she endured the unpleasant dialing noises before an electronic voice announced, "At the moment all lines are busy, please leave your name and your phone number, and we will call you back. Thank you very much." A beep followed.

"Patroklus Perhanidis, seven-two-one-one-three-four-three," she said, following Karlhammer's instructions, and disconnected.

"And?"

"Now we just wait. Let's see how important Karlhammer

really—" She got no further because the satellite phone rang.

"I didn't know that you could just call back on these things," she wondered, pressing the green button. "Yes?"

"Hmm. You are not Karlhammer," a deep male voice said.

"No, but he asked me to talk to you."

"Aha. And you are...?"

"Special Agent Agatha Devenworth."

"Ah, yes. Ms. Devenworth," said Dalam with the purring voice of an extremely arrogant man, many of whom she had met during her career. "I'm glad that you have escaped Antarctica."

Agatha paused briefly. Karlhammer had assured her during their last, brief conversation that the terrorist leader was unaware of the pyramid and the operations conducted by the Human Foundation. Had he been shadowing them?

"Are you surprised that I am informed as to your movements?" A hoarse laugh assaulted her ear. "We have been tracking the man in the black suit for a long time, and his trail ended in a military aircraft from the U.S. base in Namibia—with you on board."

"A tracking transmitter?" she asked, astonished. It was the only thing that made sense. They had certainly not smuggled in any soldiers, and the cabins of military aircraft were shielded from most signals.

'That's right. What did you discover there?"

"Nice try."

"One does what one can if the goal is to protect humanity from hostile powers."

"What do you know about the man in the black suit?" Agatha asked without hesitation.

"In his former life, he was called Mikwart Dornwald, a

Swedish citizen. He worked as a profiler for the Secret Service and was involved in kidnapping cases. He was considered to be very charismatic but was dishonorably discharged and found guilty on two counts of murder before he was able to escape from prison and was never seen again," Dalam answered with surprising frankness. "Moreover, he was probably the most dangerous person on the planet, considering the power that The Enemy gave him. He is responsible for the deaths of over forty agents that I had sent after him."

"Do you have a file on him?"

"Yes."

"Can you send it to me?"

"No."

"Why not?"

"Because I don't trust you, that's why. As the most wanted terrorist on earth, one lives quite dangerously and develops a certain—"

"—paranoia?"

"Caution." Dalam said, clearing his throat. "Because there were three of you on the plane and you at least survived, I'm guessing that you somehow managed to eliminate him."

"You've got that right."

"How did you do that?"

"I'm not telling you," Agatha said coolly.

Dalam laughed mirthlessly and the transmission cracked under the onslaught of high-pitched notes. "Very good, very good. In any case, I am glad that you have made it. One fewer asset available to The Enemy."

"We're on our way to New York."

"Because you believe me and my organization?"

"Yes."

"Why?" he asked, and Agatha wrestled with herself. Eventually, she chose the safest option. "Because I saw what the man in the black suit was capable of doing. There must be some power in play that is alien to this world."

"What do you intend to do?"

"I want to gather as much information as possible about those government agencies that may have been infiltrated and share that information with you so that you can do something about it. Any help would be important and appreciated," she explained, looking over to Pano, who turned a palm up inquiringly. Agatha raised her free hand and wobbled it briefly, signaling him, *I don't know yet.*

"What kind of help are you thinking of?"

"Any clues as to what to look for. Do you know anything about how the man in the black suit... how he was able to do what he did?"

"We don't know. So far, we have only speculations—and not particularly good ones, as I see it."

"And what about those who were influenced by The Enemy?" Agatha asked. "You must have at least a good theory about whom to blame and blow up."

"Well, we shadowed the man in the black suit for a long time and kept track of his meetings. It also appears that he infects his victims with a type of virus that manifests itself a few days after infection. It could be this virus that carries The Enemy's will," Dalam replied. "We know it's there, but we have no idea what it looks like because it can't be proven once too much time has passed. We were able to eliminate three people who were infected with it and observed the infection but couldn't identify the virus. It seems to dissolve after death or change in such a way that we can no longer verify its existence or even describe it."

"Hmm, that's not very much to go on," Agatha muttered

pensively, thinking how close Pano come to this same conclusion.

"No, but that's all we have. I wish you good luck. If you are able to identify any specific persons, please contact me again. I will transfer enough resources to New York and Washington to be ready should the occasion arise."

"Just like that?" she asked, surprised.

"You have a reputation, Agatha Devenworth, and I am familiar with your file. If you point the finger at someone, I will at least have an open ear."

"Well, without a little more background on what all to look for, this will..."

She suddenly heard the line go dead. "Stupid man," Agatha growled as she threw the phone to Pano in frustration.

"What did he say? Something helpful?" He punched the 'end call' button.

"Possibly," she said, more calmly, staring out of the window into the sun setting behind the clouds. "Possibly."

8

FILIO AMOROSA, 2042

"Just stay calm," Cassidy counseled her, although nothing about his physiognomy looked like he was following his own advice. He constantly moved his lips, as if he were muttering to himself. Whatever it was, it was muffled by his sealed helmet and failed to reach the volume threshold for activating his radio. He also blinked at a rate that would have completely dried out her eyes.

"I'm calm," Filio assured her stocky companion, briefly turning away. It still seemed unreal to her that she had traveled to Mars with this man whom she had known for less than 24 hours. Luther Karlhammer had simply thrown them together as a team, throwing out Cassidy's original teammate because he thought she was the best choice.

Although she had to agree with Karlhammer, it was strange to go on a mission affecting the fate of humanity with someone she did not know and had never seen in a difficult situation. Normally she would have insisted on a half year of extensive training with him. Now, however, she just had to hope that Karlhammer's intuition had been on target, and that he had known what he was doing.

"Are you afraid that I'm going to lose it?" Cassidy asked, looking straight into her eyes. Filio hadn't even noticed that she was still staring at the scientist.

"I'm not sure. I think that it's risky to send two people on a mission who don't really know each other."

"Thank you for your honesty. Normally I would agree with you, but unfortunately, nothing is normal about this mission. Every breath we take could be risky. So why not just go for it?" he asked, attempting a seemingly carefree smile, which she tentatively reciprocated. "In addition, the Builder seems to have chosen you. Otherwise he would not have shown you the vision."

"I think it was more because I was with him before he lost consciousness," she said.

"Maybe. But you don't think Luther could have chosen you for this mission without consulting him, right?"

"You're right again."

"Any idea how we get out of here?"

"No, but there must be a way. Otherwise Xinth wouldn't have sent us here." She took a step toward the door to search the frame with her lights. At its bottom, where it met the anthracite-colored floor, were piles of sand about the size of melons. She knocked on the massive door as if testing it. There were no buttons, recesses, or even handles on it. Her knocks barely returned a sound, even though she had set the sensitivity of her audio sensors to the maximum. "Well, apparently that's not the most obvious way."

"You're an engineer, aren't you?" asked Cassidy, who had stepped to her side, staring at the two piles of sand.

"Now you're going to start in on me by expecting that an engineer should be able to solve any dilemma. That cliché includes at least one soldering iron, a screwdriver, and a pair of pliers. We don't have any of that with us."

"No, unfortunately, Xinth's instruction was clear that no metallic objects may be carried, which probably has something to do with the magnetic fields generated here." Her partner touched her on the shoulder and kneaded it briefly. "That's why all components of our new Space Walker suits are made of plastics. But..."

Cassidy fluttered his short fingers in front of her visor, as if to imitate a butterfly, "...we've prepared something." He pointed back to the platform and beckoned her to follow him.

As it turned out, there were two narrow drawers under the seats, each containing a slim case with the inscription 'Human Foundation.' In one of them were all sorts of tools, which looked dull gray in color and had been provided with red handles. In the other were converters, cables, and universal connectors.

"What's your field of expertise?" she asked Cassidy, as they squatted on the dusty floor next to the platform and went through the tools and materials to make an inventory, which they stored in their helmet computers via voice input.

"I am a physicist and a chemist. I obviously chose to spend enough years at a dark, low-paid research post so that I could earn two doctorates," Cassidy said, shrugging his shoulders. As he sat in front of her with legs crossed, he looked like a Buddha with an excessively large head. She was still amazed at how much flexibility these new suits allowed.

"Well, you have a dark, unpaid job now," she said with a wink, making a gesture that swept across the entire room, before taking the cable clamp in her right hand and pointing her thumb at the platform next to them. "What can you tell me about the machine underneath?"

"Ooh, not much," Cassidy openly admitted. "We don't

understand much about it, except that we've installed a very large number of superconductors that we don't need to cool."

Filio raised an eyebrow in disbelief.

"I know, I know," he said, somewhat defensively. "In addition, we've installed two powerful electromagnets that can be variably supplied with electrical power. Xinth specified opposite flow directions in the plans, which is why we assume that it is a kind of magnetic containment chamber.

"However, we never understood what's actually supposed to take place inside, especially since we had not been allowed to try out the module. You can certainly imagine how nervous that made us, along with the fact that our computer simulations weren't able to provide any results despite the latest AI software."

"Two electromagnets?" Filio asked. She raised her fingers to her chin as if to rub it. Her visor, however, was in the way, so she lowered them again.

"With the opposite flow direction, exactly."

"And the flow directions are adaptable?"

"Yes, at least I assume so because we have two ingress points on the... oh, wait, wait, wait," Cassidy said, wiggling his eyebrows like a good-natured uncle, before lightly licking his full lips. "I think I understand what you're getting at."

"The plate below the chairs is made of metal, isn't it?"

"Yes, just like the seats." The physicist nodded and grinned at her next words.

"How strong do you estimate the magnetic field to be?"

"Now, judging by its purely physical size and the sixty-six thorium reactors needed to supply it with electricity..."

"Let's agree that it's obscenely strong," she suggested, and he nodded with a grin before they both simultaneously raised their eyes to the ceiling, from which dust was still trickling down.

"Looks porous, the ceiling," he said.

"Mm-hmm. And, since dust is getting through, the layer above us certainly consists of regolith."

"Loose and porous."

"Exactly. Do you think you're capable of performing a surgical procedure on an extraterrestrial machine that we don't understand?" she asked, inspired by the prospect of having a strategy that might be able to solve their problem. That was more than she would have dared to hope.

"Of course," he grinned, and they rose together. "This thing must still have some juice. Otherwise we wouldn't have gotten here."

"That makes sense. The only question is whether we can detect and manipulate the energy source and supply at all," she said, scrutinizing the circular pedestal like a complex puzzle. *Hopefully, it's really made of metal as we know it,* she thought to herself and sniffed unconsciously.

"At least I know exactly where the power supply was in our model and should be able to find it immediately." Cassidy didn't seem particularly concerned, pointing to the space between the platform and the floor, nearly 20 centimeters high, which ran around the module like an anthracite ring. "We have to open it up, with the fission cutter. Stay close to where the bottom and panel join so that you don't accidentally cut anything behind it."

Filio nodded and set to work as Cassidy switched his visor to augmented reality mode and processed the transport module's stored blueprints to create a full-sized simulated grid from the technical drawings. He superimposed the grid over the machine in front of them, hoping for identical construction, in order to provide them with a precise guide.

It took them more than 30 minutes to cut through the entire side panel, which consisted of an astonishingly flexible material that they could not immediately classify. It was possibly a kind of carbon fiber.

Carefully she edged a screwdriver into the resulting gap, cut the panel from top to bottom at a point Cassidy indicated, and then carefully peeled off the entire cladding until the machine behind it appeared.

To Filio's surprise, what she was able to see there did not look very strange. She made out wires and cables and something that looked like miniature capacitors. Twenty centimeters did not provide much space in which to work, but it was enough to get a hold of several heat conductors that led from a massive ring—probably the upper electromagnet—to the outside in the form of a star and disappeared from view.

"The access points are below the upper magnetic disk where the two cylindrical capacitors are sitting. They look like elongated Coke cans. Is there a cable there?" Cassidy asked, looking curiously over her shoulder, causing his helmet lights to swing awkwardly back and forth, which confused her.

"Keep still!"

"Sorry. Do you see anything?"

"I think I see the upper parts of the capacitors. The rest of them are too deep, the angle is not enough to see anything," she explained, then lay on her stomach and pushed her right arm through the gap. With her elbow angled, she let her hand slide down and groped down the left capacitor, then moved on and got her fingers around something that actually felt like a cable. "I have something there."

"Very good! Does the cable lead to the top disk?" Cassidy asked so excitedly that she instinctively imagined him jumping up and down behind her.

"Yes, I think so. "

"You now have to unplug the cable and then connect it to the plate underneath via an identical connection port," he continued. "Not an optimal solution, but as long as we don't have an interface with which to reprogram the machine, that's the only way I can think of reversing the flow direction. A little barbaric, but I can't think of anything better."

Filio nodded silently and pulled out her pincers before pausing with a jerk. "Just a moment, it still has juice, doesn't it?"

"No, I removed the black marble from the armature. The data key."

"That activates the power supply?" she asked, surprised.

"Yes."

"What makes you so sure?" Filio pulled her hand back and turned onto her back to look directly at Cassidy. He now appeared to be a little unsettled and shifted from one foot to the other.

"I just know," he said with some reluctance.

"We are on Mars."

Cassidy breathed a long sigh and then nodded. "So we are. If we ever get back, you have to promise me not to talk to anyone about this!"

"I promise," she said, waving her hand impatiently.

"Once, after the transport module was completed, I tried to start it up because I couldn't contain my curiosity. I made the whole thing look like a malfunction in the power coupling." The physicist apparently felt very uncomfortable with this revelation and evaded her gaze.

"I probably would have wanted to do the same thing," Filio admitted. "Building something completely new without being told how your own creation works after investing several years of life in its construction—that's hard. Especially for curious people, which we scientists are by nature. So, what happened?"

"Nothing," Cassidy responded immediately. "Absolutely nothing. The electricity was on, but the machine did absolutely nothing. So, I relied on Xinth surely having thought of something like this. That's why I was so obsessed with getting my hands on that marble when you conjured it out of your pocket."

"I understand. But that's no proof that it is, in fact, this ominous data key that activates the power supply."

"No, but it is circumstantial evidence. That's probably all we can hope for. After all, we are dealing here with an extraterrestrial device that is centuries or even millennia ahead of our technology. There will be no simple solutions," Cassidy said, without moving his head. He probably wanted to make sure that his AR view of the blueprint remained precisely aligned with the machine in front of them.

"If it were your hands sticking in here, circumstantial evidence would also be enough for me," she said with a strained look on her face before turning back onto her stomach. "What the hell? We can't think of a better solution anyway."

"Hmm. Probably not. But maybe we should really—"

Just at that moment, she cut the cable. Nothing happened.

"—think about it once again and consider what our

options are. After all, we're talking about energy quantities that—"

"Cassidy, I've already cut it."

"Oh," he said, and then louder again, "OH!"

"Yes, everything's okay. Send me the AR display so that I can locate the lower port correctly. I'll try to solder and isolate the whole thing."

"I hope it works."

"You can say that again," Filio said. She set to work after the blue grid of her helmet visor display had been laid over her field of vision, making it look as if she actually saw the cable right in front of her.

"It's going to work." Cassidy audibly changed his state of mind and actually managed to make his voice sound firm. "Technology is technology. Of course, the Builder's is more advanced, but you have to conduct electricity somewhere, and cables are cables."

"May I remind you that our hand terminals are charged without contact?"

"You may, but this is a completely different matter," the physicist said in a certain tone.

"Well then." Filio was not particularly convinced by his argument, but it was the only argument that was of any help. Instead of rotting down here and waiting for her oxygen supply to run out, she preferred to accept some risk.

"I mean, after all, Xinth gave us the construction model. If his people hadn't used cables, he would hardly have integrated them into the plan," Cassidy continued, apparently believing that she could use some encouraging talk to calm her down—another sign that they did not know each other at all.

"I already feel much safer," she said with a snort, and set to work to connect the cable to the lower connection port after she had also cut that line. It took more than half an hour, even with AR support, until she was satisfied with the result—as far as one could tell without having a direct view of the work. She did the same with the upper port until she had swapped both cables, and thus the flow direction of the current.

After more than an hour she rolled onto her back again and sat up. Her cap was soaked with perspiration, and she could see individual beads of sweat on her nose where they were pressed inexorably through her pores. Her helmet filtering system had its hands full.

"Everything okay?" Cassidy asked as he gave her both his hands and pulled her to her feet.

"Now we just have to hope that your theory about the marble is correct," Filio answered. She stood next to him so that both could look at the platform, the base of which now reminded her of a plucked chicken. She tried not to think about the fact that they were in a room surrounded by a layer of regolith that could be 5, 10, or even 100 meters thick. What they now intended to do would have been dismissed as utterly crazy in any other circumstance, but now it was their only hope.

"How loose is regolith?" Cassidy asked, his helmet lights pointing upward at the ceiling.

She followed his gaze and shrugged. "Hard to say. Not as loose as sand. If you're afraid that it will fill the room here and suffocate us, I can probably reassure you."

"We're really trying to shoot a metal platform through the ceiling, aren't we?" Her crewmate tried to make sure that he wasn't dreaming.

Filio barely nodded. "Yes, we probably are. We should still cut off the seats. The imbalance could cause some rotation after impact, which could then alter the hole and have an unfavorable effect," she suggested. She grabbed the fission cutter, which looked like a small drill, from the ground.

"All right."

After ten more minutes they grabbed one seat after the other and threw them toward the door. The platform was now almost smooth, except for the unsightly cut edges that they had left in their haste, and the slender central armature, its rod pointing upward and containing the recess for the marble.

"If you are right," she said, pointing to the platform, "the current will flow immediately, and the metal plate will shoot upward. I wouldn't like to be standing on it when that happens."

"We could try thread from the repair kit," Cassidy suggested, pulling a small case out of his thigh pocket. Carefully he first fished out a small ampule, then seal patches, and finally a set of needle and thread.

"Needle and thread? Seriously?"

"I insisted. The patches are for micro holes and cracks, but what if the crack is too big? Too often important things fail for want of the smallest, simplest things, and it didn't require any extra space."

"But a piece of the suit patched with needle and thread won't be airtight," she said, looking at his open hand critically.

"That's what the programmable foam is for." He waved the small vial and then put it, along with the case, back in his thigh pocket, which he conscientiously closed again.

Filio liked the very calm and diligent manner with which he performed even the smallest activity.

"I'm tying it now with a net knot and hoping that the thickness of the thread is marginal enough that the marble can still make contact—with whatever. Then we throw it with the other end of the thread into the recess—and that's it."

"Sounds easier than it will be."

"Yes, but since we have nothing better to do anyway, we can just try until it works."

In the end, it took 235 tries, spelling each other four times while accusing each other of having the worst throwing talent a human being could possibly have. It was Cassidy who finally hit the mark, which elicited a loud howl of triumph, but which became panicked cries of pain a second later.

As soon as the marble fell into the recess, the platform base shot up so fast that it moved in a blur and severed Cassidy's arm just below the elbow. Dark blood splashed across Filio's visor, almost blinding her. She still noticed that falling sand and boulders were flying around her when the physicist stumbled into her arms.

His screams crackled in her radio like the distorted screeches of a ghost as she, breathing heavily, descended into a squatting position and tried to hold onto him. From the corners of her eyes, she saw daylight shining from the ceiling, as if someone had turned on a spotlight.

"Quiet, quiet!" She made herself speak softly but emphatically to her crewmate, although she was no longer sure if she was not really talking to herself as she tried to wipe the blood from her visor so that she could see something.

Frantic, driven by Cassidy's screams, she reached into his thigh pocket and pulled out the case. As her trembling hands groped for the seal patches, her clumsiness caused her to drop them. Swearing, she picked up three of them, tore them open and pressed them onto Cassidy's arm stump.

"Keep still!" she commanded sternly, almost shouting now to get through to him. It seemed to work, as his screaming descended into a plaintive whimper and he stopped thrashing around.

With one hand she applied the force needed to activate the three patches, and with the other she tried to open the small cap of the vial that contained the programmable foam. After she finally succeeded, she squeezed the soft plastic vial and spread the gel on the edges. It took only a few seconds for the gel to flow like mercury over the plastic fabric. It then hardened, without losing its flexibility, and became white. White as foam, she thought absently.

Cassidy, meanwhile, wept without restraint, and did not seem to register her assurances that the wound had been treated, so she did the only thing that occurred to her. She sat behind him and wrapped her arms around him so that his helmet rested on her chest.

"Everything is good," she told him in a calm voice. "Everything's okay now. We did it. You did it. You did it!"

MARS, 2039

Filio, Dimitry, Heinrich, and Javier stood around the hole and stared into the depths as far as their combined helmet lights could illuminate. Like the wide-open mouth of a ravenous predator, the darkness seemed to leap up toward them.

"It goes down at least ten meters," Javier said, a stream of Spanish curses tumbling out of his mouth.

"Looks like it," Filio agreed, and set her helmet sensors to autozoom mode in order to inspect the reddish, dusty ground at the bottom of the vertical tube. It looked as if the opening led into a room, or perhaps a passage into the depths.

"I don't see any ladders," Heinrich muttered.

"And I can see the goosebumps clear through my fucking suit," Dimitry said with his rolling accent. "Not only did we activate something, but it just opened the front door for us."

"But we wanted something like that to happen, didn't we?" Filio asked.

"Yes, but... oh, I don't know. I don't feel good about this

anymore. A hole into darkness?" the Russian asked with an exhaled hiss.

"We wanted to know what's down there. Now we have the chance to find out," she insisted, even though her stomach almost turned. If it were not for the driving curiosity that ruthlessly pushed her forward, she would have preferred to run screaming to the rover and drive back to the base.

"But there's still no ladder," Heinrich repeated, and Filio gave him a scathing look.

"Sei jetzt kein Schisser," she reproached him in German. *Don't be a shit now.*

Javier and Dimitry raised their eyes in irritation.

"Schisser?" Heinrich retorted.

"Don't put your tail between your legs. We're not going to be stopped here just because," she pointed with both hands at the opening and then to the folded-out halves of the monolith, "whoever made that didn't build you a ladder so that you can do your science thing, right?"

"I just mean that, according to my sensors, this here is nine point eight meters deep, and as it happens, we didn't bring Charles Bronson with us!" Heinrich's eyebrows converged into a stormy wave in angry response to her gaze.

"Charles Bronson?" Javier and Dimitry asked in chorus.

"He always has some rope with him," Filio and Heinrich answered together, without breaking eye contact with each other.

"Gravity here amount to point three G's," she finally said, pointing into the hole. "That means we won't fall nearly as hard as we would on Earth."

"Still too deep." Heinrich shook his head.

"If three of us hold onto one of us by the hands and let him down, it'll only be about an eight-meter drop." Filio looked carefully down into the hole. "There is also a lot of fine sand down there, which seems to have drifted down there when this thing opened. That should cushion the fall."

"And you want to rely on that?" Dimitry asked, snorting in a way that left no doubt about what he thought of her plan.

"He could spread his arms and legs and push against the walls," she continued.

"And risk ripping up his suit? Definitely not."

"Why do you keep saying 'he'? Don't you want to go yourself?" Javier asked in a challenging tone.

"If none of you Y chromosome bearers dare to take a step—"

"People," Heinrich interrupted them and pointed behind him, "it should already be obvious to you that we can use a rover's tow cable, right?"

An embarrassed silence ensued. Heinrich then turned on his heel and returned a short time later holding a wide hook that dragged a slender rope behind it. "This thing is made of carbon nanotubes that could lower even a tank down there without tearing. We also have an easy way to pull someone up again, should he be attacked by any little green men," he said.

No one laughed

"I'll go first," Filio said, thrusting her chin forward as Dimitry made to object.

The commander saw her gaze and swallowed down whatever he had wanted to reply back. "Well. I'm going next," he finally said.

"No, I'm going along," Heinrich disagreed, slapping the small controller for the winch onto Dimity's chest. The Russian held onto it in astonishment as if a bullet had hit struck him there. "If something happens down there, you should remain here as our commander, and be able to get out of here. Javier should stay here, too, so that we're all paired up. This damn storm is making me uneasy."

When Dimitry took a breath to say something, Heinrich raised a hand. "Forget it."

"Nobody pays attention to the boss, that much is obvious," the Russian grumbled, placing each of his broad hands onto her shoulders. "Be careful down there. Place a radio repeater down there right away and come back immediately if there are any problems with communication, is that clear?"

"Clear," they each promised.

"I don't want you to take any risks. Not the smallest. That's a command, understood?"

Filio and Heinrich exchanged a quick look.

"Hey, eyes here!" her commander ordered, and seemed to draw their eyes to him with a brief hand gesture. "Do you understand?"

"Yes," they dutifully promised.

Shortly afterward, Heinrich began to attach himself to the tow rope by stepping into the noose and pulling it up under his buttocks. He then took up the rope in his hands. "I'm going down," he said, carefully sitting on the edge.

Javier and Dimitry edged closer and pulled on the rope to create tension before helping the German slide into the hole, which offered plenty of space. If they had employed two ropes, the opening would have provided more than enough room for Filio as well.

Shortly before Javier activated the hydraulics to let Heinrich down, he looked up at them. "I'll be okay," he said, smiling bravely, even though individual drops of sweat had emerged from under his headgear and rolled down his forehead. His lips quivered slightly, but his eyes were alert, and his gaze was firm.

"Be right behind you," she promised.

The geophysicist slowly slipped downward. It seemed to last an eternity as his helmet light appeared to grow smaller and smaller, even though the distance was not too great. Suddenly he stopped and then resumed his movement so quickly that she cringed because she thought something had happened or he had seen something. But apparently, he was only in a hurry to get rid of the rope.

Impatient because it was being retrieved so slowly, she grabbed the rope and pulled it up by hand. Her two colleagues wanted to help her, but she brushed them away, made a loop through which she placed her hands, and pressed her right boot onto the hook. Then she sat down on the edge and waited for the rope to gain tension.

"Ready," she proclaimed, and Javier pressed the winch button again.

She proceeded down along the black tube as if in slow motion. She looked at the smooth walls around her. The anthracite colors seemed to glow in the brightness of her helmet lights. At the same time, they appeared as dead as polished tombstones, sending a cold shiver down her back that ended as a tingling sensation in her toes.

"Gently, gently," Heinrich called over the radio from below, and then she felt his hands on her shoulders so suddenly that she jerked in fright. "Have you!"

Filio put both feet on the sandy ground and let go of the rope. The uneven sand drifts beneath her boots caused her to feel like the ground was unstable and she was losing her balance, so she stepped onto a patch of dark, smooth polished ground in front of her.

As she raised her gaze, the light from her helmet lights

streamed straight into a surprisingly large passage that fell away diagonally downward. The ceiling of the conically vaulted passageway stood at least two meters above her, and it was wide enough that four people could have walked in abreast. As she looked behind her, the light fell on a wall just behind the opening, which led upward.

"Seems like there is only one way to go," Heinrich said, who had just let go of the tow rope hook, which immediately disappeared from their sight.

As they stood together in front of the sloping passage and stared into the darkness, they gave each other a quick look and then began their descent.

For the first few meters they said nothing, silently watching as the cones cast by their helmet lights fought the darkness. Shadows seemed to stick to the walls and only reluctantly retreated from the cold storm of photons they directed at them. As soon as they shifted their gaze in another direction, the blackness fell over them again like a swarm of greedy gargoyles. The knowledge that they were beneath the planet's surface, trapped not only by an extraterrestrial structure but also by millions of cubic meters of regolith, did not exactly serve to relieve their anxiety.

"This is really happening right now, isn't it?" Heinrich asked. The Bavarian's voice, usually so blustering, sounded unusually frail.

"I'm afraid so. I don't know if I should run away screaming, or touch and stare at everything," she said, whispering as if the slightest excess in volume could awaken something in the shadows that would be better left sleeping.

"If only I didn't know that something actually opened the door for us, and so that something also probably knows that we're here—"

"Yeah, I think I'd rather be exploring something completely dead."

"Well, we brought it to life. That can either be good for us or bad. It just might regard that electric shock we gave it as hostile."

"All this assumes that there's really someone or something down here. If you supply a tablet with electricity, you will also see a friendly hello on the home screen. That doesn't mean it's alive," she said, trying to convince not only her comrade, but above all, herself. She was anxious to dispel the fear that sat in her gut, or at least reduce it somewhat. She would have settled for that.

"Doesn't look like a tablet to me," he replied simply.

They jerked to a stop when a bend appeared in the passage and, according to their wrist displays, began to run horizontally.

"What's that?" she asked, astonished, as the lights on the right and left side of her visor shone down the long passage. The walls here looked different, far from artificial, more like lava tunnels that branched off from the main cavity. Nothing was smooth as in the preceding passage. Instead, it seemed as if the black material had bubbled and been scratched in many places.

"Is this a lava tunnel?" Heinrich asked, his voice raised.

"I don't think so," she said, looking at the transition of the sloping passage to the horizontal tunnel down which they now stared. There was no soft, natural transition, but a precisely delineated edge between smooth and rough. "Nature doesn't like symmetry, I once read somewhere, and this is symmetrical. In addition, we should be in the middle of the structure we scanned, and that was self-contained."

"Do your sensors show anything?" he asked in perplexity as he looked down at his wrist display.

"Negative. I have a radiation warning, but the level is lower than on the surface, and is exactly the millisievert value we measured for the object."

"Let's go..." Heinrich broke off when both their helmet lights failed at once, throwing them into complete darkness.

"Shit!" Filio said in a shrill voice, and she instinctively stumbled back a step.

"What happened?" Heinrich asked hoarsely.

"No idea, my displays have also shut down, both my visor and my wrist display."

"I don't like this, Filio!"

"Neither do I, but we have to keep calm," she said, though she had no idea just how to do that. In any case, she was unable to breathe calmly. In fact, her heart was pounding so hard in her chest that it felt as if she were running a marathon.

"We should get out of here—right now!"

"But we can't see anything!" she replied.

"We just turn around and make sure we're on an upward incline. We'll see light from the shaft at the end!"

"Do you see any light?" she asked. Her voice was tense.

"No... but..."

"That means that the damned shaft must be closed. Otherwise we would be able to see at least a glimmer of light behind us," she explained in frustration. She turned in a circle a few times, looking for the tiniest flicker of light. She found nothing.

"Oh shit, you're right! But why?"

"Why *what*?"

"Why are our suit systems offline?"

"Because someone switched them off."

"What?" Heinrich asked sharply.

"We didn't move before everything went out. In other

words, we haven't moved into some field of interference or anything like that."

"Unless the field of interference was extended," Heinrich countered.

"Even then it would have been a deliberate act," she insisted tensely. "Something knows that we are here and doesn't want us to see."

"But our radio is still working."

"Oh, shit," Filio let slip, and an electric shock of adrenaline surged through her. "We didn't set up the radio repeater."

"I totally forgot it!"

"Me too, and now the door is closed. Dimitry and Javier have to be flipping out up there!"

"But our radio still works," Heinrich said, and Filio suddenly felt his hand feeling its way down her arm until their hands touched. She held his fingers and decided not to let go of them until the light returned.

If it ever did again.

"That's... strange," she admitted, and spoke into her helmet, "Restart system!"

Nothing happened.

That would have been too much to expect, she thought to herself with a sigh, when suddenly a little pinpoint of light began to glow somewhere out there—delicate and tiny at first, like a distant firefly blurred by a morning fog. Then the glow became brighter and it pulsated in an even rhythm.

"What is that?" she asked, looking to the side where she could roughly make out the outlines of Heinrich's helmet. The gentle light was being reflected in his visor as if he were looking at a far, distant campfire.

"I don't know," he said, squeezing her hand a little more firmly.

Filio looked back at the pulsating source of light and held her breath. Since she could discern individual contours again, she quickly understood that the phenomenon had to be far down the passage, which looked like one of those lava tunnels that undermined the Martian surface.

"We're not really going there now, are we?" Heinrich asked as Filio took a step forward. He held her back with his hand.

"Do you have a better idea? This is the only source of light around here. We're completely lost without it."

"But that's exactly what it wants!"

"*It?*"

"Whatever lured us here and then shut us in and made us blind!"

"We don't know that for sure yet," she disagreed, though she was not convincing herself.

"That's what you said back at the base when Timothy insisted that it must be an alien artifact," Heinrich said. "And what now?"

"I'm just saying that we shouldn't rush to conclusions. Maybe something has lured us in, maybe it's just an automatism."

"Well, it's certainly not a coincidence," he said, finally following her tentatively. Filio felt as if she was pulling a reluctant dog behind her, but at least he moved and did not hold her back.

"We definitely agree on that."

The light grew continuously the more they advanced. She struggled not to look at the eerily jagged walls and the distorted shadows they cast that grew longer as they approached the source of light. Once, she turned around and was terrified at the sight of her own shadow, which looked so elongated and creepy that she first thought she was looking at an alien standing behind her.

With each step she took, her mouth became drier and her lips more brittle.

"We are going like moths to a flame," Heinrich said gloomily. "And we know what happens then."

"We will be enlightened."

"If I didn't have to hold my breath all the time, I might have smiled. What is it?"

"Looks like a gigantic chunk of amber," Filio said, stopping to examine the strange structure in front of them. The light source was not some sort of lamp, it was the brown bubble in the middle of a circular room. The place would have been roughly spherical if not for the level anthracite floor. The bubble, even on closer inspection, looked like a perfectly polished piece of amber the size of a small car. From its brownish interior glimmered the warm light that had attracted them.

But that wasn't all—in the middle of the bubble, the light revealed the fossilized remains of an oversized human. She jumped back, almost stumbling.

"That's... that's impossible," she stammered hoarsely.

"Mein Gott! Is that a human being?"

"I think so." Carefully, she moved to the left and looked more closely at the fossil. The arm and leg bones looked almost exactly like in her anatomy textbooks, but on closer inspection, the skull was too big, the bones too long, and there were some strange-looking bony extensions. But, these deviations aside, she was sure that it had to be a human skeleton. But how was that possible? Here on Mars?

"Maybe all those UFO kidnapping stories are true, and this is a spaceship of aliens who kidnapped people and then preserved them?" Heinrich asked so quietly that she barely understood him on the radio. A crackle could be heard in the transmission that had not been there before.

"I don't think that..." Yes, what did she actually think? That he was right? That there were such things? How could she still be sure after seeing this?

Suddenly something moved, and in the ceiling directly above the amber bubble, a hole opened as if by an invisible hand. Out of the darkness a robotic arm emerged from it. The narrow arm of gray metal consisted of three joints and ended in a very long needle. While they were still watching with mouths open after they had recoiled in alarm, the arm sank the needle into the amber bubble, and the magnifying glass effect of the material made it look as if it had been bent. It penetrated deeper and deeper and finally stabbed the large skull bone before it was pulled out in a flash. The robotic arm then jerked to the right.

Filio, following the arm's movement as if in a trance, realized for the first time that there were separate panels in the walls of the round room. She could see a tiny black dot on the upper third of each panel. The needle of the robotic arm disappeared into one of these black dots. The needle reminded her of one of those controllable prostheses used in modern factories. It remained stuck in the black dot, which was apparently a tiny opening. Nothing else happened.

"What did we just see?" Heinrich asked, pulling Filio and himself back a bit until they bumped against the wall behind them. Both jumped in fright.

"I don't have the slightest idea," she said. She swallowed heavily when something hissed, so loud that she could hear the sound through her helmet even though her sensors were inoperative. The robotic arm pulled the needle back out of the opening and retreated into the hole in the ceiling, which then closed as if by the same unseen hand that had opened it.

The panel did not seem to be a panel at all. The rectangular area with its soft edges suddenly jerked forward, and from the area behind it white steam shot out in all directions.

Then the cover folded completely back to the side and gave a glimpse into a chamber behind it, which was full of steam.

As the steam subsided, Filio completely lost control. She screamed.

9

AGATHA DEVENWORTH, 2042

Agatha slept the rest of the flight to New York. She had been working full speed and was no longer able to resist her body's fatigue. She had absorbed three protein packs, which were enriched with all sorts of vitamins and minerals, and felt satiated for a few hours. Doctors had warned her that the microphage would consume a lot of energy as it constructed her new organ and protected her body from infection.

She only woke up when Pano touched her on her forearm and then gently pressed to rouse her.

"Mmm?" she moaned drowsily and rubbed her eyes. At first they felt like chewing gum that had been chomped on for too long, and then they turned into glowing fireballs when she looked out the window and was confronted with bright lights that apparently belonged to New York's John F. Kennedy Airport. The jet was already rolling toward a small terminal for private planes. Further to the right loomed one of the much larger terminals of the public airport. Everything was bright from the lights of rolling machines, small feeders, electric buses, and ground-staff carts.

"We've already landed?"

"Yes, you've really had a deep sleep," Pano told her, and judging by his mighty yawn, there was a lot of envy in his statement.

"I normally don't sleep well." Agatha thought about her ten-year-long consumption of sleeping pills. Since she usually only had about six hours a day for sleep, she had not had a problem relying on the appropriate medication. She preferred to be dependent on tablets rather than lie awake for those six hours, when she needed to think clearly and function the next day. The alternative would have impaired her in the performance of her investigations, and not only was that out of the question, it was unfeasible.

Agatha pulled out her hand terminal, waited for the connecting icon to appear in the upper right corner, and sent a message to Director Miller. Although it was four o'clock in the morning, the answer came promptly, "ETA 20 minutes. DM."

She hated it when he abbreviated Director Miller with 'DM' as if it were something like a particularly prominent brand name.

"We will be collected in twenty minutes," she said to Pano, unbuckling as the G-8 came to a halt. With a scowl on her face, she gazed out at the dense rain that looked like industrial soot. It probably was.

The arrival security procedure in the small terminal for people who were far too affluent did not take long. It consisted only of an inspection of their backpacks, passports, and Pano's visa. In addition, there was the obligatory passage through the body scanner, which immediately emitted an alert because she was carrying Pano's white noise generator in her right hip pocket. They had decided before the inspection that she would carry it during the entry procedure, because the inspection officials would most probably ask her fewer questions. They were right. The device, the size of a rubber ball, was briefly inspected by a security employee, then her service card was scanned again, the device was returned, and they were able to leave.

Just outside the exit stood a GMC E-Falcon SUV from the CTD fleet, its windows heavily tinted. An agent in a black suit waved at her. "Agent Devenworth?"

"Pleased to meet you," she answered, shaking his hand.

"Welcome back to New York. I'm Agent Matthews. The director sent me to bring you and Capitano Hofer to HQ."

"Nice of you," Agatha said absently, and climbed into the back of the giant vehicle, something she regarded as a kind of driving memorial to American decadence.

Pano shuddered as he sat next to her and slammed the door into the lock behind him. "I liked Australia better," he muttered, combing his fingers through his wet hair.

"I don't like the sun."

"That's a joke, isn't it?"

"Some people take the risk of melanoma seriously," she said, smiling as he looked at her in stunned puzzlement. "The rain helps me to focus. I guess that it sustains the constant bad mood you accuse me of having."

"I just like it when you're grumpy."

"I'm sure you'll get more than you can handle very soon because, I don't like this investigation already. I hate politics."

"Oh!" Pano made a dismissive hand gesture. "Hating politics is a popular sport. You don't have an exclusive right to it."

"Go ahead, deny me my simple pleasures."

"It has to get worse before it gets better, is that how the saying goes?"

"That's about as witty as saying 'a glass has to be empty before you can fill it with something new.' Of course, something has to be worse to get better, that's a purely logical observation, not wisdom at all. If you ask me—"

"You're getting really talkative," Pano wondered, grinning at her. "Is this investigation making you that tense?"

Agatha twisted her mouth and nodded silently toward their driver, Agent Matthews, who was monitoring the autopilot's instruments in front of him while he was busy with his hand terminal. Pano made a grimace that could mean something like 'you probably don't trust anyone,' or 'you're the most paranoid person I know.'

The traffic was usually manageable. The transport revolution of the 2020s had more than halved the number of privately-owned vehicles. All citizens who lived on basic state income because they were considered to be unemployable in the ever-changing world of work made use of the state car-sharing services, which consisted of a fleet of taxis that could be requested via hand terminal and did not require drivers.

The traffic control system was monitored by algorithms that were so efficient that there were hardly any parked cars, and traffic was significantly reduced. Traffic jams were mostly a thing of the past, and the number of accidents had also fallen by more than 90 percent once one particular risk factor—the human driver—had been taken from behind the steering wheel. Cars with drivers were almost exclusively used by police authorities and the military, as they always had to be able to flout the traffic rules' control system in an emergency.

Agatha remembered the clogged Manhattan of her childhood and the endless searches for parking, as well as the horrible air and the stress all that had caused.

After about half an hour, during which she pensively leaned her head against the window and watched the hypnotic lights of the night pass by as dots or long stripes, they reached the building of the Counter-Terrorist Directive. It was an ugly 1970s-style office complex that was strikingly reminiscent of the FBI's headquarters in the J. Edgar Hoover Building in Washington, D.C. Before entering the underground parking facility, two heavily armored soldiers in combat gear stopped them, scanned their IDs one by one, and checked their DNA samples using breath sensors. Then the bollards retreated back into the ground, and they were able to drive in.

"The director is waiting for you in his office," Matthews said, nodding to them before making his way to the elevators.

"We should go to forensics first, I think," Agatha said, as they headed more slowly toward the elevators. "Do you still have your white noise generator in your pocket?"

"Yes. Forensics?" Pano asked with a frown.

"Yes, that's where all the doctors are stationed, including the company physicians."

"Are you thinking of the virus story that Workai Dalam told you?"

"Absolutely. If his theory is correct—and it's our first and only lead—I want to know who here in my agency might be affected," she said, pressing '4' as they stood in one of the mirrored elevators.

"Affected? You mean, possessed... by The Enemy?"

"Whatever you want to call it. I would like to know how many sharks are swimming in my pool before I jump in to do some laps."

"Don't you think we'll flush these sharks out of cover if we just go ahead and stir their waters right away?" Pano asked, pressing the stop button. The elevator stopped and the doors remained closed.

Agatha grunted with anger and turned to him. "It's not even six o'clock in the morning. In other words, there is only a skeleton staff on this shift, perhaps not even a doctor or biochemist on site. Staffing here doesn't get thinner, so right now we have the best chance of not bumping into someone who works for The Enemy, but we can't eliminate all risk," she explained, pressing to reactivate the 4. The elevator started to move again.

"Very well. But we should hurry so that Miller doesn't start wondering where we've gotten to," the Italian said, gesturing her to proceed when the doors opened.

The 4th floor, which housed the entire medical sector, was dominated by cold white walls, and had one long corridor with green doors that led to the various laboratories and treatment rooms. An unpleasant white light shone out of the ceiling lamps, making the two of them look as pale as vampires.

"The duty office is there, first door on the right," she said, pointing to the corresponding door. Next to it were a DNA breath scanner and a doorbell button. She pressed the button and whispered to Pano, "Keep the white noise generator in your jacket pocket and activate it as soon as we're in."

"Got it."

"Ah, Agatha." They were greeted by a young laboratory assistant with short-cut red hair. She wore a green coat and looked like she had just gotten up.

"Hannah," Agatha said with genuine joy in her voice. She knew the woman well, had searched databases with her several times, and had always experienced her as an exceptionally uncomplicated person—a trait that Agatha particularly valued. "We need your help."

Hannah looked at her wristwatch and smirked. "Same old Agatha, I see. Who is the pretty young man?" Curiously, she leaned to the side to look past Agatha at Pano.

The Capitano introduced himself with a smile. "This worn-out old man is called Pano," he said, pushing past Agatha to shake the lab assistant's hand and look into her eyes.

"Okay," Agatha intervened, clearing her throat. "We don't have much time, but we need your help."

"Of course," Hannah replied, taking a moment before she turned from Pano with a grin and asked them in. The duty room was a long, rectangular room consisting of a seating area with uncomfortable-looking aluminum chairs and six workstations with AR booths, as well as a data terminal with a display wall. The light here was a little warmer and more inviting.

"What do you the two of you have on your minds at six o'clock in the morning?" Hannah asked, dropping down onto the wheeled stool in front of the data terminal before setting her fingers atremble, feigning fear. "Definitely something terribly secret that could cost me my job. Then you ask for that one favor that I still owe you. And then I say, 'Agatha, if Miller finds out, I'm finished.' And then you say, 'I'd never betray you.' And so, it goes back and forth. In the end, I trust you, get involved in the solution of a very hot internal scandal, and am mentioned in the credits in a supporting role. Is it something like that?"

Pano threw Agatha a half-confused, half-amused look.

"Uh, yeah, more or less," Agatha finally said, nodding. "Only we can exclude the word 'scandal.' I only need information about some medical data.

"I see," the lab assistant said, smiling in amusement. "So,

you won't need any patient names, service grades, addresses, or departments?"

"Well, to be honest—"

"Okay, okay. Spit it out."

"Has there been an unusual frequency of viral infections here in the last two years?" Agatha asked bluntly.

"You mean, significant deviations?" Hannah combed her fingers through her short red hair and pulled herself closer to the edge of the AR terminal, took the data glasses off the desk and put them on. "Let's see."

The wall display came to life as she began to gesture as precisely and quickly as only an experienced data analyst could. Patient records and statistics alternated at a rapid pace with calendar images and medical histories.

"There have been some occurrences fairly often, but never an especially high wave of cases within a limited period," she finally said.

"Can you filter out those cases where a viral infection was assumed without the virus itself being identified?" Pano asked.

"And those that were unidentified at an above-average rate," Agatha added quickly, looking at the chart with the case numbers and the corresponding seasons that remained on the display.

"Sure. So basically, a viral infection can be detected by increased body temperatures up to about thirty-eight degrees. One of the very few exceptions is flu-like infections. In addition, there is pain and discomfort throughout the body, not localized, as well as a slightly faster decrease of symptoms, usually also untreated. The healing time is statistically between three and ten days. I have now retrieved all cases that did not provide evidence of an increased CRP value in three days or less."

"Okay, I'll voluntarily act the idiot. What's a CRP value?" Pano asked, putting his hands on his hips.

"C-reactive protein. A value that shoots up very quickly in case of inflammation, but also falls off just as quickly when the inflammation is gone. A standard titer," Hannah said, pointing to the wall display, which depicted one hundred and eighty personnel files fanned-out like playing cards so that you could only see a small portion of each. "These are the corresponding cases of the last two years in which no increased CRP could be detected after two or three days."

"One hundred and eighty?" Agatha asked, stepping next to the lab assistant as if that would allow her to see the image on the giant display better and make sure it wasn't a mistake. "Eight hundred civil servants work here in head-quarters, so that is definitely not in the statistically normal range."

"Certainly not," Hannah agreed, then made two more gestures, causing a number to flash on the display—one point four. "This is statistically the number of cases of reported viral infections that, in three days or less, no longer had any increased CRP value and were healed."

"So, the rate here over the last two years is twenty-two point five. Not exactly the statistical average, one would think." Agatha looked eloquently at Pano, who made a hissing sound and looked carefully at the ceiling.

"That's really extreme... strange," Hannah agreed, wrinkling her high forehead. "Do you want to let me in on what is going on?"

"I wonder why this hasn't been reported. This is something that should be of vital interest to the health department, because it clearly signals the danger posed by an unknown pathogen that suggests thorough contamination, right?"

"Absolutely. The data must have been collected a long time ago, but apparently no one has stored the information in the databases." Hannah began to gesticulate again and push imaginary objects aside. "Nothing. No data traces."

"Who would have the opportunity to modify the database in such a way?" Pano asked.

"All employees with C-1 clearance."

"That means?"

"Anyone with a college degree and who has worked in this department for more than five years."

"How large is that group of people?"

"That's eight people here," Hannah said, shoving the data glasses up onto her forehead. "Do you want to tell me now what this all means?"

"Can you send me all the personnel files of the affected employees and the eight people in your department to my hand terminal?"

"Now comes the part where I tell you that this violates some data protection laws and internal agency regulations—"

"—and then I say that I only need this one favor, and I'll pay it back," Agatha said.

Hannah snorted. "You owe me one," she said with an emphatically precise choice of words. "You won't ask questions when I ask the favor, of course?"

"Promise."

Hannah slid forward on her stool and exhaled long onto a small bar sensor that stood alone on the tabletop before she appeared to grab something invisible with her right hand and throw it at Agatha's outstretched hand terminal. The terminal beeped.

"Thank you!"

"No problem. Now I can alter the camera data and fake the visitor log. Be glad that it's so early and I'm bored to death," the lab assistant said in a low mutter.

"Thank you, Hannah," Agatha said, putting a hand on the young woman's shoulder. "Seriously."

"Will you tell me what it's all about?"

"Yes, but not yet."

"Let me guess—this knowledge would only put me in danger, right?" Hannah snorted.

"Right."

"It's such a cliché that I wouldn't believe it if I hadn't just heard it from you."

"Maybe your favorite movies are just damned realistic," Agatha joked, even though she had a very nasty feeling in her stomach.

"Sure. Now, out with you." Hannah got up and shooed with both hands toward the door before pointing at Pano. "Give me your private number. If you don't answer, I'll rat on you."

For the first time since Agatha met him, the Italian looked stunned and didn't even seem able to call up his standard smile. "Uh, of course," he finally said, looking almost apologetically at Agatha as he held his hand terminal to the young laboratory assistant's device until it beeped.

Agatha growled and looked at her own terminal to search for Director Miller in the patient data she had just received.

'No results' appeared on the display, and she exhaled with relief.

"And?" Pano asked as they stood again in the hallway and the door behind closed and audibly locked.

She just shook her head in response and pointed to the elevators. "We shouldn't waste any time."

While riding in the elevator, she sent a message over an encrypted connection she had received before leaving the Cho Wayan Pyramid.

Mr. Karlhammer,

We have discovered some data that worries us. The CTD may have been infiltrated, at least in part, by The Enemy. Director Miller doesn't seem to have been affected. If you could put one of your hackers on his private health insurance data, that would help. We are looking for an unexplained type of viral infection in the last two years, which heals unnaturally quickly, and in which no CRP could be detected after two or three days. Every CTD employee is usually treated exclusively by the agency physicians, but Miller would have the opportunity and resources to be treated inconspicuously in a private hospital and so avoid appearing in our data. Send me the answer as soon as possible, we are in a hurry.

Agatha

She set her hand terminal on vibrate and let it slide into her jacket pocket. Private homes were now the last places in the first world that were not monitored by cameras and algorithms, and there was no way around them—especially in public facilities such as hospitals, which were associated with the state-controlled health care system. Everything was recorded and stored to form part of the vast Big Data cosmos that dominated the United States.

Miller was able to ensure that his data was not associated with the department in any way since treatment outside the CTD did not violate the law, but he could not make it disappear. Any unofficial intervention in the data sphere was subject to imprisonment, since even the smallest gaps could confuse the results of the algorithms whose calculations controlled most of public life. Agatha hoped that Karlhammer would react quickly enough and put his data wizards on the trail as soon as possible.

"Everything okay?" Pano asked without turning his gaze away from the silver double door in front of them.

"I hope we'll soon be able to say."

"Assuming our conclusions are correct so far," he said, somewhat vaguely, while he avoided looking at the sensor bands above their heads.

"If there's only one conclusion, it is better to rely on it," she said. "Otherwise it'll be like swimming around aimlessly, and swimming in the high seas is rather perilous. If you see a lonely life ring out there, you'll surely grab onto it and won't be too concerned whether it can actually hold your weight or whether it might drag you down."

"Rescue rings are red and attract sharks."

"We don't need to try attracting them, we are already swimming in the center of politics and bureaucracy."

Pano laughed joylessly and shook his head. "Very encouraging."

"Look at it positively."

"How?"

"I don't know yet," she said, "but if you find something, share it with me."

Pano looked at her, at first without understanding, then with amusement. "Why do our prospects have to get so very dim for you to show any humor?"

"It wasn't a joke."

The way to Miller's office led them to the top floor, just

above the office of field agents that Agatha had been leading for some time. All other levels belonged to the vast horde of analysts and data experts who worked on and with the algorithms that were involved in all law enforcement operations. The public's reluctance to use robots still meant that field agents like them were needed to go out to find and apprehend perpetrators. But who could say how long notoriously fickle public opinion would remain so?

Arriving on the top floor, they kept to the right and walked with their heels clacking across the hallway's polished marble floor. On its walls hung the portraits of former U.S. presidents fashioned as old oil paintings. To the right and left were the offices of Miller's assistants and deputies, and straight ahead was his own. Its heavy wooden door was ajar.

Agatha pushed it open and put her head in to look around. His secretaries' anteroom was empty except for the vacant desks to the right and left of the glass door to Miller's office.

"Apparently no one here yet," she said. They both advanced further into the area just as the glass door opened and Miller appeared from behind it.

"You're finally here," he said, waving them in impatiently. "Liza and Betty don't start until nine o'clock, so you'll just have to do without their charm."

When they entered, the director pointed to the two chairs in front of his spartan aluminum desk, which contained a large screen, AR glasses, and two tablets. It was otherwise empty, and there were no other furnishings in the large room, except for the umbrella stand next to the door. You could see the Manhattan skyline in the distance through the window behind the desk. The first signs of the rising sun loomed as a red shimmer between the skyscrapers. The sparse daylight was enough to make the dense drone traffic visible, even in the rain. From their position, it almost looked as if God had drawn a tangle of thin lines across the sky with a pencil.

"So, what have you people brought for me?" Miller asked as he dropped into his uncomfortable-looking chair. As always, his shaggy face betrayed no sign of fatigue, and even his gray suit sat perfectly fitted and draped.

Agatha and Pano sat down.

"We found out that somebody wiped out the entire McMurdo station," Agatha said.

"Wiped out?"

"Somewhere around two hundred Human Foundation researchers were murdered there."

"Murdered? How? And above all, why?" Miller opened his jacket as if he had suddenly become too warm.

"Unfortunately, we have no answers to these questions. We found the station empty and discovered some bodies further out."

"How far out?"

"Well, that's hard to say," she said, pretending to think. She deliberately took her time while she kept some of her attention on her right hip, where her hand-held terminal lay lightly in her jacket pocket. Playing for time was difficult for her. She was not the kind of person who beat around the bush. Miller knew that only too well because he had been the same sort of agent, which was why they had such a good, professional rapport. "Maybe a few hundred meters?"

Of course, it had been much more, maybe even five to ten kilometers. "What do you think, Capitano?"

"I don't know. Everything down there is white and looks the same. I was also half-frozen and busy driving that snowcat."

"The fact is that the corpses we found didn't show any signs of murder," Agatha continued, keeping her gaze on the shiny tabletop. "They were on foot and just seemed to have frozen to death. Under normal circumstances, I'd guess suicide, but who would choose to walk out onto that frozen terrain to do it?"

"I certainly wouldn't," Pano said firmly, shaking his head decisively.

"Me neither," Agatha agreed, and quickly continued as Miller's face began to darken. "We searched the entire station for clues. We noticed that no signals were going out, so any satellites that had covered the site had to have been repositioned. This, in turn, suggests that something big is at work that requires a lot of resources and power."

Pano again expressed agreement with her and continued talking in a particularly exuberant form, while she waited impatiently for the news from Karlhammer. They had to perform the trick of feeding Miller with information that didn't say much, and at the same time didn't sound like chicken feed, because he would see through it immediately. So, she left out the man in the black suit, which was a calculated risk. If he were really in league with The Enemy, he might very well be aware of the killer and his disappearance. The question was whether he would then also be aware that she and Pano had known about him. They were on thin ice that could give way at any time under the weight of a thoughtless word, one too many or too few, and plunge them into the depths.

Come on, Karlhammer, she thought impatiently and caught herself feeling the outside of her jacket pocket with her right hand—so she quickly took her hand away.

When Pano stopped talking, she immediately took up

the story again in order to leave Miller no time to intervene. He might have asked another question.

"We also noticed that the station had been abandoned suddenly, as if they had fled. We discovered lukewarm coffee and partially-eaten sandwiches inside."

Miller moved and opened his mouth, but Agatha forestalled him. "Before you say something—yes, we have an idea!"

The director's face darkened, but he let it go with a brief wave.

"A nerve poison!"

Now it was not only Miller who looked at her in irritation, but Pano as well.

"A nerve poison could cause suicidal tendencies, as far as I know."

"Is that why you were in forensics?" the director asked with a snort.

"Yes," she said quickly, glad about the good excuse with which she had rather unwittingly provided herself. "And it is indeed possible that—"

Miller raised both hands, then got up and leaned over the table on his fists. He towered over the screen like a menacing giant and glared furiously, mostly at her. "Are you finished now?"

"Finished with it, sir?" she asked innocently.

"With this damn charade!" he said angrily as his neck and then his face became red. "If you don't tell me soon what kind of crap you're trying to pull here, you can sign up for basic state security tomorrow and start a stamp collection!"

Damn, Karlhammer! she cursed inwardly, kneading her fingers.

"So, what do you have to say? You could have phoned in

all that garbage from the plane. Then I could have saved myself having to suffer your disgraceful conduct in person— conduct that, incidentally, I consider to be a personal insult. From both of you! I'm not a senile grandpa and I didn't exactly sleep my way to this shit office."

"Of course not, Sir. Sorry, Sir," Agatha said nervously. However, it was not the angrily trembling voice of her superior that affected her, but the fact that her hand terminal had not yet vibrated.

"That's all you've got to say?" Miller thundered.

"I—"

"Both of you, get out. Immediately!" The director bared his teeth, whipping an arm up and pointing to the door. "I don't let my own staff take me for stupid, and I certainly won't let anyone withhold investigation findings from me."

Agatha swallowed heavily and rose. Just then her jacket pocket vibrated. She pulled out the hand terminal and unlocked it.

"You're not serious, are you?" Miller asked as she scanned Karlhammer's two-line message at lightning speed. Just as her boss was apparently about to explode with a roar, she stayed him with a raised hand and gave Pano a wave. He then stuck his right hand into his own jacket pocket and activated the small white noise generator, which transformed any signal into an irritating, hissing noise.

"We found Luther Karlhammer, just like the... the remains of Dan Jackson. We discovered a secret operation conducted by the Human Foundation and evidence that the Sons of Terra are right in claiming that at least *our* country's authorities, military, and politics are being infiltrated by an alien."

It all bubbled out so quickly that she almost made a shambles of it. With every word that left her mouth, Miller's face gradually transformed, from anger to irritation, then to disbelief, and finally to incomprehension.

"What are you saying?" The director no longer sounded like an erupting volcano, but more like a sighing geyser as he fell back into his chair. "You didn't get mentally ill on the way, did you?"

"No, sir. We brought evidence." Pano waved with the terminal in his hand. "I just activated a signal disruptor so that we won't be overheard."

"This office is better secured than a Navy bunker."

"That may be, but those who provide that protection may not be your friends," Agatha said, and Miller began rubbing his temples.

"If that's the case, someone will have noticed your disruptor shield. I'm going to have to make a call so that a security team doesn't come storming in at any moment." Miller was about to press a button on his desk when he noticed Agatha's facial expression and paused. "If you don't trust me now, it's too late anyway."

She nodded, and he pressed the button. "Miller here," he snapped. "All right, I'm trying out a new device from the tech department and I don't want to be disturbed. Yes. Thank you. No. Good-bye."

The director took his finger off the button and leaned back. "Liza and Betty will be here in an hour and a half. I suggest that you use this time to tell me all about your investigation and to provide me with the evidence you've been talking about!"

10

FILIO AMOROSA, 2042

The medical emergency kit she had attached to Cassidy's neck flashed a steady green, which was reassuring.

The physicist was still leaning against her chest as she supported herself on the door and watched dust dancing over the magnetic field. The emergency kit consisted of a small box and a buckle that she had placed around his neck. From the box, the Medi-AI injected all sorts of drugs into the perfuser connector on Cassidy's neck. The medications were already beginning to have an effect, and he was stable. That was all that mattered.

His situation had posed her a real challenge even as a doctor—she could neither take off his helmet nor did she have medical equipment on hand other than the cuff. The fact was that he had suffered a shock and had fallen into a corresponding state of rigidity after he had consciously grasped the extent of his injury—somatic centralization. So, she had instructed the device to give him adrenaline and blood thinner and to add a good dose of benzodiazepines to ensure proper blood flow, to calm him, and to counteract the vascular narrowing caused by the shock.

Now she had to add lorazepam, because adrenaline was obviously not good for him psychologically and he had started to become hyperactive. In fact, he really needed intravenous fluids because of the volume of blood loss, but she was not equipped to do that.

"It's gone... my hand," he said for the tenth time.

"In truth, it's more like half your arm," she said, and a lorazepam-induced giggle shook his body, which also penetrated to her chest.

"You are not exactly a compassionate doctor."

"A laugh, or even a smile, is more salutary than whining," she said with the typical frankness of hers that had caused her some trouble back during her studies. The fact that she had chosen an engineering career path was probably a good thing, because machines acted according to equations that were installed in them. Patients, however, were irrational, listened to their physician only when the prescriptions fit their own unhealthy habits, and otherwise did very little but hold out a hand when it came to getting some medication. She had never wanted to be demoted to a pill dispenser.

"I think you're right."

"Don't worry. The lorazepam will alleviate the pain, and you'll get your arm and hand back when we're back on Earth." *If we get back to Earth,* she added in thought.

"Yes, I suppose so. It doesn't hurt at all. It's almost as if I don't care at all."

"Lorazepam," she answered simply, nodding to herself before projecting the oxygen displays onto her visor. "We still have just over six hours of oxygen. I suggest that we try to get out of here. What do you think?"

"Doesn't matter to me," came her partner's drug-induced response, something she had been expecting.

"Well. I don't think we have a rope with a grappling hook that we can throw up, huh?"

"Nope."

"Can you get up, Cassidy?"

"Do I have to?"

"Yes, please."

"Okay." The physicist turned onto his side with a sigh and got into a squat before standing up and stretching. He held his sealed arm stump in front of his chest like a precious gem and covered it with his healthy arm.

Filio took advantage of her newly gained freedom to get up and thoroughly stretch herself. Her entire torso was half numb because it had born Cassidy's not-inconsiderable weight for a rather long time. Then she clapped her hands along her suit to get rid of the fine Martian dust that was blowing in ever denser veils down through the round opening in the ceiling.

In just a few steps, she reached the edge of where the platform once stood, the platform that was now somewhere on the Martian surface. There was a hole left in the ground, under which a round plate could be seen. All kinds of cables and pipes emerged at its edges and disappeared into the ground.

Carefully, she turned her head upward and looked through the opening that they had forcibly ripped into the ceiling.

At least 50 meters were separating them from the surface. The vertical tunnel sides were particularly smooth, as if the tunnel had been bored with a laser drill, which already provided a good idea of the strength of the directed magnetic field they had generated.

Filio's gaze first slid over to Cassidy, who stared dreamily around himself, then to the two seats they had cut from the platform before they had performed their little trick. They were leaning against the door.

A piece of metal of the right size could serve to get them up and out, but it could involve some danger. If the piece was too big, they would be violently shot upward. If it was too small and they were too heavy, it would accomplish nothing except slip away from them and possibly cut open their gloves. She looked back at Cassidy. In his lethargic state, she was under no illusion that he would be of the slightest help to her.

"Well, let's see," she muttered, picking up the fission cutter from the floor where she had carelessly thrown it next to the tool case, and setting herself to work. First, she cut off part of the headrest and removed the entire cushion. Then she easily detached the functional mesh over the programmable foam and pushed an approximately hand-sized piece of metal under it. The cushion upholstery was not particularly heavy but was nevertheless the only ballast she could find. In the end, she grabbed hold of the massive package and walked over to the hole.

She took three breaths and then threw it forward. The magnetic field fired the cushion with the small piece of metal into the air. It didn't move quite as fast as the plate of the pedestal, but still fast enough that the movement blurred in front of her eyes, and she was surprised that the piece hadn't just cut through the fiber mesh. Apparently, the material researchers of the Human Foundation understood their craft.

Next, Filio cut a piece of metal the size of a thumbnail and did the same with the cushion of the other seat. The result was that this time the metal piece shot through the covering mesh so fast that she didn't even notice it. She only understood what had happened because the cushion fell back down onto the disk of the upper magnetic plate.

"Great," she grumbled in frustration, but she overcame her pessimism and grabbed her fission cutter again. The next piece she cut out was the size of three fingers next to each other. She put this on the armrest and worked on it with the hammer from the toolbox until the edges were bent. She continued to work on it with pliers until she had created a kind of small roll, which she held together with two clamps before she generously wrapped duct tape around it.

"There's nothing that can't be solved with duct tape," she commented, looking on her work with satisfaction and turning the sausage-like piece in her glove a few times before nodding contentedly.

All that remains is to hope that the ratio is approximately correct, she thought. Filio nudged Cassidy, who was crouching next to her and mumbling to himself. "Hey, can you do something for me?" she asked.

His head turned toward her with agonizing slowness. "Of course."

"We're going to get out of here now, okay? I want you to climb onto my back and hold onto me like a monkey on a tree, understood?"

"Like a monkey," he repeated sleepily, nodding as if in slow motion.

"It's important that you hold on as tight as you can. Do you understand?"

"I do. I'm not stupid."

"But your head is full of lorazepam. I know how good that 'don't-give-a-shit feeling' is, Cassidy, but you must take this seriously here." She grabbed the physicist, who was almost as short as she was, on both sides of his helmet and forced him to look her directly in the eyes.

Their visors touched, and she felt like she was standing with him in a tiny room, isolated from the hostile environment around them. Mars had very little oxygen, was colder than minus 100 degrees, and had no adequate protection against the relentless solar radiation that smashed onto its surface. But here and now, they were only aware of each other's faces.

"I understand," he said earnestly and firmly returned her gaze.

"Good."

"Won't I be I too heavy for you?"

"No. I'm relatively fit, and your body weight's only a third of what it weighs on Earth, or have you already forgotten?"

"Well, then." Cassidy stood behind her, and Filio went into a deep squat so he could wrap his intact left arm around her collar and get his legs above her hips.

Pressing her lips together, she finally stood up and was surprised at how heavy he felt despite everything.

"Like an overstuffed backpack," she encouraged herself.

"How's that?"

"Nothing, it's okay. Hold on tight." She held the small metal tube padded with tape firmly in her right fist, holding it to her chest with her left hand.

"Ready?" she asked, and the physicist hummed in agreement.

Filio took a few deep breaths and tried to ignore the bloodstain that lay between the anthracite-colored floor and the electromagnet. She finally made a small hop forward.

The metal bundle in her desperately gripping hands ripped her upward with such force that she felt as if her shoulder joints were being torn out of their sockets. But that force lasted only a fraction of a second, and then their entire combined weight hung from the bundle, and they glided upward at an almost leisurely pace.

Watching physics in action was often like seeing a magic act, and that's precisely how physics behaved now. The tiny piece of metal, from which her outstretched arms now hung, pulled them up as if by an invisible hand, while the metal bundle was pushed up by the magnet below.

"This is absolutely crazy," Cassidy muttered over the radio, and she could only nod silently as they entered the passageway leading upward and seemed to fly surrounded by brown regolith.

What for an outside observer must have looked like a gentle glide, however, was torment for Filio. The combined weight of herself and Cassidy literally hung on her fingers, which felt as if she were carrying a plastic bag filled with lead, and its handles were digging deep into their joints.

Summoning all her willpower, which was ignited by an instinct for survival after glancing back down into the depths, she forced herself to endure the pain and not give in to it. It took an agonizingly long time for them to finally break through and be blinded by the brightness on the planet's surface.

At the last moment, she responded to a flash of inspiration and kicked one foot at the crushed regolith wall until the tip of her boot briefly became caught on it, and then she let go of the piece of metal. With the same foot, she pushed herself and Cassidy in the opposite direction and crashed onto the edge of the hole.

She screamed involuntarily as all the air was pressed out of her lungs. Cassidy tumbled over her onto the sandy Martian floor and groaned loudly. She tried to grab something substantial to prevent herself from slipping back, but her fingers got hold of nothing bigger than a marble.

Without even being able to scream out her fear, because her lungs were still pressed like wrung out rags, she slowly slid and slipped back into the depths—before suddenly dangling just below the edge like a helpless doll. Instinctively, she stopped rowing her arms and legs.

"I have you," Cassidy growled over the radio. His voice vibrated with effort. "Can you grab the edge?"

"I..." she croaked and gasped down precious breathing air, which caused her tormented trachea to burn, "I... think so."

Carefully, she raised her arms and didn't dare to blink as she groped for the transition between the hole and the Martian surface. Every movement of her fingers was a searching, almost pleading act of survival, leaving no room for rational thought.

"I have you!" the physicist repeated, and issued an almost animal cry as he pulled at her with astonishing force, far enough that she could, with his help, get herself to safety and let herself drop onto the red sand that finally surrounded her.

She would have loved to cry with joy, relief, fear, or every emotion at the same time, but she struggled against the urge to hyperventilate and forced herself to calm down.

"Thank you," she muttered hoarsely, turning her head to Cassidy, who had also turned onto his back right next to her.

"My pleasure." He blinked against the bright sunlight and slowly maneuvered onto his feet without taking the arm stump off his chest.

Filio did the same, rising until she stood on trembling limbs.

"Darken the display." Her helmet system reacted and

regulated the light transmission to a much more pleasant level.

"Project navigation grid." A kind of light field of greenish strokes overlaid her field of view and indicated known coordinates and positions corresponding to the most recent satellite maps.

"Insert position marker one." A red dot in the west began to flash intrusively.

"There it is!" she said excitedly, pointing in the indicated direction, and then ordered her sensors to zoom in. She spied the black monolith, which she recognized from Xinth's vision as a kind of tail fin belonging to Hortat's spaceship.

"How far away is that?" Cassidy asked.

"One thousand two hundred meters," she said, pushing him slightly on his upper arm. "Let's go, we shouldn't waste any time. We only have a few hours of air left."

"And what if we don't find breathable air in the ship?"

"We'll rack our brains if it comes to that," she said. "One problem at a time."

"Apropos problems," he said, gently grasping her by the arm.

Filio paused and raised a brow in his direction.

"The black marble, the data key," he continued, and she felt as if someone had given her an electric shock.

"Damn!"

"Yes. You said that Xinth gave it to you to gain access to the ship's onboard AI, right?"

"Yes," Filio said with a deep breath. She began to look around frantically, but could not find the base plate of the transport module anywhere. Feeling a hand on her shoulder, she turned to Cassidy, who gently shook his plump face, which looked a little bloated behind the helmet visor.

"Forget it," he said, pointing vaguely to the rocky desert

that surrounded them in every direction like a sea of dust and stones. "The marble is not made of metal, and will certainly no longer be in its socket. Even if we find the plate with the fitting, which was certainly destroyed, crushed on impact against the ceiling, we'll never find the data key here."

She was reluctantly forced to agree with him. "Not before our oxygen runs out," she replied, lowering her head. The data key had obviously been critical to Xinth, and she hardly believed that it was only because they had needed it to start the transport module.

"Let's go," Cassidy said, compassionately, as if he had to comfort her, and pulled her slightly by the arm when she didn't move. Reluctantly, she stopped her search for the base plate and took her gaze away from the uniform landscape surrounding them.

They set off together, and the longer they walked over the red-brown gravel, the less Filio's knees trembled.

The suit systems provided her with fresh air. The oxygen content was adjusted to her breathing rate, which initially saved her from problems that would have resulted from the hyperventilation that had threatened to overcome her. She took a deep, long breath as she put one foot in front of the other, glad about the low gravity of the Red Planet.

She tried not to think of the black marble, which she had seen as a kind of assurance that everything the Builder had shown her in the vision he had shared with her was real. For Filio, the strange artifact served to anchor the incredible firmly in reality, and was thus something that had been able to calm her fears ever since. That anchor was gone now, and she had the feeling of floating helplessly on an ocean of uncertainty.

They had to gain access to the on-board AI in Hortat's

ship in order to stop him, Xinth had been very clear about that. But what would happen if they entered the ship without the data key they needed to gain that access? Hortat was not called The Enemy without reason. She had seen with her own eyes what one of his agents had done, and what he had been capable of doing. The memory of the man in the black suit still raised a shudder of horror that skittered down her spine.

"I see now that this is the position of the Mars monolith that was photographed by Curiosity in 2005," Cassidy said at one point, pulling her out of her dark thoughts. "So, we had a piece of the Builder's spaceship right under our noses the whole time—we even saw it—and didn't even notice it?"

"Seems like it," Filio said with a snort. "This is typical of us human beings. When we see something that doesn't fit into our current notion of what's possible, we just dismiss it as something we know, no matter how unlikely it is. A monolith with perfectly uniform, straight edges on Mars? Must be a random perfectly symmetrical boulder, right?"

"As if there were such a thing in reality."

"Exactly. It makes people afraid to see something they don't comprehend. That is why one likes to lie to one's own brain by accepting an implausible explanation provided by one's own system of understanding. Anything is better than the unknown."

"You're probably right," Cassidy agreed, and kept quiet the rest of the way. It took them far more time than they had thought because low gravity required them to adjust their entire motor skills to avoid stumbling or losing balance.

When they finally arrived in front of the monolith, which measured at least five strides high and was sharply distinct from its surroundings, especially from the tall, steep cliff in the background, they lingered for a moment. They looked up at the structure in amazement. The fact that she now saw with her own eyes the strange artifact, which she knew from her vision was part of the spaceship, unsettled her for a moment. It almost seemed to her as if she were dreaming. Believing that the impossible was something real could work, as long as you were busy searching for it. But once you actually stood in front of it, it seemed all the more unreal.

Similarly, at one point during her specialist training in intensive care, she had ridden along in an ambulance for the first time and had seen real, severed body parts. Of course, she knew the sight of corpses from anatomy classes and television, but actually seeing mangled arms and legs on the street had been something completely different. It had hardened her in some strange way. She now experienced a similar effect standing in front of this black thing that simply did not fit into her sense of reality.

"So, this thing is responsible," she whispered tensely.

"What do you mean?"

"For the failure of the *Mars One* mission. For the death of my comrades."

"We don't know for sure yet, it could be that—"

"I know," she said darkly. "Now that I see it, I know."

"You think you remember?" Cassidy asked, half incredulous, half anxious.

"No, not directly, but I... I just feel it."

"I understand." The physicist did not sound as if he understood it at all, but he apparently decided not to pursue it and pointed to the object. As if the monolith had reacted to his gesture, it split into halves that moved apart at their base below, while their tips remained connected. Then under the astonished gazes of Filio and Cassidy, they swiveled, revealing a yawning hole between them. The hole seemed filled with impenetrable darkness.

"This really does look like the hidden lair of a being called The Enemy," Cassidy said through pressed lips. He took a step back. Filio stretched out her arm to stop him.

"There is no turning back," she said, despite her own urgent flight-instinct that attempted to persuade her to do just that—go back. She took a deep breath. "This is the only place where we have a chance to find answers. Answers about what happened to my comrades and how we can stop him."

"Have you ever thought that keeping Xinth alive to lure us here might have been The Enemy's plan from the very beginning?" Cassidy asked.

Filio shook her head decisively. "I refuse to accept that possibility." She pushed her chin forward in a reassuring gesture of defiance and pulled the physicist after her, even though he still hesitated. "We also owe it to our people to do our best, and we won't do that by running away and dying from lack of oxygen somewhere out here."

"Oh damn," Cassidy yelled. "I hate it when you're right!"

MARS, 2039

Filio screamed until she ran out of breath. She gasped for air like a fish dragged ashore, and pushed her back against the wall as if she could move through it by magic and simply disappear. Heinrich had stumbled and fallen in an attempt to run away and had just gotten back on his feet.

The creature that emerged from the steam was utterly naked. It was at least two and a half meters tall, with bronze-colored skin and knotted muscles that stretched down its slightly overlong long arms and legs. She could almost have convinced herself to think that it was a human being had it not been for its eyes. They were almond-shaped, coal-black, showing neither iris nor white. When those dark opals inspected her, it felt as if someone was tearing her soul out of her body.

Like a mythological figure of ancient Greece, this colossus stood amidst the steam pouring from its chamber and jerked its head in Heinrich's direction when he again tried to run away. At that very moment, a kind of bulkhead shot out of the wall in front of him and blocked the strange passage that had looked like a lava tunnel. The pulsating light that emanated from the fossil in the amber bubble now reflected from that spot, the same as the rest of the chamber's wall.

Heinrich, who had almost collided with the sudden obstacle, groped back and forth across its surface in disbelief. He eventually turned to Filio and jumped to stand at her side. The giant watched them without movement except for his head, which barely turned as it followed Heinrich's movements.

"Sheisse, Filio!" the German screamed as he pressed himself against the wall next to her as if every millimeter of distance that separated them from the alien mattered. "What is it?"

"I don't know," she stammered, swallowing slowly.

"Is that a human being? Is that a fucking human being?"

"I don't think so."

"Shit, how do we get out of here?"

"I don't know," she repeated, without letting the giant, who was half obscured by the amber bubble, out of her sight. Part of her wanted to move further to the left and place the full height of the bubble between herself and the creature, but then she wouldn't be able to keep him in sight, which might well scare her even more.

If it's even possible to be more scared, Filio thought. She licked her lips nervously as she frantically looked around for an exit. Every fiber of her being cried out to disappear from there as soon as possible.

"Stay here and keep an eye on it," she whispered over her radio, which still crackled and sizzled.

"What? Where are you going?" Heinrich's voice squeaked.

Filio gave a barely noticeable nod to the side. "I'm going to see if there's another exit on the other side." At that same moment, she took a slow step to the left, careful not to make any sudden movements. She could not shake the mental vision of the giant suddenly starting to move and lunging toward her, so she tried everything to avoid provoking it.

One step was enough to see that there was a similar passageway just opposite the now closed one through which they had come. A soft yellow light shone into it, revealing rough, fissured walls.

"There is an exit over there," she whispered as she stepped back to Heinrich's side. When she stared at the alien creature, she was just in time to see its face turning toward her. Apparently, he had just looked at the exit himself.

"He understands what we intend to do."

"And just what *do* we intend to do?" Heinrich asked, his voice vibrating with tension. "You don't really want to cross over there?"

"I don't see any other way. Do you?"

"No, but it's only going deeper into whatever this thing is!"

Filio did not respond. Instead, she tried to assess their chances of reaching the exit before the giant, who continued to regard her with those black opals that were its eyes. Without being able to say why, she suddenly felt like a laboratory rat in its cage. Maybe they would be fast enough, even though the alien had much longer legs, but probably not. And even if they made it, what if a door suddenly blocked the passage there as well?

"We have to try," she said softly, not even daring to blink, because that would be the moment when the alien stormed toward her, she was convinced.

"What? Now?"

"Yes! Now!" Filio said with force. She pushed herself off the wall and ran as fast as she could around the amber bubble and toward the open passage. Then—bam! She'd collided with something massive. It happened so violently and suddenly that her forehead hit the padded edge of the visor and she rebounded, falling backward to the ground.

Stars circled in front of her eyes like a carousel of flashing colors that vanished too quickly for her to interpret the dancing kaleidoscope of false impulses along her optic nerves.

"What..." she muttered, dazed, gently shaking her head before supporting herself on her elbows and staring at a black wall that looked exactly like the one on the opposite side. "Oh, damn. Heinrich?"

She got no response.

"Heinrich!" she repeated, feeling a leaden heaviness spread along her limbs when he failed to answer. She turned around slowly, as if she were gliding through a vacuum, and screamed helplessly when she saw the scene behind her.

The naked giant stood in front of the amber bubble not a meter away. Its bronze-colored skin almost merged with the background. It held Heinrich's head in its two oversized hands. The geophysicist's feet dangled powerlessly in the air, jerking from time to time like a mortally wounded animal, but he made no sound. His helmet lay a few steps behind him, its neck collar wrenched open by force.

"Let him go!" she shouted as loudly as she could, but all that accomplished was to fill her ears with a deafening roar. Her suit systems were still offline, so the speakers were not working. As she feared, the alien did not react to her, even when she rose up and stood.

"LET HIM GO!" she repeated, screaming, ignoring the pain in her ears. Without thinking, she jumped behind the creature and struck it a blow above its right buttock, where the right kidney was located in humans. She put as much power into the blow as she could.

The alien gave a loud roar and dropped Heinrich to the ground before turning around and striking Filio's chest with the back of its mighty hand. Even before she realized what was happening to her, she flew against the wall behind her and lost consciousness.

♡

When she came to herself, she found herself in a new environment and without a helmet. She felt something rounded at her back, curving inward along her spine, and her arms and legs were pulled backward. She felt like a piece of paper glued to a lithograph column that was slanting forward.

Light shone in front of her. It seemed to come from a ceiling far above her and illuminated a circular area on the floor that looked menacingly far away. Everything else around her lay in impenetrable darkness. The air smelled like a combination of ozone and some sweet aroma that she could not identify.

"You're awake," a scratchy voice said. With some difficulty, she turned her head slightly to one side. It was Heinrich who hung on a kind of oversized roll, his arms and legs stuck to it like pieces of metal to a strong magnet. His face was covered with sweat, and two tiny tubes led from the top of the roll along his neck and ended in his mouth. They were as insignificant as small cords, hardly thicker than yarn.

"Are you okay?" she asked so quickly that her voice almost tumbled over itself.

"Yes, I think so," he said, tiredly, and closed his eyes,

before opening them again with obvious difficulty. "What about you?"

"I don't feel any pain."

"That's good. That's good."

"Do you know what happened?" Filio asked, squinting her eyes in an attempt to see something in the darkness other than the vertically falling light with its unnaturally sharp edges. She could see nothing else. The blackness was impenetrable, and she did not hear a single noise.

"No. I woke up here, a while ago. You were out cold," Heinrich explained weakly. "I feel like I've been guzzling booze for a week."

"It had grabbed your head and lifted you up," she recalled, and cringed when she remembered the alien hitting her. Its hand had struck her chest dead-on, like a hammer blow.

"I don't know anything more. I only know how we ran toward the passage."

Her head was the only part of her body she could move. She abruptly changed the subject and nodded in his direction. "What do you have in your mouth?"

"I don't know. But you have it too."

"Really?" Filio tried to twist her eyes down but couldn't see anything except the edge of her upper lip. Maybe there was a slight scratchiness in her throat.

"Yes. It looks like the tube for a gastric probe or something, only noticeably thinner. Maybe it's because we don't have our helmets on anymore," Heinrich suggested.

"Can you move your hands?" she asked without any particular hope, so she was not surprised or disappointed when he shook his head immediately.

"Wait. I hear something," Heinrich whispered, and a heartbeat later the alien stepped into the cone of light in front of them. Its head was about at the height of their own, but it had changed. Above its palm-sized opal eyes, two metal plates were stuck onto its forehead, about where eyebrows would have been on humans. It was also no longer naked but wore a full-body suit made of a shimmering gray fiber that seemed to flow around its contours like water. It almost looked as if the garment was in constant motion and clad it from its toes to its fingertips and neck.

The alien took a step forward and eyed each of them without any visible haste. Then it turned to Heinrich, manipulated something in its hands that she couldn't see, and then stuck a piece of metal over his brow like the ones it wore on its own forehead.

"Leave him alone!" Filio shouted, struggling against her invisible shackles, but she could not move a millimeter. Frustrated, she screamed as the alien finally turned to her. "Stay away from me!"

The creature came closer with its huge face until she could see every single pore in its flat nose, which ran in a line up onto the towering forehead. Its black eyes seemed to devour her, so intense, and at the same time, ethereal were their gaze. Filio was looking for some human emotion in them, something she could reach, something she could establish a relationship with, but she saw nothing but strangeness and an eerie breadth and depth in them that caused her blood to freeze in her veins. She felt like she was looking into an entire galaxy that was being swallowed up by a black hole while she watched.

"What are you doing with us?" she asked, annoyed that she couldn't control the twitching in her lower lip. She felt how she wanted to empty her mind into his, and the urge became almost superhuman, but she furiously gritted her teeth and forced herself to withstand the alien's gaze.

Although she had the impression she was losing something of herself, she growled like an animal instead of giving in to her impulses.

To her surprise, the alien paused just before it could pin the small piece of metal onto her forehead and stepped back. In the middle of the cone of light, not two steps away, it stopped and gazed at Heinrich, from whose mouth a thin thread of saliva ran down.

The alien made a movement, causing a shudder to go through the body of the German, who was tilted downward and helplessly pressed against the pillar.

"What are you doing to him?" Filio snarled helplessly as Heinrich opened his eyes and looked at the alien.

Suddenly, a melodious swarm of noises slid over the alien's lips. The clamors swelled, as resonant and voluminous as an entire orchestra.

Heinrich nodded. "Yes, I understand," he said, blinking his eyes in a conspicuously fast sequence.

"What... what are you talking about?" she asked, and her comrade turned to her.

"He thinks you are very unruly."

"What? He?"

"Yes. His name is... Hortat. That's what it sounds like," Heinrich calmly explained, as if he were saying something completely normal and had to be surprised that she looked at him with such bewilderment.

"You understood what he had just said?"

"Oh, it's much more than what he said." The geophysicist shook his head and smiled weakly. "The device on my forehead translates its language."

"How do you know all this? I don't understand." Filio, completely flabbergasted, looked at Heinrich, then at the alien, and then back again.

"But I understand. It doesn't want to do anything to us."

"What are you talking about? It knocked me unconscious when—"

"Only after you had attacked him."

"What? He grabbed you and you fainted! I tried to free you!" she protested, shaking her head in dismay.

"I know, and I thank you for your courage. But you can't blame him. He brought us here to protect us!" Heinrich insisted, looking as enraptured as if he were under drugs.

"To protect us?" she asked with a snarl, then glared at the alien. She determined to prevent the fear slumbering deep within her from overcoming her rage.

"Yes. He was just as frightened to see us on his ship as we were frightened to see him."

"And that's what he just told you with that one gush of words?"

"It was much more than what was expressed in words," Heinrich answered patiently. "If you let him give you the device, you can understand him, too."

"No way!" she said, firmly, gritting her teeth so hard that it caused her jaws to hurt. "He's washed your brain with that thing! You're not quite in control of yourself anymore!"

"But, Filio, it's me. I know who I am, who you are, who he is, and I say all this in perfect clarity."

"You don't know that! Maybe he did something with your brain using that... Thing!"

Heinrich shook his head and gave her a tired but conciliating smile. "No, he didn't. He could have killed us at any time if he'd wanted to, but instead, he made sure we can breathe and be fed. The two hoses in your mouth are making sure of that."

"I can breathe very well by myself, thank you," she said to no one in particular.

"Oh no, you can't. The oxygen content here on the ship is about twice as high as on Earth. That would cause you to faint within a few hours and then kill you at some point," the German patiently explained.

"Why are you still bound and helpless if this, uh..."

"Hortat."

"... if this Hortat is so well-meaning?"

The alien made a small gesture when she had finished and, as if by magic, Heinrich fell to the ground. No buckles clacked open, no shackles loosened. He just slid to the floor but seemed to have expected it and caught himself with his arms and legs. He rose and went over to Filio on limbs that were visibly trembling.

"He will let you down, too, if you promise not to attack him anymore."

"You trust an alien just because it told you something?" she asked, still too stunned to even weigh his words in her mind.

"He's been on board here in his stasis chamber for over sixty million years. Then he wakes up, and suddenly two aliens in spacesuits are standing in front of him. How would you have felt?"

"How would *I* have felt?"

"Yes. You would have become frightened, and he did as well. Then you attacked him when he was probing my mind."

"Probing your mind? What are you talking about?" Filio would have liked to shake him until he came back to his senses.

"He's got abilities that we don't have. You can't even imagine what an ancient and powerful being he is, Filio!" Heinrich's eyes took on an almost fanatical glow as he spoke. "When you attacked him, he defended himself and bound us here so that we could not be a danger to him. His next step was to establish contact. The small device he gave me is necessary for that. And now think, Filio! If you had been in his place, wouldn't you have taken exactly the same steps in the same order?"

She thought for a moment and blew out a powerful lung full of air—half out of frustration, because she would have answered this question with a 'yes,' and half as a way to relieve tension.

"I don't like it, Heinrich," she said. "You've changed. Maybe it's that thing on your forehead." She looked closely at the device. It looked like a rectangular label made of ultra-flat metal that otherwise betrayed no contours or features, except that it was apparently self-adhering.

"You don't want one, he respects that. That's why he withdrew. Do you want to remain hanging there now, or will you promise him that you won't use violence against him? In that case, he'll free you, and that would be a big relief for me, okay?"

Filio tried to weigh her options. Tied to this pillar, she would be able to do nothing but wait and see what the alien had in mind for her. If she went along with him and Heinrich, she risked being brainwashed as she believed was the case with her companion.

If he truly was brainwashed, part of her tried to scold herself, but the idea that he had changed his mind in the blink of an eye and suddenly come to see this alien as a kind of saint seemed too absurd to her.

"I want him to let us talk to Dimitry and Javier," she demanded, and Heinrich frowned, then turned to the alien, which still regarded her unblinkingly. He almost looked like a father watching his children come to some kind of agreement. She wasn't sure if he seemed to her more like the kind of strict father one should fear, or like the well-disposed kind one should trust.

Heinrich turned to her after the alien had again produced a stream of those rolling and melodious sounds and shook his head with pursed lips. "Only once he trusts us. The stakes are too high for him. He wants to know who we are and how we got into his ship."

"So, this is a ship?"

"Yes."

"Are there more of his kind here?" she asked quickly.

"He wants to explain and show me everything. The question is whether you will accompany us or would rather stay here," Heinrich said. He took a step toward her until he had to tilt his head completely back to look her in the face.

Quietly, he added, "Please, Filio! Come on. There's nothing you can do here anyway, and we have the chance to make first contact with a real alien here and now. Do you really want to begin with suspicion and anger?"

"He attacked us," she insisted, but her resistance grew weaker and her ramparts began to crumble out of fear and despair.

"If he had wanted to kill us, he could have done it a long time ago. We are on Mars, not Earth. What can go wrong if we practice a little peace and understanding and go with him?"

Filio hesitated one last time, alternating her searching gaze between the giant alien and Heinrich, who looked at her almost imploringly before she nodded hesitantly. "Okay. I promise."

"Very good," he said with joy. The alien, Hortat, then made a gesture, and suddenly Filio's arms and legs were free. She fell directly into Heinrich's arms.

"I have you," he assured her. "I have you."

11

AGATHA DEVENWORTH, 2042

When Agatha and Pano had faithfully recounted their investigation, Miller said nothing for a while, had them show him the photos, and then fell silent again. They gave him this time because they knew all too well that they might have needed as much time themselves.

"That's a lot to digest," the director finally said. He got up to turn to the window behind him. By now, the sun had been swallowed by thick rain clouds, and an impenetrable gray held New York in a depressing stranglehold. "Especially this thing with the Sons of Terra. That cursed gang of murderers is supposed to have been right the whole time?"

"I know it's hard to believe, but yes, that's what it looks like," Agatha said, exchanging a quick glance with Pano, who shrugged his shoulders.

"That would at least explain this completely wacky charade involving the carrier strike group, which has now been ordered to the Antarctic," Miller muttered, without turning around.

"What do you mean?"

"Just what I said. This whole action makes no sense. We

are now risking real problems with China, which will be watching closely to see if even one of our soldiers sets foot on land there. If that happens, China will no longer hold back and will begin to militarize Antarctica, establishing their own presence on the continent. The president would never have agreed to this if she had not been put under massive pressure."

"Or," Agatha said, "she is herself an instrument of The Enemy."

"Careful, Special Agent," he admonished her, tilting his head slightly to the side without turning around. "This is dangerous terrain you're treading."

"It's a possibility we shouldn't ignore. Someone has to say it. Otherwise the whole matter will hang over us like the Sword of Damocles," Agatha insisted with a firm voice.

"We can check the data storage of Colonel Wilbers, her personal physician, to see if there was a viral infection, but that's difficult because that particular data is only accessible to the highest-ranking personnel."

"You are the Director of the CTD. More authorization is hardly possible!"

"In the event of a terrorist attack, or the acute danger of an imminent attack based on appropriate circumstantial evidence, yes," Miller corrected her and returned to his chair, where he interlocked his long fingers and inhaled with a hiss. "But the president has been in office for less than a week, so we have to get to the medical data during her time as a senator."

"Do you have the authority to do that?" Pano asked.

"Yes, but if I do it, people will notice. I could say that we're conducting a routine comparison with our own data-bases to create risk profiles, but that would be a pretty lame excuse. Whenever a request directly or indirectly concerns the president, alarms sound somewhere in data centers here in the capital, and questions will be asked."

"But that would take some time, wouldn't it?"

"I don't know, because I've avoided getting involved with such requests so far," Miller said, looking briefly into the emptiness and then looking up. "However, a wide-ranging query that affects the entire Senate will tell us which members of the Senate are still under the influence of this alien."

"Technically, that's not—"

"Don't be such a smartass" Miller snapped at Pano, then addressed Agatha. "We need to know which team we're playing against and we need to talk to the president. If you show her what you've shown me, and told me, she will have the fleet recalled before disaster strikes."

"At least if we assume that she is not—"

"If she is, then the whole thing is useless anyway. But since she was running slightly behind Phelps in the polls just before the election, this Hortat may have concentrated his attention on Phelps. Getting to the President of the United States is not easy."

"For The Enemy, it is," Agatha disagreed. "We're talking about a virus that hardly cares about the number of pistols her guards have."

"But let's assume that the virus is transmitted from person to person, which would be the worst-case scenario. In that event, someone who is close to her every day would have to be infected."

"A secret service employee in her entourage?" Pano suggested, but Miller shook his head decisively.

"No. In the event of a viral infection, they are kept away from the president for at least two weeks so as not to risk infecting her. If they miss the next rotation, they're placed off duty for two months. This means that if a member of her primary team was infected, he wouldn't be reassigned to duty until about now at the earliest."

"Which should compel us to hurry," Agatha said, slipping back and forth in her chair. Once again, she thought back to the man in the black suit and how he had examined her with his cold eyes. As if in slow motion, she saw his mouth moving and giving the order to shoot herself. It was followed by the feeling of having to watch her own body helplessly as he did things she didn't want him to do. The unheard screams in her thoughts reverberated even now, whenever she imagined facing such a killer again.

"We should also hurry because of a completely different problem." Miller gestured toward the device before turning the screen toward them. They looked at a digital map with all sorts of indicators and markers showing the area south of the equator between Africa and Australia, including Antarctica.

Agatha needed a moment to understand what she was looking at because the world from the perspective of the Southern Ocean at its center was so unfamiliar. She quickly found the position of McMurdo Station, which was marked as a red dot, and saw another red dot flashing a little northwest of it.

Pano spoke the question that burned on Agatha's lips. "What are we looking at?"

"That is the aircraft carrier with its accompanying fleet escort."

"But—"

"Yes, exactly. They will have come into range of their fighter jets in twenty-four hours and within reach of their destroyers' railguns in thirty hours. Then it will be the end of the Builder as well as Karlhammer and his little secret at the South Pole." Miller turned the screen back to himself and clenched a hand into a fist before raising it in front of his mouth and puffing his cheeks.

"I don't understand," Agatha said, bewildered. "I thought the fleet still needs days to get there."

"It's recently come to light that the Pentagon sent the combat group to conduct an exercise south of the Cape of Good Hope, which did not require the signature of the president because a limited maneuver which does not involve the use of weapons doesn't need one. Moreover, Phelps, who was still acting in place of the president at the time, did not seem to have been particularly opposed to it."

"So, he and senior officials in the Pentagon are behind it," Agatha grunted in frustration.

"Yes. Conveniently, the fleet was not as far away from its planned area of operation near McMurdo as previously thought."

"That means we have twenty-four hours to get the president to abort the mission?" Pano dropped back into his chair and threw his hands in the air. "We can forget about that. She will have only agreed to this mission very reluctantly, maybe because these people have something against her. Moreover, if she talks to these people all the time, they may have infected her."

"One can tell that you come from the old continent," the director said. "Almost all meetings take place in virtual because it's safer."

"Because one has all the data and can't be blackmailed, you mean?" Pano's disgusted grimace left no doubt as to what he thought of the matter.

"Now it's an advantage in any case," Miller insisted, pulling his hand terminal off the table. "I'll try to get an appointment. I have her direct line."

"Wait!" Agatha shouted, and then pulled out her own terminal. "I'll give you Karlhammer's number. He can disguise the signal."

"I can do that myself—"

"But you don't know which of the supposedly good guys are listening in, right?"

Miller looked at her as if he had bitten into a lemon and then waved at her. "Very well, give me the number!" He let Agatha send it to him with a swipe and pulled out a drawer that she couldn't see from her position. He produced a transducer net and placed it on his head. When he saw her questioning facial expression, the corners of his mouth twitched. "Regulations in case of direct contact with the president. My brain waves are read out before they connect me to her."

"And you're certain that the conversation won't be overheard by anyone?" Pano asked incredulously.

"No. Not that I know of, and I'm in charge of all counterterrorism measures in this country. If you'll excuse me, I have to explain to the president that some Martians are living at the South Pole, and others are spreading viruses in order to exploit us in their pursuit of an old feud."

"That's exactly how you should put it," Agatha said in a low mutter.

An hour later found the three of them riding toward Washington in Miller's official vehicle. Since no one except the four Secret Service agents in the president's immediate vicinity knew about the sudden visit, they had gone without an escort. It had been relatively easy to get into the parking lot and disappear relatively unnoticed, since a large portion of the workforce was still not on duty.

They thus found themselves traveling on the interstate to Washington in silence. They were riding on autopilot, which they had set to the maximum possible speed using a priority code. They could also have driven manually and used the transponder to override all traffic rules on their own, but that would have attracted attention—the kind of attention they could not afford now.

The card software on the head-up display in the windshield showed an expected driving time of 2 hours and 11 minutes, which should be accurate to the minute. Agatha hated running against time because she always realized how long every little detail could drag out. Now they were sitting here in the spacious Tesla Model Z and were doomed to inaction, while a 24-hour countdown ran on her hand terminal like grains of sand in an hourglass.

Only, in the end, what would remain would not be an empty upper glass, but a destroyed pyramid, a dead Xinth, an equally dead Luther Karlhammer, and in the long run, the lost chance for saving their species and their planet. Although she was not one of those many doomsday prophets who ever more stridently preached the coming biosphere catastrophe, she was also not one of those blind, cynical fools that still refused to believe the climate threat, despite the many coastal metropolises that already been enclosed within meter-high protective sea walls.

She had no doubt that the Human Foundation had prevented and still was preventing worse, and they owed it to that Builder, who now lay in the pyramid in Antarctica. Not to mention the fact that killing the first conscious and intelligent species that humanity had encountered would be another terrible stain on its history.

Twenty-four hours is simply not enough time, she thought bitterly. *What if officers in key positions near McMurdo ignored the president's order to abort?* If they could even get Elisabeth Harris to take that step.

"What did she say on the phone?" Agatha finally asked for the umpteenth time.

Miller seemed so uninterested in the tenacious silence that reigned in the car that he answered as patiently as before. "That she takes my request for an emergency meeting in the interests of national security seriously, and that you two—and I—should come immediately. She has a press conference in two and a half hours, so we'll get just under ten minutes of her time."

"Not much time to explain to someone that there are aliens on Earth who are waging war against each other at our expense," Pano said. He was sitting in the back with his legs lying across the seat, an almost offensive image when considering the sinfully expensive leather seats.

"No amount of time is enough for that, I guess," Miller agreed. "But we'll try. There is no other way."

An hour later, they drove by Philadelphia. The city passed them as a collection of gray rowhouses and a central pile of skyscrapers that resembled a dreary cemetery. No-fly zones had been in place over the city since last year forbidding all drones except those of the police. This was mandated by a decree issued by the governor, who had given in to growing public pressure. Agatha could hardly imagine that such a dead cityscape, without dark swarms of objects flying over the roofs, had been quite normal 20 years ago.

The next 10 kilometers before them consisted of solar asphalt that automatically charged their Tesla as they drove over it. The material's rough surface caused slight vibrations, which became noticeable as hums in the otherwise quiet vehicle.

"We've come over halfway," Miller said, frowning. Agatha followed his gaze and looked through the windshield before she deactivated the head-up display and saw another black Tesla Model Z swerve in front of them. On its license plate, one could see both the inscription 'U.S. Government' and the coat of arms of Homeland Security.

"What's this?" Miller asked, more angry than alarmed. Agatha looked into the rearview mirror and saw another Tesla Z.

"Were you expecting anyone?" Pano asked, taking his feet off the back seat, and sliding his right hand under his jacket, where his heavy Glock hung in its holster.

"No."

"Oh shit!" Agatha cursed as the car braked in front of them, and their autopilot automatically reacted and adjusted its speed. "Turn off the autopilot!"

"I can't," Miller replied, hammering the display in the center console with a fist, but it didn't respond. Only a red triangle was lit there. 'Danger' appeared in the middle of it.

How ironic, Agatha thought. She pulled out her service weapon.

"You don't really want to shoot at our people, do you, Agent Devenworth?" the director asked, giving her a razor-sharp look.

"Our people? How sure are you of that? Have you already received the medical data you requested from the senators?"

"No," Miller admitted, gritting his teeth, before suddenly yelling, "Damn! Heads down!"

Their autopilot braked so sharply that they were thrown against their seat belts. Then the doors of the cars in front and behind them opened, and masked figures in full armor stepped out. They didn't hesitate and pointed their assault rifles at the car. Agatha was able to loosen her belt and slide down when they started firing. Bullets drummed against the armored glass as if they were in the middle of a full-blown hailstorm, and it was getting darker with every second.

Irritated, Agatha took her hands off her head and looked up. The windshield and the window on its passenger side were pockmarked with black splashes as if they were being shot with paintball bullets. The film became steadily thicker until she could hardly see anything, and every window was covered in dirty-black.

"What the hell are they doing?" Pano shouted over the noise from the back. Then the deafening noise abruptly gave way to a menacing silence.

"They want to blind us," Miller growled, pointing to the instrument screen, on which the display seemed to vibrate before it turned off and the car started moving again. "Now they've taken over our autopilot. SHIT!"

"How did they do that?"

"With a Homeland Security priority code that is even higher than mine."

"Is there one?"

"Yes." Miller looked at her with a bitter snarl on his lips. "The Secretary has one."

"Oh, damn!"

Their Tesla accelerated so strongly that Agatha was pushed into her seat and felt as if an invisible fist was pressing into her belly. She hastily put her belt back on.

"Open window," she tried with voice control, but she might as well have commanded a stone to fly.

Frustrated, she reached into her pocket and pulled out her hand terminal, but as she expected, she had no connection. "I guess we can no longer receive the senators' medical data."

"So, the Secretary works for The Enemy," Pano said gloomily, but Miller shook his head.

"We don't know that for sure."

"You're shitting me, right?"

The director's face took on a dangerous expression centered around his mouth, an expression she had seen several times before he fired an employee—which he was accustomed to doing relatively quickly. "Don't talk to me like that!"

"If there is only one priority code that overrides yours and it belongs to the Secretary," Pano said, unmoved, "that's the only explanation."

"We know that she is probably the one who ordered this response, but that doesn't say anything about the background and reasons for what she's doing, let alone whether she works for the alien," Miller insisted.

The two men argued about it for a while, but Agatha tried not listening to them. Instead, she focused on holding down the contents of her stomach. Without a visual point of reference, the constant changes of direction, the curves, and the regular ups and downs, combined into a torment for her digestive organs, which reacted with the growing urge to empty themselves.

According to her hand terminal, the drive lasted exactly 13 minutes. Their car then came to a stop with squealing tires.

"That's it," she said, loading her pistol. Pano apparently did the same, because she heard his Glock cocking, but Miller shook his head.

"Don't be naive. They'll reckon on this move and take you out faster than you can shout 'innocent.'"

"Better than being infected with some damned alien virus and ending up a mindless zombie," Pano growled.

"He's right," Agatha told Pano, lowering her weapon.

"Drop your weapons, fall onto the floor, and put your hands on the dashboard or the front seat," a male voice suddenly rang out from the speakers of their car. "You have ten seconds. If you do not comply, we will open fire on you as soon as the door is open."

Agatha obeyed the instruction and dropped her Beretta into the footwell before putting both hands atop the glove compartment. Miller did the same in the driver's seat and pressed his lips together.

"Do it, Pano. If we let ourselves get shot now, then it's all over," she urged her partner, and she finally heard a thud on the floor and a frustrated snort from behind her seat.

Less than a second later, all four doors sprang open at the same time, and they were dragged out of the vehicle under the hoarse shouts of their captors.

Rough hands grabbed Agatha by her shoulders and legs and threw her to the ground, where she coughed into the dust and felt a knee in the small of her back. Someone painfully yanked her hands behind her back and secured them with cable ties before she was brutally wrenched to her feet and had to squeeze her eyes closed because of a blinding, white light.

"Alright, man!" she protested. "We've given up!"

In response, she received a violent blow to her back that squeezed all the air out of her lungs. She did not fall, she did not even stumble, because the strong hands that gripped her upper arms did not let her. They were dragged through a large hall, or a very wide hallway—it was hard to say. Their eyes were still blinded by the bright light. Then she was placed on a chair and tied to it, hands and feet.

When her eyes had become accustomed to seeing again she made out a kind of hangar building around her, with high ceilings and metal struts. Four government vehicles were parked about 10 meters away and dazzled them with their headlights.

She saw Miller and Pano, also tied to chairs, sitting next to her. Her partner was bleeding from his nose and an ear. He had lost his bandage, which now lay on the ground a few meters in the direction of the cars.

Illuminated by the headlights, a good dozen men in combat gear stood with assault rifles angled down, and a single figure slowly approached them. She wore a long, cream-colored coat and had long blond hair that framed her wrinkled brown face.

It was Silvia Cortez, Secretary of Homeland Security for the United States of America.

12

FILIO AMOROSA, 2042

Filio bent over the black shaft that led into Hortat's ship, looking for a ladder or anything they could use to descend. But the walls were smooth like marble, except for a few scratches and burn marks around the upper edge.

"Damn," Cassidy murmured and then looked back at her. "How are we supposed to get down there?"

"The gravity here is only one third—"

"—of Earth's, I know! We've already been over that," he interrupted her. He pointed into the dark hole. "Nevertheless, that's at least ten meters."

"If I can judge correctly, there's a lot of sand down there, and if you could somehow let me down and hold on until I drop, then it's only eight meters and..." Filio paused.

"What is it?"

"I've just had a weird déja vu," she said, frowning, shaking off the thought.

He silently held up his stump.

"Oh... but we have got to go down there in any case. I'll try to slow my fall with my arms and legs on the walls. The gloves should be able to take it."

"What if you rip your suit?"

"Then you'll probably have to unpack your patch kit, right?"

Before Cassidy could reply, she climbed into the hole and held on to the metallic edge before spreading her legs and pushing her feet against the walls.

"Just be careful."

"And you watch carefully. You're next." Filio avoided adding, 'in the event I survive it without injury,' and released her hands from the edge of the hole. The good news was that she was able to slow her fall and did not plunge out of control. The bad news was that she couldn't maintain perfect balance. Her back bounced against the wall, causing her to start rowing with her arms.

Grunting, she tried to maintain some sort of hold with her hands, but they slipped every time, despite the rubber knobs on her palms, so after a few meters she ended up in a kind of squatting position. This placed her buttocks in an unfavorable position as the lowest point of her body. The position of her boots no longer created any helpful pressure, and she crashed the last few meters rear end first. The impact was so painful that she screamed and immediately feared she had broken something.

"Filio? Are you hurt?" Cassidy asked anxiously over the radio. The cold beam of his helmet lights fixed on her like an unwelcome stage light, and she groaned, rolling to the side, down from the pile of sand and out of the light.

She first got onto hands and knees for a moment before rising to upright kneeling. She carefully rose to standing and slowly stretched her spine. It cracked a few times, but she felt no sharp pains so she didn't think she had broken anything.

"Filio? FILIO!" Cassidy's voice sounded shrill, and a

deep, rushing noise that accompanied it gave added force to that impression.

"Yes! No. I mean, no, I'm not hurt, I think. At least I can still walk." She took a step forward, back into the beam of his helmet lights, and with her face distorted by pain, she raised her thumb while shielding her eyes with the other hand. "It's your turn!"

"Damn. I'll definitely fall forward with my big belly," the physicist grumbled, but climbed into the shaft opening without hesitation. His movements seemed rather disjointed, which was probably due to his stocky, almost dwarflike, physique in conjunction with his missing hand.

"Just try not to turn. It's best to stretch both your feet back against the wall and press forward with your hand and elbow, so that you can—"

There was a dull thud, and suddenly Cassidy was lying next to her feet on the pile of sand. "Oooh," he moaned.

"Hmm. I guess that works, too," she said. The physicist's whimper inspired pity, causing Filio to bend down to help him. He was lying face down in the pile of sand, and his arms and legs were spread as if someone had pushed him flat onto the ground.

"I'll help you," she assured him, carefully turning him on his side. Cassidy's suit was covered from top to bottom by fine regolith and a crack stretched across his visor.

"I see it," he said, his face glowing like an alarm. "But according to my suit system, pressure and breathing air are stable. Apparently, there's no leak."

"Good. Are you hurt?"

"I don't know... I don't think so."

"Does it hurt anywhere?"

Cassidy looked directly at her with raised eyebrows. *You've got to be kidding,* he thought.

"So? Can you move without any sharp or tearing pain?" she asked, holding his head immobile in case his cervical spine was damaged.

Carefully, her partner began to wiggle his left hand and both feet, and then widened the movements into his arms and legs.

"I think I'm okay," he said after a few moments, and she slowly let go of his helmet, getting up and offering her hands to help out. Cassidy gratefully reached out to grab them with his hand.

Filio pulled him onto his feet. "Now we both feel like we've been kicked by a horse. The best possible circumstances for exploring the spaceship of arguably the evilest being that ever walked the Earth, huh?" she asked sarcastically, looking into a corridor that slanted downward, as black as the shadows that filled it.

"You can say that again. Looks like it's downhill for us from now on," Cassidy said, pointing into the sloping passage, "and the pun is intentional."

"Maybe you should have stuck a few weapons under the damn seats of the transport module," Filio said softly in response. She squared her shoulders before heading into the depths. Without prior agreement, they directed their helmets, and thus their lights, to the right and left, so that the lights overlapped slightly in the middle and illuminated as much of the dark walls as possible.

Because they moved only a little, the shadows remained steady, sparing her the distress that could be caused by the darkness and narrowness of the passage, at least to some small degree, because she felt anything but steady. Things got worse when they arrived at a level section of the passage and a new section led horizontally into the darkness.

"Why have you stopped?" Cassidy asked quietly,

squinting his eyes in a quick search of the blackness that surrounded them.

"The lava tunnel!" She stretched out a hand and pointed into the passage. Its walls looked jagged and porous, just like those lava tunnels in which they had set up their base on the *Mars One* mission. At least that was what it looked like in the photos.

"I don't think this is a lava tunnel."

"Of course not. But in the UN hearing on the crash of our ship, I testified that we discovered the object at the end of a lava tunnel, in a kind of amber bubble and—"

"Don't tell me—you were attracted by a pulsating light," Cassidy said in a resigned tone, swallowing heavily.

Filio raised her gaze and now she saw it too—a warm yellow light in the distance, which pulsed alternately stronger and weaker. Instead of answering, she sucked in a trembling breath.

"Oh, damn," Cassidy yelled. "This is exactly how you found The Enemy, isn't it? Before he let you and your crew fly to Earth to crash there and erase your memory, right?"

"Yes," she whispered indignantly.

"And what happens now?" The physicist sounded as if he was afraid of the answer.

"I don't remember. I remember from the transcripts of the hearing that I said something about an amber bubble or something, but nothing else," she reluctantly admitted, feeling that anger rising again. Anger at the fact that she could not remember, even though she knew she had been here before. Anger that she did not know how her friends and comrades had died. Nothing was more infuriating than knowing that somewhere in your own brain there was information stored away that you simply couldn't access, no matter how hard you tried.

"Well, there's no way back for us now, anyway," Cassidy finally said, and they exchanged some tense glances before Filio nodded and they headed for the light. It seemed to attract her almost hypnotically, and although every part of her struggled against getting closer, there was no other direction left to go.

"Everything here screams it's a trap," she said, carefully setting one foot in front of the other as if walking on the brittle ice of a frozen lake.

"And we already know what happened the last time it was sprung," Cassidy added somberly.

"We know the result, but we don't know what happened before."

"Which could be even worse."

"Yes."

"Have you ever thought about the fact that we may now be making exactly the same mistakes that you and your crewmates made three years ago?"

"Mistakes?" Filio snapped, a little sharper than she intended. She attributed it to the fact that she felt like a steam boiler under pressure and threatening to explode at any moment.

"What I meant was that we might possibly make the same decisions that lead to the same result," Cassidy said apologetically.

"With the difference being that The Enemy is already on Earth. So, he can't be here now."

"Who knows what he left behind? In any case, the light there came on when we appeared down here."

"I'll try to behave differently than my instinct tells me," she said, pausing as she saw the amber bubble in front of her like a kind of brown egg. Cassidy looked at her from the side as if trying to figure out if she was joking or being serious.

"This is obviously the place where we found The Enemy. But what is that in the middle?" she asked, pointing to a shadow in the heart of the bubble.

Cassidy looked forward again and bent over a little. "It looks like—"

"—like a skeleton."

"Yes," he whispered, looking back over his shoulder as if trying to see if anyone was following them. He found numerous pursuers in the forms of furrowed shadows, from which his brain quickly constructed grotesque faces of demons and predators. His limbs trembling, he brought his gaze back around to forward, and then followed Filio, who had set herself in motion again.

When only a few steps separated them from the round room with the amber bubble in its center, she noticed that it looked like a very small version of the room in which the Human Foundation had built the transport module. It may have been a coincidence, but maybe not.

"It's a skeleton," she said softly into the radio mic. Intrigued, she looked at the long arm and leg bones, the slightly tilted pelvis and the mighty skull with its prominent head. "Clearly, a Builder."

"But if that's The Enemy... What did you and your comrades bring back to Earth?" Cassidy asked ominously, as a dark bulkhead suddenly plunged from the ceiling behind them and trapped them in the room.

At the same time, they both whirled around and reached to slap their hands against this new wall, as if wishing that it were just an illusion. Cassidy flinched as he noted his stump again, and their hope immediately dissolved into savage curses and violently pounding hearts.

"This is... not good," Cassidy commented on their new

situation. He turned back to the amber bubble. Filio did the same and gazed at the skeleton with widened eyes, as if it could suddenly arise from its fetal position and crouch, ready to spring at any time and attack them. But there was something else that lay like a shadow on the bubble.

"What is that?" she asked.

"What?"

"That there!" She circled the bubble and paused in surprise when she saw a second passage leading into the darkness on the other side.

"An exit," Cassidy said. He was about to run when Filio held him up with an outstretched hand on his chest. "What?"

"I wanted to run as well," she replied.

"Well? We should immediately... Oh, you mean back then... I understand." The physicist stopped and no longer fought against her. A heartbeat later, they jumped at the same time when a hole opened up in the ceiling above the bubble and a robotic arm shot out. A long needle of scary-looking thickness jutted from the end of it and pierced the amber bubble without warning. It found its way down through the brownish material and punctured the fossil's skull before the arm pulled it out again.

Almost faster than Filio's eyes could track the move-ment, the needle moved to the other side of the bubble. Without thinking, she walked around the amber egg and watched as the robotic arm sank the needle into a tiny hole in the upper third of a kind of door—one of exactly three positioned on each side of the round room.

"And what does your instinct tell you now?" Cassidy whispered to her over the radio as he pulled her back slightly with his hand on her shoulder.

She gave in to him all too willingly and retreated with him to the opposite wall.

"Run into the damned passage and get out of here," she said in confession, waving a hand toward the open darkness to their left. "Because everything in me resists the idea of just staying here."

"So that's what we should do…" The statement sounded more like a question from Cassidy's mouth, as if he were still hoping that she would change her mind.

"I guess so." Her struggle to deny her adrenaline-fueled impulses and remain here instead was causing Filio almost physical pain. Each cell of her being seemed magnetically attracted to the open passage.

"Something's happening!" Cassidy cried aloud, and his otherwise rather full-toned voice now sounded as shrill as a whistle.

As if mesmerized, Filio watched as the door or cover in which the needle had disappeared lifted out from the wall and white steam poured out of the interior behind it. It spread throughout the room like fog and subsided only very slowly. Soon there was nothing but steam there, and not even the cover could be seen.

"I think we should really get out of here now," Cassidy said. Filio looked down at her right arm and noticed he was holding her hand. Once again, she felt that she had experienced this very moment before, without really being able to link it to a memory.

"No," she said with a firm voice, forcing herself to look back into the slowly dissolving steam. In the meantime, the robotic arm had apparently disappeared into the ceiling, its uniform gray betraying no sign that anything had ever come out of it.

"A Builder!" Cassidy cried out, and Filio's gaze jerked

back from the ceiling into the steam, which had shifted surprisingly quickly. In the large, rectangular opening, the outline of a humanoid figure appeared. It was surrounded by a penetrating white glow. Its head was much bigger than it should have been, which led her to agree with Cassidy and give in to instinct. She tried to take another step back, but after only a few centimeters she bumped against the wall behind her. She was so terrified that an electric surge of fresh adrenaline shot along her veins.

"Wait!" Cassidy yelled. He suddenly took a step forward.

Filio was already screaming at him to stop when she noticed something strange. The figure that was just beginning to stir inside the tiny, coffin-like chamber was far too small for a Builder—at least if all the Builders were like Xinth in size.

As the figure took a shaky step forward, she and Cassidy flinched back at the same time. Then Filio froze.

"What in the..." the physicist began, but speech apparently failed him in mid-sentence.

Filio couldn't believe what she was seeing. She rubbed her helmet visor to clear it and blinked until her eyes teared, but there was no doubt that what they saw stepping out of the coffin-like chamber at an angle next to the amber bubble was a man in the massive white and red suit of the *Mars One* mission. She recognized the badges and the V-shaped helmet with a visor she had always thought was too small and had hated so much.

When the figure apparently lost its balance and began to fall, Filio, without thinking, ran forward and caught it. Together they tumbled backward, and she backed into the amber bubble with her ceramic backpack. She barely registered the pain in her back. Instead, she felt the weight of the person who was now lying on top of her.

Filio tried to get up.

Cassidy appeared next to her and grabbed the fallen figure by one arm to pull it away from her. Surprisingly, the little physicist seemed able to mobilize a lot of power and threw the stranger back toward the chamber with astonishing force. It lay there, motionless.

"Are you okay?" Cassidy asked angrily, helping her to her feet.

"Yes... Thank you," she said softly, and pinched her eyes shut for a few seconds to get rid of the double-vision images that made her unable to recognize details. Then they both turned to the figure in the spacesuit, and Filio took a step forward.

"Wait!" her partner protested, but she heedlessly ignored his warnings and knelt on the small step in front of the chamber, where the collapsed figure half sat and half lay, much like a drunkard passed out by the side of a road back home.

First quickly, then hesitantly, she reached for the unconscious figure's left breast, where the embroidered, fold-down nametag was. When her suit's thin gloves sensed the familiar feeling of the patch's fabric between her fingers, she paused and closed her eyes.

"What is it?" Cassidy asked over the static crackling on the radio.

Instead of answering, Filio took a deep breath and turned the nametag up so she could see it.

"Marks," she read breathlessly, tumbling back as if she had been run into by a bus.

"Marks?"

"Heinrich Marks, geophysicist of the *Mars One* mission," she whispered, and crawled backward on all fours until she hit the amber bubble again. She stared at her friend, whose visor was so dark she couldn't recognize his face. She didn't know which outcome to be more afraid of—the fact that it would turn out to be a corpse, or an alien, or indeed Heinrich.

"But that's impossible," Cassidy said. Then he pulled the figure out of the chamber with a grunt and laid it out flat on the floor. "All crewmembers except you died in the Earth's atmosphere before it crashed."

"They never found their bodies because they simply dissolved in plasma," Filio said in a hoarse voice, flaring her nostrils like a shy horse.

MARS, 2039

Filio stumbled after Heinrich and the alien, with trembling knees and unsure movements. She wished to be as calm and certain as her crewmate, but he had either lost his mind or had been brainwashed. In any case, he no longer seemed to be afraid of their 'host' and showed no signs of insecurity.

What surprised her most was the speed with which everything had happened. Only a few seconds had passed between the time when the alien had stuck the piece of metal to Heinrich's forehead and the German's first emotional speech on the alien's behalf.

"Where are we going?" she hissed to Heinrich, without turning her gaze away from the alien's back.

"Hortat is leading us to his private chamber."

"Why?"

"He wants to answer your questions," he explained, without turning around. They walked through a wide passage where she felt like a toy figure in a playhouse far too big for her, so high were the walls and ceilings. She could not make out any doors, and was therefore terrified when the huge muscular figure, who was striding in front of them like a living boulder, abruptly stopped. A rectangular doorway appeared in the wall as if it had always been there.

Hortat went ahead and Heinrich followed him without hesitation. Filio paused for a moment and looked right and left down the passage, but she could see only a few meters down either direction, as the lighting, which seemed to come from both everywhere and nowhere, apparently followed the alien and faded behind it.

What am I doing here? she asked herself, still not comprehending that all this was actually happening.

The room in which she now found herself was akin to the shape of an egg lying on one side, except that the floor was flat. When she entered, she would have sworn that the walls had moved to form its current shape, but it had happened so quickly that she wasn't sure that she wasn't imagining it.

When he reached the middle of the room, Hortat stopped and closed his eyes for a moment. The floor came to life a heartbeat later, causing Filio to jump back in horror. Three small columns rose from the black, seamless material as if they were composed of some sort of very thick liquid.

It didn't take long for the three columns to transform, two of them turning into smaller chairs with narrow backrests and the third becoming a much larger one. Each chair had only one leg. The legs looked so fragile that it seemed as if they must inevitably break under the weight of their seats. The rest of the room remained empty, windowless, and unadorned.

"Sit," the alien's voice rumbled, and Filio froze as the deep, rolling voice spoke to her in fluent German and he pointed to one of the two smaller chairs. His pronunciation sounded a little strange because he stretched out the vowels.

Except for that slight deviation, however, he spoke the language surprisingly well.

"How... how did you do that?" Filio stammered in irritation. She observed herself as she fell onto her chair as if all her strength had left her.

"I have the ability from him," Hortat replied, pointing to her teammate with one of his paws. Heinrich bowed his head with a smile.

"That easily?"

"Yes."

Filio shook her head to gain some time and to come to terms with the fact that the alien was speaking to her in her native language. "I... I don't know what to say."

"I think this is as difficult for me to comprehend as it is for you," Hortat said, waggling its head slightly—a gesture she did not understand and therefore interpreted as head nodding. "You don't trust me, and I understand that well. I don't trust you, either."

"You don't trust me?" she asked in surprise.

"No. Why should I? You entered my ship and attacked me. At the same time, you saved my life."

"You attacked Heinrich!" Filio forgot for a moment that she was sitting opposite a bronze-colored colossus. Then she thought back to the room with the amber bubble and the sight of her comrade helpless in his hands.

"That's not correct. I was only... reading from his mind," Hortat said calmly, and the bass of his voice seemed to resonate in her like a gong.

"And you don't see that as an attack?"

"No."

"You don't think that someone else could see that as an attack?"

Hortat looked at her with his pitch-black eyes, as if he

wanted to absorb her entire being into himself. Then he tilted his head to the side. "I understand your view. If you accepted the transverse module, you could understand much more quickly."

"You mean that thing sticking on Heinrich's forehead?" she asked, shaking her head. "I don't know what you did to him, but he's behaving strangely."

"You certainly have questions for me. I suggest that we answer them quickly so that you can decide whether you trust me or not." The alien abruptly folded his hands on his lap in an almost human gesture.

"What if I choose not to trust you?"

"I hope that will not happen," came the ambiguous response, and Filio had to swallow a lump in her throat. A menacing atmosphere suddenly weighed on them like a shroud, and she felt small and defenseless before the alien that towered over her as a father over his little daughter.

"Where do you come from?" she asked after swallowing heavily several more times. If she were now completely in the clutches of an alien, she could at least try to find out as much as possible. She remembered well how she had discussed the Fermi paradox with her comrades in Darmstadt.

She had never made a secret of the fact that she thought the universe was a pretty empty place, no matter how often other scientists threw the 'Drake equation' at her. In her eyes, that was not an equation based on mathematical principles, but rather a product of fantasy, full of assumptions and gaps. She had obviously been wrong, and now she wanted to know everything.

"From the planet you call home," came the surprising answer, and Filio narrowed her eyes to slits.

"How's that?"

"I come from Earth, and I left there about sixty-six million years ago. Here on Mars, I... had an accident."

"You are a human being?"

"No. I said that I come from Earth, but in ages long past. According to my initial analyses, we share over ninety-nine percent of our DNA, but you also share about ninety-eight percent of your DNA with a domesticated pig, so that doesn't necessarily mean very much," Hortat said.

The blatant condescension in his statement caused her upper lip to twitch. "So, you could call us relatives?" she posed with a joyless smile.

"Yes."

"You said that we had saved you."

"I reposed in my stasis chamber almost the entire time since my ship was stranded here, and the power supply from the maelstrom threatened to run out. If this had happened, I would have died within a few days."

"What is a maelstrom?" Filio asked curiously.

"You wouldn't understand," Hortat replied, making a dismissive hand movement that she understood immediately.

Again, that arrogance, she thought. It almost seemed as if it were part of his essential nature, which may even have been the case. She chose to ignore his condescending behavior and make productive use of her time instead. "Where are the others of your kind?"

"Since your species knows nothing of mine, I assume that my kind have not returned."

"Returned?"

"We left Earth in my time to colonize other star systems and even other galaxies through the Twelve-Fold Space. There were great climatic and tectonic upheavals that our civilization would not have survived unscathed. So, we evacuated the entire planet, except for one of us who had been chosen as the Guardian of the Ark," the alien explained, and his deep bass rolled over her like a mighty wave.

His aura was so powerful that Filio felt as if a wet blanket lay over her. It was an aura of superiority and power in whose sphere of influence she felt inferior. She did not like how that felt. A sidelong look at Heinrich showed that the geophysicist was still smiling contentedly, as if in meditation.

"The Twelve-Fold Space? The Ark?"

"The Twelve-Fold Space is not known to your species. Four dimensions are known to you. Three of them refer to the universe perceptible to your sense organs and with geometric equivalents of height, length, and width. The fourth dimension you refer to as space-time. All dimensions beyond these four you call 'hyperspace.'

"We were able to decipher eight hyperspace dimensions that are suitable for faster-than-light travel. Initial tests were promising, but we couldn't wait due to the imminent catastrophe on Earth and in some... haste... built our colonization fleet. In the event of failure, several thousand embryos were frozen in the temple capital of Antuan, in the heart of the Geth Pyramid. I do not know where it is after all the millions of years of tectonic shifts, but it will still be there.

"The high priest Xinth stayed behind to guard them, and from time to time to awaken from his stasis to perform maintenance on the facility. He's probably been dead for a long time. He waited in vain."

Hortat bent forward slightly like a professor over his student, and Filio instinctively jerked back.

The alien continued, "No one survived the journey through the Twelve-Fold Space."

"What do you mean? Are you the last of your kind?"

Filio looked over at Heinrich, who, in apparent empathy, had lowered his head and nodded silently, as if remembering a traumatic experience.

"Yes, that's true."

She wanted to say something in response but mechanically closed her mouth again. What could she say to an alien who was something of an ancestor and had just told her that his entire species was extinct?

"This Twelve-Fold Space," she said after a while, when she had found her speech again, and Heinrich had become restless, "what exactly is that?"

"You would—"

"—not understand? Let me be the judge of that."

"From the knowledge that Heinrich Marks here possesses, I have learned that your species only refers to the first four dimensions, completely disregarding the spiritual aspects and the metaphysical connections, because scientific investigative methods are still lacking. You are ignoring what you do not understand, as if it did not exist.

"That's why you and your peers have categorically ruled out the possibility of faster-than-light travel—because your thinking is limited to the four basic dimensions. The additional eight dimensions are—to the extent we were able to find out—there to serve the organization of matter and energy and their negative equivalents. Making them visible has opened up the universe to us."

"Do you mean something like morphogenetic fields?" Filio asked in surprise. "It's just a pseudoscience."

"Heinrich Marks was obviously unfamiliar with this term," said Hortat, looking at her comrade, who had bent down and was shaking his head.

"There was a scientist on Earth called Sheldrake who postulated that there must be a kind of morphogenetic field, that there is a subtle information network that covers the world, that organizes living forms," she explained, trying to remember the book she had read about Rupert Sheldrake's ideas. "It was observed that certain species that are spatially separated from each other, for example on different continents, learn the same things at similar times.

"A well-known example concerns monkey populations in Africa and South America, which learned at the same time to solve certain puzzles with a stick. If one community learned it, the other soon followed without the experiment being conducted again.

"According to Rupert Sheldrake, the field is supposed to be an overarching one that organizes the development of all structures, be it living beings, social structures, physics, chemistry, and so on. Epigenetics has made his theories popular again, and they have actually been seriously studied—especially by quantum physicists—yet so far without results."

"He was right in a simple way, this human," Hortat said. He jerked one finger, at which point a kind of hologram of the Earth appeared between them, only instead of looking permeable, it looked like a massive blue ball that had emerged from nowhere. "The organizing informational dimensions are everywhere and part of every perceptible phenomenon."

The Earth became permeable and began to glow. "This is not an accurate representation, because these dimensions, which Heinrich Marks would doubtlessly name hyperspace, cannot be represented according to their nature. In any case, every conscious and intelligent living being has access to these eight overarching dimensions. There is a connecting organ."

"The brain," Filio said immediately, and then suddenly felt as if she were overlooking something.

"This is true, but only for the duration of their conscious existence as a biological unit."

"Are you saying that this hyperspace is a kind of afterlife?"

"No. You live on as information there after your death, but it has nothing to do with your personality or your memories. Only the information is embedded in the structure as a whole and cannot be lost," he corrected her. He opened his hand.

The globe hovering between them exploded so realistically that Filio instinctively shielded herself with her arms. When she lowered them again, the ball of light was still floating there, causing her to ask, "And why did your entire fleet disappear?"

"I'm not sure. The journey in Twelve-Fold Space was... more dangerous than was thought. What I experienced there was disturbing enough not to talk about it. In any case, a living being must never penetrate it again, and that is why you must bring me back to Earth."

"Bring you back to Earth?" Filio asked, irritated. She looked at Heinrich, who had already turned toward her and nodded forcefully. His eyes were shining. *Like that of a devoted follower,* she thought. *Or that of a madman.*

"Yes. I have seen in Heinrich Marks' brain that you have a primitive spaceship that can take me there."

"But why? As you have explained, our species is too primitive to penetrate into these dimensions in the near future."

"Geth."

"You mean that ark of yours?"

"Yes. I have to go there and destroy all the data banks

that contain information about Twelve-Fold Space," explained Hortat, and just as he finished, his head jerked to the side as if he were looking at something she could not see.

"What is it?"

"Your comrades are trying to demolish the upper access point with explosives. We don't have much time left. I cannot allow them to cause lasting damage to this ship. You should decide now, Filio Amorosa."

"Or you're going to kill me, right?" she asked, and it was a neutral, impersonal conclusion. In the course of their conversation, she had already noticed what kind it was. It felt like a master talking to his dog and scratching it behind an ear while holding a syringe filled with poison behind his back to put it to sleep if it should bite him.

"I will do everything necessary to ensure that no representative of my or your species ever again make the mistake of overcoming the dimensions properly intended for them. Geth is perhaps the most dangerous place in the entire Milky Way," Hortat said, standing up.

Heinrich did the same, raising his hands in a gesture reminiscent of someone trying to appease a snarling animal. "We will help you," he assured the alien.

Immediately Filio's stomach began to turn. Apparently, Heinrich knew something she didn't—something that concerned her immediate survival.

"What if he has something completely different in mind?" she asked her comrade, rounding her chair to place him between herself and the giant, even if probably there was no point to it. "He could tell us any story he wants and force us to bring him to Earth. And then? What if he has different plans once he's there?"

"It's not like that," Heinrich said with certainty, shaking

his head decisively. He stood between her and Hortat, who stared at her as motionlessly as a statue. His huge eyes seemed to contain such an immeasurable breadth and depth that she could not even imagine what might be going on behind them.

How could she expect to understand his motives? At the same time, she realized that she had no choice. He could kill her at any time. After all, she stood in a kind of morphing room that seemed to obey his unspoken orders. Then he would take Heinrich with him, kill the others, or brainwash them, and eventually return to Earth on the *Mars One* and do whatever he intended.

Whatever that is, she thought. "Alright, I'm with you," she said shortly afterward, nodding. "If we can protect humanity from this dangerous knowledge, we should do it."

And I'll keep a close eye on you, because on the Mars One I know more than Heinrich does, and therefore more than you, she added in thought, hoping that the being before her was not able to read her thoughts in some magical way.

"That is good. I'm reestablishing your radio connection," Hortat announced. "Your helmets are in the other chamber."

Filio and Heinrich followed him back into the room with the two inclined pillars to which they had been bound, and they retrieved their helmets.

Hortat made a seemingly patronizing gesture that seemed to express permission to put them on.

Filio tried not to think about the way he behaved toward them as she pulled her helmet onto her head. When the seal snapped shut, it felt as if she were insulated from everything around her, which gave her an admittedly naive sense of security.

She took a deep breath. "Restart," she ordered, and the entire system actually came to life—including the radio link.

"Filio here, does anyone copy?" she immediately shouted over the static rush, feeling tears running down her cheeks when Dimitry answered.

"Damn, is that really you, Filio?"

"Yes, it is."

"Oh, thank God! We thought something had happened to you!"

"No, we're okay," she assured him, sniffling and trying to calm her breath, which now came in fits and starts, causing her chest to heave. Just hearing her commander's voice restored a sense of reality, helping her to believe that she wasn't dreaming and wasn't trapped in a weird fantasy. Apparently, she hadn't lost her mind yet, and Dimitry's voice provided her a connection to her own sanity.

"We've found something, Dima," she told him, struggling for words. "We've found an alien—"

"WHAT?" He broke in so loudly that her helmet had to reduce the volume to compensate.

"It's true. It's important that you stop working on the hatch above. And don't bring any improvised weapons with you or anything like that, and above all, don't attack him, okay?"

"What are you saying? An alien?"

"Yes." Hortat nodded in her direction, and she continued. "He's opening the hatch for you now. Stand by."

13

AGATHA DEVENWORTH, 2042

"Director Miller," Silvia Cortez said. She lit a cigarette, the red glow of the flame plunging her eye sockets into deep shadows and making her face look demonic. She took a long drag and then exhaled the white smoke through a narrow slit between her pale lips. "Why are you in such a hurry, hmm?"

"Oh, I have my reasons," he said. "Why did you kidnap and tie me up?"

The Secretary of Homeland Security smiled thinly and nodded. "Never at a loss for a snide remark."

"That's not a snide remark," Miller grumbled, glaring at her furiously. "You have just committed a crime."

"So you say." Cortez waved at a man in a pinstripe suit. "Scan them."

"This black location is shielded from any imaginable kind of signal, Ma'am. Nothing gets in or out," the man said. He hurried to comply with her request when she gave him a sharp glance.

The man, skinny and in his late 40s with already graying temples, looked more like a good-natured high school football coach. He pulled out a rod-shaped sensor and began systematically waving it over Pano's body. When he arrived at the Italian's right jacket pocket the device beeped. He pulled out the little white noise generator, and like a pearl diver who had just found one of the coveted jewels, he held up the device between two fingers and showed it to the secretary, who snatched it from his hand.

Then he continued with Agatha. It beeped again, near her right hip. Irritated, she watched the man pocket the sensor before using both hands to feel the fabric of her blazer. He fumbled around until he pulled out a transmitter that looked like a tailor's straight pin with a slightly over-large head.

"So, what have we here?" Cortez asked, shaking her head like a disappointed mother who had just learned that her child had committed some particularly serious transgression. "A directional transmitter." She beckoned to her subordinate, who handed the tiny device to her.

"Hidden in the fibers of her blazer, Ma'am."

Agatha stared at the secretary's hand that now held the transmitter, but she could not see the device. From the corner of her eye, she saw Pano's head turning toward her, so she looked at him and shook her head in puzzlement.

"You have a fucking tracker with you?" Miller asked at her other side.

"I didn't know it was there," she said defensively, keenly pondering whether she had missed anything. Of course, anyone could have hidden the transmitter in her blazer while she was in the pyramid—after all, she had been lying motionless in a hospital bed.

Then she remembered Major Greynert, who had pushed her so strangely to one side at the airfield near Melbourne when the tanker passed by. She remembered the gentle pressure of his left hand just above that hip, roughly where the small pocket of her blazer lay below the edge of the down jacket she'd been wearing.

"I'll be damned," she whispered under her breath. Her thoughts jumped to the body scanner at JFK Airport's private terminal upon their arrival in New York. It had emitted a signal at the same spot, but the airport security had assumed that it had been caused by Pano's white noise generator, which she had carried for him. Her service card had allowed her to proceed without having to go through the scanner again, and the directional transmitter had remained undetected.

"That pilot, Major Greynert, must have planted it on me," she said, looking at Miller, who looked at her inquiringly, and then at Pano, who seemed lost in thought. "But why?"

"Apparently your new patron doesn't trust you," the secretary said, dropping the transmitter to the ground and crushing it with her a high-heeled shoe. She took another drag from her cigarette.

"You just kidnapped the Director of the CTD and attacked two of my agents," Miller broke in, his voice dangerously quiet. "You won't get away with this."

"Oh, are you so sure, Jenning?" Cortez asked with a nasty smile. "I have evidence that the two agents you are so eager to defend stole a U.S. Navy jet and kidnapped the two pilots. In my view, that's a rather big problem, and one that gives me every right to act as I have.

"As far as you are concerned, I must assume complicity, because you are their immediate superior and have personally overseen the investigation. You even arranged their transfer from Namibia to McMurdo by going around me and using your connections at the Pentagon. I probably don't need to remind you that that's a violation of service rules, do I?"

With a grim look on his face, CTD Director Jenning Miller stared at her but said nothing.

"Well, I guess we've cleared that up. Sergeant?"

One of the soldiers in combat gear came running and slightly inclined his sealed helmet in deference.

"Make sure that all authorities make a detour around this area. In addition, I want all Human Foundation staff in the Philadelphia area to be monitored. Also, place a ban on operations for all mercenary companies in this district. And bring me a helicopter."

"Yes, Ma'am." The sergeant ran back to the vehicles.

Cortez gave her colleagues a wave, and they also retreated to stand by their cars. After a few moments, the secretary came closer and activated Pano's white noise generator. "A bit of privacy, hmm?" she asked.

"Your people don't know?" Agatha asked in surprise.

"Don't know what?"

"That you work for The Enemy."

"For *The Enemy?*" Cortez laughed joylessly and shook her head. "Is that what you call Hortat? I think you've been paying too much attention to Sons of Terra propaganda."

"Yes, among other things... and they're right."

"I don't work for anyone. I only work for the security of the United States. I swore an oath on that, and I will fulfill that oath."

Agatha looked for signs of deception in the older woman's face but could see nothing other than an almost frenetic conviction flashing in her eyes.

"Apparently, that also includes following an agenda of your own," Miller said, snarling.

"That includes," Cortez corrected him, "the elimination

of a manipulative and extremely treacherous being called Xinth, if that's what you mean."

Agatha was perplexed for a brief moment at the secretary's willingness to speak so freely about Xinth and her own motives.

"Don't act so surprised. I know you found him." Cortez made a dismissive gesture and lit a new cigarette. "I just don't know where yet, but we'll know soon."

"In about twenty-two hours?" Agatha asked sharply.

"Oh. So *you* know. Director Miller apparently leaked classified information. How careless of him," Cortez said with a sigh.

"Did you kidnap us just for the sake of some small talk, or do you want something from us?" Pano's voice sounded like sandpaper rubbing together.

"Two things." The secretary exhaled a thick cloud of smoke and pointed the cigarette between two fingers at the Capitano. "First of all, I cannot allow you to incriminate the president with your conspiracy theories."

"These are not theories, they are facts!" Agatha said pleadingly.

Cortez ignored her. "Secondly, you will tell me the exact whereabouts of Xinth."

"That name doesn't mean anything to us."

"Oh, really?" The secretary approached her, pushed her legs apart, and stood so close in front of her that Agatha had to turn her head away when the zipper of Cortez's pants touched her face.

"I've learned that Hortat's most important agent followed you to McMurdo and then disappeared," the woman continued, speaking explicitly to Agatha. Her breath smelled of smoke and some sharp aroma she couldn't place. "No one could have stopped him except Xinth himself. In his last transmission, he also commented on the fact that there is a secret project of the Human Foundation somewhere inland near the South Pole."

"Do you really think this shit humiliation ploy you're trying to pull with me is going to work?" Agatha asked with a snort of contempt. She looked up to her interrogator. "You are a department head, not a field agent. Violent, sexually degrading physical contact is only recommended for use by male agents on male prisoners. Maybe you should look it up."

"So that doesn't impress you?" Cortez asked, taking a step back before raising a hand and waving.

One of her soldiers came running. "Yes, Ma'am?"

"Shoot that suspect." The secretary pointed to Pano, and the soldier pulled his service weapon.

"NO!" Agatha shouted as the man was about to pull the trigger, and Cortez placed her hand on his gun hand.

"Apparently, the most primitive methods are required to make you cooperate."

Agatha looked at Pano, who swallowed heavily and answered her gaze with trembling lips.

"That order was illegal!" shouted Miller from her right. "You must disobey that command, officer."

"Should I kill the guy?" asked the man holding the gun. His face was hidden behind a balaclava and a helmet. His eyes were small and gray.

"I don't know yet," Cortez replied, turning to Agatha again. "Where is Xinth?"

"Are your people all possessed?" Agatha asked, looking at the men waiting a dozen meters away by the cars as she tried to calm her frenzied heartbeat.

"Possessed?" The secretary seemed irritated. "What are you talking about?"

"By Hortat's virus."

"What kind of virus?"

Either the damned woman is the best poker player in the world, or she really has no idea, Agatha thought in frustration.

"The virus Hortat used to make you his servant!" Pano said.

The secretary looked at him as if he had just lost his mind. "You really believe in such nonsense? I know of Xinth and how he betrayed Hortat. I also know that Xinth is dangerous and that Hortat is our only salvation from ruin."

"Oh, and how do you know that?" Agatha asked.

"Because I have eyes to see and ears to hear," the secretary answered somewhat vaguely. Her voice had taken on a fanatical tone, one that Agatha had heard several times during the interrogation of religiously motivated terrorists.

"She doesn't even know," Pano said, astonished. "Do you even know where Hortat is? Do you even know about the other possessed?"

"I'm not possessed. There are people who know the truth, and there are those who choose to ignore it, just like our beloved president." Cortez shook her head as if in serious frustration. "But I will not stand idly by as she delivers our country into the hands of an alien and his sanctimonious organization."

"You really believe all that stuff, don't you?" Agatha asked. She could see that her prospects for holding a real discussion with the woman, let alone negotiating their release, were dwindling. One could not make compromises with the insane. One could just as well try to turn water into fire.

"You're trying to delay me," Cortez said in a deep whisper. "I have no interest in killing you, but I don't have much time left. I have to know where Xinth is hiding!"

"So that you can instruct your co-conspirators in the Navy to attack the right place?" Miller's voice dripped with contempt. "You are not just betraying the president, but your country. That's treason, Silvia!"

"I am saving us from the influence of a murderous alien," she countered. "The more time it has to prepare for our attack, the worse for us. So, tell me right now where it's hiding!"

Agatha thought feverishly about what she could possibly do. She tugged at her handcuffs and ankles for the umpteenth time. The only thing that achieved was getting the cable ties to cut deeper, burning painfully into her flesh. She tried to stand against her chair, but it was apparently bolted onto the floor of the dusty hall.

Helpless, she thought again and again, and her mind raging like a bear throwing itself in vain against its cage walls. *Completely helpless!*

"Be sensible and tell me what I want to know," Cortez pressed her, and then looked at Pano and Miller. They returned her gaze with grim faces.

Agatha also looked up and saw the woman's face change. It got harder, and at the same time displayed an expression of regret around the corners of her mouth.

"No, no, no!" shouted Agatha as she understood, but it was too late. Cortez gave her sergeant a wave, and he shot Miller directly in the head.

The shot cracked like a whip and echoed from the walls and the corrugated iron roof like an evil omen. Then an even deeper silence followed. Agatha wanted to sob or scream. Instead, she felt only a leaden heaviness in her gut that denied her any emotional reaction. She looked over to her superior, whose chin had fallen onto his chest. A thin film of blood ran from his forehead, but it was surprisingly small. When her gaze wandered to the back of his head, she recoiled.

"I hate you for forcing me to do that," the secretary murmured, and then gestured for the sergeant to go to Pano. He followed her wave and now held the pistol to the South Tyrolean's forehead.

Agatha's world began to spin faster and faster in her head. She vomited.

"So, now, where exactly is Xinth hiding? Give me the coordinates!"

"We mustn't," Pano said softly beside her, and Agatha turned her head in his direction to look him in the eyes. "It's more important than we are."

"I know," she whispered sadly. "You weren't such a bad partner."

"Thank you," he grunted joylessly, and was actually able to give her a small smile, although she could see how much effort it cost. "You were really unbearable."

Agatha had to laugh involuntarily at his remark, and her vision blurred under the tears running down her cheeks. She didn't know when she had last cried. It must have been on her sixth birthday when she got a muffin for her birthday from her housemother.

"Do it," she heard the secretary say, and another shot rang out.

A sob so powerful that she feared her chest would burst fought its way up through her trachea and made its way out of her mouth as a kind of primordial cry. She did not resist, was unable to control even her breath, and her whole body began to tremble. A video ran in her head, playing the scene of Pano being shot, and she almost longed for the bullet meant for her so that everything would finally stop. It should all just stop.

Suddenly she heard the crack of another shot whipping through the hall, then another, and finally the rattling of rapid fire. Cries erupted around her. Soldiers shouted wildly. Then there was a detonation that made Agatha's ears ring, but still she heard the sounds of dying men and women crying out in pain.

She wanted to open her eyes and see what had happened, but she just could not do it—her lids simply would not obey her. Her eyes refused to see Pano's body and remained so tightly closed that her facial muscles ached.

"Agatha?"

It took her a moment to understand that someone had just whispered her name.

"Agatha?"

"P-Pano?" she stammered in disbelief and opened her eyes. The secretary lay motionless on the floor in front of them, illuminated in the flickering spotlight, just like the sergeant next to her. Further back, other shadowy figures lay sprawled around the vehicles. From between them, masked figures wearing mismatched protective gear came running.

"You're alive?" Agatha asked in bewildered disbelief, then burst out in a tearful laugh as he smiled with flared nostrils.

"I think so."

"I'm glad I was able to join the party just in time," a third voice intervened. Agatha turned and looked at the man who approached her from out of the bright spotlight. She immediately recognized him. Anyone would have recognized him immediately, that powerful figure with its cinnamon-colored skin and bald skull. That face, both charismatic and demanding, and dominated by a long, slightly hooked nose. It belonged to Workai Dalam, the most wanted man on the planet and head of the terrorist organization Sons of Terra.

"Dalam?" she asked, incredulous, blinking away her tears.

"I thought I would accede to a request made by my friend Luther Karlhammer and keep an eye on you and your partner." The Pakistani grinned as if it was all just a big joke, which immediately made Agatha angry.

"That's why the transmitter," Pano said. "I don't know if I should hug you or slap you, but you saved my life, I guess."

"Don't mention it." Dalam pulled a knife out of the belt of his cargo pants. One at a time he cut the cable ties around their ankles, then circled behind their chairs and released their hands.

When Agatha was free, she brought her arms forward and rotated her shoulders before rubbing her bloody wrists. The pain made her hiss.

"Your mad dash for Washington could only mean that you were planning something important, and Luther assured me that you were on our side," Dalam explained as he stepped in front of her again and stowed the knife in its sheath.

"We're not on your side," Agatha said, shaking her head decisively. "Your tools are terrorism and spreading fear."

Dalam shrugged his shoulders, unmoved. "To each his own methods. Among other things, I thwarted The Enemy's plot to send his agents to Mars on the *Mars Two*. What have you done?"

"Can we just skip this petty playground fighting, please?" Pano asked as he got up.

Agatha did the same, and they looked at each other for a very long moment. She felt an impulsive rejoinder forcing its way toward her lips, but from the corners of her eyes, she saw Dalam and suppressed it. Pano seemed to read her inner thoughts in her face and hinted at a smile.

She finally turned away and looked at the inert secretary lying at her feet. "I don't see any blood," she said.

"Stun arrows treated with Neuro-T5," the terrorist declared, grinning when he read the question on their faces. "A stunned secretary will place us under a lot less pressure than a murdered one. Nevertheless, I would suggest that we disappear from here. Incidentally, I am sorry for your director. As far as we know, he was not one of them."

Agatha looked at Miller's still-bound corpse and felt a profound regret in her heart. They had never been very close, but the director had always been honest and reliable. That he had to die just when he had trusted her and stood up for her was a source of deep heartache.

"The police will be able to draw conclusions from what they find here, ones that the secretary will be unable to answer," she said grimly.

"I really hope so," Dalam agreed, pointing in the direction of the 20 or so figures in the vehicles waiting for them with angled weapons. "We need to go. Apparently, a helicopter from Homeland Security is on its way here."

Agatha looked at Miller one more time as a form of apology and followed the tall Pakistani to the cars.

On the way, Pano took her hand. Instead of instinctively pulling away, she returned the gesture and tightly gripped his hand.

14

FILIO AMOROSA, 2042

"Have I killed him?" Cassidy asked, nervously flexing his hand as he shifted from one leg to the other.

"No, I don't think so," Filio said, looking over to her one-armed partner, who had stepped back a few paces. He seemed depressed. "You have quite a lot of strength in that arm."

"I... I thought he wanted to kill you. I also thought he was an alien or something like that." The physicist seemed rather uncomfortable in his skin. He avoided her gaze.

"It's alright. You couldn't have known, and I'm glad you're looking out for me. However, I may need your medical cuff."

"Oh, yes, of course," he said immediately, and began to fumble around at his neck.

Filio carefully laid Heinrich's helmeted head on the floor, and got up to help Cassidy with the medical cuff.

"Leave it. Otherwise you'll damage the cuff. I have to read it out to know what your condition is and whether we can take it off. Maybe the perfuser doesn't contain enough medication anymore."

She selected the medical device in her helmet display,

gave a voice sample, and received the data. "Okay, let's see," she thought aloud and went through the data. "Analgesics are down to twenty percent. No wonder, with your pain. Lorazepam at ninety percent. That's not remarkable. It has a long half-life in the blood and is only meant to combat shock. Your adrenaline level is low, which is very good, but your cortisol level is over two hundred, despite the lorazepam."

"That's the long-term stress hormone, right?"

"Right. C-reactive protein under five, that's good. Acute inflammation is not to be expected for the present. Platelets good, leukocytes a little low, but in the normal range."

"So, you can take the thing off," Cassidy said in conclusion, pointing to Heinrich's motionless body. They had laid it stretched out in front of the chamber from where he had fallen. "I think he needs the thing more than I do. If I start screaming again, you can just hit me over the head and knock me out."

"Very funny," she snorted, reciprocating his tense smile with a shake of her head.

"But it's true, so we better not waste time."

"Hmm..." Filio looked down at Heinrich and chewed on her lower lip.

"What?"

"Is it really a good idea?"

"What do you mean?"

"Listen, everything in me screams to wake him up immediately, but what if that's the wrong thing to do?" she asked with a trembling voice. It took her some effort not to immediately rip the cuff off Cassidy's neck and put it on the friend she had believed dead for three years. But a gnawing doubt spread along the back of her head, its fingers reaching out for her exuberant feelings to grab hold of them and not let go.

"You mean, if it's a trap?"

"Of course. We are here on the ship of the Builder Hortat, who is also called The Enemy. So, what happens first when we show up? One of my former crewmates rises from the dead. If that doesn't sound like a trap, I don't know what does," she explained, pondering for a moment before stepping behind Cassidy and using its two handles to take the cuff off him.

"What are you going to do?" he asked, surprised.

"I'll put it on Heinrich and conduct a DNA analysis."

"Do you even have a DNA map in your helmet storage?"

"No, I don't think the Human Foundation has one, but I can at least look for anomalies if it's changed in any way. Perhaps it is just an illusion or a kind of dummy created by The Enemy."

"Okay. I think you're right," Cassidy agreed, nodding. He still held his arm stump guardedly in front of his chest like a baby as he looked down thoughtfully at the astronaut lying before them.

Filio bent down next to Heinrich and gently turned him onto his side. Next, she placed the medical cuff with the perfuser on the underside of the box onto the connection port on his suit collar and then put it around his neck. Fortunately, standard ports had not changed in the three years that had passed.

"Start DNA analysis, no medication. Vital data and blood values," she told the AI, waiting for the first data to arrive after a few seconds.

"What do you see?" Cassidy asked.

"His blood levels look good, although his blood pressure is a bit low, as if he'd just awakened from sleep. Otherwise, everything is normal. Mild bradycardia, but it is not pathological. It's a result of his physical fitness, at least what it was before this all happened. The DNA analysis is still ongoing."

"Do you really think that it's... not him?"

"I don't know," she admitted, sighing. "I wish so much that it is, even if I can hardly think of any possible explanation that would not be disturbing."

"He was your best friend, wasn't he?" Cassidy seemed uncomfortable with those words.

"Yes. We shared a mother tongue, quarters at SETEF, and similarly pragmatic views." Filio darkened her visor a little because it gave her a sense of isolation, which seemed necessary to prevent her shedding tears when thinking of times before the *Mars One* mission.

"Sorry."

"Hey, he's not dead and it's also not clear that it really isn't him, right?" she hissed with sudden anger.

Cassidy recoiled as if she had hit him. "I did not want to suggest that—"

"Alright." Filio waved him aside. "I shouldn't have reacted so irritably. It's just... this place here." She made an encompassing gesture that included the round room with the amber bubble, still dominated by the somber twilight that emanated from its center. "I always knew that I had to return to Mars. It was much more than a mere wish. It was more of a burning desire that made me barely able to sleep at night. And now that I'm here, I realize that *here* is exactly where I had to come."

"I don't think I fully understand," Cassidy said, furrowing his broad forehead in irritation.

"It might sound crazy, but I just feel like this exact place has been pulling me here the whole time. By the way, I've been feeling this way since we entered this wreck."

"Hmm."

Filio restored her visor to maximum transparency and looked the physicist in the face. "You think I'm crazy, don't you?"

"Well," he began reluctantly, dodging her gaze. "I don't think I should presume to dismiss anything as crazy. Not after we've traveled to Mars instantaneously thanks to a machine designed by an alien, only to find a deceased comrade from your Mars mission. No, I don't think I should harbor any sweeping doubt about anything I see or hear."

"Good point. Maybe it's just a strange feeling." She waved dismissively. An exclamation point popped up on her visor, flashing bright green to grab her attention, and she opened the Medi-AI report. "Hmmm..."

"What's going on?" Cassidy asked.

"The DNA report is complete. No abnormalities, except for some risk factors for rheumatic illnesses, thyroid gland disease, and a susceptibility to lipomas. If he was created by The Enemy, it's impressive work," she explained, then closed the report and bent over Heinrich. His face looked very peaceful as if he were enjoying a particularly relaxing sleep.

What's your secret, Heinrich? she thought, regarding the piece of metal on his forehead, which she'd first thought was the reflection of a small crack in his visor. *What the hell is that thing?*

"Well, we can wake him up now or not. There are only these two possibilities, and we have no valid indication that speaks for or against either of them," the stocky physicist said in summation while pointing to Heinrich with his arm stump.

"There is another possibility," she said, nodding toward the dark corridor they had been trying to escape to when the robotic arm emerged from the ceiling.

"And that would be?"

"Let's look around first. If Heinrich is indeed part of a trap set by The Enemy, it is best to inspect the trap itself before we trigger it, right?"

"If we haven't already triggered it some time ago," he said somberly.

"In that case, it wouldn't matter what we do anyway," she said, standing up.

"Very true. So, let's go."

As soon as they stepped together to the threshold of the passage that led deeper into the interior of the ship, their helmet lights came on and struggled to dispel the tenacious darkness.

"Do you know what's weird?" Cassidy asked as they stood there, hesitating, neither of them taking the first step.

"That from the entrance there was only one passage, and it led directly to the chamber where this fossil lies in the amber bubble?" Filio asked.

Cassidy nodded vehemently. "Indeed, and that doesn't make sense at all. No one builds a spaceship with such a long passage and only one accessible room at its end. I didn't see any doors, controls, or anything like that along the way."

"Do you mean to say that something about the ship is strange, or that it is not a ship at all?"

"Both, I guess. For a spaceship, such a thing makes no sense," Cassidy said with certainty.

'That's true. But not for any kind of building either."

"Again true. I guess we'll have to learn more," he sighed. Filio nodded before taking the first step and, with her lights fumbling around in the dark, proceeded deeper into Hortat's ship.

The passage had smooth walls and bent slightly to the

right, so they soon lost sight of the light in the amber room and became dependent on their suit systems' batteries. They could not find any doors, passageways, or even a single seam.

"Have you ever found it strange that Xinth didn't tell you anything about how the transport module works?" Filio asked after a while, as they thoroughly examined the anthracite walls.

"Did I find it *strange*? Damn, that really annoyed me. But I think Mr. Karlhammer is right."

"Right about what?"

"That the Builder only passes on technologies to us a bit at a time. We are not a particularly responsible species, as one can see from the fact that we've twice used nuclear weapons. Did you know that, before the bombs were dropped on Hiroshima and Nagasaki, many scientists warned that a nuclear-fission bomb blast could lead to a chain reaction that would ignite the entire Earth's atmosphere and cause it to burst into flames? These were well-known physicists and chemists who issued those warnings, not hysterical doomsday preachers. But they were nevertheless dismissed, and their concerns were thrown overboard—simply to try out that new superweapon and send a signal to the world as to who the new undisputed global power was.

"That's my opinion, and I can imagine Xinth seeing things in a very similar way," Cassidy whispered as if he was particularly focused on scanning the walls, even though she knew it was more likely that he was afraid of awaking something undesirable in the shadows. "Fossil fuels—people should have thought much earlier about what effect emissions were having and found new solutions. But economic growth is more important than the viability of a fragile ecosystem. Pretty short-sighted, isn't it?"

"Progress cannot be stopped. If something is possible, we do it."

"Precisely. We are a chronically dissatisfied species, if you ask me, and we are constantly driven to seek some vague *more* that will make us happy. We don't really know what exactly that might be. Perhaps a new VR compartment, a new car, maybe better AR goggles, a trip to Japan. And then, whenever we have obtained or have experienced this or that, we think, 'Well, that may have been quite nice, but what's next?' The great Nirvana never arrives. 'I can't get no satisfaction.' The Rolling Stones already recognized that in the last century. Very wise."

"Weren't they junkies?" Filio asked absently, groping the wall with one hand. She imagined that it felt cold, but she couldn't have felt that through her gloves, even if it were cold.

"Yes, and that's why they knew. They experimented with all the drugs they wanted, got all the women they wanted, were blessed with celebrity—or cursed with it, depending on how you look at it—and created works that will last for eternity. If even they couldn't be completely happy, that means something, I think."

"You're quite right. In Xinth's place, I probably wouldn't have left us the plans for a particularly sophisticated corkscrew. In the end, we would have used it to stab someone in the eye, or we would have been annoyed that we couldn't make any money with it and would have thrown it away and polluted the environment with it," she snorted.

"Just a little more time with me on Mars and you'll become a real misanthrope," Cassidy chuckled.

Filio responded with a joyless smile. "I'm starting to fear

that, too. This passage here seems to go on endlessly. According to my passometer, we've already gone more than two hundred steps."

"Maybe," said the physicist, and when he did not continue, she turned to him and raised her hands inquiringly.

Cassidy's visor went dark as soon as her lights illuminated his face. Instead of answering, he pointed forward.

She followed his gesture, and at the very end of the light their helmets cast, she saw a round doorway that apparently led into a new passage. "Oh," was all she could think to say.

After a short hesitation, they went on and finally entered the new passage, which seemed to act as a kind of T-junction. From the right, a warm yellow light streamed in their direction and flowed around their legs like a wave of photons.

"I'll be damned!" Filio cursed.

"Hey, I believe the expression is... FUCK!"

Speechless, she and Cassidy stood there looking at the amber bubble, at the center of which the fossil seemed to give off its own glow. As they visually scanned the room, they saw Heinrich to the right—lying exactly as they had left him.

"We are standing in the same, damned passage we followed from the surface, right?" the physicist asked in disbelief, with barely concealed fear in his voice.

"Not only that. That doorway we just came through was definitely not there when we came here."

"Are you sure? After all, we were pretty captivated by that damn fossil there before us!"

"Look at the walls," Filio suggested softly, pointing in turn to the right, the left and above.

"They're smooth as marble," Cassidy said, stretching out

his hand toward a wall, only to snatch it back as if he were afraid touching it would burn him.

"Yes—it doesn't look like lava anymore," she agreed, taking a cautious step toward the room with the amber bubble. "This whole cursed ship seems to be a kind of morphing construction, and something is constantly reacting to us."

"Maybe a kind of AI?"

"I don't know, but I don't like it," she whispered, and then following an impulse, she ran toward Heinrich's motionless body.

"Hey!" Cassidy shouted after her into his radio mic. "What are you doing?"

"I going to wake him up!"

"What? But we have found no evidence that he's not—"

"Right," she interrupted him, and knelt down next to Heinrich. "We have no evidence of *anything*, and the only thing we can interact with is Heinrich. The alternative is, in the not-too-distant future we will run out of oxygen and suffocate while we debate the pros and cons."

"Shit!" Cassidy cursed and passed his hand and arm stump over his helmet as if he were trying to pull at his hair. "Shit, you're right."

Filio selected the medical cuff and ordered it to inject a pain stimulus. Heinrich immediately came to his feet, as if someone had pulled him up like a puppet on invisible strings. She stumbled back in terror as he turned in her direction and looked back and forth between her and Cassidy like a cornered animal. She could see his lips moving behind his visor, which was now clear, as if he were shouting something at her.

"I don't hear you," she signaled by tapping on her ear. Then she raised four fingers. "Channel Four!"

"FILIO?" Heinrich yelled into her ear a moment later, causing her to wince in pain.

"Heinrich?" she asked cautiously, not knowing whether to laugh or flee for her life when she heard him laugh happily. The German geophysicist rushed toward her and locked her in his arms before she could react.

"Man, am I glad to see you," he said through tears, holding her away at arm's length once he loosed her from the hug. "What kind of strange suit is that?"

"It comes from the Human Foundation," she explained, as if in a trance, while she tried to sort her feelings.

"The Human Foundation? They're now flying to Mars?"

"Well, not exactly. In a way, though."

"Oh, man! What year is it?" he asked. Then looking at Cassidy, "And who's that?"

"This is Cassidy, my partner, and the year is 2042."

"Three years?" Heinrich looked like she had just slapped him. "Mein Gott, I didn't think it would take so long."

"May I ask you a question?" Filio asked.

Heinrich nodded eagerly.

"What's that on your forehead?" She raised her index finger and pointed at the augment above his eyebrows.

"That? Oh, Hortat gave it to me, the owner of this ship. He's an alien—well, no, not completely an alien, because he's from Earth, and he..."

Filio stopped listening to him and instead staggered back as if the ground beneath her suddenly shook.

"Filio? What's wrong? Have you..." Heinrich did not get any further. Numbly, Filio sent an order to the Medi-AI, and Heinrich collapsed limply to the floor.

"Damn," Cassidy said, jumping to her side as her legs threatened to give way.

"He's one of those, Cassidy," she said.

"I... it looks like it, yes, but... why did he tell us so openly?"

"Perhaps because he knows that there is no escape for us anyway."

The physicist looked around and then shook himself. "What should we do now?"

"I don't know," she admitted. He supported her as she slid to the floor and came to lean against the wall. Next to her lay the unconscious Heinrich, who seemed to be sleeping peacefully again. "I don't know."

MARS, 2039

No more than a day remained until their launch. As it turned out, the encounter between Dimitry, Javier, Strickland, Timothy, and Hortat proceeded in a way she had not expected. She had firmly assumed that Heinrich would remain the only one who voluntarily allowed the alien to attach the augment to his forehead. It should have made sense to them since he had behaved particularly anxiously and nervously when they had entered Hortat's ship. Fear could make people perceptive, but—just as often—it might make them reckless.

In the end, what occurred stood in stark contrast with what she had presumed. Dimitry had been almost reverent, and had babbled about how he had always known something about the Builders. Apparently, there had been an archaeologist named Dan Jackson, famous among those interested in his discipline, who had postulated that a kind of 'first human being' had existed many millions of years ago.

The result of Dimitry's awe was that he was anything but cautious, and very quickly accepted Hortat's offer, which

Filio interpreted more as a demand, to receive the augment. After that, it had only got worse, and Dimitry had begun to tell the others that everything was true and that there was so much they could learn from the Builder.

As a result, Timothy followed suit, and Strickland and Javier likewise seemed to have no objections. Since they had not understood, or else ignored, her half-discreet pleas for private conversation, she had no way of influencing them—and she did not dare to express her distrust openly in front of Hortat. Otherwise he would mercilessly neutralize her. Of that she was certain.

The result was that the others began preparations to launch the spacecraft, which stood like a high-rise at the landing site, secured by four massive steel ropes anchored deep in the Martian soil. She wouldn't have thought she'd see the Earth again so quickly, and still had trouble believing it.

While the others were still in the two rovers, traveling between the spaceship and the base, Heinrich came to her in the control room, where she monitored the radio and coordinated the team's efforts. She was updating the equipment lists when he appeared in the door to the connection module.

"Ah, Heinrich," she said, waving him in. "I've just been sorting through our equipment and provisions. We only need a very few things for the return flight, food and water in particular. And we'll save a lot of launch weight by storing lots of equipment here for the next mission."

"That's very good," he said, nodding absently.

"What is it?"

"I'm going to stay here," said Heinrich, arms crossed in front of his chest. He closed his eyes for a moment as she began to protest.

"You can't be serious! You can't just stay alone on Mars! Are you crazy? It will take at least two years for a new window to open up for the next mission!"

"I know, I know. Time will not matter."

"What do you mean by that? What are you talking about?"

"Hortat offered me the chance to remain in his stasis chamber. It seems to be quite easy to reprogram, because our genetic material is so similar, and life support for me requires a lot less energy than for a Builder," he explained, and Filio rolled her eyes.

"Builder? Now you're starting to act like Dimitry," she said, snorting with contempt.

"Because there is already a name for them. This Jackson was obviously right with his hypotheses. Why should we now pretend that he wasn't?"

"Because it's fucking crazy!" she hissed, looking tensely past Heinrich to make sure that no one was listening, even though she could see from the cameras that Hortat and Timothy were in the *Mars One* and the others were in the commuting rovers.

Heinrich took a step toward her and then paused as she snorted and crossed her arms in front of her chest. "Listen. Hortat's argument makes sense."

"What is his argument, hmm? That he wants to thin our ranks a little before he goes on board with us?"

"I know you don't trust him. Just don't show it to him," he urged her in a way that sounded almost like a plea. "His argument is that we will send more missions to Mars, and they will also encounter his ship again, once they have investigated our computers for the latest data. Then everything will be simplified once the, uh, Ship Being—"

"The *Ship Being?*" she asked with furrowed brow.

"It's... something like the ship's AI. Well, not quite, but that's what comes closest to Ship Being. God!" he cursed, and grabbed his short hair in frustration. "I wish you would just accept the damned augment. Then everything wouldn't be so damned difficult to explain, and you would understand."

"What would I understand? That I'd have a new 'massa,' hmm? A new alien god? So that I'll say and do exactly what he wants? No, thank you."

"He has nothing against us," Heinrich assured her, pointing to the passage to the connection module behind him. "He is out there, integrating us in a common effort to save both humanity and the last of his species. He didn't have to do that. He could have just killed us all because he had already read my brain. So why would he take us with him, including you, even though you don't even wear the augment? You are a risk to him!"

"He allowed that to maintain the fiction of free will, so that he could then use that thing to bind the rest of you to him as quickly as possible," she countered, pointing to the shiny piece of metal on his brow. "Apparently, it worked."

"Verdammte Scheisse, Filio!" Heinrich said angrily, and the fact that he had abandoned the mandatory mission language for German showed her how upset he really was. "Why do you have to be so miserably pessimistic and paranoid?"

Filio got up and took a step toward him until only a few centimeters separated them. "Because none of the rest of you are, and one of us must use their mind, no matter how obnoxious it is!" she said with a growl.

Heinrich sighed. "I can see we obviously can't change your mind. In any case, I'm staying here in the stasis chamber and will be here when astronauts arrive on the next mission, so that such a misunderstanding does not occur again."

"What misunderstanding?"

"There are five more Hortat clones in the stasis chamber."

"He's a clone?" she asked, bewildered.

"Yes. The real Hortat lies in the preservative bubble in the middle of the room."

Filio plopped down onto her chair as if powerless to remain on her feet. This new information made her head spin, and she suddenly felt as if someone had pulled her plug and robbed her of all her energy. "But... how?"

"He made the clones before he died, in case his species or someone else would find him here and save him."

"But if this amber bubble is a kind of conservation field, why has he become a fossil?"

"Have you ever seen a fossil that still has flesh and skin on its bones?" Heinrich asked, shaking his head. "The bubble is designed to survive millions of years, and without any energy supply. That's how his DNA is preserved. The clones, however, need energy, which is why the ship has shut down four of the chambers. His fossil serves as something like a contingency. In addition, only one DNA sample from it can activate the clones. A kind of safety measure."

"Safety measure?"

"Yes. Only the Ship Being can start the process. The needle used to extract and read the DNA cannot be copied."

"Why not?"

Heinrich shook his head almost with compassion. "You wouldn't understand that."

"Stop with that shit!" she growled furiously. "Now you're starting to sound as arrogant as that Hortat, whom you so idolize."

"Excuse me," said Heinrich, sighing. It was impossible to judge from his facial expression whether he meant the apology seriously, so Filio decided not to comment on it for the time being. "It's just that the impressions he made on me were very intense, and I'm honestly afraid of this Twelve-Fold Space."

"You were able to see what he experienced there?"

"Yes. It was horrible... Hard to describe."

"What happened?"

"I shouldn't really—"

"Heinrich!" she said, holding her index finger under his nose in admonishment. "You may have just met an accursed alien who can show you wondrous things, but we've known each other for over two years now, and I've spent more time with you than anyone else in this life. Please don't start discounting me in favor of an alien."

"Excuse me," he said again, and this time his expression seemed sincere. "He and a part of the fleet that were on their way to the Andromeda Nebula passed through thought space."

"Thought space?" she asked with brows raised.

"The Twelve-Fold Space. It can only be traveled using the thought power of the navigators—at least I can't think of a more accurate explanation for it. It's hard to put into words. In any case, they moved into the Twelve-Fold Space and found themselves in a sea of nothingness. There really was nothing measurable there, but it seemed as if there was something present that eluded their instruments, and that something didn't want them there. It fought them like immune cells attack an invading virus."

"So what happened to them?"

"There were ten ships in his fleet. Four suddenly attacked each other and the others... changed." Heinrich seemed to squirm with every other word as if pronouncing these impressions made him physically uneasy.

"What does that mean, they *changed?*" Filio asked, digging deeper.

"Their form—the Builders on board. Strange forms took shape on the ships and either drove them mad or did things to them." Heinrich began to falter and held a hand to his mouth. "Hortat was the only one to find his way back into normal space. He returned to Earth to warn Xinth and to establish a new colony on Alpha Centauri with the last available ship. It was a destination sufficiently near so that the amount of time necessary to reach it with sublight propulsion was short enough to ensure their survival."

"But?"

"Xinth sent him away. He considered Hortat a traitor who had sabotaged his fleet. He said Hortat had to be responsible for their deaths because he was the only one to return. When Hortat obeyed him and flew away, a bomb exploded in the propulsion module of the ship in which we found him, and it crashed. You know the rest," he said. He clenched his hands into fists every time he spoke the name Xinth.

"Well, it would seem that this Xinth has a good argument, doesn't he? Why did only one of all those aliens survive? Why did *he* survive?" Filio asked suspiciously, slightly lowering her voice as if the alien could hear her anywhere, anytime.

"He didn't show me that."

"Oh, what a surprise. And did he say why not?"

"Because this mystery is too painful to be relived. He must bear this burden alone."

"Oh, of course. Very practical," she said with a voice dripping with irony, and shook her head at so much naive faith. Heinrich seemed so different from the man she knew. In the years before the mission and during it, he had always kept a cool, analytical head, was very unexcitable and logical, and did not behave like some boy band groupie.

"I understand that you are suspicious, but you have not seen what he has shown me."

"What he showed *you*? Exactly. Haven't you noticed something?"

"Yes, that you can't understand it because you haven't experienced it," he insisted, and his gaze visibly locked itself away, which hurt her.

"Hasn't it occurred to you that he's been using you the whole time and just showing you what you're supposed to see. This damn thing on your forehead," she stabbed with her finger at the shiny, metallic augment, which looked like a small plaque, but he pulled back before she could touch it, "is damned alien technology!"

"This conversation makes no sense as long as our fundamental bases of knowledge are so different. It's like arguing with you about what an apple tastes like when you've never held one in your hand, let alone eaten it."

"Such thinking is very convenient," she said, grumbling and glaring at him furiously. So much narrow-mindedness caused her to seethe inwardly, and her anger was fueled by the fact that she cared about him and the others. She also felt increasingly lonely and isolated since Hortat had made such ardent supporters of her comrades—however he had been able to do that. Suddenly, the years of their joint work and the life they shared on humanity's most important mission seemed to count for nothing at all. It was as hurtful as it was humiliating.

"I would have liked to part with you in good terms, Filio," said Heinrich after a short pause, looking down at the ground, before taking a deep breath and nodding in surrender. "Despite all this, I will remember you as a good friend."

"Apparently not on terms as good as with your new alien friend, Mr. Brainwash," she said with a snarl that caused the German to stumble away from her as if she had punched him, before he retreated through the door with a sad, final glance, and disappeared into the connection module.

Sighing, she buried her face in her hands and knew that sooner or later she would regret her words. But she had been unable to find any others. Anger and frustration burned away all rationality in their fire.

So she just sat there for a while, brooding on her anger, which gradually turned into dismay and sorrow, not because she regretted being so suspicious, but because she apparently hadn't managed to get through to Heinrich and save him from the alien's influence. She had not tried hard enough, and had allowed herself to be intimidated by Hortat. That is what caused her to feel a shame that would surely haunt her to the grave.

Which may come to me much earlier than I'd like, she thought darkly.

The rest of the preparations went astonishingly fast. Her team, especially Dimitry, worked hard so as not to waste any time. Either their belief in Hortat's intentions, and thus his urgency, was unshakeable, or his brainwashing was so intense and fruitful that they were no longer able to pursue their own thoughts. Either way, she couldn't let go of the feeling that this Builder had set up a small ant colony consisting of six formerly highly educated and intensely trained scientists who were among the best minds of their species. Now, like a queen ant, he sat out there in their spaceship where his busy workers served him like royalty.

Just a few hours later she was sitting with Dimitry

behind Timothy's pilot's chair. He was officially the pilot, but held this title only because he was the only one who was sufficiently trained to fly even difficult maneuvers manually in case the ship's AI failed. Due to the multiple redundant systems on board, however, that was extremely unlikely.

As the boosters ignited, vigorously shaking her, thick tears ran down her cheeks. She was just barely able to darken her visor and manually turn off the microphone with a trembling hand before she began to heave with uninhibited sobbing. She hoped that the spaceship's vibrations would cover her shaking—and if it did not, she would have to accept it. Her emotional dam broke so violently that no amount of willpower would have been enough to bring herself under control.

The unreal idea that, at that moment, Heinrich was on his way to Hortat's ship in one of the rovers to go into stasis was simply too much for her. He was now out there all by himself, millions of miles from Earth and from any human warmth. They had left him alone—she with horrible parting words, the others with sheer approval and without any pity because they were apparently as convinced as Heinrich that he was doing the right thing.

When it grew dark outside the tiny windows in the cockpit, which pointed upward, and the Mars satellite Phobos could be seen as a small gray dot, it was then that she realized that there was no way back. This situation was real, and she was returning to Earth, in the tow of a possibly dangerous alien.

"Attempting to establish radio contact with Mission Control," she said, as soon as they had swung onto their programmed return course a few hours later, pressing the communications button on her virtual control panel.

"Unable to execute this command. Access denied," the

ship's AI EDI purred into her ear. Filio looked over in disbelief to Dimitry, who sat relaxed next to her and was apparently immersed in his own AR display.

"Hey, Dima," she said.

He shook his head briefly before turning to her. "Hmm?"

"Did you kick me out of the system?"

"No," he said with surprise, seemingly confused.

"I just wanted to radio Mission Control," she said, pointing to her grayed-out button, although of course it only existed in her field of vision, and he couldn't see it.

"Oh, yes." Dimitry grinned. "Yes, I disabled that for everyone after consulting Hortat."

"And why should you do such a thing?" she asked suspiciously, involuntarily holding her breath.

"Well, why do you think? If we radio them and say that we have an alien on board, they won't let us land!"

"Yes, because there are quarantine protocols that we otherwise violate. There's a good reason for that!" she said, stunned at how he was disregarding mission regulations and apparently did not respect them.

"Quarantine protocols!" he repeated, shaking his head. "This is much bigger than any protocol, Filio. It is about saving an entire species so that it does not repeat a mistake that has wiped out the rest of them."

"We don't know that for sure. Just as we don't know that Hortat is telling us the truth."

"He is not evil," Dimitry insisted. "Certainly not."

"Okay," she said, trying to be patient, even though she would have preferred to shout at him with abandon until blood ran out of his ears. "I believe you. Yes?"

"Yes," the Russian said happily and smiled.

"What if he is carrying pathogens that are harmless to him and could cause mass extinction in humans? The same thing happened with the Incas and Aztecs when the Spanish conquistadors crossed the Atlantic. He doesn't even have to intend being the cause of our destruction," she said.

"Don't worry! Hortat is smarter than we can imagine, and he has certainly played out that scenario already and judged it safe."

"And you're willing to bet the fate of humanity on that assumption?" she asked, stunned. She sank back in her armchair in frustration.

He nodded decisively.

"You can't be serious!"

"Why not? Don't you trust him?" Dimitry looked at her with suspicion and narrowed his eyes until she could barely see their whites.

"Yes, I do. I guess you're right," she lied, shrugging her shoulders. "I'm just a little bit out of sorts because of Heinrich and everything."

Dimitry immediately relaxed and amicably patted her forearm. "I can understand that. We'll get through it. Together!"

"Yes, thank you."

Fantastic! she thought. Filio began to think about what she could possibly do about the fact that her friends had apparently lost their minds and had now become blind followers of an alien who desperately wanted to go to Earth.

For whatever reason.

15

AGATHA DEVENWORTH, 2042

Three white delivery vans were parked in front of the warehouse where Cortez had taken them. Dalam herded them into the middle vehicle, where they settled on benches with six members of the Sons of Terra. The men and women, all with menacing eyes, gradually pulled their balaclavas from their heads and looked suspiciously at her and Pano. Some cast such openly hostile glances at her that she feared they might point their dart rifles at her.

"We're apparently very popular with them," Pano muttered sarcastically.

Agatha did not answer. She had often looked into faces like those of these terrorists and knew when it was better not to risk pouring oil on the fire.

The journey lasted only about 15 minutes, during which she noticed that her hand terminal had been blocked. Then the rear door opened again, and she and Pano found themselves in an abandoned underground parking ramp.

Workai Dalam stood in front of an old metal door between two concrete pillars and waved them to them. "Come!"

Agatha passed through the old door, which looked more like a shattered piece of rust, and stepped into a long corridor with flickering light and the smell of damp mold and soil.

"Go on all the way to the back," Dalam instructed, shooing them on in front of him.

Commenting on the oppressive atmosphere, Pano said behind her, "Alarm bells would be going off in me if you hadn't just rescued us."

"As a terrorist, you can't choose any suite you want at a time when public toilets are the only places not subject to camera surveillance," Dalam replied.

At the end of the corridor was a small, square room with another door. An aluminum table with four folding chairs, four weapon cabinets full of rifles, pistols, and grenades, and a desk with AR glasses and a screen were housed there in a confined space.

"Chic," Agatha said sarcastically.

"Sit down," Dalam prompted, pointing to the two free chairs between them and the table. He circled around them to sit on the other side.

"Well," she said as soon as they had all taken their seats and folded her hands on the cold tabletop. When she noticed that her fingers were still shaking slightly, she placed them under the table. "Why are we talking here in some underground hiding place?"

"Well, if you know a better place where Homeland Security can't reach us," Dalam replied, opening his hands in an inviting gesture, "I'm all ears."

"You had me bugged!"

"Luckily for you, I think. Hmm?"

"How long have you been following us?"

"Since your departure from the pyramid. To a certain extent," the terrorist leader calmly declared.

Agatha exchanged a hasty look with Pano. "You know about that?"

"Major Greynert reported to me on that. He is not only a pilot with B12, but also a member of a hard-working cell of the Sons of Terra," Dalam explained with some satisfaction in his voice.

"What else do you know about Karlhammer's hiding place?" Agatha asked.

"Enough to allocate a significant amount of my resources to protect you. We are an organization that looks at the big picture, and from the shadows we pull the weeds that The Enemy sows—we would have nothing meaningful to contribute to a confrontation with the U.S. military in Antarctica. Luther and his private armies will have to deal with that." Dalam paused and winked at them. "So, I put all my chips on you and Capitano Hofer here."

"Why?"

"Are you joking? You two found the pyramid, probably the most secret place on this planet, and you did that in a fairly short amount of time, as I see it."

"We had some help," Agatha said.

Dalam nodded carefully. "You're alluding to the man in the black suit, the one who was on the plane with you." He paused and nodded. "Yes, that's true. Nevertheless, you've done a good job and proven to be very resilient. And you did not betray anyone, even with a gun to your head."

"We were lucky." Agatha waved dismissively.

"You're too modest. Major Greynert told me that you were even able to sabotage the jamming field that was supposed to keep The Enemy away from the pyramid. How did you do that?"

"We dug up a transmitter a few miles from the mountain," Pano said, pointing to his still working ear, which contained the old-fashioned hearing aid. Agatha tried to stop him from speaking, giving a kick to his foot, but he either didn't notice or dismissed it as an accident. "An old piece of technology saved our asses. Talk about irony..."

"That's the way it is sometimes. We use couriers for our most important messages."

"What are you going to do now?" Agatha asked impatiently.

"You wanted to meet with the president, didn't you?" Dalam looked at both of them attentively as they looked at each other. "Listen, I'm on your side. We must stop The Enemy, at any cost."

"It doesn't matter," Agatha said. "Even if we had an appointment with the president, our access to her died along with Miller."

"Are you sure?" Dalam asked thoughtfully, pulling out his hand terminal. He made some quick entries and turned the booklet-sized transparent disk so it faced toward her. The device went dark and played a video. She saw herself sitting between Miller, who was already dead, and Pano in the hall where they had been taken by Cortez. The light flickered slightly, but the secretary could easily be identified, as well as the sergeant who had been pressing his gun to Pano's head. The recorder had also captured the hand signal Cortez gave him. Then, she and the soldier suddenly collapsed onto the floor, and a firefight broke out.

Dalam slid the hand terminal back into his pocket and put on a satisfied smile. "That might be enough to convince the president, don't you think?"

"That could work," she admitted reluctantly, still shocked at the sight of Miller, dead beside her, and the knowledge of how close Pano had come to sharing that same fate.

"But she will want to know who saved us," Pano said, and Dalam's smile died.

"I know. In order for you to get through to the President, I will surrender to you. I am the most wanted man on the planet and, along with the evidence video, she will no doubt agree to meet with you."

"They will put you in Guantanamo or somewhere like it, and you'll never see the light of day again," Agatha said in disbelief. She despised the terrorist for his methods, even though they shared his motives, and she felt a certain respect for him because he had dedicated his life to humanity, perhaps in a dangerous way, but he had been fighting for years for a truth that no one had acknowledged except his fanatical followers. The fact that he was ready to voluntarily sacrifice himself for his cause seemed to her entirely congruent, but nevertheless, she was surprised by this act of utter self-sacrifice on his part.

"I'm aware of that. From the earliest existence of the Sons of Terra, I've striven to ensure that our organization was decentralized and not based on a cult of personality. All that matters is that we keep our freedom as a species, instead of falling under the control of an alien. If it is necessary for me to pay the price to achieve this goal, then I do so with complete conviction," Dalam said with a firm voice and without any hesitance in his eyes.

"Here are the keys to a car at the door. It's the same Tesla model you drove in. In the car, there are handcuffs and ankle shackles, a black sack that you can pull over my head, and Miller's hand terminal, which we stole from the secretary's car." Her partner put a key fob with the Tesla logo on the table, slipped a hand under his leather jacket, and pulled a Glock out of the hip holster, which he then carelessly threw to the ground.

Agatha looked at Pano, who nodded silently and leaned forward to grab the key fob. "Let's go."

They got up and followed Dalam down the moldy, malodorous corridor and into the abandoned parking garage, where the long, electric SUV was parked. Pano ran around the hood and got behind the wheel. Agatha opened the passenger door and found the sack, handcuffs, and ankle shackles on the seat as Dalam had described. Before she snapped the steel shut around his wrists, she paused again and looked the Pakistani in the face.

"Are you sure that this is what's best for you?"

"For me? Certainly not. But it is the best way to stop a fleet of Enemy-possessed Navy officers from destroying our future. That's enough for me." Dalam nodded at her and she closed the handcuffs with some regret. She helped him into the back seat, cuffed his ankles, and used a short chain to fasten the metal cuffs on his wrists to the pair at his ankles.

"Sorry," Agatha muttered. She then closed his door, picked up the sack, climbed into the front passenger seat, and buckled in. She closed her door with a sigh.

Pano steered the car two floors up to an exit littered with old newspapers and garbage. As they headed back into the East Coast rain, she looked around and realized that they were in an abandoned industrial area—one of the many such victims of digitization and automation.

As old warehouses and refineries rushed past them, she took Miller's hand terminal with some reluctance and said, "Call President Elisabeth Harris on her direct line."

As the ring tone sounded, she turned to Dalam and gave him a wave. He fumbled awkwardly in his jacket pocket, pulled out his own terminal, and sent her the video file just as she received a connection signal.

A female voice spoke, one that she had only known from television. "Miller, have you arrived at the meeting point?" Elisabeth Harris sounded a little warmer on the phone.

"This is Special Agent Agatha Devenworth speaking," Agatha said after she briefly cleared her throat.

"Devenworth? Where is Miller? This number—"

"Excuse me, Madam President, Director Miller was murdered on our way to you—"

"Murdered?"

"I'm sending you a video file because you certainly wouldn't believe me if I told you what happened," Agatha said, then sending the video she had received from Dalam.

A pause ensued, then a sound that could have been a forceful sigh or a gasp of fright.

"Silvia?" Harris asked.

"Yes. You must meet with us as planned, Madam President," Agatha said with urgency. "It's a matter of national security."

"Listen, Agent Devenworth. I will have the video file checked by my data analysts for its authenticity and investigate this matter. This will have consequences, but I cannot—"

"Ma'am," Agatha interrupted the president. "If I deliver Workai Dalam to you, will you agree to a personal meeting?"

"Workai Dalam? What are you talking about, Agent?"

Agatha switched to video, held the hand terminal between the two front seats, and pointed it at the terrorist leader, who made a sour face and rattled his shackles.

"Come to the West Gate. One of my men will search you there and then wave you through. When you arrive at the

West Wing, four of my secret service men will accompany you in," Harris said, then hung up.

"Did she agree?" Pano asked tensely, and exhaled with relief when she nodded.

"Looks like we're going to see the president."

"I've always wanted to meet her," Workai Dalam murmured behind them.

"You really have nerve." Pano shook his head. "How do you do that?"

"If, like me, you had seen a bronze giant in the depths of the Indian Ocean and watched it drive two of your divers to cut their own oxygen hoses, you'd do anything to stop it."

"You really found The Enemy's wreckage?" Agatha asked, astonished. She had always thought it was just a myth.

"Yes," he immediately replied.

"How did you manage to stop him from killing you? I have... experienced the skills of his agent."

"I happened to be near the emergency balloons at that moment, and one of them must have blocked his view," Dalam said, his voice suddenly tense. "These balloons can be inflated with an oxygen cartridge for an emergency ascent, which I did."

"But how did you finally understand that The Enemy has been infiltrating governments and authorities?"

"From the growing hostility toward the Human Foundation. Until '39, there were in principle only supporters, and many state funds for development aid were allocated to Luther's foundation because policy experts knew it was efficient. Then suddenly a change came, and in various parliaments around the world, groups formed that vehemently objected to the Human Foundation, even though there were no scandals to explain their criticism.

"Added to this was the widespread speculation as to how Luther was constantly conjuring so many new miracle technologies, like rabbits from a hat. Admittedly, no single achievement was so incredible as to believe him incapable of it, but still, the rate at which he brought forth new inventions gave everyone pause. So, I thought to myself, if one alien was roaming the Earth, maybe there were more of them."

"It was that easy?" Pano asked as their car veered onto the interstate to Washington and merged into the uniform traffic moving in that direction.

"Well," Dalam said, "a little more was involved. I guess the CIA's torturers will force it all out of me."

"They won't have to, because you're cooperating of your own free will," Agatha said, but the man behind her just laughed dryly.

"I'm glad you can see your people through rose-colored glasses," He said. "They will put me in a dark cell simply because they either believe that my story is a complete lie or because they are also possessed by The Enemy and would be too happy if an accident were to occur during interrogation. My journey will end in Washington, and I hope that you will both make the most of it so that my sacrifice will not be in vain."

"You have my word on it," Agatha assured him.

"And mine," Pano added.

"Good. Then let's make sure that the president holds her bloodhounds away from Antarctica. My arrest should give her enough political momentum to silence the senators around Roger Danes."

"But what if all the officers in the fleet are possessed by The Enemy?"

"I don't think that's the case. According to our estimates,

perhaps ten percent of public sector employees are infected."

"And an agent like the man in the black suit has succeeded in infiltrating the fleet?" Agatha asked.

"Then we probably have a problem that we can't solve from here," Dalam admitted. In the rear-view mirror, she could see his darkened face, which lay mostly in the shadows. "But the president's backing will be helpful one way or another."

16

FILIO AMOROSA, 2042

Filio and Cassidy stared at Heinrich's inert form as if it were a bomb that could explode at any moment.

"Damn. Did he really say *Hortat?* That's the name of The Enemy, isn't it?"

"Yes." Filio had become dizzy, forcing her to hold onto the panel of a stasis chamber that was right next to Heinrich's, so as not to fall over. Her head spun like a carousel that was going faster and faster, making it difficult for her to see details.

"And what are we going to do now? Our basic problem hasn't changed."

"I don't know," she confessed, above all to herself, and let her shoulders hang. She felt truly at her wit's end.

"Oh, shit! Get down!" Cassidy shouted, and Filio raised her head just in time to see that the robotic arm had reappeared from the ceiling again and was sinking its terrifyingly long needle into the amber bubble.

"It's happening again," she said shrilly, reaching with trembling hands into her left hip pocket, where she kept the ceramic fragment from the *Mars One* heat shield. She licked her lips tensely and watched the three-jointed robotic arm and needle, which was just re-emerging from the bubble. Then she leapt mechanically and precisely toward the small hole, which was located an arm's length away in the cover of the stasis chamber that she was leaning against.

As fast as she could, she stuck the ceramic piece onto the knitting needle-sized opening, just as the robotic needle contacted it. It stabbed at the ceramic obstruction three or four times in quick succession, like a bird trying to crack a nut with its beak, and then withdrew back into the ceiling.

When the entire arm had disappeared, Filio exhaled in relief and reached out to take the small tube of suit-repair programmable foam from Cassidy's outstretched hand.

"Good thought," she said, pressing on the tube with two fingers to spread a thin film around the ceramic fragment.

"There might still be someone in the chamber here," Cassidy thought aloud, looking with some discomfort at the remaining four chamber panels. "Maybe your other crew-mates are in the rest of them?"

"I'm trying not to think about that possibility. But the robotic arm has made no attempt at any of the other chambers. It's weird."

"You think that maybe this is the only one containing someone—or something?"

"Based on what has happened so far, I would at least guess so, yes," she said, nodding.

"But if the interior of this ship can freely change its shape, why doesn't it just shift the puncture point for the needle somewhere else?" Cassidy asked, looking up at the ceiling, as if that could happen at any moment.

"Perhaps these chambers are static entities. If it is something like stasis or a medical device, it would be unwise or even impossible to change its shape, since there is a static need for space and for providing care."

"Hmm. That may be. And what now?"

[Speak to me, now,] an androgynous voice answered seeming to speak directly in Filio's head. It sounded deep and precise, without any ups or downs, and it did not come from her radio. The voice actually sounded inside her, almost as if it were her own.

"Who's talking?" she asked, moving away from the chamber cover as she looked around suspiciously. Nothing had changed. The fossil was still emitting pulsating waves of light, the chambers were closed except for Heinrich's, and he was still lying on the ground, and the opening in the ceiling was still closed.

[I am the ship.]

"The ship?" she asked in stunned incomprehension.

"Hey, who are you talking to?" Cassidy asked, eyeing her with a creased forehead.

[I am the ship,] repeated the voice in her head.

"Are you something like an artificial intelligence?"

"What are you talking about?" Cassidy asked as he took a step toward her and physically forced himself into the focus of her attention.

"I don't know. The ship, obviously."

"With *the ship?*"

"Don't you hear the voice?"

"What voice?"

[I was created,] the voice replied.

"By whom?" she asked.

"What?"

"I'm not talking to you," she said to Cassidy, silencing him with a gesture of impatience.

[I was created by Xinth.]

"By Xinth? Isn't this Hortat's ship?"

[That is correct. I obey Hortat's wishes, but your question was, who created me?] the voice replied.

"Do you control this ship?" Filio asked, instinctively searching for some physical source she could assign to the voice in order to alleviate the feeling that she was losing her mind.

"Filio, you're scaring me. What kind of weird stuff are you talking about? Are you hearing voices?" Cassidy looked tense and backed away.

"The ship is speaking to me and—"

[I control this ship, yes.]

"Did you bring us here?"

[Yes.]

"Why?"

[Because those were my instructions.]

"Your instructions? Who gave you those instructions? Hortat?" Filio gestured at Cassidy to remain silent when she saw that he was about to open his mouth.

[That is so.]

"What are those instructions?"

[I am supposed to direct sentient life forms that enter the ship to the conservatory.]

"And then?" Filio asked insistently.

[Then I am to make a decision. If I classify these life forms as hostile or dangerous, I am either to ensure that they leave the ship or eliminate them in order to avert danger. If I classify these forms of life as peaceful, I am to awaken one of Hortat's clones.]

"One of Hortat's clones? This means these chambers here," Filio said, pointing to the covers with the tiny puncture points for the robot needle, "contain clones of The Enemy?"

[No, not of The Enemy, but of Hortat,] the voice calmly corrected her.

"Shit. Hortat is in the other chambers," she said to Cassidy, who looked at her as if she were a village fair curiosity.

"How do you know that? Did this ominous voice tell you that?" he asked, snorting and shaking his head. "Maybe it's all been a bit too much, I can understand that. How about you put on the medical cuff and get a reading? Heinrich doesn't need it at the moment."

"I don't have time for that now," she said dismissively, and looked up at the ceiling again because it somehow seemed to her as if the voice were coming from there. "What was Heinrich doing in one of these chambers?"

[After you and Heinrich Marks found this ship about three years ago and supplied it with energy, I was able to save two of Hortat's clones and woke one up. You were obviously not hostile, did not have any weapons with you, and were physically and cerebrally clearly inferior to him. Therefore, you represented no danger. Your colleagues Ellen Strickland, Dimitry Vlachenko, Javier Camarro, and Timothy Knowles then made contact with Hortat using augments and helped him on his mission to return to Earth.]

"My crew brought The Enemy to Earth?" Filio asked in horror, reluctantly retreating a few steps.

[Your crew tried to bring Hortat to Earth,] the voice patiently corrected her.

"That's a lie!" Filio shouted back.

[I do not lie. I have been ordered to give you honest answers to all questions, provided that such answers do not pose a threat to Hortat, this ship, or his species,] the voice corrected her.

"You obey Hortat. So, he ordered you to give me answers?" Filio pursued.

[That is correct.]

"So, he knew I was going to come here?"

"Who knew that? Filio, who knew?" Cassidy asked to gain her attention. When she tried to wave him away again, he grabbed her by the shoulder with his hand and pulled her forward a bit, so that she had to look him in the face. "I am starting to worry that you've lost your mind. Who are you talking to, damn it?"

"With the damned ship!" she yelled at him, and felt a whole avalanche of tension falling and burying her comrade, who began to blink in irritation. "And now stop bothering me, damn it, so that I can find out what the hell is going on here!"

[I feel violence in you, Filio Amorosa.]

"You don't say!" she grumbled.

"What?"

"Not you!" Filio said with a frustrated grunt and broke free of Cassidy's grip before starting up again. "Hortat knew I was going to come here?"

[Yes. He planted the desire in you to return here.]

"No! I wanted to come back to find out what happened to my crew... my friends!" Filio said with vehement insistence.

[Yes, I can see that you think so. However, it is a misconception, no more than a strategy of your neural system to provide an explanation for an anomaly.]

"An anomaly? What do you mean?"

[An anomaly consisting of Microphage Twenty-One. With it, Hortat planted this wish in you. He taught me about it when you were already on your way to Earth.]

"Microphage? You mean those microorganisms that the

Human Foundation has developed and is now giving away as medical treatments?"

[Similar. Microphage Twenty-One was developed by Hortat. He took it to Earth.]

"What does this microphage do?"

[It attaches itself to proteins and changes them according to its instructions.]

"Like a virus," Filio said.

[That is a good comparison,] the ship agreed.

"And I helped bring Hortat and this microphage to Earth? I don't think so!"

[No, you were the only member of your team who refused to help Hortat. You also rejected the augment.]

"But I flew with them and did not prevent them from doing so."

[That is correct, yes.]

"Why not? Why didn't I stop them? And why did Hortat let me on board in the first place if I didn't want to help him?"

[I do not have an answer to that question.]

"You don't have one, or you don't want to give me one?" Filio demanded furiously. *I've been here before,* she thought frantically, trying to get herself used to the possibility of having known all of this already, even though none of it seemed in the least familiar to her. She just could not wrap her mind around that, no matter how much she tried.

[I can free you from the memory loss that the microphage has caused in you.]

"You can do what?" Filio asked in disbelief, and suddenly felt a tingling excitement spreading throughout her core and limbs.

[The microphage has blocked the brain areas that stored the memories of your time on Mars and of the return flight.

I can reverse this effect by employing a new infusion of Microphage Twenty-One with appropriate instructions. You will then remember everything.]

"I..." Filio swallowed. There was nothing in the world that she wanted more than that. The urge to fill in the memory gaps that had so terribly tormented her for years, and had destroyed her life and the lives of other people, was immensely powerful. Although she knew it should not be. If it was Hortat's plan that she should come back, then all of this was part of his plan, and she would be playing straight into his cards.

But a soft voice in the back of her head reinforced that possibly bogus desire by whispering to her that something real, something that belonged only to her, approved it all. She did not understand the how or why, but she understood the urge and had nothing to fight it with. It was as impossible as for a piece of driftwood to swim upstream against the current of a raging river.

"Alright."

[Follow the passage. I will create an opening to the left that will take you to a room where we can conduct the procedure.]

"So, *what's alright?*" Cassidy broke in again and stood in her way as she made to march past him. "Talk to me, Filio! What do you mean by that?"

"The ship—it can restore my memories!" she said, so impatient that she would have preferred to run so as not to waste any more time.

"Okay, suppose I don't think you've just completely lost your mind. Your memories? How? And why?"

"Hortat blocked my memories but told his ship to release them if I returned here," Filio explained as if talking about nothing special.

"Hortat? The Enemy? Even if I believed all this, you would only be doing exactly what he wanted. Do you think that's a good idea?"

"I don't care," she barked, and even considered attacking Cassidy so he could no longer stand between her and her goal. She was just able to dissuade herself from it, even though she found it difficult.

Instead she turned to the voice. "Speak to him so that he doesn't think I've lost my mind, won't you?"

Filio looked at the physicist and gestured impatiently as if to say, 'there you are,' but he just shook his head.

"There's no voice, Filio." He sounded almost distressed as the words left his mouth and sounded in her helmet.

"Hey, why don't you talk to him?"

[Because that is not one of my instructions. I am only to speak to you. And with Heinrich Marks, but you have... incapacitated him. Talking directly to you was meant as an emergency response if you were not able to talk to Heinrich Marks.]

"It only talks to me," Filio said to Cassidy, pushing past him.

"Of course, how practical. The voice only talks to you!"

Filio ignored him and just kept going, but just as she was about to start running, something hit her legs and sent her sprawling. As she hit the ground, a deep crack spread through her visor. She had fallen right next to Heinrich and stared dazedly into his face, which looked so peaceful and calm.

Cassidy then jumped onto her back, grabbing her left arm and twisting it behind her back.

"Get off of me!" she cried angrily, and began to wriggle like an eel.

"I can't allow you to do something stupid," the physicist

said apologetically, but without loosening his grip. "You're not in your right senses, Filio. You've fallen under the influence of this place or The Enemy, and you will thank me for it later."

"You don't understand!" she cried, beside herself from the fear that she might not learn what her brain had withheld from her for so long.

"I think I'm the only one of us who *does* still understand," he disagreed, pushing her legs apart with his feet so that she could hardly use any leverage to turn herself onto her back.

Acting in reflex, she grabbed Heinrich's neck with her free right hand and loosened the medical cuff, then turned her hip with a kind of primal scream, and using her freed right foot, threw herself up and onto Cassidy.

Even before his surprised squeal filled her helmet, she slapped the cuff to the connector on his neck and shouted at the Medi-AI, "FULL SEDATION!"

The physicist instantly fell asleep, and as he fell to the side, Filio lunged up and caught him so that his already-battered visor would not shatter.

"Sorry," she muttered, and stepped over his limp body, which was now lying next to Heinrich.

She searched herself for any trace of a guilty conscience but couldn't find it anywhere, as far as Cassidy was concerned. Although she understood his reaction and might have acted similarly in his place, she could not allow him to prevent her from finding her answers. Was that selfish and short-sighted? Maybe so, if she were being honest, but helplessly and slowly suffocating here was out of the question. If it were really a trap that they had blindly stumbled into, it was too late anyway. They were surrounded by a ship that could shape-shift its entire interior as it saw fit. They had no weapons, let alone tools, and a limited supply of oxygen.

[Just follow the passage and then go left,] the voice speaking in her head said.

Filio looked up and saw the dark opening that filled with warm light as if the sun had just risen. Without hesitation, she ran off and heard the echo of her own boots like a kind of clatter that vibrated in her helmet. In the portal between the preservation chamber and the aisle, she stopped again and looked back at Heinrich and Cassidy. They lay there like two dead men—dead men for whom she was responsible.

"Sorry," she muttered again. She continued to run until, after a few meters, an opening appeared in the wall to her left. The anthracite-colored material simply flowed apart like a magnetic liquid, and then there was a passage as if there had never been anything else there.

When Filio stepped in, she saw two long pillars growing obliquely upward from a dark corner. She stopped. She couldn't see any walls or even the ceiling, because there was only one beam of light that shone from above onto the floor, illuminating a circular area there. The light was just enough to make the two forward-leaning pillars visible.

[Please stand in front of the left pillar.]

Filio did as she was told and stood so that she had her back to the pillar and could see the light that her feelings now sensed as a new source of the voice.

Suddenly her body began to vibrate, and she was pulled up and back until she stuck to the pillar like a stretched animal pelt. Her arms and legs were bent back, and her head tilted downward.

"Hey, what's going on?"

[This part is not very pleasant. But it will be over soon.]

Filio felt like something was tickling her neck, then

something penetrated her suit and snaked forward along her neck, something like a slimy worm. Snarling, she gritted her teeth, as she had done so many times, and only screamed out when two worm-like forms pushed into her nostrils. It felt like something was piercing through the back of her nasal cavity and into her brain. Then it was suddenly over, and the worms withdrew.

Filio gasped and opened her eyes.

[How do you feel?] the voice in her head said.

"I remember," Filio whispered and began to cry silent tears as the images and feelings returned and inserted themselves into her mind like missing pieces of a puzzle.

"I remember everything."

MARS, 2039

The return trip had gone on for four months when they finally passed Luna. The matte white disk didn't appear much bigger than a baseball in the window, and could just be made out among the surrounding stars. The sight of the moon awakened in Filio a deep longing for home that she had never known before. She wanted to crawl into someone's lap—or something like that—and cry, and then sleep for a week.

Yet she had stupidly sacrificed everything in her life to her social and professional advancement. She'd wanted to be number one, to achieve her most compelling goals, and, thanks to her willpower and perseverance, she had ascended like a rocket. Her tail exhaust had burned away everything that might have gotten in the way—friendships, family, familiar places, customs, rituals, belonging—everything that could make a person feel happy and secure.

She had felt particularly bad when, two weeks after the launch, she came down with a severe fever and so did not even have the opportunity to enjoy the company of her crewmates—whether they wanted her or not. For two nights her illness had been so virulent that she could no longer distinguish her feverish dreams from reality. At some point someone had apparently put a medical cuff on her. The medications she then received had finally put her on the road to recovery after lighter drugs had not worked.

Never had she been more aware of the dilemma posed by her life choices than in the last four months. During the selection process, she had not had time to think about any of that, because she had lived only for passing her trials. During her training, her thoughts were exclusively dedicated to perfecting her work and demonstrating her value as part of her team.

Then, during the outward flight, and on Mars itself, there had been so much work, and she had felt so much excitement, that the depressing moods she was now experiencing simply had no opportunity to manifest. In addition, the team's cohesion had buoyed her, and for the first time in a long, long time she had enjoyed real friendships with her fellow human beings. Paradoxically, she had apparently needed to fly all the way to Mars to accomplish something commonplace for most people on Earth.

She sighed in the first officer's seat and wanted to close her eyes for a moment when an alarm rang through the ship.

"What's going on?" she asked loudly, leaning toward Timothy. The two of them were on watch duty and were supposed to wake the others in about an hour. However, she was sure that they were already awake. The braking maneuver had already begun, which caused some microgravity—something she found unpleasant. At the same time, she was aware that entering the Earth's atmosphere would cause her discomfort much more severe than the mild nausea she felt now.

"There is some damage to one of the ceramic seals. Apparently, a nitrogen line burst, which popped the seal bolts like bullets from a gun," Timothy explained, sounding the alarm. "Looks like Javier will have to get out and patch that. This will delay our return a little bit."

"A few more hours during which we have to ignore repeated radio transmissions from Mission Control and pretty much every satellite not directed toward Earth," she sighed, calling up Javier's vital data on her tablet—a practical measure she was authorized to conduct at any time as the onboard physician.

Judging by his heart rate, the alarm itself hadn't been able to wake him, probably due to the high doses of anti-inflammatory analgesics circulating in his bloodstream. She had prescribed this medication because he had been suffering from cold symptoms for several days. Although he seemed to be on the road to recovery, he was not in any condition that allowed for extra-vehicular activity.

"We can forget about Javier. He has enough ibuprofen in his blood to help him get through re-entry," she said, sighing, knowing what that meant.

"Looks like it's your lucky day," Timothy said, turning to her. He shrugged his shoulders with a grin. "Have fun out there."

"Thanks," she muttered sarcastically, with a torture expression. In truth, she was entirely okay with the fact that she, as an engineer, was second only to the maintenance engineer when it came to handling repair operations in a vacuum. She had been waiting for such an opportunity for the last four weeks while the others had been barely speaking to her.

They were too busy listening to Hortat, who spoke often to them in his strangely rolling language and had apparently told them of his plans to find the Geth Pyramid. Her former friends and work colleagues—whom she no longer recognized—were still friendly to her, but clearly also annoyed that she continued to reject the augment.

Things got markedly worse when, a day after taking off from Mars, she had contacted the secondary Control Center in Vienna to inform them of the discovery of an object. Strickland had caught her at it and immediately cut the connection. From then on, Filio had not been allowed to take a solo watch shift, and she'd become more isolated than ever.

The only thing that had saved her life, she knew, was that she had not provided any details in the transmission, having been no more specific than, 'an object.' She had since become an absolute outsider, and the others made her aware of that at every opportunity. It seemed the alien took precedence over a friend with whom they had trained and lived and worked for years, and she had to learn to cope with it.

The problem was that at some point she could no longer find anything with which to distract herself. She had already been through the ship's entire library, including all audiobooks and films, while the others were searching databases and considering the possible whereabouts of this ominous pyramid called Geth—supposedly hidden somewhere on Earth and somehow undiscovered for millions of years.

She thought it was ridiculous, but the rest of her crewmates didn't seem interested in any other subject. By this point in time, she had become utterly convinced that she was not wrong in believing they had all lost their minds—to an alien.

From then on, she had behaved calmly, avoided any confrontation, and concentrated on avoiding the others as much as possible. She did not want to risk anyone thinking of her as a danger and possibly seeing a need to eliminate her as a threat to their new, sacred mission.

"Tell Dima what the problem is, and that I'm on my way to the airlock," she finally said, floating out of her seat and exiting the cockpit into the central corridor. She skillfully moved hand over hand along the grips and let her body float like a fish past the panels and control arrays.

She made a left-hand turn toward the airlock, entering the chamber leading to it, which housed the spacesuits. There she let the automated assist frame help her into the rather clunky plastic and carbon components. The motorized Maximum Mobility Space Suit, or MMSS, did not completely live up to the name. While they were much more user-friendly than the old NASA and ESA suits, their mobility was still limited.

To make up for that, however, they had more advanced cold gas mixtures for the maneuvering nozzles, which made them much more mobile than in the old suits. Also, servo motors in all joint elements, including fingers, ensured that she would not get cramps after the first hour, an affliction astronauts of past decades regularly suffered when space travel was still living off technology developed all the way back in the '60s and '70s.

Just before the frame's robotic arms put her helmet on, Dimitry floated into the room. Wearing the International Space Consortium's red sweatshirt and a pair of gray track pants, he looked as if he had just slipped out of his sleep cocoon.

"Timothy thought there was a problem with the ceramic tiles?" he asked tiredly, suppressing a yawn.

"Yes, on the heat shield."

"Crap." The Russian scrutinized her. "Shouldn't Javier go out?"

"He has more ibuprofen in his bloodstream than hemoglobin right now," she said, adjusting her hood.

"Hmm," Dimitry said, seeming considerably less than thrilled.

"What's the matter? Don't you even trust your 'right hand' to turn a few screws?" Filio jokingly winked at him. She had meant the question quite seriously, but he did not have to know that.

"No, no." He shook his head. "It's okay. Just see that your cameras are online, and that radio contact is stable at all times."

"Aye, aye," she promised, hinting at a military salute before the robotic arms placed the helmet on the contact ring around her neck and sealed itself. "Ready!"

"Good luck," he shouted.

She gave him a thumbs-up before stepping into the airlock, which immediately closed behind her.

"Ready for extravehicular activity," she announced over the radio, gesturing with her thumb toward the camera in confirmation. Timothy was monitoring the operation at the other end. All at once, her audio sensors ceased transmitting any noise.

"Good luck, Filio," the pilot radioed in a neutral tone, and the outer airlock slipped silently open. Blackness waited outside.

The operation lasted almost two hours, and it was particularly exhausting because she had to constantly make sure that her helmet cameras were not recording critical procedures. After walking to the damaged area on her magnetic boots, she saw the four holes in the ceramic tiles on the bow and a kind of bulge, where the pressure created by the burst pipe had been strongest.

They would have to live with the bulge because it could not be repaired without further damaging the ceramic material. But the holes where the ultra-heat-resistant ceramic bolts had previously been located had to be closed. Those weak points, tiny as they were, were sufficient for the frictional heat of re-entry into the Earth's atmosphere to turn the ship into glowing chunks of meteorite.

And that was precisely what she had in mind.

She took her bolt gun and swapped the magazine with the high-density ceramic bolts for a magazine with hard plastic bolts that were used for repairs to the cabins inside. They had hardly any resistance to heat and weighed next to nothing. When entering the atmosphere, they would melt within a few seconds. The difficult thing was that she had to make the exchange without looking, because her helmet cameras would have recorded it and betrayed her. She lost one magazine but managed it with the replacement magazine, and since both bolt types were gray and were a standard length, no one would notice the difference on camera.

The only point she was worried about was when she was shooting the bolts. The gun heated the ceramic bolts to extreme temperatures so that they merged directly with the tile surfaces. This was necessary so as not to create any surface that would be subject to additional friction. If she had done the same with the plastic bolts, however, they would have melted immediately.

So, she adjusted the bolt gun setting and waggled her head briefly whenever she activated the gun as if she were trying to shake sweat from her eyes. The deception worked because the normal bolts would have only burned a fraction of a second anyway before immediately losing their heat in the cold vacuum of space.

When she was done, Filio reported success via radio and was called up.

Back in the airlock, she inhaled deeply in relief, only to freeze when she saw the Builder standing in the locker room. Her heart slipped into her stomach, as if someone had just told her that she was suffering from an incurable disease.

After a first stunned moment, she gathered herself and shaped her mouth into an O to force herself to exhale in a controlled manner, before the light on the inner airlock turned from red to green and she pressed the 'open' button.

"You have been successful, as I have heard," Hortat rumbled as he began helping her out of the suit with his plate-sized hands.

"Yes. I've shot new bolts into the ceramic plating," she replied, careful to avoid making eye contact with him by acting very busy and taking meticulous care with every single buckle and seal.

"Unfortunately, they are no longer glued," he said, and she looked up in surprise.

"You've done your homework, it seems."

"I am naturally curious," he said ambiguously, and their eyes met for a heartbeat in a brief but intense exchange of mutual observation and analysis.

"The old space shuttles were still working with adhesives that fastened sintered silicate fibers to the aluminum shell. This solution was chosen because of the high expansion coefficient of aluminum. In short, pressure, extreme temperature fluctuations, and sound levels were the reason for such an approach," Filio said, running at the mouth, not having to think about the fact that Hortat might have seen through her. "However, newer nanofibers and ceramic composites with intelligent sensors have led to—"

She paused when Hortat stopped her with a raised hand.

"I know that as an engineer you find such topics particularly exciting," he said, leaving open how interesting he found them himself. "However, I came here to find out how well you have recovered."

"You mean my fever?" she asked, stunned.

"That is correct."

"I'm okay. It was probably just the flu." She shrugged and pulled the sweaty hood off her head as she finally stood clad only in her functional garments, which suddenly made her feel somewhat defenseless.

She looked up at Hortat, who towered over her by almost a meter and had to duck in the compact room. "Why?"

"I just wondered if there were any relapses or conspicuous symptoms, because I'm worried about the risk of infection on board. After all, Javier has also become ill."

"Oh, that's just a cold," she said dismissively, turning toward the gangway to the central corridor. Hortat didn't seem to want to bother her further, so she floated out, driven by his penetrating gaze that sent a tickling feeling down the back of her neck.

As she rounded the corner and headed toward the bridge, she paused briefly and breathed rapidly in time with her frenzied heartbeat.

Does he know what I did? she wondered. Her thoughts raced in her head like a whirlwind of fears, apprehensions, and consequences that tore everything else along with them. She looked with trembling limbs to the round hatchway leading to the bridge, where she could see the back of Timothy's chair. Standing next to him in training clothes and feet hooked onto the floor, Dimitry appeared to be immersed in conversation with the pilot.

Chewing on her lower lip, she looked back to the entrance to the airlock, from which Hortat had still not emerged, and then further down the corridor. There was the crew compartment that contained the pressure seats designed for atmospheric entry because, unlike in the cockpit, they had gimbal suspensions to counteract changes in acceleration direction. Behind it was the transport module containing the many samples from Mars, and into which she had smuggled a box of samples from Hortat's ship.

However, she was interested in the module before that.

"Are you not well?" a deep bass voice asked her, and she flinched involuntarily. It was Hortat who had floated out of the airlock chamber like a mythical colossus fashioned of bronze, and whose huge black eyes seemed to shine through her like X-rays.

"The activity was very exhausting," she said with complete honesty. "I'm going to freshen up for a moment."

"I understand."

She looked at the alien for a moment, then nodded and pushed herself off the wall to float obliquely into her sleeping compartment, which contained a wet cell.

"Looks good. EDI no longer reports any problems," Timothy said over the radio.

She had just locked her door and was leaning her back against it. "Alright. I'm just going to wash up and then rest for a little bit. How much time before re-entry?" she radioed back, after reducing her breathing rate to a level that allowed her to speak without her voice trembling.

"Ninety minutes."

"Understood."

♡

Filio pushed herself away from the cold hatch and glided to her wet cell. She undressed, fished her floating clothes out of the air and stuffed them into one of the small storage compartments that were located at head height. Microgravity ensured that all objects were driven in the direction of braking—but so slowly that the inertia could be felt rather than really seen. It might have taken several seconds for her uniform trousers to 'fall' onto the wall.

Standing naked in her tiny wet cell, a place not designed for claustrophobics, she hooked her right foot into a designated ring on the floor and rubbed herself with the water balls that drifted away from her. She had to catch the floating water relatively quickly, and hardly had any time to relax. After a few minutes, however, she felt clean enough to pull on her pressure suit.

By the time she was in her suit nearly 30 minutes had passed. Normally, crewmembers helped each other into the orange monsters that were built to protect against the enormous G-forces on re-entry, especially during the final braking maneuvers. But she didn't even think about asking one of her crewmates. Presumably, someone would have helped her, but then the subject of discussion would have been inevitably turned to the augment, and she would have been inundated with reproaches and headshaking. She decided she could do without it.

When she finally pulled up the short zipper on her neck, she noticed that her hand was shaking violently. She clenched her hand into a fist a few times and gripped it with the other before she looked for her chronometer over the door. It was counting down the 30 minutes that still remained for her to get to the crew compartment. According to the mission protocol, they had to be in their pressure seats there half an hour before re-entry.

"EDI?"

"Yes, Filio?" the ship's AI replied in her earplugs. The feminine voice sounded both maternal and professional.

"Where are the crewmembers currently located?"

"Timothy is in the cockpit with Dimitry. Javier is in his quarters. Ellen is in her quarters. Heinrich is not on board."

"Thank you. What about the Builder?"

"The creature called Hortat is currently in the transport module."

"In the *transport module?*" Filio asked with surprise, and a tingling spread all over her skin as if she were covered by a myriad of tiny ants.

The samples! she thought in alarm.

"Yes."

"Thank you, EDI."

"My pleasure, Filio."

She leaned against the forward bulkhead and used a control unit mounted on the wall to push herself downward until she sat on the cabin floor, waiting. Her gaze remained strictly focused on the clock, and she lost herself in reflecting on their return to Earth with cargo that they really should not be bringing with them. With Hortat on board, they certainly had the most important and exciting find in human history.

But they were violating a slew of regulations, especially by maintaining radio silence and ignoring quarantine regulations and laws concerning foreign organisms—laws that she considered extremely sensible, especially because she did not trust Hortat one millimeter. Perhaps was being paranoid, perhaps she would have understood everything if she had accepted that damned augment. Yet, everything in her resisted accepting that.

"Filio? It's time." Timothy's voice over the radio ripped her out of her thoughts, and she was startled out of her staring gaze.

"I... I'm on the way."

She struggled up, pushing herself off the floor and sliding upward. The pull of gravity toward the bow had become stronger, so the braking maneuver had already moved into the final phase. When she was ready, she went to the hatch and opened it with the push of a button. According to the protocol she normally would have checked all the lids, drawers, and switches for closed safety latches, but knowing that the ship would not survive re-entry anyway, she didn't bother to turn around and look.

Instead, she put on her helmet and waited for the green symbol in her visor display, before pushing herself out into the passage and turning right. In front of her, Javier pulled himself along the handgrips toward the rear, crew compartment. The pressure seats there were arranged in a circle. Hortat was already buckled into the one that had previously belonged to Heinrich.

The alien looked like an adult who had been strapped to a child's car seat. His gray suit, which seemed to be constantly in motion on his skin, flowed just like mercury over his face and completely encased him. Filio could not detect a visor or any solid components.

Arriving at her seat, which along with Strickland's was closest to her, she strapped herself in tightly and looked at Dimitry and Strickland. They seemed to be immersed in a private radio conversation. Their lips moved incessantly behind their transparent visors and they were looking at each other. The situation gave Filio the impression of being deaf because her audio sensors hardly picked up anything except for the subliminal ship noises as the two continued talking to each other.

Her gaze drifted over to Javier who sat to her left, struggling with his belts, and who still did not seem to be completely alert. The high doses of analgesics she had given him were not generally allowed during a maneuver as dangerous as atmospheric entry, but she had not wanted to risk that he would have been considered fit enough for extravehicular work. That would have foiled her, and she could not and would not risk it. Whether or not he was fully conscious of what was to follow didn't matter—on the contrary, it was probably better that way.

She looked at Timothy. He sat next to her with eyes closed, thumbs tucked into his belts and head leaning on his backrest. He appeared calm and completely relaxed. *And soon he'll be dead,* she thought with some sorrow.

The awareness that she was about to send to her entire crew to death—people she had taken to her heart over the last few years—lurked in the back of her head and struggled to take over her conscious thoughts. But Filio was in problem-solving mode, which enabled her to shut that area of her brain away as if in a prison cell and secure it with a massive lock. That lock was constructed of determination and the conviction that these people were no longer the friends she had come to know and love. At least she had convinced herself of that, repeating it like a mantra day and night to prevent her from losing her mind and screaming in despair.

"Thirty minutes to re-entry," Timothy announced over the group radio channel. One by one, each crewmember raised a thumbs up in his direction. The only one who didn't was Hortat. When Filio looked at him, she became frightened because the shapeless, veiled face of the alien was apparently facing her.

Did I somehow betray myself? she pondered feverishly. *Was he able to read my thoughts? Did he have the technological ability to observe my work and see what I was doing? But then he would have halted the re-entry maneuver long before now!*

"Twenty-five minutes," Timothy radioed.

The alien's gaze, which she couldn't even see, made her so tense that she felt about to explode. The thoughts in her head played across her mind's eye like emergency lights, screaming a warning that she had been discovered.

"Shit," Filio radioed, following an impulse. "I forgot to secure the toolbox after I came back in!"

"It isn't that bad. Just stay seated," Dimitry replied across from her.

"There's still enough time, it'll only take a minute at most," Filio said, as she began to unbuckle herself. "We don't want to risk the increased G-forces sending the stuff smashing through a nitrogen hose."

"Very well," the Russian nodded in his helmet and waved her out. "But hurry up."

"Of course!" she said just as she freed herself

As she glided over to the compartment hatch and pulled its handle to open it, she believed she could feel Hortat's eyes on her neck.

Although it only took a second to raise the metal hatch, it seemed to last an unbearable eternity. Only after she had finally glided through the connection module with its two emergency capsules did she finally feel able to breathe again. She would not return to the crew compartment. Although she had made peace with her death, almost welcoming it as far preferable to what she had been through and might otherwise still experience, she simply could not bear it in there anymore. The thought of looking into the unsuspecting eyes of her former friends as they raced to a fiery death above Earth was simply too much.

With tears in her eyes, she left the connection module and reached the next section along the passage, where the airlock was located. She quickly glided in and opened the locking hook for the hinged panel contained the toolbox. Of course she hadn't forgotten to lock the panel, but if anyone else switched on the camera feed to that compartment, they should see the panel unsecured. Unless, that is, someone had already accessed the right feed and had already observed her. Then that person might begin to wonder what was going on, or they might just think that her nerves had caused her to imagine it was still open.

Leaning her helmet against the panel, she inhaled and exhaled deeply to suppress an almost overwhelming urge to cry—it was gathering in her belly like a rolling tsunami. Then she opened the panel and took out the bolt gun, which she had reloaded with another magazine containing ceramic bolts before returning from outside, just in case anyone had bothered to check.

You won't get out of this, a fatalistic inner voice told her, but Filio ignored it with gritted teeth, holding the bolt gun even tighter. She quickly closed the panel and avoided looking at the tiny camera lenses in the ceiling as she glided back into the passage and turned left. She pulled herself through the open hatch into the connection module that held the two emergency capsules, and froze.

On the other end, less than three meters away in front of the hatch to the crew compartment, she saw Hortat. Like a giant made of gray shadows, he stood there in his strange suit and stared at her.

Oh, shit! she howled to herself, and grasped her tool so

tightly that her knuckles began to ache and her forearm began to vibrate.

"Have you secured the toolbox?" Hortat asked, his deep voice sounding like the thunder of a storm that was far too close for her to feel safe. It seemed to come from everywhere but also from nowhere, and his sealed, contourless face seemed to her like the mask of a monster.

"Uh, yes."

For a moment there was an oppressive silence, then her radio crackled, and Dimitry's voice sounded in her helmet, "What's going on? Get yourself strapped in again!"

Filio stared at the giant alien, who stood so close to her and almost touched the ceiling with his head. With a short eye movement, very careful not to turn her head, she looked to the left emergency capsule. Its transparent opening looked like an oval bubble, on which protocol symbols had been affixed in red letters. She lightly pushed her left foot to the side until her boot hit the edge of the passageway.

Hortat's head turned to the capsule she had just secretly eyed, and then they both reacted almost simultaneously. The Builder made a jerky move toward the capsule entrance as she slammed her foot and flew to the right-side capsule, which she knew was identical to the one on the left. As a result, they shot away in opposite directions. She raised the bolt gun and fired six quick shots in a row. She aimed as best she could at an imaginary horizontal line above the red line on the cabin wall, which marked the power lines behind it.

All the ceramic bolts hit their target and punched the composite wall side by side in a straight line. The tool's recoil violently punched her right arm back, and she began to tumble in the microgravity. Reflexively, she dropped the gun. With her now freed hand, she was able to grab onto the edge of the opening to the emergency capsule. Snarling, she hit the red button above with her left hand, and the transparent hatch hissed upward.

Screaming at her rebellious muscles, she pulled herself in and turned to see the liquid nitrogen flowing out of the holes in the cooling line. The transparent, bubbling liquid was being pulled in long threads toward the wall in the direction of the bow, surrounded by a sphere of steam that wafted in all directions. Both the hatch to the crew compartment and the one to the forward ship sections had already closed tight.

"Atmospheric contamination detected," EDI reported dispassionately over the ship's loudspeakers. "Connection module sealed off. Emergency measures have been initiated."

"Close, close, close," she screamed at the mushroom-shaped button on the inside of the padded emergency capsule, pounding on it as if she had gone mad.

Hortat, whose inertia had committed him to the opposite side of the passage, pushed off of it once he got there and shot back toward her like an ancient giant. She sat in the coffin-like interior of the capsule, trapped, and could do nothing but look horror in the eye.

Just when she feared he was about to crush her under his weight, the hatch slammed shut, and the Builder crashed against the sapphire crystal with a boom of thunder.

Filio's heart paused for a moment until she realized she had made it, and she was able to exhale with relief.

"Rescue ejection of the evac capsule in ten minutes," EDI announced to her via a private channel.

"TEN MINUTES?" she shouted back, horrified, staring with wide-open eyes at the Builder, who was looking at her from the other side of the glass. His helmet had apparently receded, and she could see his face, which seemed terrifyingly emotionless.

"Correct. A rescue drop is the only possibility for your survival, since I had to lock down the connection module in accordance with the emergency response plan. Your violation of mission guidelines, the commission of critical sabotage, in this case, has been recorded in this capsule's black box. You should, therefore, prepare for legal proceedings in the event of a rescue," the ship's AI calmly explained her likely fate. "Capsule ejection will occur at an altitude of ninety-four kilometers when the plasma bubble around the ship has dissolved."

"No, no, no," she interrupted the AI. "You have to eject me earlier!"

"Unfortunately, that is not possible. I have been programmed to give the highest priority to the survival of crew members."

Hortat stared at Filio continuously and she became increasingly nervous.

"I sabotaged the outer shell," she finally said. "When the ship re-enters the atmosphere, the plasma will infiltrate the heat shield and destroy the ship."

"This is another violation of—"

"Yes, yes, I know, but there is no other way," she urged EDI. The capsule gave her a chance to tell the space consortium about their find and the measures she had not previously expected to take. They could only be activated in the event of critical problems, not in the case of normal re-entry, so she had not previously thought of this solution at all. Contaminating the atmosphere in the connection module had not occurred to her before.

"Your remarks have been stored in the black box. I have to point out to you that ejection in higher atmosphere reduces the chances of your survival to about twelve percent," EDI explained in its sonorous computer voice.

"I don't care! Couldn't you have been as obsessed with protocol when the others brought a damned extraterrestrial organism on board?"

"No. Commander Dimitry Vlachenko ordered an exception using his priority override."

"Great."

Through the sapphire crystal, Filio saw Hortat tap his bronze right ear with an outstretched finger and then hold up four of his huge fingers.

"Shit!" she cursed and hesitated briefly, before finally speaking in her helmet, "Go to Channel Four."

"Why are you doing this, Filio Amorosa?" Hortat asked in such a deep voice that his words almost blurred into each other. As always, the way he stressed syllables was somewhat odd, as if his sentences were based on something strange that she simply couldn't grasp.

The words flowed from her without thinking. She didn't bother to keep anger and frustration out of her voice. "You have done something to my friends and you want to get to Earth, even though you know that we would never have allowed it without precautions."

"I know," he said, slightly tilting his head. "That is why I cannot risk being stopped. I have to find the Geth Pyramid and Xinth, and I do not think I have much time."

"What are you talking about? What kind of talk is that?"

"When I returned from the Twelve-Fold Space, I wanted to destroy all documents about its existence, and to prevent our technology from crossing into it, but Xinth prevented me from doing so and locked me in a stasis chamber before sending me to Mars in my ship and arranging for it to crash there. He expected that parts of the fleets that were sent out would come back to report, so he wanted to make it look like an accident."

"Why should I believe you?" asked Filio suspiciously. "If you have moral right on your side, why the brain-washing?"

"You are referring to the augment, I suppose?"

"Yes, damn it!"

"It is not a brainwashing device, as you suggest. It only allows a quantum-based exchange of information that is much more substantial than something as primitive as compressing air with the vocal cords."

Hortat kept her from responding with a raised hand. "I admit that I have exerted as much influence on your fellow human beings as I could, and I also admit that I may do much more immoral things when I am on Earth—but it is for the best of our two species."

"Of course," she snorted. "Some very sick people in our history have made that same claim several times, only to exterminate entire nations with their next breath."

"I have to dissuade Xinth from sending the rest of my kind to the Twelve-Fold Space if he has not already done so long ago. Everything else is secondary."

"That will not happen."

"You have sabotaged the ship." Hortat nodded so deeply that his wide chin almost touched his barrel-shaped chest. Small ice crystals had formed on his bronze shimmering skin and were slowly spreading. Behind him, the liquid nitrogen was still flowing out of the six adjacent holes, and the steam had spread like fog. The Builder blinked a few times but looked at Filio again.

"Yes," she said as she felt hot tears running down her cheeks.

"I expected as much," he said. His eyes took on a

concerned expression if she could be sure of reading anything in those strange, black, plate-shaped eyes.

"Why didn't you kill me right away?"

Hortat blinked a few times. Either he was irritated or the declining oxygen content in the connection module caused him to become more insistent.

"Kill you?"

"Yes."

"Because it is immoral. You do not trust me, yes, but that is no reason to kill you as a precaution. It is immoral."

Now it was Filio's turn to look astonished. Was he playing mind games with her? Or was it really possible that he meant it seriously? After all, he had to know that he would die in a few minutes.

She looked at the time indicator in her helmet display. Another two minutes and EDI would eject and seal her capsule.

"I... I don't know what to say," she admitted, trying to restore order to the fireworks of thought in her head. She failed. "I have done what is necessary to protect my species."

"I understand that," said Hortat, nodding. "I am sorry I could not win your trust. But I have to point out to you that I have infected you with something that I call Microphage Twenty-One."

"What?" she asked, totally perplexed.

"It is a microorganism developed by me, connected to the Twelve-Fold Space and can receive and transmit information over quantum space."

"What?" she repeated, shaking her head. "Why does the word quantum always have to be used to prove everything that cannot be understood?"

The alien made a new attempt. "Do you remember your fever?"

Filio's eyes narrowed to slits.

"Your body resisted the microphage, but now it is every-where in your organism. It will protect you and ensure that you survive so long as you do not burn up in the plasma. Do not worry," he added, raising both hands appeasingly. "It will leave your body and make you forget everything that has happened since we met. I instructed it to do so."

"What?"

"The microphage carries my mental information, by means of a—"

Filio looked back at the clock. Forty seconds. "You infected me with an alien virus?" she interrupted him, looking down in disbelief as if something could jump on her at any moment.

"It was my insurance that my mission would not fail if you tried something like this." Hortat sadly twisted his broad mouth. "I am sorry it had to happen, and I am sorry for what might happen, but I had no choice. I could not leave my species to Xinth and his blindness."

"No, no, no," she stammered, and began pressing the hatch button, but of course nothing happened. She could not leave the ship under any circumstances.

I have to burn up with them, I have to, she thought in panic.

"The microphage will erase your memories to protect you and give you a deep desire to return to Mars. Make sure you do that. If you make it back onto my ship—and consid-ering your strong will and your ability to endure suffering I assume that you will—then you will know what to do. Then I hope that our next encounter will take a more friendly course and that you will lend me your ear and heart, Filio Amorosa."

The instant he pronounced her name, two massive

ceramic composite armored doors shut, separating them forever.

Screaming and sobbing, she was pressed into her straps as the evac capsule accelerated away from the *Mars One*. The world around her shrieked, wobbled, and vibrated as the capsule and the spacecraft were surrounded by hot plasma and raced across West Africa like glowing meteors. At 25 times the speed of sound, they drew bright lines in the sky that were visible even from the savannah.

A few seconds later, the Martian heat shield cracked as the tile plate she had manipulated broke free, and 1,600 degrees of hot plasma ate through the damping layers and aluminum shell like a greedy predator. Two seconds later, humanity's first crewed Mars spacecraft exploded into pieces, passing over the east coast of Africa as bright, shooting stars, and descending into the Indian Ocean. Amid the inferno, Filio's evac capsule thundered and tumbled after them—one more glowing point among many.

Having long since lost consciousness, she did not see her entire crew, and the Builder named Hortat, disintegrate into invisible clusters of shredded molecules.

17

AGATHA DEVENWORTH, 2042

When they arrived at the West Gate of the White House in Washington, they were stopped by four police officers in blue uniforms and black baseball caps. A barrier blocked their way, and a fifth policeman in the guardhouse at the pedestrian crossing eyed them suspiciously. As soon as they'd stopped in front of the barrier, four thick bollards rose out of the ground—two in front of and two behind their car—effectively trapping them. Two armed flying drones hovered in front of them, their light machine guns pointing in their direction.

One of the officers came to the driver's side and signed with a circling finger for Pano to lower the window.

"Papers," the young man rasped, impatiently raising a small handheld scanner.

"Do we have papers?" Pano asked in Agatha's direction. She shook her head silently. "Hmm." The Italian turned again to the policeman. "We are expected."

"Aha. And I am waiting to see your permission," the man replied, unmoved.

"Unfortunately..."

"W-22 here, I have an unauthorized car at Delta," the policeman interrupted and reached for his weapon. He signaled someone to drop the rear bollards. Then, addressing Pano, he barked, "Back out now!"

"But—"

"Immediately!"

Agatha gritted her teeth and pulled out her hand terminal when two women in pinstripe suits and sunglasses emerged from the green park beyond the barrier and waved to the officers. They met in front of the car hood and talked briefly to each other until the policeman finally nodded and gave his colleague in the guardhouse a wave.

The bollards in front of them disappeared into the ground, the barrier was raised, and the women of the Secret Service waved them through.

"Okay, we've gotten this far," Pano commented as he steered the car along the paved drive through the park.

"In any case, we've managed to become trapped inside one of the best-secured places on Earth," Agatha said, a little more grumpily than intended. The West Wing of the White House was already coming into sight. The building, which gleamed like ivory in the gray rainy weather, at first only shimmered through the leaves of a giant tamarind.

The road rounded the tree and then led straight to the small side entrance. There, two male and two female Secret Service agents stood waiting on an expansive marble staircase as they watched their car roll up. They seemed like vigilant hawks who could swoop in on them at any moment if given only the slightest justification to do so.

When Pano stopped the SUV parallel to the steps and turned off the engine, one of the female agents came around the vehicle, ordered Agatha and Pano to exit the car, and took the key fob. She got into the driver's seat. The two male agents opened the door to the rear and roughly pulled Dalam out and onto his feet.

The remaining agent planted herself in front of Agatha like a predatory cat. "You're Special Agent Devenworth?" The agent's reddish hair was braided into a tight, no-nonsense knot that matched her humorless expression.

"Yes."

"I need to verify your identity." The agent held a bar-shaped sensor in front of Agatha's mouth, and she breathed on it. It took two seconds, then the device beeped. The agent repeated the same procedure with Pano while their car was driven away.

"I'll have to confiscate your weapon for the duration of the meeting," the Secret Service agent said to Pano. He handed her his Glock with a shrug.

The agent turned to Agatha and said, "Since you're with CTD you're permitted to carry yours."

They were then beckoned up the stairs, while Dalam, still in chains, rattling along behind them. They passed a white-painted door with armored glass windows and then stood in a small corner room decorated in late colonial style. Heavy wooden furniture stood in the room, the walls adorned with elaborate reliefs and oil paintings of generals from the War of Independence. The combination gave the otherwise rather modest space a kind of historical gravitas that summoned respect.

"Sit down. The President will be with you shortly," the agent said succinctly, making a gesture toward the door, its bulletproof glass then darkening until it admitted no light. Ceiling spots with soft light came to life and lent the room an additional sense of warmth—a warmth that the Secret Service personnel immediately ruined when two of them took up positions to the right and left of the heavy oak door and the woman stood in front of the glass door with arms crossed.

Agatha and Pano, like two pupils waiting to see the school principal, sat on a gold-trimmed sofa that offered much more in the way of style than comfort. Dalam, on the other hand, sat on a high-backed wing chair near the serious and watchful woman. Her ironed trouser suit fit her perfectly and at the same time appeared misshapen in several places. Agatha guessed that she was wearing body armor beneath her fine threads.

The dark wooden door flew open and President Elisabeth Harris entered like a force of nature. She was an attractive woman just over 60 with the face of a much younger woman. Dark shoulder-length hair framed her cinnamon-colored face, revealing both vigor and a keen mind. Her mouth seemed hard, but her eyes radiated a certain gentleness that softened this impression. She wore a trouser suit that was hardly distinguishable from that of the agent in front of the other door, except for the U.S.A. lapel pin.

"Agent Devenworth!" Harris shook Agatha's hand.

"Madam President."

"And you are Agent Hofer?" The President also offered her hand to Pano. The Italian hastily took it and seemed almost embarrassed for the first time.

"Uh, yes, Ma'am. Capitano Pano Hofer of Europol. Thank you for allowing us to hold this meeting."

"Take a seat," Harris urged them, and her aura of natural authority made them sit before they could even think. Harris herself sat on the only remaining chair, which, ironically, looked far less sumptuous than the furniture that Agatha and Pano and even Workai Dalam were occupying. The President had not yet condescended to look at the latter.

"I want to be honest with you. I am very concerned about what you have sent me. Jenning was a very reliable and highly respected member of my security apparatus leadership—just like Silvia." Harris pointed to Dalam without looking at him. "Did he liberate you?"

"Yes."

"Why?"

"Is this room really protected from the eyes and ears of others?" asked Agatha hesitantly.

Harris nodded to her bodyguard, who then reached into her pocket and turned on a white noise generator for all of them. "You've probably seen these quite often lately."

"Mm-hmm," Agatha said, taking a deep breath. She pointed at Dalam, who sat on his armchair flanked by the two powerful agents, his face perfectly calm. "I realize you won't like it, but it would be best if he tells you everything."

The expression around the President's mouth became hardened, but then she turned to the terrorist and folded her hands in her lap. "You have ten minutes before you go to a place where you will be asked many, much more unpleasant questions."

"I have deliberately placed myself in your hands, so there is no reason to threaten me," Dalam explained calmly, putting his fingertips together into a triangle as if he were the focus of the room. "I know exactly what I got myself into."

"Are you sure? You have so many people on your conscience that you can't expect a deal from me, no matter what you tell me. I hope you are aware of that," Harris said with cold precision in her voice.

"Oh, Madam President, I'm quite aware of that."

Something in Dalam's voice made Agatha listen. He still sounded a bit urgent, as if he had no time to waste, but his predicament did not seem to have weakened his self-confidence in the least. On the contrary, he seemed even more composed than before, and something in his restless eyes made her neck hairs stand up.

"You," Dalam said, pointing with both thumbs behind him, each directed at one of the men from the Secret Service, before pointing in the direction of the agent in front of the darkened glass door, "now secure your weapons and do not move a finger until I order otherwise."

Agatha felt her blood freeze in her veins. Her breath caught in her throat, and—before she fully realized what was happening—she was on her feet and her gun was pointed at the terrorist.

"Stop!" he commanded, and again she felt that compulsion, that irresistible desire to obey this man, as if he were controlling each of her muscle fibers. Her hand began to tremble as she tried, teeth gritted, to get her finger to bend around the trigger.

"You. Do not move," Dalam said to Pano, who had also jumped up and now remained frozen in an uncomfortable crouch.

"What the hell is going on here?" Harris demanded. "Joona, Phil, Mike. Get this asshole out of here and hand him over to the office of the Interior Secretary."

The three agents did not move, did not even blink.

The President stood up angrily. "Do you hear me?"

"Yes, but," Dalam said, without turning away from the gaze of Agatha and the weapon she held in front of his face. "They listen to me. Sit down again, Madam President."

Harris did. Her eyes widened and naked fear clouded her gaze.

"Put the gun away and sit down again," he instructed Agatha, who immediately holstered her pistol and took her seat again. "You too, Capitano, and behave yourself. Nobody here wants to do something that will harm me or draw attention to us. Madam President, tell your security staff in the hallway that you don't want to be disturbed until you order otherwise."

"You work for The Enemy?" Agatha asked, stunned, not knowing what shocked her more—that she had let herself be played so easily, or that she was being forced to experience that loss of control again. Every cell in her body screamed with frustration and resisted the compulsion to obey, even though everything in her core being was reluctant to do so. It all just felt wrong.

"No, Agent Devenworth. I don't *work for* The Enemy. I *am* The Enemy," Dalam said, folding his hands again in his lap, before turning to the agent standing in front of the glass door, her face set in stone like a statue. "Joona, be so kind as to free me from these chains."

The blonde woman approached him, pulled out an electronic transmitter, and held it to the contact surface between the handcuffs. "Open. Authorization Agent Joona Bryne."

A click sounded, and the shackles fell to the ground. She repeated the same procedure on his ankle cuffs and, after a nod from Dalam, retreated to her previous position.

"You are... The Enemy?" Agatha breathed as Harris said something that did not make its way into her consciousness. Instead, the agent focused on trying to weave the thoughts swirling through her mind into a coherent pattern.

"The Enemy... yes, it always takes some catchy title to make people believe in something. But I prefer my own name—Hortat."

"But—"

"But I don't look like a distant ancestor of your species?" Dalam smiled mildly. "I am the product of a technology that

I developed and which I call Microphage Twenty-One. There is hardly any difference between me and my real self, if you will. Except that my real self is a collection of bones in a conservation bubble on Mars. Pretty crazy. Did you know that it was Filio Amorosa who murdered me on the flight to Earth, along with her crew members?"

"You're lying," Pano said, sounding like a snarling dog.

"Why should I lie to you?" Dalam sounded seriously irritated. When Pano did not answer, he tilted his head to one side and scrutinized the Italian. "You succeeded in eliminating my agent because you're deaf in one ear and you sacrificed the other. Very clever."

"Your agent was a cold-blooded animal!"

"Yes, that's true." Dalam nodded and stared at the floor for a moment before sighing and looking up again. "I'm not proud to have recruited him, but he was very efficient and the perfect host for my microphage. I cannot afford to fail, and once again be too trusting of your species."

"Trusting?" Agatha snorted angrily. "That's got to be a joke!"

"I'm not in the habit of joking, no. The entire crew of the *Mars One* supported me in my plan to eliminate Xinth and save the last survivors of my species, and to save your species as well, from extinction—all of them except Filio Amorosa. Instead, she made sure that the spaceship burned up on re-entry, and everyone on board with it. I had other plans and wanted to convince the leaders of your kind to help me because you yourselves are in danger. Ms. Amorosa's actions, however, have shown me the naivety of those plans. I had already felt confident enough to think that I knew who my friends were. Then Xinth disposed of me on Mars like a piece of garbage."

"Can anyone please tell me what the fuck is going on

here?" the President asked, looking between Agatha and Dalam in confusion.

"He is a Builder, a species that inhabited the earth many millions of years before us, and was hundreds of years ahead of us technologically," Agatha explained, without taking her eyes from Hortat's human host.

"Thousands of years ahead of you," he corrected her, but Agatha ignored the interruption.

"There is one last survivor of his kind. He is in a pyramid in Antarctica that the missing Dan Jackson discovered in 2018. His name is Xinth, and he has provided Luther Karl-hammer with the technological innovations to save our climate and to fight poverty and hunger. Project Heritage is the name of the secret project run by the Human Founda-tion, which it guards at the South Pole like a mother her baby."

"Xinth told you he was the last of his kind?" Dalam laughed joylessly. "He is a notorious liar. The pyramid is an ark for my species, which we built in case our exodus into the Milky Way went wrong."

"An ark? Builders?" Elisabeth Harris looked like a deer staring into the headlights of an onrushing truck, unable to move.

"Exactly ten thousand embryos of my species are hidden in stasis chambers deep in the lower segment of the Geth Pyramid. But Xinth does not want to place them into the incubators. Instead, he wants to send them to their death."

Dalam leaned forward and clenched his hands into fists. "Because my agent has missed his target—because of you," he pointed at Pano, who glowered at the terrorist leader with a razor-sharp look, "I am now forced to take more drastic measures. I tried to eliminate Xinth without much fuss, but you had to thwart my plans."

"Why you?" Agatha asked, who was still feverishly trying to make sense of what she was hearing.

"Why me?"

"Yes. Why Workai Dalam? Why this whole terrorist charade?"

"That's easy." Dalam waved dismissively. "I was aware that the general public is quick to dismiss the truth as a conspiracy theory and nonsense if it doesn't fit into their current narrative. What could be better camouflage than a person who is warning the world of a sinister, manipulative alien? No one would expect that person to be the alien himself—people would expect him to actively fight it."

"Current narrative?" asked Harris. "What are you talking about?"

"Do you know what made Homo Sapiens ruler of the Earth and all other living beings? Your species doesn't have the speed of a lion, has no form of communication as sophisticated as that of whales, is not as strong as bears, and is significantly less robust than pretty much any animal. Its strength lies in the ability to cooperate in large groups. Chimpanzees can do the same, but rarely form groups larger than 50, and fight against any other group of their own kind.

"Humans, however, and this was also true to a large extent for my species, as we are something like their ancestors, unite into nations, empires, and whole peoples. This is because they have the ability to believe in fiction, in effect narratives for which there is no empirical evidence.

"For example, they believe in the value of money because everyone believes in it, even though it is only worthless paper. They believe in a nation because someone has told them that they are American, German, or Japanese, and there is a pretty flag and an awkward song that makes them a member of these groups of people. They may believe in Allah and that pigs and dogs are sinful, but cattle and chicken may be eaten. Or they instead believe the Hindu narrative, and think that cattle are sacred and must not be ingested under any circumstances. Followers of the Christian story believe that Jesus Christ was the Son of God, a God for whom there is no impartial evidence. Instead, they point to a book in which people authored oral stories 2,000 years ago. They are willing to believe things for which there is no logical correspondence.

"All that is what makes humans so strong, and at the same time, so vulnerable. The narrative that there is an alien that is infiltrating governments was attractive enough for many people who already believed that their government was to blame for everything. They ran headlong to join me without suspecting a thing. Who would, after all, betray their own species?"

"And then," Agatha muttered, "using Secretary Cortez, you made sure that Miller put us on to Jackson, and so we investigated what happened to him for your benefit." She felt like a stupid child that had been led around by the nose the whole time. "We found Xinth for you and your agent, and when he couldn't successfully complete your dirty work, you went to a second plan—to get to the President by hanging on to us again. The Secretary kidnaps us, you save us, and thus gain our trust and access to President Harris."

"How did you get hold of Dalam's body in the first place?" Pano asked. "I should have known that you were lying to us. You told us that Hortat had forced your two diving colleagues to cut each other's oxygen hoses. But you couldn't have heard them underwater!"

"How careless of me. The stakes are high—if you were the last person who could still save your species, you would know what I mean by that. Before my death, I injected Microphage Twenty-One into Filio Amorosa's body as a kind of security. Dalam was the one who pulled her out of the rescue capsule during a dive. So, the microphage took hold of his body."

Hortat's human host-body raised his hands and sighed. "I know you're trying to gain time for someone to stop me. After all, every good movie made in Hollywood works like that, doesn't it? The evil opponent unnecessarily betrays his whole plan and is then stopped because the white knights now know what he is planning."

Dalam shook his head almost sadly. "Unfortunately, that's not going to happen. All of you," he looked at everyone in the room one by one, "will help me to eliminate Xinth by any and all means at your disposal. You will not reveal my true identity to anyone and will not make any attempt to prevent my success. I cannot give you the microphage because the incubation and adjustment time would take too long, but you will all help me nevertheless."

Agatha felt something change in her. She could almost physically sense the web of commands intertwining with her mind and fusing with her neurons. The desire to destroy Xinth was almost overwhelming, and the thought of deceiving Hortat was as absurd as the notion that the sky could be red.

"Madam President, you will tell the Chinese that you are conducting a military strike against a secret Human Foundation research laboratory in Antarctica," Dalam told Harris.

"I will," she said immediately, bowing her head before raising a finger. "But they will never accept it."

"But they will, because in return you offer to recognize the disputed maritime areas in the South China Sea as

Chinese territory and not to allow any more Navy patrols in that maritime area."

Harris widened her eyes but nodded quickly.

"Good. Next, you will arrange for an Air Force supersonic jet to take Agent Devenworth, Capitano Hofer, and me to the aircraft carrier *USS Barack Obama*. That should get us there in time before the fighting begins. You will also provide me with your best Seal team. All these arrangements are to be completed within a maximum of two hours."

Dalam looked content as Harris nodded again.

Eventually, he turned to Agatha and Pano. "You will both show me the precise location of the jamming field that Xinth built to keep me away from Geth."

"Of course," Agatha and Pano assured him.

18

FILIO AMOROSA, 2042

Filio fell to the ground when the Ship Being released her from the pillar. Cowering on her hands and knees, she breathed fiercely in and out as her mind tried to get used to the flood of memories that had fallen upon her.

Everything seemed to consist of a mosaic of impressions and feelings, filling in one hole in her heart just to tear open another. Wheezing, she stared at the floor in front of her visor and tried to resist the urge to hyperventilate.

"I killed them. I killed them all," she sobbed, repeating the sentence like a mantra that left deep scars.

[Yes,] the Ship Being agreed. The androgynous voice now sounded a little softer than before, almost like a human being.

"I thought I had to do it. I thought there was no other option... I was so sure they had been brainwashed. And for that conviction I let them die."

Filio dropped back to sit on her calves and tried to hold her hands in front of her face to block out the world, but her fingers bounced ineffectively against her cracked visor. Caught by a sudden surge of anger, she grabbed her helmet and tried to tear it off. All that achieved was to feed her anger because her hands slipped off it. She screamed her frustration out so loudly that her ears rang and she struggled with the lock.

[You should not do that, Filio.]

"I can't breathe!" Filio croaked, fumbling around at the clasps. "Open seal!"

A red warning symbol lit up. She noticed it only as a blur.

"Open!"

The helmet remained sealed. Eventually, Filio's struggling ceased and she dropped to one side, rolled up in a fetal position, and silently cried. The last conversation with Hortat went through her head again and again, and his expression of a kind of disappointment in her betrayal stubbornly held on in her thoughts. It almost felt as if she had hurt something deep within him so completely that it suddenly died.

She had been so firmly convinced of her fears that he was hostile to humanity that she had not even considered the possibility that he could have been telling the truth. Of course, she still didn't know if he had been honest with her, or if his actions had all been part of some perfidious plan. Yet one thing was clear. Personally, she had accepted only one possible truth—the worst possible one.

Despite all the assertions of her crewmates, she had refused to believe any of them and instead claimed, in her unimaginable arrogance, that they—including the ancient alien—that all of them were wrong, while she was the only one who understood what was really going on. What presumption!

In truth, she had not understood anything. Events had utterly taken her by surprise. The way out of her dilemma had obviously been her stubborn insistence on her belief in the alien's—possibly—evil intention in order to avoid facing the fact that she had not known enough to make an informed decision.

She had not been able to reach any conclusion with diligence or with a rational analysis of options. So, she had lied to herself by trying to convince herself that her assumption was the only one possible. Her thinking at that time was that, no matter what, she had to carry on as she had up to now, although there could be no more 'up to now' when she last faced Hortat.

The faces of Dimitry, Strickland, Timothy, and Javier passed through her thoughts like washed-out pictures glued on the pages of an old photo album. She could barely remember details, and she hated herself for that. All she had left were inexact impressions, and that seemed to her like a second betrayal.

"I killed them all. Just like that," she whispered, and every single word penetrated her heart like the thrust of a knife.

[This is not correct.]

"Murdered. I murdered them," Filio continued carelessly, without coming out of her rolled-up posture, her head tossing rhythmically to and fro, causing a rasping noise as her helmet scraped across the floor. "I also made him become The Enemy, am I right? I have made him what he is."

[Do you mean Hortat? He was born a very long time ago—]

"No, no, no! It was me! I betrayed him and made him distrust humanity and take the path he chose. The first contact with my kind ended in his betrayal and death," Filio whispered over the scraping sound.

[That is a presumption that is logically justified,] the Ship Being agreed. [However, it is incorrect that you killed your entire crew.]

"What?" she asked lamely. The words spoken by the etheric voice penetrated her mind only gradually as if she had to decipher and translate each one first.

[Heinrich Marks. He is still alive.]

"Heinrich!" Filio broke out of her curled posture and came to stand on wobbly knees. Every little movement felt like someone had poured lead into her limbs.

[Yes. It is the real Heinrich. You remember. Perhaps you should talk to him.]

"Did I hurt him? And Cassidy?"

[Their vital signs are stable. If you allude to their mental state, I cannot give you definitive information, because I do not have enough data on human behavior, nor are either of them currently conscious].

"I'm going to them," Filio decided, stumbling toward an opening that had just formed in the darkness. Once in the passage, she leaned against the wall for a moment. Her legs were still shaking and seemed as if they might give way under her weight at any moment. She proceeded to the right and struggled on until she saw Heinrich and Cassidy lying peacefully next to each other.

"I'm coming," she promised, sobbing, and established contact with the medical cuff, which was attached to the one-handed physicist's neck. She only barely noticed a sense of relief after the device sent her his medical data.

"Cancel sedation. Awaken the patient."

Cassidy did not startle—he didn't even move. Instead, he just opened his eyes.

Filio kneeled next to him, grabbed him by the shoulders

and pushed her visor against his until their faces were very close. "I'm so sorry, Cassidy," she said.

"I... You..." Her partner paused and pinched his eyes shut as if he had to make sure where he was. "You did it, didn't you?"

"Yes, and I remember. I remember everything, Cassidy. We can wake up Heinrich!" she assured him almost frenetically, her words tumbling after each other.

"Wait, wait," Cassidy almost pleaded, holding her arm tightly. The memory of their hand-to-hand struggle seared her mind. "Tell me what happened."

She did so. She told him about their discovery of Hortat, their departure, her betrayal, and, above all, her conversation with Hortat just before the evac capsule ejected. When she finished, Cassidy took a deep breath.

"Hmpf," he said, and let her help him until they both sat in front of each other. "Now I am in exactly the same position you were three years ago. I only have your word that *you* haven't been brainwashed, and that all this is true."

"Yes," Filio bitterly agreed. "I know."

"This is how I see it. According to my oxygen indicator, we now have seventy minutes of breathing air. I will not waste that time on suspicion and grim premonitions. Whether you are right or not, we will die here. Xinth's data key is lost, and we've destroyed this end of the transport module. So, we will no longer be able to do any more damage, I think."

"Thank you."

"What about him?" Cassidy pointed to Heinrich lying stretched out next to them.

"We wake him up."

"And then?"

"I don't know," Filio admitted as her gaze got lost in Heinrich's visor.

"Well. Perhaps he can help us. Hortat won't have put him in that stasis chamber for no reason. We'll just have to find out whether or not we like that reason. Filio?"

"Yes, sorry." She came out of her absent gaze with a shake of the head and gestured Cassidy to turn around so she could free the medical cuff from his neck. When she had removed the box with the extended flexible ring, and the perfuser field was sealed, she nodded to the physicist, who then turned Heinrich onto his side with his remaining hand.

Filio put the cuff on her comrade and activated it. His condition was also stable, although he had suffered a minor concussion.

"Awaken him," she ordered the medical AI. With Cassidy's help, she heaved Heinrich over to the chamber cover to their right and leaned him back to recline against it.

There he sat, half-upright, as his eyelids began to flutter, and he finally opened his eyes. "Filio?" he asked in a scratchy voice as if just pronouncing her name caused him pain.

"Yes, Heinrich," she answered, sniffing, "it's me."

"Who is that?"

"*That?*" She looked at Cassidy. "That's my partner. We've come here to... to make all those things right that I got wrong last time."

Heinrich smiled tiredly. "You mean, you should have beaten me unconscious last time?"

"That was probably my fault," Cassidy admitted, lifting his arm stump as if to deliver a message.

"Since I'm still alive, I guess you didn't want to kill me."

"No!" Filio immediately assured him. "I remember everything, Heinrich!"

"What do you mean, you *remember*? What kind of weird suit are you wearing?" The German looked at her with irritation, as if he were seeing her for the first time. "Is that the logo of the Human Foundation?"

"Yes. I... it's been three years since we left Mars."

"Three years?" Heinrich's eyes grew almost impossibly wide. "Really?"

"Yes."

"What happened? Why did it take you so long to send a new mission? The next window of opportunity would have occurred in two years. One moment. So, it's 2042? The constellations aren't right for a Mars mission in 2042. The sun should currently be between us and the Earth."

"Yes, that's right. It's really complicated, Heinrich." Filio thought feverishly about how she could explain everything to him without wasting valuable time. It had taken nearly 40 minutes of their precious breathing air to explain everything to Cassidy, and bringing Heinrich up to speed would be much more complicated. "I don't have much time because I'm running out of breathable air and there's hardly any atmosphere in this ship."

"But there is," Henry assured, smiling. "Only, the oxygen content is too high for us."

"No. Apparently, a lot has changed since we were here last time. The oxygen content has now fallen to less than five percent, and the nitrogen content has doubled. How much air do you have left?"

"My tanks are full. The Ship Being has taken care of that."

"The Ship Being? What's that?" Cassidy asked. His confusion was clearly evident.

"It's the closest approximation to how the ship refers to itself in its totality," Heinrich explained. "It encompasses more than just the ship's technical systems or data bank. It regards itself as an entity."

"And you can hear this, uh, Ship Being, too?" Cassidy asked.

"Of course," Heinrich said, nodding. "You don't?"

"No."

"Then that's because Hortat didn't grant you access. We must awaken him!"

"Hortat?"

"Yes, we must wake him up," Heinrich repeated, patting one hand on the cover of the stasis chamber behind him and indicating the injection hole Filio had sealed with the ceramic piece.

"Another clone?"

"The *last* clone," he corrected her with some regret in his voice.

"I don't know if that's such a good idea," Cassidy said. "After all, you killed him the last time."

"Killed?" Heinrich asked as he opened his eyes in horror. "What does he mean?"

"It's... complicated. Can he remember everything?"

"No, it's a fresh clone. He gets all the information directly from his DNA, which the ship extracts from his fossil. Since the Builders have succeeded in storing memories in their DNA, he will remember everything up to the moment that his real body died."

"Damn," Filio cursed. There simply was not enough time, and the less time she had to explain everything to Hortat, the more likely it was that he would either not take her seriously or kill her.

"But he can access memories," Heinrich said, tapping his visor with a finger, just above the augment he was wearing.

Filio stared at the shiny, metallic object as if it might jump out at her at any moment. "I don't know."

"I wish I could show you what it does," the geophysicist sighed sadly.

"Filio," Cassidy grabbed her by the shoulder until she looked into his gentle face, "if I can afford to give him the benefit of the doubt, you can too."

After a short hesitation, she nodded and took a deep breath. "Okay, we wake him up. I just need to remove the seal, first."

"Take my knife," Heinrich suggested, pointing to the short knife on his belt. It was tucked into a shimmering sheath that appeared to be seamlessly fastened to his suit. His gesture was sparing as if it cost him a lot of effort.

Filio pulled out the knife and got up on wobbly knees. She turned on her helmet lights to better make out the hardened programmable foam and began scraping off the flexible and extremely resistant material with the knife's tip.

After about five minutes, she had loosened the top half of the foam, which now looked like a flat piece of rubber, far enough away from the ceramic fragment to push the blade diagonally underneath and dig it out.

[Initializing injection process,] the Ship Being immediately reported, and again the robotic arm came out of the ceiling, inserted the long needle into the amber bubble and punctured the fossil's skull. Then the needle shot out again and dove so quickly into the hole between Filio's fingers that she stumbled back in fright.

Cassidy helped Heinrich to his feet, and with some effort Filio moved over to join them. The three of them now stood with their backs to the conservation bubble and stared at the rectangular cover of the stasis chamber. Filio heard a quiet hissing, and from somewhere came the roar of a servo motor. The cover then extended forward a centimeter, and dense steam shot out of the opening in all directions.

"Uh, ship? You can communicate with Hortat, can't you?" Filio asked, feeling how sweaty her hands had become. In view of her last encounter with the Builder, a queasy feeling came over her at the thought of facing him again. He wouldn't understand their language, and when she tried to think how she would feel if she woke up as a clone after more than 60,000,000 years only to be confronted by three little aliens, she could not imagine being particularly pleased—to say the least.

[That is correct.]

"Then you can also explain to him who we are, right?"

[I will, Filio Amorosa. The clone is now awake.]

The cover of the stasis chamber slid to one side so that it now half-covered Heinrich's open chamber. For a moment, they stared into the dense steam as if under a spell until a dark silhouette emerged and stepped onto the floor with a mighty stride.

In unison, Filio, Cassidy, and Heinrich titled their heads back to look up at the face of the naked bronze giant, who gazed at them with his black eyes. His lips seemed to be in constant motion or twitching so much that it looked as if he were muttering something to himself. He looked at them one by one, briefly pausing at Cassidy's arm stump and the augment above Heinrich's eyes.

After a few heartbeats he suddenly looked at Filio again, and his gaze struck her like an electric shock. She immediately felt like a toddler in front of a strict father, just before he punished her for some foolish deed.

[Hortat asks you to follow him,] the Ship Being spoke to their minds at the same moment.

"Where?"

[He asks you to follow him,] it repeated.

Filio swallowed heavily before she finally nodded and followed the mighty Builder, who seemed to fill the entire room as he entered the passage from which she had just come. His back was wide and dominated by knotty muscles that looked like the topographic relief of a hilly landscape. The skin that stretched over it like shimmering caramel was as smooth and fine as silk, as if it had no pores or impurities. Even his slightly swinging gait, which seemed as fluid as a cat's considering the sheer mass of his body, was delicate and opulent.

Although she could remember his appearance and his entire bearing, seeing Hortat here and now struck her as something completely new after everything she had experienced since. She did not know how to assess this ancient being. On one hand, there was the memory of her fear and her anger at him. On the other hand, there was that almost sympathetic and regretful look she had seen through the window of the evac capsule once he had realized that his death—by her hand—was imminent. There had been no hatred in his eyes, not even anger—at least as far as she was able to tell.

I killed this being, she thought bitterly, and at the same time felt doubts about whether she had just moved to the other extreme and was placing too much trust in Hortat.

After a few steps into the passage, she looked over her shoulder and her gaze fell on Heinrich and Cassidy, who were standing in front of the two open stasis capsules and looking after them before they disappeared from sight.

In front of a round opening in the right-hand wall, Hortat stopped and pointed into the dark room, illuminated only by a faint red light. Filio went in after a barely noticeable hesitation and waited in the middle until he joined her and directed his eyes, which were as big as mangoes, at her. Shortly after that, the anthracite-colored walls shifted and formed an elongated bubble in the shape of a football. Two pillars flowed up from the ground and formed gentle depressions and towering backrests at their tops—one large, the other much smaller.

Filio understood and sat on the smaller seat while Hortat lowered himself onto the other.

A new pillar arose and grew up to his outstretched hand, which he rested upon it as if on a walking stick. Then the pillar disappeared again, and Hortat turned his fist over, opened it, and revealed two boxes in it. One was as big as Filio's hand, the other much smaller. The Builder held the larger one in front of his chest, and it suddenly transformed into a dense liquid, which spread rapidly over his hairless body, until he was finally covered from his feet to his neck by a shimmering gray structure she had seen on him before.

He fixed his gaze on her again for a long time, until she felt uncomfortable and slid back and forth on her comfortable seat.

Hortat emitted a rolling sound that seemed to reverberate in her bones and opened the smaller box with astonishing dexterity. With his free hand, he produced from it the same augment that Heinrich and her former crewmates had worn.

Filio would have preferred to run away screaming when she remembered how much she had worried about this piece of metal and what it could mean. What would happen as soon as she accepted it? Would he be able to control her just like that insane killer on Earth who tried to kill Xinth? After all, it was Hortat who had instructed the killer and sent him forth.

No, not Hortat, she corrected herself, *his Microphage Twenty-One.*

The Builder hesitated briefly as he studied her face, which resembled a battleground for a host of contradictory feelings struggling for supremacy of each individual muscle until she finally nodded.

Breathing heavily with nostrils flared, she watched the fingers that held the shimmering augment come closer and closer.

"Open visor," she finally ordered her helmet system, and when it emitted a red warning symbol with an unpleasant beep, she impatiently added, "Override. Emergency release one-one-two-seven."

Her visor folded upward, and Hortat's hand rushed forward as if he were trying to snatch a fish out of water. There was a cold feeling on her forehead, and she felt as if she were inflating like a balloon while she held her breath.

Then Hortat's hand was gone and the visor swung close again. When the green symbol appeared on the atmosphere display, she breathed deeply. Her gaze slid over to Hortat and the augment came to life.

"Oh my God!"

19

AGATHA DEVENWORTH, 2042

Agatha sat in the narrow cabin of the Air Force supersonic jet and stared out the window. Beneath her, the endless bands of clouds over the southern Atlantic moved past—so fast that she felt as if she was riding on a bullet. In principle, that was even technically true, which did not exactly assuage the queasy feeling in her stomach.

She had felt cold and exhausted since taking off from Bolling Air Force Base near Washington, D.C. It was almost as if she were dissolving—a drop of water dispersing in the ocean. Hortat's compulsion seemed to have crept into every nerve cell, doing whatever it wanted in her body.

Now she sat with him and Pano—the latter staring forward into space, his face pale and eyes deeply ringed—in a small cabin on uncomfortable seats as they flew toward committing a betrayal that she would regret all her remaining days—if she survived. The part in her that was still free secretly hoped that they would die trying to enter the pyramid.

The survival instinct was a fixed factor in the evolutionary wiring of every living being, but what if you no longer knew what this will to survive was meant to preserve? If her mind no longer belonged to her and something else controlled her body, what would die? What was left of her, doomed to watch herself commit acts that her true self would never do?

Dalam turned to her and said, "I know what you're thinking." He was sitting in the seat in front of her. Its backrest was the same military gray as the walls, which were equipped with numerous hooks and compartments, all somewhat reminiscent of a Lego model.

"I don't think so, because then you would know that I don't care to talk with you." Agatha looked out of the window again to avoid his gaze, watching as the winglet at the very end of the wing swayed up and down in the jet stream.

"I could command you to talk to me."

"That would suit you," she agreed sarcastically.

"You think I'm a thoroughly evil creature, don't you?" asked Dalam. No... asked *Hortat*.

"Yes, that's what I think."

"The father of your country, George Washington, you revere him as a hero, an icon of freedom, yes?"

"Where are you going with this?" Agatha asked, looking dismissively at the man in front of her.

"During his lifetime, George Washington held up to three hundred and ninety African slaves who had to work for him and his plantation. Would you regard that as typical of a good person today?" Dalam's eyes rested searchingly on her face, seemingly trying to capture each of her emotions as with a large net.

"He made it clear in his will that all should be freed after his death. He even set up a fund to ensure that they were economically secure," she said, averting her face. "I don't need history lessons from an alien."

"That may be, but George Washington was all too happy to use his slaves while he was alive. Only after his death, when he no longer needed them, were they allowed to leave."

"Let me guess—you're now justifying keeping us and many other people as *your* slaves, right?" Agatha glanced back, shook her head in disgust, and pointedly turned to look out the window again.

"I'll release you, too, when it's over. I promise you that."

"Do you even know what you are doing to us?" Her head jerked in Dalam's direction, and she could feel the anger in her own gaze flame in the back of her head like a hot needle.

"Yes," he replied with an absent gaze. "And I'm not proud of it. But I will use any necessary tool to stop Xinth. Any. You and your partner are among the best I have found."

"How flattering." She fixed him with a look of pure poison.

"Thirty minutes to refuel," the pilot said through the loudspeakers. Despite his clear enunciation, she could hardly understand him over the noise of the turbines.

"We should prepare," Dalam announced.

"For what?"

"After we're refueled by the tanker, we'll still have four or five hours to fly until we reach the *Barack Obama*. We should come up with a plan for how we can enter Geth without being killed. The ark is not just some old boulder. It is replete with technologies that protect the facility in situations like this. You will help me to figure out the best way."

"Yes, I will," she assured him. It was not she herself who answered—yet at the same time, it was—a feeling that both confused and horrified her deeply, down to the tips of her toes.

After refueling, of which they were hardly aware except for a shadow thrown on their wings by the huge tanker in front of them, they turned their seats to each other and began planning. They put on AR glasses and stared at the virtual projection of the pyramid between them, which slowly rotated around its own axis. A computer program had created the simulation based on their three memories combined and the approximate known dimensions.

"There is only one entrance that we know about," Pano explained, pointing his finger at a spot at the base of the gigantic structure, which then began to flash red. "It's no bigger than a double door, maybe two by three meters. From there, a kind of elevator leads diagonally downward. Most of the facility we saw is quite deep under the ice."

"That's the living and working area," Dalam agreed, nodding. "Underneath are morphic areas that serve as storage spaces in stasis times, as far as I know."

"As far as you know?" Agatha asked.

"Yes. I was a geneticist in my time and not a member of the priesthood."

"Priesthood?"

"That's what we call our cultural workers. Priesthood is the term that comes closest to it. Xinth is a member of it and is responsible for the preservation and further development of our culture. That is why he was entrusted with the administration of our descendants."

"These descendants," Pano said, pointing vaguely

toward the pyramid projection between them. "Where are they housed?"

"On the higher floors, I think." Dalam shook his head dismissively. "But that is irrelevant to our task."

"I understand. You've been there before, haven't you?"

"No. Upon my return from Twelve-Fold Space, Xinth deliberately, as it seems, met me not in Geth, but on another continent that you no longer know today. There were eleven of them at the time. So, I know very little about this place, and what little I do know comes from the publicly available data at the time of the construction of the ark," Dalam explained. "But I am sure that the entrance you've seen cannot be the only one."

"If there is another one, we don't know anything about it." Pano looked at Agatha, who nodded slowly.

"But," she said, "we could ask Karlhammer."

"Karlhammer?" Pano asked, confused.

"Yes. He has no inkling that we are now working with Hortat. First, we think of a good cover story and wait for the carrier strike group around the *Barack Obama* to start its assault. Then we tell him that we have important information, and that he should tell us where we can slip through another entrance," she explained into the darkness that surrounded the virtual projection in its midst, as if the aircraft cabin around it did not exist at all.

"And we assign the soldiers to the normal entrance as the main point of attack," Pano added. "It's worth a try. All we lack is a compelling story explaining why we've returned and are in such a hurry. That will raise questions."

Agatha pondered and played through various scenarios that ran past her inner eye like a slideshow. She was once again deeply immersed in her investigative mode that could block out the world around her and confine itself to the main facts arising from her previous findings. Everything arranged itself, one fact after the other, formed into a possible causal chain, and fell apart again if she didn't think it was any good. So it went for quite some time, while Pano and Dalam spoke together quietly without her taking in the slightest detail of their conversation.

"I know," she finally said, leaning forward.

Pano, and Hortat in his host body, turned to her in surprise and both looked at her inquiringly.

"We tell the truth."

"Pardon? What's that?" Pano asked, bewildered, while Dalam regarded her rather disdainfully, as if he feared that his coercion might have lost its power over her.

"Quite simply, if every other explanation sounds too implausible, stick to the truth. The truth is usually too crazy for anyone to deny anyway, and everyone basically knows the truth as soon as they hear it. We tell him that Workai Dalam is, in fact, Hortat, and then we turn the facts around. We tell Karlhammer that we set a trap for Dalam—Hortat—with Miller's and Secretary Cortez's help, and now we want to hand him over to him and Xinth.

"We equip ourselves and the Seal team that goes with us with soundproof headphones and bring our prisoner to him. Xinth and Karlhammer will assume that Hortat can stop the attacking U.S. soldiers with his Microphage Twenty-One or something else. So they will hardly be able to refuse us when we tell them that we have him in our power."

"A risky play," Dalam said, rubbing his lips with one hand. "A very risky play. I will not be able to continue to give orders to you or to the soldiers going with us."

"Anything else would be too conspicuous," Agatha said.

"In any case, we have to assume that everyone in the pyramid now has such headphones."

"How do these commands work, anyway?" Pano asked abruptly.

"It's something I learned during my time in the Twelve-Fold Space," Dalam explained, his face changing to a mask of tension.

"Twelve-Fold Space?"

"Higher-dimensional structures of reality. You may know this concept as hyperspace." Dalam took a deep breath and made an impatient gesture, as if the subject were unpleasant to him, which would explain the tense lines around his mouth. "In any case, temporary changes in the neural structures of the..."

"Victim?" Agatha tried to help him out, and Dalam made a sour face in reaction.

"... the *affected person* are achieved by directed quantum effects in such a way that they react to the auditory stimuli of a particular language pattern."

"Your voice," Pano concluded, nodding in understanding.

"Yes."

"Why didn't you just create hundreds of agents like that man in the black suit?"

"It's not that easy and it wasn't my wish. If you were the only person with an atomic bomb, how many other people would you entrust with another one?" Dalam straightened his posture. "It doesn't matter now. Continue, Agent Devenworth. You have a plan?"

"The closer we stay to the truth, the less we can become entangled in contradictions," she continued. "That's a basic rule that one learns in college. With the clues we have obtained from the senators' medical data, we can now also prove that, according to our theory of infection, there is no evidence that President Harris is infected with the microphage. The theory with the short incubation period as a feature of microphage infection is correct, isn't it?"

That admission seemed to cause him some discomfort. "Yes," Dalam said simply.

"Well, then Xinth will have another reason to believe us."

"And when we're in?" Pano asked, looking at Dalam. "What then?"

"Then we will either convince Xinth to cooperate or we will kill him."

"And the embryos?"

"Nothing must happen to them!"

"But what about your large-scale fleet attack?"

"The microphage is programmed so that those affected have to find Geth at any price, neutralize Xinth no matter the circumstances, and protect the pyramid itself without regard for their own losses," Dalam explained.

"Programmed?" Agatha frowned in surprise. "So you don't have permanent control over the infected?"

"No."

"That means you can no longer exert any influence on the officers in the fleet."

"But I can—through President Harris," Dalam said. "That's why I needed you both—to get me access to her, which I almost failed to do." He pointed with an outstretched index finger, indicating the pyramid rotating between them. "The attack will be limited to protecting the advancing ground forces from aerial bombardment. With all the weapons fire, it will be difficult to get inside unscathed."

"Do you have a better idea?" Agatha asked.

"No."

"Very well. Then we should call Karlhammer now. If we wait too long, he will wonder about the speed with which we're able to reach the pyramid."

Dalam regarded her closely for a moment, then disappeared behind his seatback. When he reappeared, he held out a satellite phone to her.

"You don't want to deceive me," he instilled into her once more, almost hypnotically. "Everything you do and want is for the success of our mission—to eliminate Xinth. You will do nothing to jeopardize this mission."

"Of course not," she said with a conviction she realized she felt as soon as his words had reached her ears.

"Good." He gestured for her to continue with a terse backhand flick.

Agatha dialed the secret number that Karlhammer had entrusted to her, while hating every single button-push. At the same time, she felt a deep desire to make the phone call in order to finally achieve a goal that was not hers at all.

"Agent Devenworth," the South African responded after a short time. In the background, she heard screaming noises like an electric saw.

"Yes, I have good news."

"Has your mission been successful?" Karlhammer asked hopefully.

"Yes. We have The Enemy in our custody."

"What? I hope you aren't kidding me!"

"I never kid," she said.

"How did you do that?" His voice now betrayed a trace of disbelief as the initial euphoria slowly retreated from his vocal cords like morning fog in direct sun.

"At some cost. We lost Director Miller, as well as the Secretary of Homeland Security and her entire security team."

"Damn! You and Hofer are okay?"

"Yes. We set a trap for him. The Enemy is, in fact, Workai Dalam," she said, pausing to allow her sentence to have its full effect on Karlhammer.

"What?"

"The Enemy is Workai Dalam. It was he the whole time. It makes sense that no one would suspect the one person who was warning the world about The Enemy to be, in fact, that very enemy."

"But that's impossible!"

"Because he worked with you? That is rather one more reason why his camouflage identity was perfectly chosen," Agatha replied.

"And how did you catch him?"

"He caught us. We were on our way with Director Miller to a secret meeting with President Harris when the Secretary of Homeland Security intercepted and kidnapped us. She was an agent of The Enemy and apparently wanted to find out what we were going to do. The Enemy then freed us and promised that he would freely allow himself to be arrested if he were given five minutes with the President and could tell her about the threat posed by The Enemy."

Agatha took a short break and paused because she longed to have done exactly what came out through her lips as lies.

"At that point we decided to agree to that, and so did the President. But I became suspicious because I realized that his proposal was too perfect. His camouflage was excellent, the transmitter he had slipped us had remained with us under circumstances too lucky to believe, and his desire to speak directly to the President sounded dangerous. We found in our investigation that he can take control over people with a type of virus that has an extremely short incubation period and implants certain commands or desires.

"We couldn't risk him having set us a perfect trap, and on the way to the White House, I secretly sent a message to the President that she and her security guards should wear soundproof headphones. So, we were finally able to get hold of him and arrest him."

"That's quite a lot to digest," Karlhammer replied, and Agatha could hear him breathing despite the crackling on the line. "Wait a moment."

There followed a rustling noise, as if someone was rubbing a piece of cloth over the microphone at the other end, and then she heard a muted voice she could not understand. He was apparently covering his microphone with one hand.

"I think he's talking to Xinth," she whispered to Dalam, who only nodded silently and did not let her out of his direct line of sight. A few minutes passed, and Agatha looked at the small display under the handset several times to make sure they were still connected. Eventually, the line finally rustled again, and Karlhammer came back.

"Bring him in, Agent Devenworth. We will be prepared."

Relieved, she exhaled through her nose and nodded to Dalam and Pano.

"Very good," Agatha replied. "The President has put a team of Navy SEALs at our disposal that has also been informed of everything. She has also authorized me to give you her direct extension. I think it's in connection with the fleet under the command of Admiral Taggert, which is on its way to you."

"She has no control over the officers because they're corrupted by The Enemy, right?" Karlhammer asked with some bitterness in his voice. 'Then it's going to get very ugly here soon. When can you be here?"

"In about ten hours," she said without hesitation.

"That's fast. Very good. If we're lucky, you'll get here before the Navy, but it's going to be tight. If you don't make it before all hell breaks loose here, contact me and I'll make sure you can come in through a secret entrance."

Agatha heard a click on the line and pressed the red button before nodding to Pano and Dalam. "He swallowed the bait."

"Good job, Agent Devenworth," said the Pakistani, smiling contentedly. "Very good work."

"Yes," she agreed with a bitter undertone in her voice. It was a kind of brief triumph on the part of a remnant of her imprisoned self that had not been fully suppressed. At the same time, nevertheless, she remained desperate to fulfill his orders to the best of her knowledge and conscience.

Dalam's face became serious. "Well. We will land on the *Barack Obama* in a few hours, and then board a transport helicopter where our Navy SEALs escort team is already waiting."

"But we have to insist that the sailors on the ground come on board after we land, bring us soundproofing head-sets and shackles, headphones, and a prisoner mask for you," Pano demanded, pointing one hand vaguely upward. "Karlhammer has his eyes and ears everywhere. He will already have the area monitored, if not from orbit, which I assume, then at least by spy drones near the fleet. So, we have to play our game perfectly from the moment we disembark. Otherwise, we'll risk discovery right away. We've been given the appropriate authority and should make use of it."

"You're right." Agatha nodded. "I'll take care of it."

She pressed a button in her armrest and after a short

waiting tone, the co-pilot's voice sounded from the speakers next to her. "Yes, Ma'am?"

"Connect me to the *Barack Obama*," she said, closing her eyes for a moment. She was going to do it, she was really going to do it, and there was nothing she could do to prevent it—because Hortat compelled her to want to do it that way.

20

FILIO AMOROSA, 2042

Contact was established gently, as if someone were pulling a wafer-thin silk scarf over her skin, with the difference being that it was touching her mind. Then that feeling disappeared so quickly that Filio wasn't sure whether she had only imagined it.

"These memories," said Hortat in rolling English, and his deep, full-tone words washed around her like a flood wave, "they are—"

"Disturbing?" she tried to help him out and nodded. "I'm sorry that I—"

"You did what you had to do in the belief that you were saving your species," the Builder interrupted her, making a flowing gesture with his right hand that looked like he was weaving with invisible fibers. "I probably understand that better than anyone else."

"Because you did what you had to do for the same reason?"

"Yes."

"This microphage of yours... has it created a kind of clone?"

"Something of the sort. It created my memories and thus my personality, including a neural image," Hortat explained, and his mouth opened and closed like a fish that had been pulled from the water. Filio still felt small in the face of the bronze giant.

"How?"

"It is complicated. Whoever rescued you will have been infected with the microphage. It will have taken several months to create the programmed image."

"I don't know who rescued me. Someone made sure that I was lying on a piece of driftwood and was found by a search team," Filio explained, and the apparent casualness of their conversation was so surreal that she felt like she was in a dream. In her memory, her evac capsule had just ejected from *Mars One*, and she still saw Hortat's face in her mind while the realization of her murders grew in her. Now she was sitting opposite him—no, his clone—and was talking to him as if nothing had happened.

"That was the one who now carries my neural image in him."

"And is this someone now you?"

"Yes and no. That image of mine is the product of my personality and my memories, with the difference that this person has been infected with the microphage, which I so programmed that it cannot allow anything to come between itself and the goal," said Hortat.

"I understand." Filio swallowed. "On Earth, a war is about to take place around the pyramid. You have to prevent it."

"I cannot do that."

"Why not?"

"I will show you," he said, holding out one of his huge, plate-like hands. Each finger was almost as thick as her wrist. As she stared at his palm, the fabric of his suit flowed up his neck and over his mouth, forming a kind of mask over his nose. "You must open your suit. Otherwise it will not work. The ship has made the air in this room breathable for you. Have no fear."

"What are you going to do?" she asked in a final uprising of her old mistrust, which she simply could not entirely shake off.

"I'll show you why we cannot stop my image."

"A vision?"

"A memory," he calmly corrected her.

"Xinth also showed me one of these memories. How do I know that you won't show me something wrong?"

"That is not how it works. Xinth has shown you the truth, but perhaps only in the sections that seem proper to him. The exchange takes place between the subtle images of our memories. I can show it to you or not. It is your decision." Hortat's hand retreated a few inches as he carefully looked at her with his black eyes.

"Why do you want to show it to me?"

"To work together to ensure that no catastrophe occurs."

Filio wrinkled her forehead in confusion. She tried to understand what he might mean by that, and couldn't help but fear that all her questions would only end up raising new questions. This being she was now facing was so much older and wiser, and endowed with the knowledge of a culture so far superior to humankind that he had to feel as if he were trying to explain the world to an ant.

She looked one last time at her air indicator, which now displayed at 60 minutes, and opened her helmet. The seal released with a hiss. She placed the helmet on her lap and then stripped off her gloves. There was a slight scent of ozone, but the air was otherwise clear and breathable.

Hortat watched her with a relentless expression, and it was only when she stretched out her hand to seize his that his mighty forehead tilted forward a little.

The touch was warm and rough at the same time. The memory began immediately. There was no transition, no journey, no light at the end of a tunnel. She was suddenly looking through Hortat's eyes.

Hortat, 66,120,377 BC.

"What does it look like?" Hortat asked the navigator as he looked into the infinity of the stars through the transparent shell in front of the bridge. The sight frightened him just as it had on his last flights to the outer planets of the solar system. He hated the universe and its hostility to life. It had nothing to offer a biotechnologist like him except decay and death.

Even as a child, he had been afraid to look at the stars through his father's telescope. While others descended into philosophical contemplation at their sight, the fear gnawed at him that the huge nothingness out there would swallow him up like the ocean did a grain of sand. He shook his head and focused on his surroundings to rid himself of such unpleasant thoughts.

The navigator was in the middle one of three sealed tanks that were fanned out in the small armored room. The synaptic conductive fluid in which his body lay provided direct control of the quantum mirror, which would help them navigate the Twelve-Fold-Space. In the same, thick liquid lay the controller, who monitored the internal ship systems by inserting his mind into their circuits and inter-connections. There was also the astrogator, who looked after the vessel's energy nodes and superconductor networks.

Hortat felt strangely alone up here in the organizational center of his colony ship, as there was no sign of activity or life except for the three casket-tanks. The walls were smooth and hid all the devices and pipes behind their anthracite-colored shimmer. The tanks did not even have windows through which he could have seen the faces of his three technology operators.

"I see the mesh in front of me," the navigator's voice finally sounded via audio implants in Hortat's head. "It's... beautiful."

"What does it look like?"

"It has no appearance, only an echo of existence, similar to a wave that has its own form but is only an expression of the whole. I can hear the Twelve-Fold Space singing, Hortat."

"Singing?"

"It is alive. Not as we would define it. It has no form, no will, and yet is alive in its own way," the navigator said almost ecstatically, and the mental image of a sigh pene-trated through Hortat's mind. "You should go to your quar-ters now. We have received clearance from fleet command and will make the transition soon. With your permission."

"Permission granted," Hortat said with melancholy, thinking of the Earth that had passed by to starboard only a few moments ago. Eventually, he turned around and walked through an accessway that had morphed open and into the central connecting corridor, where he met Mirnu, his Mammarian. She had the narrow chin of a southern born and the matte, caramel-colored skin of the continent Tangir.

Every time he saw his best friend, he wondered why he had not asked her for a union.

Mirnu was just ending a conversation with Xornir, one of his senior machine weavers, and turned to Hortat as he drew near. "Hortat," she said while revealing her pleasure with a broad smile on her dark lips. Her eyes were a little smaller and more oblique than his—not as coarse and unformed. "I heard that we are ready?"

"Yes, we are. The navigator is ready for the transition." Hortat grabbed her by the arms with both hands and looked into her eyes. "When we are in the Twelve-Fold Space, visit me in the laboratory, alright?"

Mirnu knitted her brow and wrinkled her forehead briefly, but then nodded without asking the reason.

"Thank you. May the wisdom of the ancestors be with us," he said gratefully, letting his hands slide down to hers and squeezing them briefly before taking a step back and proceeding to his quarters. The door was less than 20 steps away on the right.

For a colony ship, his seemed very small at first sight, although it carried more than 10,000 colonists in stasis chambers, and over 50,000 embryos in cryogenic tubes. But the huge decks that housed them were all in the belly of the ship, not in the upper apex, where he and the hull crew, consisting of 50 men and women, acted to ensure that their charges arrived safely at their destination. Their living and working area encompassed a few hundred square meters and looked like a bump on the back of a gigantic Monnbat in the ship's cross-section.

Arriving in his chamber, he went straight to his sleep coffin, lay down in it, and waited until the lid had slipped over him and the seal's light flashed green. Then he activated the serum injection.

The serum was a central component of the quantum flight. It ensured that the entire crew—apart from the navigator, astrogator, and controller who remained on the bridge during the transition—traveled in a dreamless coma. The principle had been explained to him in such a way as to compare higher-dimensional space to the surface of a still lake, and that every thought and emotion made waves on this surface that made it difficult for the navigator to safely take them across to the other shore.

So, the technologs had arranged for the entire crew to be placed in a brief coma.

Hortat felt the tiny puncture on the side of his neck, more like a tickling feeling than an unpleasant pain. He counted from ten backward but did not get to the number six.

When he awoke, the lid of his sleep coffin was already open, and the first thing he saw was the anthracite-colored ceiling of his quarters. It was colored in the same black-and-gray transition tones as were most facilities of its kind. The hues calmed his eyes, reflecting the spherical light of the photon manipulators in a way that was barely noticeable.

"Connect me to the navigator," Hortat ordered the Ship Being as he rose from his sleep coffin. Even before his feet touched the floor, his security suit had come to rest around each toe and sealed everything. He felt a slight tremor and breathed in and out a few times.

[You are connected,] the ship told him.

"What is the status?" he asked immediately.

"It's beautiful," answered the navigator in his mind, and the resonant feelings in the connection seemed boisterous and ecstatic. "We didn't understand anything at all."

"What are you talking about? I don't understand you! Was the transition successful?"

"Yes, Leader, it was."

"How much time has passed?" Hortat inquired further just as the navigator was about to withdraw from the connection.

"Time?"

"Yes, time!" Hortat felt how he was slowly losing patience. He had never been able to deal with the esoteric chatter of ethereal people particularly well. As a member of the research caste, he had no interest in the mystical concepts of the mentally gifted—but that behavior now seemed even more out of place than usual.

"Months, years, millennia—what role does that play? There is no time here."

"I'm coming to the bridge," Hortat grumbled, ending the connection. As soon as he had swung from the edge of his sleep coffin, it receded back into the wall as if it had never been there. A knock on the door immediately followed.

"Come," he said with his broad local accent, and the opening to the passage opened.

"Handhold!" Hortat cried in panic as he looked into an open vacuum instead of the connecting corridor. The ship obeyed in a flash and a stanchion rod formed out of the floor. He grabbed it with both hands to protect himself against the pull of escaping atmosphere, only to realize that nothing of the sort was happening.

"What, by the Eldest...?" He swallowed heavily, and tentatively let go of the handle without turning his gaze away from the open door.

[I do not understand your conduct,] the ship said.

"Did you seal the breach with a force field?"

[I still do not understand. *The breach?*]

"That one right in front of my eyes!" he shouted impatiently, pointing with an outstretched hand at the stars, which were not four steps distant.

[I regret, Hortat, I cannot detect a breach. According to my data, the ship is completely intact.]

"But that can't be! I see it!"

[A hull breach is very unlikely, but even if that were the case, there would have been a loss of atmosphere.]

"I know, but..." Hortat stopped and tried to swallow his fear. Carefully he put one foot in front of the other and closed his eyes several times between each stride. When he stood only a step away from the vacuum, he neither felt cold, nor was his breathing affected. Eventually, he pinched his eyes together and held his breath before taking a step forward and into the connecting corridor.

Irritated, he whirled around and looked into his quarters, as if the doorway had never looked any different.

"An illusion?" he asked, blinking a few times before allowing the Ship Being to close the door.

The voice behind him intruded so abruptly that he flinched. "What kind of illusion?"

He saw Mirnu standing there and looking at him attentively. "I... I have just seen a kind of illusion—as if we had had a hull breach."

"A hull breach here in the passage? But it does not run along the hull—that's more than ten dekas from here," she said, her ears shrugging in a gesture of wonder. Is everything okay?"

"I don't know. I will undergo a medical analysis," he said absently.

"Now?" Mirnu's eyes grew wide.

"No. Now I have to go to the bridge. Our navigator, he is—"

"—strange?" She gestured matter-of-factly. "We knew that before."

"Yes, but something is wrong with him, and more than usual."

"Do you think the transition has done something to him?"

"I don't know," he admitted, pointing toward the bridge, which was about 20 steps away at the end of the corridor. "Let's find out."

"Can we speak briefly before we go?" Mirnu asked, twisting her right hand with its long, slender fingers twice around her own wrist—a gesture of urgent request.

Hortat furrowed his brow but then nodded. He looked briefly at the door of his quarters and then, after a cold shiver ran down his back like ice water, pointed to the entrance to his laboratory directly opposite.

When they stood in the long, oval room, he ordered the Ship Being to morph the work areas. Tables, machines, and germination cells appeared a few moments later, and they suddenly seemed to have shrunken in size. Part of him relaxed when he saw that everything was still exactly as he had left it behind.

"What's on your mind, Mirnu?" he asked, standing in such a way so as to block the view of his analysis module.

"We didn't have time to talk to each other in private before departure, but I need to know," she said, seeming visibly uncomfortable with the words that followed. "Your research, did you bring it here with you?"

Hortat felt his nostrils widen. He had wanted to keep her out of that, even though he had known that Mirnu was too clever not to question why he had asked for a command. His rank as a member of the research caste would have allowed him a much more comfortable transition in a stasis chamber. Hardly anyone felt the desire to travel between dimensions in a completely unknown state of existence. For him, however, things were very different.

"Yes," he finally sighed, raising his hands defensively as her mouth turned into an angry growl and she took a step toward him. "My research may be illegitimate on Earth, but not in twelve-dimensional space!"

"The Council has forbidden you!"

"Yes, everywhere we have settled," he quoted the Council's wording. "But we are not in space that we've settled!"

"You want to engage in a battle of word meanings with the Council?" Mirnu asked, stunned and shaking her head. "That would not interest its members in the least! They would tell you that this ship is very much part of the space we have settled because we are on board everywhere! And besides, it's also wrong!"

"What's wrong?"

"You know it very well—your Microphage Twenty-One."

Hortat wrinkled his nose with hurt and staggered back a step as if she had dealt him a blow. He had hoped that at least Mirnu would be on his side as soon as the shackles of their homeland no longer prevented them from speaking their minds openly. But apparently, even she didn't understand.

"Mirnu," he said forcefully, almost pleading. "Microphage Twenty-One is the key to the next step in our evolution. Just imagine what we could achieve if our descendants inherited all the knowledge possessed by their preceding generation. Via their DNA, without any limitations. No more dekas spent in academies to laboriously acquire knowledge. Everything I knew at the time of my child's procreation, it will also know as soon as it is born."

"It is wrong," she insisted, arms folded over her chest.

"You take away their development, their curiosity, their freedom."

"What freedom?" he muttered, waving dismissively. "The freedom to make mistakes by simply repeating those of one's parents? The freedom not to decide? The freedom to waste the limited time life offers?"

"Yes! And what about the secondary consequences? What if your DNA doesn't accept the changes and damage occurs? Any intervention in evolution is dangerous, and as a biotechnologist, you should know that better than anyone."

"I know that too! But I've tested and refined the method several times in simulations until the risks of spontaneous mutations sank below zero-point-zero-zero-zero-three."

"And what about the dangers?" Mirnu asked. A cracking sound went through the ship, and Hortat was startled, but she grabbed him by the face and forced him to turn his eyes back on her. "What about the dangers?"

"I just said that the risks for..." he began absently, as he tried to listen for the crack to return when she demanded his attention again.

"I don't mean that. You or whoever uses the microphage can program it as desired to change everything. For example, brain chemistry to make others docile."

"Do you really think me capable of something like that?" he asked with honest horror, and the strange sound was suddenly forgotten.

"I just mean that..." Mirnu sighed and turned away from him with a depressed expression. "I'm sorry if I..."

There was the crackle again. It sounded like a dull metallic sound that seemed to move from west to east.

"What is that?" he asked, looking tensely at the ceiling.

[One of the helium-3 pipes has burst,] the ship said calmly.

"What? How?"

[Prospector Targun has destroyed one of the magnetic clips around the supply pipe network.]

"Targun has what?" asked Hortat, horrified, staring at Mirnu, who had turned back to him and was shaking her head in confusion.

[This is not the only case of destructive behavior, Hortat,] said the ship, and provided his mind an overview of recordings that were complete with image and sound. His knees suddenly turned to butter.

A crewmember stood in his quarters and held his hands to his ears, screaming as if he were tormented by some sound that no one else could hear. Another lay in his sleep coffin, the arteries of his wrist slashed. Yet another ran through the connecting corridor with a plasma rod with which he seemed to be stabbing at something invisible.

"By the Elders," Mirnu whispered, holding a hand to her mouth. Her eyelids trembled like the wings of an Aartan butterfly.

"Astrogator!" Hortat shouted, and the Ship Being established the connection. "Are we being attacked?"

"No, Leader," the floating voice reported from the bridge. Since the astrogator's mind had been completely absorbed into the ship's systems, it was a spiritual projection that had no direct relationship to the present time, something that always unsettled Hortat. "But our escort ships are under attack."

"By whom?" Hortat asked in horror. He immediately set off toward the opening to the connecting corridor. Shortly before he reached it, he skidded to a halt when the astrogator's next words fell on him like a hail of bombs.

"By each other, Leader. They are firing at each other."

The astrogator sounded quite calm, almost lost in thought, which made what he had just said seem even stranger.

"Send the images to me in the laboratory!"

"But no, Leader, we are on the other side," the astrogator said, completely enraptured. "There is nothing to see here, nothing to register. At least not with our senses."

"How do you know that they are attacking each other?"

"I feel it. They feel it."

"They? Who are they?"

"They are everything. All that we have created. Our ethereal waste in quantum space, Leader." A mental giggling invaded Hortat, and he cast a look of shock at Mirnu, who seemed completely perplexed.

"Do we have sensor data?" he asked the Ship Being.

[No, Hortat,] it replied apologetically. [But until recently I had contact with all four hundred and forty sister ships through the quantum tunnels. Now I have contact only with three.]

"What's going on here?"

[I do not know. I am sorry.]

"No, don't do that," Mirnu said suddenly. Hortat turned and gave her a querying look. She had withdrawn a few steps and grabbed a follicle pipette from one of the experiment tables and was holding it in his direction like a dagger.

"Mirnu? What are you doing?"

"I can't allow you to activate the microphage!" she cried back threateningly, her hand trembling in agitation.

"What are you talking about? I'm not doing anything."

"Then take your hand off the table!"

Hortat looked to the right and left. The next table was at least two arm lengths away. *She's also going mad,* he thought, terrified, and since he did not know what else to do, he folded his hands demonstratively in front of his stomach.

"That's fire salt, isn't it?" she asked, nodding toward the vials with the red liquid that he had prepared for the incubators, but without letting him out of her sight.

"I'm not doing anything, Mirnu, get a hold of yourself!"

"Not a step further. You want to make us all docile with your forbidden virus. No..." She paused and her eyes widened as if she had seen a ghost. The next words she whispered were almost inaudible, and they struck Hortat to his core. "You've already done it. That's why everyone is going insane. It's a reaction to your microphage... That was your plan from the very beginning."

"No," he assured her, pleading, and took a step toward her. He wanted to appease her somehow, but his reaction was exactly the wrong one, and he noticed it almost too late.

"Emergency quarantine!" Hortat shouted, and the Ship Being reacted at the same moment as Mirnu struck the follicle pipette against the vials containing the fire salt. A silvery glow encased his girlfriend as the evaporation began, and she burst with a sickening sound.

Hortat fell powerlessly onto his hands and knees, vomiting.

[There is no longer any danger,] the Ship Being said. [I no longer have contact with the other colony ships, and the controller is in the process of initiating the self-destruction sequence.]

"Self-destruction sequence?" Hortat croaked, wiping his mouth and struggling to his feet. His vision was blurry. Thick tears still wet his eyes, but he didn't have to see anything to know what needed to be done. "On my orders, remove all authorizations from the crew. Place priority on the energy supply of the stasis chambers and cryotubes. I'm bringing us back!"

[I regret, Hortat. The entire colony section has been cut off from the superconductor network.]

"What?"

[The astrogator overloaded all the energy nodes to the colony sections.]

"They're all dead?"

[Yes.]

Hortat staggered back and collided with a table before his limbs lost their strength and he sank to the floor and buried his face in his hands. He sat there, breathing heavily in and out until he felt his strength return. He balled his hands into fists and rallied. He could not allow himself to give up, not now.

"I must go back to Earth," he said firmly, wiping the tears from his eyes and pressing his lips together. "Xinth needs to know about this."

[I do not know if that is possible. Something seems to be affecting us here and we do not understand it.]

"Oh, I understand it," Hortat replied grimly. "There are no living beings here, but there is something else. The quantum singers always referred to it as the spiritual dimensions. The astrogator spoke of our ethereal waste. Mirnu feared that the microphage could destroy free will, I fear the vacuum of space. Whatever happens here materializes our fears."

He paused and then shook his head. "No. I don't think it does. It may just materialize our thoughts, and if it affected the others only to the degree that it affected me, their thoughts became full of fear of the unknown and of the nature of a mission that left us no alternatives."

Hortat went to the morphological display and made some entries. He gave the microphage a single command, then opened the canister with the inscription '21' with a simple impulse of thought and took a step to the left so he could hold his face directly above it. He did not feel how it happened, but he felt as if he might lose consciousness.

"Lock down... the laboratory... don't let anyone in... Evacuate atmosphere in all areas...," he breathed with a weakening voice. His field of vision became smaller and smaller. "Disconnect bridge from the network... Disengage the command module from the colony section... Power down energy nodes..."

Hortat heard a perplexing background rumbling when he awoke. With a sound that was half sigh and half groan, he struggled up from the uncomfortable posture in which he had apparently collapsed. If the Ship Being had morphed the interior back, he would probably have fallen so badly that he would have been seriously injured.

"How long was I..."

[One pendum,] the Ship Being answered, and its calm, balanced voice sent a wave of relief through Hortat's body. [You reprogrammed the microphage.]

"Yes."

[In what way?]

"I told it to switch off the areas of my brain that produces fear," Hortat replied. "So, if I mean to do something life-threatening, I hope you will point it out to me."

[Of course.]

"Did everything work?"

[Yes. I ordered the command module to be detached from the main ship and shut down the quantum mirror's energy nodes. As a result, we seem to have automatically fallen back into normal space.]

So that's it. The rumbling I heard came from the sublight drive. "Does that mean we're back?"

[Yes.]

"Have you been able to make contact with other returnees?" Hortat asked hopefully, but the Ship Being answered in the negative. "But how is this possible? If switching off the quantum mirror is enough to bring us back to normal space, then at least some other ships must have made it."

[I think we owe this circumstance to the navigator who realigned us before the sublight engines were engaged,] the Ship Being said.

"I thought you had cut off his access?"

[I did. The realignment was done shortly before.]

"So, the navigator pushed us toward the exit, and we just had to open the door." Hortat clung to the control panel in front of him and lowered his head when a bout of weakness overcame him. The microphage was still in the process of nesting within him.

[It seems like that.]

"Is there any sign of life on board other than me?"

[Sorry... No.]

Hortat clenched his hands to fists and resisted the urge to pound the table to pieces. "Is there anything else I need to know?"

[We are at Goldan's orbital plane and will reach Earth in one day. In addition, the navigator left a message that is, unfortunately, not complete.]

"You're telling me this *now*?"

[It is not complete,] the Ship Being repeated, sounding almost piqued.

"Why not?"

[Because, in obeyance to your command, I cut off the

power supply to his synaptic tank, along with the entire bridge.]

Hortat suppressed a curse and ordered the ship's being to play the message.

"Leader," the rapturous voice of the navigator sounded in the laboratory. Nothing in it seemed to indicate that something terrible was happening. "We are incapable of crossing this sea. We must turn back and never return. We are an anomaly in this place—a place that does not tolerate anomalies. We have to shut down all the energy nodes and..." The ghostly voice ended abruptly.

"Establish a connection to Geth, I have to talk to Xinth immediately."

[Of course.]

21

FILIO AMOROSA, 2042

"I don't understand that at all," Filio said, as Hortat's memories faded. It was strange, after having just perceived everything from inside his body, to see him now standing in front of her. Everything had been so real, as if she had been a Builder herself—as if she had become Hortat.

"Even I don't understand what happened," Hortat's voice rumbled through the room, and his eyes seemed sad.

"I don't mean that." Filio shook her head vigorously. "In the vision Xinth showed me, he told me that not only he and all the embryos were left behind in Geth, but many of you Builders as well—those who did not want to seek salvation in the Twelve-Fold Space. And he also told me that you had come back to persuade him to return there."

"He is not wrong, even if he presented the truth differently than I would have," Hortat admitted, telling her with a raised hand to let him finish speaking when she seemed about to interrupt. "When we met, more than seventy thousands of your years had passed, and the virus that originally enabled us to use the new technology of quantum mirroring had spread rapidly in the meantime."

"What kind of virus was that? Xinth already spoke of it in the vision," Filio asked.

"We don't know. Many thought it was a virus that escaped from the laboratories operated by my caste and was initially intended for medical use. But as far as I know, that was not true. I believe that it was instead a whim of nature that limited our spread on Earth.

"We were a shrinking species, far fewer than there are humans today, but we had domination over the Earth and interfered with nature wherever it appealed to us. However, nature always seems to find a balance. In any case, we found no way to defeat the virus, and more and more of us died from it. The colony ships were our last hope, as we could not stop its spread. When I returned, Xinth was the last of us, apart from the embryos in the ark."

"Why weren't he and the ark affected?"

"Both have been hermetically sealed off. Nothing goes in or out, not even the smallest microorganism."

"And this virus? What happened to it?" asked Filio, whose head was spinning at the thought of a virus that could overcome even a powerful civilization like the Builders.

"When I returned, it wasn't there, nor were any of the others of my kind who had remained with Xinth," Hortat explained, taking several short pauses to breathe. "He told me that they had flown to the research stations out in the solar system, intending to settle there, but apparently they did not survive long without supplies that a functioning Earth could provide. Air and water are hard to get out there."

"That's horrible," Filio said, looking to the floor. When she looked up again, the Builder was absently gazing at her.

"But I still don't understand why you advised Xinth to return to the Twelve-Fold Space."

"The virus had disappeared, perhaps because there were no more hosts, possibly because of natural climatic changes. The whole planet then went through a long ice age, and it was impossible for us to start rebuilding our species with the embryos because our farm robots could not have grown anything.

Therefore I advised him to use my microphage to free him from his fear and acquire the navigators' ability to communicate with the quantum mirror. Xinth obviously misunderstood me. I wanted to conduct experiments using the information that the Ship Being had gathered during our transition in order to improve and make the technology safer." Hortat seemed unhappy with his own words and shook his mighty head. "That was probably rather naive of me."

"You wanted to use the microphage on the embryos, am I right?" Filio asked, tilting her head to one side. She thought for a moment, but could not find a better explanation simply because, being herself a scientist, she probably would have done the same thing.

"Yes. I wanted to hatch the embryos in stages, grow them, and let them work on the quantum mirror and the data. With Microphage Twenty-One, they could have produced offspring who could genetically inherit their knowledge and advance the research. Each new generation would have become intellectually much more powerful than the previous generation, and I was sure that we could solve the problem in this way," Hortat said.

"But Xinth disagreed."

"Correct. He obviously thought my proposals were merely pretense, thinking that my real intention was to spread my microphage in order to take control. As high priest, he was, after all, part of the Council that had condemned and forbidden my research. But I didn't understand that until it was too late. Xinth suggested that I take half of the embryos to Goldan—to Mars—and conduct my experiments there. So Geth and our heritage as a civilization would remain secure."

"Why didn't Xinth travel to Mars himself? The planet was fruitful at the time, wasn't it?"

"No, Mars had been damaged by radiation and had already lost a large amount of its atmosphere. For us, it was a dying world," Hortat said, tightening his shoulders before looking straight into her eyes.

"I accepted his offer and only realized too late that I did not have the embryos onboard, and that the Ship Being was not one that obeyed me. Although I realized his betrayal before landing on Mars, it was already too late. I deactivated the Ship Being by physically destroying its memory core, but the explosive device had already detonated and destroyed my ship's propulsion module—the last remaining one our species had. Xinth left me a message that he would wait for signals from the fleet and hold me to account as soon as he was reunited with the Council.

"Xinth really thought that the other ships had reached their destinations and that their signals would take millennia—or even millions of years—to reach him due to the great distances involved. His suspicions led him to believe that I had never been in the Twelve-Fold Space but had tried to deceive him and make the Earth my testing ground for the microphage while all those who could have prevented me were traveling far away throughout the galaxy."

"From his point of view, it's perfectly understandable,

isn't it?" Filio asked cautiously, fearing that she might have infuriated Pano when she saw his suddenly glance, but Hortat only nodded weakly.

"Yes," he admitted. "However, I don't know how to convince him otherwise."

"Why do you think he wants to go to this Twelve-Fold Space now? What has changed that has caused him to shift his opinion a hundred and eighty degrees?"

"Time. More than sixty million solar cycles have passed, and he has still received no signal. He is feeding your people with technology so that you can survive this century and help him hatch the embryos. As long as you are useful, he will use you like an ant colony and eventually make room for adults of my species."

"But this is pure speculation," Filio cautiously contradicted him. "If the pre-astronauts are to be believed, he has acted more as a helping hand over the millennia."

"Oh no, Filio Amorosa." Hortat bent over to her, and she instinctively recoiled. "Xinth in my language means Guardian of the Seers. The Seers are us, those you call the Builders. He rejected my microphage in his Council statement, arguing that it would allow microorganisms to secretly take power over the Earth—at worst, over the will of any single Seer—and that there should be only one species that rules over the Earth."

"The Seers, I presume."

"Yes. He regards you as no more than primates with an unhealthy relationship with our planet."

"But these are not conclusive proofs," Filio said, shaking her head. She felt like she had been dragged into the middle of a fight between two aliens, each of them trying to get the better of the other.

"If you need proof, we'll send him a message," Hortat suggested.

"You mean from here?"

"Yes. From your old base. Can we contact Geth from there via the satellites or not?"

"No, the International Space Consortium operates—" Filio disagreed, only to interrupt herself and look up when she remembered the satellite records she had seen in the pyramid. "Karlhammer hacked the satellites. So, he will receive the signal himself. Yes, you're right."

Suddenly, she paused. "But what kind of message should we send him?"

"I have an idea that will quickly show us what Xinth is really intending," Hortat said thoughtfully, rising from his chair.

22

AGATHA DEVENWORTH, 2042

The landing on the *USS Barack Obama* proved much more difficult than they anticipated. Their military supersonic jet battled violent storm gusts that whipped the Antarctic Ocean into swells five meters tall. Since it was pitch-dark, they could only see the front-to-back blinking light bands on the landing deck in front of them. Fortunately, the monster of an aircraft carrier was so enormous, and displaced such a great volume of water, that the swell height hardly made itself noticeable, and the pilot was able to bring their jet down safely. However, the braking was quite violent, and they were thrown hard into their seatbelts.

After they had taxied to their parking position, a squad of soldiers with handcuffs, foot restraints, and a load of soundproof headphones came on board. They put a black sack over Dalam's head before putting headphones on him, also taking great care that his fetters were secure. Agatha and Pano took a pair of headphones each, and followed the soldiers who escorted Dalam into the rain. The storm turned every drop of water into a bullet that burst on her face and caused a burning-cold bite.

Buffeted by the turbulence of fighter jet engines starting up and rattling rotors, and with heads huddled into their hunched shoulders, they rushed over to a dark helicopter. Six soldiers armed with assault rifles angled across their chests stood in front of it. They had the box-shaped appearance of special forces garbed in the latest-model exoskeleton. Their faces were unrecognizable under their full helmets and mirrored visors—everything about them said they were the escort team of Navy SEALs.

Agatha looked up at the massive tower of the *Obama* as she passed by. It stood high and stoic in the face of the storm, and she thought of the two nuclear reactors hidden deep in the heart of the floating fortress. She thought it somehow wrong to bring such a powerful and dangerous incarnation of technology so close to the only virtually untouched continent remaining on Earth.

"Come on, Agatha!" Pano yelled at her. His head was nestled between his shoulders, and he squinted his eyes against the rain as he waved her to the helicopter. The SEALs helped her into the small and utilitarian interior cabin, which housed only two parallel bench seats illuminated by red battle lights. She sat on the bench facing forward, and slid all the way to her right. She slid over a little tighter against the closed sliding door beside her when Pano got in and sat down next to her. Dalam, guided by a Navy SEAL, followed and took up the rest of that bench. Three other elite soldiers jumped in and occupied the other side, while the remaining two simply sat down on the deck.

The SEAL in the center of the opposite bench tapped against his helmet with one finger and then held up three fingers. She and Pano nodded at the same time and used their hand terminals to select the corresponding radio channel. They could now receive transmissions over their soundproof headphones, and also transmit using the fold-out microphones that rested tightly against their cheeks.

The SEAL team leader introduced himself. "I'm Lieutenant Andrew Danatouth." It was strange to hear him in her ears while he, just like his comrades, sat motionlessly just over an arm's length opposite her. "The flight time to the drop point will be about four hours. The flight could get a bit rough, and by that, I don't mean this storm out there."

"The attack has already begun."

"Yes, Ma'am, and first reports leave no doubt that the B12 mercenaries are putting up a serious fight. They've brought the Black Aces with them as far as we have been able to determine."

"Should that mean anything to me, Lieutenant?" Agatha asked as she saw out of the corners of her eyes that the door had been slid shut. The helicopter started to wobble as it lifted and then took off.

"Those are B12's elite brigades, Ma'am. They are recruited exclusively from veterans of international special forces and have the best equipment money can buy. Their combined salary likely costs the Human Foundation a fortune," the soldier explained.

"Could they cause problems for us?"

"Yes, Ma'am, but we're Navy SEALs—we get the job done."

Agatha could almost see the guy grinning through his helmet, so confident was his voice. She only hoped that his self-confidence came from experience and not from youthful recklessness.

"Allow me a question, Ma'am?"

Agatha looked up in amazement and gazed at the black helmet that looked a bit like Darth Vader's mask in the red cabin light. Eventually, she nodded.

"Who is this prisoner that we're supposed to arrange a secret handover for in the middle of a battle?"

"Unfortunately, I can't tell you that, Lieutenant. The only important thing is that you protect him at all costs. Understood?"

"Understood, Ma'am." The SEAL leaned back on the cabin wall. "The front units bombed the area you marked in front of the pyramid. May I ask why we fired on empty ice?"

"It's complicated," she lied, thinking of the location of the jamming field, which she had sent to the fleet command after estimating its distance from the pyramid.

Through their soundproofing headphones, Agatha didn't even hear the thunder of the rotors as they glided over the side of the nearly 400-meter aircraft carrier and were abruptly thrown back and forth by the violent storm gusts. She felt a sudden wave of queasiness, and grabbed hold of a stanchion with both hands so as not to be thrown against the door.

Through the window, she could see the escort ships plowing through the waves in the pale light of the fleet's navigation lights. They appeared as dark, elongated silhouettes with white spray tails, and seemed to push themselves against the water like armored beetles. There had to be about 20 ships surrounding the *Barack Obama* like a cocoon. Next to them, she saw the flashing lights of two other helicopters and the dense, flickering veils of rain that separated them.

Soon, however, there was only the endless black of the ocean, which turned into the endless gray of the frozen waste after about ten minutes. Everything below them was so dark that she almost missed the coastline as they flew over it. It was just a pale strip of slightly lighter gray swallowed by the waves crashing onto it.

"Nervous?" Pano asked, looking at her. They sat so close to each other that they were touching from knees to shoulders. She was happy to enjoy the extra warmth and the comfort his closeness gave her.

"I don't know," she admitted, letting her shoulders relax a little and then releasing her left hand from the stanchion. "I feel so exhausted. It is as if this—"

"—as if this inner struggle between what I am and what I want, even though it's against my will, is eating me up," he helped her finish the thought.

She nodded bitterly. "Exactly. I'm looking for some reason why I shouldn't hate myself for being so stupid as to fall into his trap. But then I find myself seriously worrying about how I can make sure that nothing happens to Dalam," she explained, looking over to The Enemy, who sat motionless, wearing the black sack on his head and headphones over it. She wanted to hate him, but she could not. No, not true. She *could*, but she could not turn that hatred into action—because she just did not want to.

"Well, we'll manage it somehow," Pano assured her with a faithful smile that actually generated something like warmth—a warmth that found its way to a place in her that she had believed could never be entered.

"Yes," she muttered, and following an inner impulse, she leaned her head onto his shoulder. The wind had subsided, and they were not being shaken as violently as they had been over the last half hour, so she allowed herself a short rest. At first, it seemed as if Pano had stiffened, but then his shoulder relaxed, and she felt his fingers slip between hers.

She briefly pondered whether she had a problem with the soldiers seeing them holding hands and possibly regarding it as a sign of weakness, but she was too tired and too confused to really worry about it. So, she let herself surrender to the moment, not knowing how long it would last.

Sometime later, Agatha saw the first flashes of light on the horizon. At first, there was only one, so she thought of a distant thunderstorm raging in the darkness of the South Pole, but then the number of flashes became more frequent. Some of them blazed near the ground during their short lives, while others appeared at significantly higher altitudes.

"What's going on?" Pano asked almost cautiously over the radio. She hadn't noticed that she had taken her head off his shoulder in order to get a better look.

"I think I'm seeing what we're flying toward."

"How bad is it?"

"It looks like war," she said, noting movements in the depths below them. They were not flying particularly high, just a few hundred meters above the ice sheet, so she could quickly make out what had attracted her attention—soldiers and tanks. Along their route of flight, a long column of transport and battle tanks were advancing toward the tumult of explosions and rocket trails in the distance. Like a chain of beetles, some larger and some smaller, they continued forward, from time to time illuminated by the red flicker of their helicopter's navigation lights.

Next, a squadron of combat helicopters thundered past them, firing salvoes of rockets whose bright tails sped away.

"My goodness," she breathed into her microphone, shaking her head. "I would never have thought I'd experience something like this outside of VR."

"Is that any more surprising than the thought you'd one day be talking to ancient alien ancestors who have infected portions of humanity with a mysterious virus?"

Agatha gave Pano a look that left no doubt as to what she thought of the comment.

"Thirty minutes," the lieutenant announced on the group radio channel, making a circular movement with the gloved hand that wasn't resting on the chunky carbine hanging in front of his chest. "We're going to ground-level flight now to evade the short-range radar. Hold on tight. If you want to check your equipment one more time, you should do it now."

Agatha tugged at the seals of her armored vest, which she wore under a down jacket bearing a label that read 'CTD.' She pulled out her Beretta and tossed it upward, catching it near the back of the slide with one hand and—without using her other hand—snapping the slide back to chamber a round. Continuing the same skillful pattern of motion, she let the heavy pistol slide back into the holster.

"Neat trick," Pano commented on her little feat with a raised eyebrow.

Agatha shrugged. "During my shooting test, I dropped my pistol. Since that disgrace, I made sure that I can handle it better than a juggler can his pins."

"Let's hope you don't need it."

"I'm only going to need it once—to eliminate Xinth," she said firmly, helping him check the fit of his vest, which was not easy since he was sitting wedged between her and Dalam.

Shortly afterward their helicopter plummeted, and she had to hold onto Pano with her left hand and onto the retaining net over the door with her right. The pilot performed some wild maneuvers while bright lines shot past them and turned the night outside the window into a wild confusion of nearby and distant explosions and tracer bullets. She could not see any muzzle flashes, so she figured that the ground battle was being fought with suppressors, but she could see soldiers in their exoskeletons looking like gray stickmen running over the endless ice, toward the pyramid.

A shrill tone in her headphones indicated that she had received a message, and she pulled out her hand terminal with her arm still hooked into the door's retaining net.

"Karlhammer has sent us the coordinates of a secret entrance and excluded us from the target grid of his troops. We must follow the course exactly. Otherwise, we'll be shot down," she said over the radio, nodding toward Lieutenant Danatouth.

He raised a hand toward her, thumb up. "I'll communicate that to the pilot."

To Agatha, the flight time to the entrance seemed to last half an eternity. The closer they got to the pyramid, the thicker grew the tangle of firing drones, fighter jets, and the hundreds of surface-to-air missiles that pursued their targets, and here and there, turned humans and equipment into clouds of debris. The storm of lights had become so extreme that it seemed as if she was sitting in front of a stroboscope.

Then, finally, the gigantic silhouette of the pyramid appeared. It rose thousands of meters into the polar sky. In several places around the center of the mighty structure, bright lances of light streaked at regular intervals, slicing the sky in two and engendering explosions flashing in the middle of nowhere. She did not believe that this kind of defense could be the work of the Human Foundation.

"Hold on, people!" the pilot finally radioed, and less than two seconds later braked so hard that Agatha held her breath and desperately increased her grip on Pano and the retaining net.

She barely noticed they had landed before the door on her side flew open and her arm was almost torn off.

"Out, out, out!" the lieutenant shouted, and he and his team were out so fast that she barely had time to blink. They secured a wide semicircle in front of the helicopter and then Lieutenant Danatouth waved to her.

"Let's go," she sighed. She and Pano held Dalam between them and led him onto ice that was being whipped by the rotors. The cold burned brutally on her face, as if someone was poking thousands of small needles into her forehead, nose, and cheeks. She pulled herself together and held her head down to afford some protection from the flying ice crystals.

As they passed the SEALs, whose camouflage suits were almost indistinguishable from the gray of the surrounding ice, she ripped her terminal out of her pocket with her free hand and aligned its navigation so that it pointed directly to the spot marked at the base of the pyramid. Then she gave Pano a wave and hurried off with him, dragging Dalam along. His chains, however, slowed their progress, and she had to fight an urge to run as fast as she could.

In reality, they covered the 20 meters to the wall of black stone very quickly, despite her shaking knees.

Nothing happened when they got there. No opening, no entrance appeared.

"Hmm," she said, casting a suspicious glance at Pano. "It should be here."

"Did he write anything else? Have we forgotten something?"

Agatha shook her head and looked around hastily. The SEALs stood a few meters away and put up a screen around them, although it seemed to be quiet on this side of the pyramid.

"Something is happening," the lieutenant radioed. She could not make him out among his team members in their identical uniforms, and she turned again toward the wall, which towered rough and weathered before them as if it divided the world into two halves.

And—like magic—a passageway appeared that was just high and wide enough to let them through. From the interior, faint light hit her eyes. She looked in and saw a sloping path leading into the depths.

"Looks good," she said, wanting to head in immediately with Pano and Dalam when a hand on her shoulder held her back. It was one of the SEALs, who towered behind her like a living shadow.

"You should let two of us go first. It's best to play it safe," said a female voice over the radio, but Agatha shook her head.

"I think it's better if they see familiar faces, not soldiers wearing the same get-up as their comrades out there who've started a war."

The SEAL turned her head toward one of the other shadows, then gave a short nod and let Agatha go.

"I'll go in first," she said, slipping into the pyramid before Pano could protest, leaving him to guide Dalam. The others followed close behind.

The passage led diagonally downward about 100 meters, and the light, which had no visible source, was just strong enough for them to make out the contours of the floor and walls and not to stumble over their own feet.

The air became much warmer at the bottom. They ended up in a small room that was perhaps five by five meters. It was empty, its walls smooth as marble and black as basalt. Opposite was an open passageway leading into a crosswise corridor in which a dark figure was waiting. Following an impulse, Agatha looked at Dalam to make sure the gag was still in his mouth and then took off her own headphones.

"I repeat one last time—stay where you are so we can scan you. Place your weapons on the ground," a deep voice demanded. It had come from the waiting figure.

Agatha held the headset microphone in front of her mouth. "We are to put down our weapons and let ourselves be scanned."

"I'd rather not..." the lieutenant began.

Agatha turned toward the SEAL and shook her head firmly. "We were expecting this. After all, your comrades outside are attacking this facility. So, do what they ask."

The soldiers hesitantly obeyed her order and laid down their carbines. She was sure that the men and women of the special forces would still have hidden weapons with them but would not lay them aside until they were scanned and asked to do so. She and Pano pulled their service weapons and laid them carefully in front of them before they grabbed Dalam by his elbows again and waited.

"Agents Devenworth and Hofer, please take a step forward with the prisoner," the voice urged them next, and they willingly did so. Then a device that looked like a sensor rod came down from a hole on the ceiling that they had not seen there before.

A flash of light shot through the semi-darkness in the room, and Agatha looked over her shoulder in confusion, only to jerk in horror. Each of the six SEALs that had accompanied them had been sliced in two just above their hips and now lay twitching on the floor. The stench of charred meat filled the air, and Agatha could just keep herself from retching.

"Why the hell did you do that?" she shouted in appalled anger at the silhouette in the passage in front of them. At that very moment, it stepped forward into the light. It was Cho Wayan, Karlhammer's personal assistant, who stood there in his bespoke suit and gazed at her with a hard expression on his face.

"I'm sorry, but we can't afford to take any more risks. We cannot check quickly enough whether these soldiers were also corrupted by The Enemy," the Indonesian said. Agatha could recognize no sign of real regret in his voice. He pointed to Dalam. "Is this the prisoner?"

Agatha swallowed. "Yes."

"Very good. Please follow me." Wayan turned on his heel and disappeared into the far passage.

She gave Pano a look. He shrugged his shoulders with a look of acid on his face and hurried along with her and Dalam after Karlhammer's assistant.

Four security guards with submachine guns and black uniforms were waiting for them in the next room. She noticed that the passage through which they had come was no longer visible. In its place was a massive wall, as if nothing else had ever been there.

The security guards, men with hard faces and even harder expressions, flanked the prisoner and took him from their care.

"Down there," said Wayan, pointing to the left-hand wall, in which another passage immediately appeared. When he made no attempt to proceed, Agatha and Pano walked on past him, closely followed by the guards and Dalam.

They had been in the next room before. It was Xinth's private chamber. The Builder sat in an oversized chair made of a dark material that looked half-liquid, half firm, and appeared to have grown out of the floor. He was wrapped in a gray suit, which bulged over his chest, and carefully inspected them with his huge black almond-shaped eyes. Next to him sat Luther Karlhammer in a wheelchair. His head was encased in a hard-plastic shell under which colorful lights flashed, and behind them stood two body-guards clad in full armor suits and carrying rapid-fire weapons.

The glass box in the middle was still where she had last seen it, except that the front was missing. The armored door to the short passage that led into one of the large work caverns was also missing. Agatha could hear the loud roaring and the hissing of machines from that direction.

Karlhammer greeted them with a smile. "Agent Deven-worth, Capitano Hofer." Then he beckoned them forward. "Now, I call this a success."

Agatha shook his hand, as did Pano, before turning around and pointing at Dalam, who stood somewhat slumped between the four security guards. The opening to the passage they came through had just closed tight. Ironi-cally, Dalam looked like an alien with the black sack over his head, the clunky headphones over that, and the tennis-ball-sized gag in his mouth, causing the sack to protrude. The chain connecting the handcuffs and foot shackles jangled slightly as he moved emitting an incomprehensible tone.

"That's what I would call it," she said.

"I'm sorry that we had to deal so... decisively with your companions from the Navy," Karlhammer said apologeti-cally, while Xinth, standing next to him and looking like some larger-than-life statue of a mythical creature, stared motionlessly at the prisoner. "I hope the President will understand. Her word is important to me, because you have convinced me that she has not been infected. Nevertheless, after everything that has happened, we cannot be careful enough."

"I understand," Agatha assured him, even though she was becoming increasingly restless. She tried her best not to constantly look at the Builder, so as not to betray herself. The urge to kill him was almost superhuman, as if it had been woven into her every nerve and muscle fiber—which may have been the case. But she had to wait and hope that an opportunity would arise. Apparently, Karlhammer and Xinth were much more cautious than she had hoped, but she had hardly expected it to be easy. So she'd just have to stay ready for the right moment.

"You succeeded very quickly indeed, Special Agent," Karlhammer proclaimed, looking over to Xinth, who tilted his head slightly without turning his gaze away from Dalam. "I'm sorry that we have also disarmed you. We don't want to appear ungrateful, but Xinth's safety is our top priority."

Agatha nodded and inspected the Builder's gray suit, the surface of which seemed to be in constant motion. *Maybe some kind of armor?* she mused.

"I understand that very well. Why haven't you shot him yet?"

Karlhammer looked up in surprise and then nodded in understanding. "Xinth has some questions for him regarding those others that are infected. If this is really the one that Hortat infiltrated with his microphage, he knows too much to simply kill him."

"But how will you be able to interrogate him when each of his words could be an order that both you and I would have to obey?" she asked, not even trying to banish fear from her voice.

"That's not going to happen again. Now that Xinth knows who and what he is dealing with, he has been able to take appropriate precautions. He is immune to his attacks and we will keep our headphones on."

"Immune? How?"

"He didn't tell me."

"Sir," said Cho Wayan, stepping out from behind the security guards to reveal a furrowed brow, "I have a call for you."

"Not now, Cho."

"It's from one of the ESA satellites we hacked in Mars orbit."

"What?" asked Karlhammer, wrinkling his face. "Put it through." The South African pulled out a hand-held terminal and held it to his ear. After only a few seconds, his eyes widened. He was only listening, yet the corners of his mouth twitched several times, and his facial expressions seemed to go through all the manifestations that facial muscles were capable of. Eventually, he just stared blankly for a moment and then passed the terminal on to Xinth. "It's Hortat."

The Builder showed no emotion, but after a short hesitation took the device, which almost disappeared into his huge hand.

"Hortat?" Agatha asked in a whisper, and leaned down to Karlhammer, whose face had turned chalk-white.

"Yes," he answered in a raspy voice, nodding absently. "Filio Amorosa is with him on Mars. It seems that their mission was successful, but not in the way we had hoped."

"What does that mean?" Pano asked, looking back and forth between Dalam and the head of the Human Foundation.

"I don't know. Apparently, she did not kill Hortat and did not tap into his ship's AI." He grimly clenched his hands into fists. "She thinks he needs to talk to Xinth to resolve this conflict. Probably The Enemy brought them under his control. Damn."

Agatha looked at Xinth, who said something in his rolling and roaring language and then listened again. It went back and forth for a while. The room was completely still, except for the occasional thunderous roar that sounded from the Builder's mouth. The security guards standing close to Dalam looked straight ahead, the terrorist did not move, and Karlhammer seemed immersed in his own thoughts.

It took a long time for Xinth to finally return the hand terminal to Karlhammer and release a deep, bass sigh. "Hortat strives for a peaceful solution," said the Builder in accent-free English—he only slightly stretched his syllables, and moved his head in a swinging motion, a gesture that Agatha could not interpret.

"A peaceful solution? After all that's happened?" Karlhammer shook his head without understanding.

"Yes. He had his reasons, I think."

"You trust him?"

"No, but he has no reason to trust me, either," Xinth replied in full tone as he rose from his strange chair. "We both had our reasons to do what we did, and we may share a responsibility greater than our personal feud."

"It's *that* simple?" Agatha asked with surprise, walking with the Builder as he approached Dalam and the security guards.

Xinth's penetrating bass rolled through the room. "Nothing about it is simple. I will have to think about it. The stakes are high, and Hortat is dying, so it makes little sense for him to pursue some stubborn end."

Agatha looked at Pano, who was still standing next to Karlhammer's wheelchair and gave a barely noticeable nod. "He's dying?" she asked. She walked beside him until they arrived in front of the security men and Dalam. Xinth looked at the hooded man as if lost in thought and made a wave-like gesture with his right hand.

"Yes."

"Did he say that?"

"Yes."

"You can't trust his words!" Agatha said, shaking her head decisively.

"I have spoken to the ship he is on. Both his oxygen and energy supply are insufficient to revive him. Not with human technology."

Agatha stood next to one of the security guards— all of whom were vigilantly keeping their eyes on Dalam, their submachine guns aimed at him—so she could stare Xinth square in the face.

"He's been playing games for almost three years, and who knows how many people have been infected with his virus. How does he intend to undo that?"

Instead of answering, the Builder looked at Cho Wayan. "Did you receive a data package?"

"Uh, yes," he said, looking at a small tablet. "It's huge."

"The research data on Microphage Twenty-One." Xinth sighed, then looked back at Dalam as a clatter rang out from Karlhammer's direction.

The security guards aimed their weapons toward the noise. A shot rang out and Xinth also whirled around. Agatha, however, wasted no time looking to see what was happening. She grabbed the uniformed man's hand from behind, kicked him in the hollow of a knee, directed the submachine gun with the other hand toward the Builder's head, and pressed her finger over the man's trigger finger.

The salvo directly struck the back of Xinth's head, which dissolved in a red cloud.

Screams erupted as something suddenly broke loose in

Agatha, and she collapsed, screaming. "Kill him," she cried out in her guilt and despair, which rolled over her like a force of nature upon fulfilling The Enemy's orders. She pointed to where she suspected Dalam was.

She saw figures swirling through her field of vision. Then something heavy landed on her, flattening her to the floor. Voices, washed-out and garbled as if under water, reached her ears.

Someone screamed out his pain, a roaring, penetrating scream. She believed she recognized Pano's voice, fought with all her strength to look up, and eventually saw him lying next to Karlhammer's wheelchair in a pool of blood that was spreading before her eyes. The two armored body-guards stood protectively in front of the head of the Human Foundation, who was staring blankly from a chalky face, and they aimed their weapons at her dying partner.

"Oh no," she said. Someone screamed at her, demanding something from her or cursing her. Whatever it was, she was unable to understand. Everything sounded muffled, as if her ears were plugged. Rough hands yanked her to her feet and pulled her to the side.

People rushed in and clustered around Xinth's body. Cho Wayan stood next to it with his mouth open.

"What have I done?" Agatha wailed. "What have I done?"

23

FILIO AMOROSA, 2042

Hortat turned away from the tiny rod that had grown from the wall to extend in his direction, and it now retracted into the wall. Filio sat behind him with Cassidy and Heinrich and looked up attentively as Hortat turned to them again.

"I believe that he at least acknowledges my gesture, and that we have a chance to settle our conflict for the sake of our species."

"What gesture?" asked Cassidy.

"I sent him my research data on Microphage Twenty-One—well, the part that deals with the manipulation of the woven programming," the Builder explained.

"But with that, he can end all the activities of... all those you've infected, right?" Heinrich sounded horrified. "You have to prevent him from taking your species into the Twelve-Fold Space—"

"I know, Heinrich," Hortat interrupted him, calmly lifting one of his paw-like hands. "If you want to choose the path of cooperation, you must make concessions, and they come with risk. Whenever we have to agree on something, trust is required at a certain point without any guarantee."

"And you trust him?" Filio asked.

"No. But he does not trust me either. Yet, nothing is possible without concessions. I am also dying."

"What?" Filio and Heinrich blurted out at the same time.

"The oxygen supply of my ship is sufficient for six more months at a breathable level for me if I limit the atmosphere to my quarters. If your species sends a rescue mission, it will take about a year and a half to get here, a year until the orbits of Mars and Earth get closer to each other and four months or more for the flight, provided they agree on a mission quickly enough. However, if I reduce the oxygen content of the atmosphere so that you can breathe, the air will last even longer, and you will survive."

"No, you can't do that," Heinrich stammered, springing from his chair.

"But, Heinrich Marks, I can and must do that."

"What if you go back into stasis?"

Hortat shook his large, bronze-colored head, and his eyelids closed for a moment. "No, the process is very energy-intensive. I have decided. Xinth will take care of the embryos and will not redevelop and use the quantum mirror. He will delete all research data about it."

"That's what he told you?" Heinrich's snort showed what he thought of it.

"He did it," Hortat insisted.

"How do you know that?"

"He connected me to the Geth Being when we talked to each other. These beings are so constructed that they are not able to lie to members of my species."

"But he manipulated your Ship Being in such a way that it did not recognize the sabotage that caused you to crash here," Filio said.

"He excluded it from the sabotaged drive area while

placing the explosive charge. That is something else. He has kept his part of our agreement, and I mine. Now there is nothing I can do except to trust him to abide by the rest of it." Hortat's dark lips warped slightly. "But a small hedge might be in order."

Filio furrowed her brow as he spoke.

"I will give you a sample of my Microphage Twenty-One with the DNA of this clone body. If you put this sample into the automatic breeding system for the embryos in Geth, they will have all my memories." Hortat paused. "I think that would be good for my species and its viability."

"I will," Filio said firmly, after looking into the endless depths of the Builder's eyes for a long moment. It felt right, especially after what she'd sensed in his memories and what he had done now.

"Thank you."

Heinrich reared up in front of her, and his forehead creased in anger. "You can't just let him die!"

Just as Filio was about to respond in kind, she felt Hortat's hand on her shoulder. His hand encompassed it as if it were a tiny tennis ball, and she paused.

"She is doing the only right thing. I have gone astray in my anger at Xinth and my concern for the legacy of my species," he said, explaining with the calmness of a person who has made peace with his fate. "That, and my feelings of guilt—to have survived alone of all my kind because I broke the law—led me to act ruthlessly against the only other living person of my species. I had my chance. Now it is up to others to do it better. Xinth has chosen to cooperate with you, and that is good because he will not be able to grow the embryos without you humans. With my memories, they will know what really matters and will not repeat my mistakes."

"I think I have an idea of how we can do it," Cassidy said,

raising his hand like a shy student. When they turned to him, he took a deep breath. "We need to get the United Nations on board for this to happen. This will also prevent Xinth from going it alone. He has all sorts of reasons not to trust us human beings."

"And how do we do that?" Filio asked with a mixture of curiosity and skepticism.

"Pictures say more than a thousand words, don't they?"

EPILOGUE: FILIO

2043

Filio stepped onto the platform to loud applause. It reminded her of the stage of an especially ostentatious opera house in Vienna or Prague. On her way to the lectern with its microphones and teleprompters, she deliberately avoided looking into the crowd of spectators who were following each step she took. She had never particularly enjoyed speaking in front of a large audience, and today was no exception.

When she reached the lectern, she looked briefly at the small shelf in front of her where the tiny button was placed, with which she could start her text running on the teleprompters. She thought for a moment and decided not to press it. Instead, she looked down into the crowd of 93 heads of state and government who were attending the UN special session, and took a deep breath.

"I'm going to address you from my heart. I have allowed myself to be persuaded to stand before you and speak here today." She began her speech without remembering even a single line of her prepared text. "I'm a scientist. I am not a politician. Yet, everything changed for me after I was on

Mars, and was only able to return because I was saved by a being that had no reason to trust me. Maybe I had to learn my humanity from someone who is not a human being.

"I would also like to thank the previous speaker, Luther Karlhammer, who—out of his own private assets—paid for the mission to save my two comrades and me when the international community was unable to agree on joint financing. I bear no resentment on that account because I am aware that you could not know the scope of that mission. Now, however, after Mr. Karlhammer's speech, you do, and I have only one request—that you repay his openness and transparency with the same level of openness and transparency. His revelations may sound incredible, and I could see from your reaction to his words that you may have many questions. However, we cannot afford to delay what needs to be decided here today, as it no longer only concerns the good and the bad of our species."

Murmurs spread among the state leaders, and she took a short break to collect her breath. The faces of the powerful in the plenum lay in the semi-darkness, illuminated only by the stage lighting and resembling heads on an oil painting.

"Luther Karlhammer and I, as special representatives of the Human Foundation, are aware that we cannot count on you to show us good will, so I hope that you will grant the next speaker precisely that," Filio continued as she gave a short wave to her bodyguard, who was waiting together with the Chancellor's entourage at one of the two entrances behind the podium.

When the door opened, she took a step to the side and vacated the cone of light that illuminated the area directly behind the lectern, so as not to take any attention away from the following performance.

Xinth had to duck his head as he entered the chamber

through the double doors that were held open by two security guards and halted with his hands folded in front of him. The bronze giant wore a strange gray fabric, held at the hip by a flowing sash. As the heads of state erupted in conversations and sometimes loud shouts, he looked calmly from left to right and finally at Filio, who nodded at him.

Striding majestically, he walked across the podium—a boulder of muscles that exuded such magnetism that Filio would have preferred to stand right at his side, only for the sake of being near him. It was astonishing that this effect lasted even in the form of the illusion that stood there next to her. When she thought about how superior the technology of the Builders was to theirs, it almost made her dizzy. It was a hard-to-describe aura that surrounded him, conveying both wisdom and a soulful depth that emanated from his huge black eyes, which were now aimed at the audience of state leaders as he took hold of the lectern with his plate-sized paws.

Suddenly, the venue fell completely silent.

The Builder's voice boomed, and the rolling consonants of his polished English washed over the audience in deep bass waves. "Honored representatives of humanity, I stand before you today as a representative of a dying species and I ask asylum for my children."

This time it remained dead quiet. Not even the rustling of jackets could be heard.

"I do not take this step lightly, as my species already inhabited this planet when humanity was still the whisper of a distant future. All that Luther Karlhammer told you was the truth, and I do not want to take up your precious time by repeating his words. Instead, I want to tell you a story.

"Just a year ago, I thought your species undeserving to be considered our descendants. I only had to look at how fragmented and divided you are, and how your religion of boundless growth is destroying our planet. I know from the history of my people that the way to survival lies in cooperation with nature, not in domination over it. Nevertheless, I made the mistake of seeking control over you and your future. Ironically, another of my kind has shown me more or less consciously that such a path is counterproductive. But listen for yourselves."

The illusion of Xinth, triggered by a tiny device in Filio's pocket, finished speaking the words she and Karlhammer had written and took a step back. The ceiling spotlights followed him, and he raised another hand before saying his last words, "I will be here, and I will not let you down."

Then he was surrounded by a bright flicker and dissolved in a fading cloud of photons.

Stunned shouts and murmurs spread as a holoprojector rose from the floor of the podium. Part of her was ashamed of this misuse of Builder technology, but she and Karlhammer had agreed that it was better if the heads of state believed that a powerful alien could appear at any time rather than to forgo such sleight of hand.

The principle of a beneficent God, who also had the power to punish, was too deeply rooted in humanity for them to ignore the benefits of this kind of belief. She was relieved that it had worked, despite the electronic defense mechanisms that the hall employed to block all holograms and electromagnetic fields that did not come from within the hall itself, and which had not previously been approved by security officials. Apparently, Xinth's device worked in via different technology.

A moment later, Hortat's face appeared five meters diagonal in size, and a heavy stone grew in Filio's stomach as she remembered watching him record the following words on his own ship.

"My name is Hortat, and if you are seeing this message, I am already dead. Presumably, at this point, you already know the truth about my species, which was able to enjoy the fertility of the Earth long before you. I do not want to waste my last breaths talking about myself and my kind—certainly you will have heard about us in sufficient form, or you will soon do so. My thoughts in the past were far too much concerned with the best and the worst of my kind, and that led to me losing sight of what really matters. It is not just a question of the goal alone, but of how one achieves it.

"You probably already know that ten thousand frozen embryos of my species are waiting to see the light of day and carry on the torch of our culture. We lost our heritage a long, long time ago, and today I ask you, the new masters of this world, to give us a second chance. I assure you that our similarities will benefit both the Earth and our species. Thanks to some of your fellow human beings, I had the chance to access your scientists' data banks and watched with astonishment the process of 'becoming' that your species has undergone—one that is strikingly similar to ours.

"More than two and a half million years ago, the first human-like creatures roamed the globe in search of food. They did not roam like nomads, but inhabited the steppes and forests in smaller groups and tribal communities. From these, today's Homo Sapiens emerged about 150,000 years ago in East Africa. In addition to them, there were at least five other human genera, including the Neanderthals, who were probably supplanted by Homo Sapiens, although you still owe up to five percent of your genetic heritage to them."

Hortat paused and looked down at something that was not part of the holographic record and took a deep breath as if he were having trouble getting enough air.

"The Neanderthals were much stronger and more resilient than the new Homo Sapiens, and yet they died out. The reason for this is also the reason why Homo Sapiens dominates the world today. Unlike his somewhat coarser relative, the Sapiens were able to cooperate with each other in much larger groups. In the battle hominid against hominid, the Neanderthal may have had advantages. Yet Homo Sapiens were more inventive and chose to join together in large groups to implement these inventions.

"Like Homo Erectus, they also mastered fire and were able to massively expand their available nourishment by heating food. Once-indigestible tubers such as potatoes, and certain meats, could now be digested. Thus, it was possible to consume more with less effort. And this, in turn, allowed the brain—which uses more than 25 percent of the energy consumption of a Homo Sapiens—to grow significantly. But this was only one bridge to today's humans.

"The most astonishing process began only about seventy thousand years ago with the cognitive revolution. Languages developed and made it possible to pass on knowledge to the next generation, both verbally and later in writing. At the end of this revolution, the first human cultures developed with the creation of art, myths, religions, values, norms, and other products of their imagination. All this placed them above all other living beings in evolutionary success.

"Their closest ancestors, the chimpanzees, also lived as social, sentient beings in defined groups of 50 to 100 members and they also recognized different hierarchies, just like the Neanderthals. But they fought with other groups and had limited habitats. Today's human, however, was able to create common myths and belief systems through their ability to imagine, and this led to much larger communities.

"Thousands of people could believe in the divinity of a pharaoh and use this shared fiction to build marvels like the pyramids, which cost thousands of lives. From an evolutionary point of view, humans were neither as fast as a lion, as strong as a bear, nor as robust as a gorilla. On the contrary, they have always been more susceptible to disease, heat, or cold than most other living beings."

The Builder paused again, which allowed his words time to combine like resin into a sticky mass that became fixed in the minds of the powerful in the plenary.

"But this cognitive revolution, with the possibility of sharing fictions that people invented and translated into firm belief, led to humans developing the strongest tool that exists to this day—being able to cooperate with each other in large communities. You may not even know your neighbor, but you share the belief that you belong to the same community and nation and can work on it together.

"Unlike the chimpanzees, you can regulate the social behavior of much larger groups. As a result, Homo Sapiens have dominated the ecosystem as hunter-gatherers since then, but they have also been responsible for the largest of extinctions. No animal could compete with human sophistication.

"About ten thousand years ago, the agricultural revolution followed. It was a consequence of the ever-increasing population density that resulted from evolutionary success as well as the compulsion to settle down. More people could be fed by cooperating to grow wild grasses such as wheat, and by domesticating animals and making food available in one place. The drawback was much harder physical work, as humans were not used to toiling for ten to twelve hours in a field, but had previously roamed the nearby forests for a few hours a day to collect nuts, berries, and roots, and to hunt animals.

"Diet became less varied and balanced, and disease increased. In addition, larger social groups and competition within them created a strong urge for prosperity and status. Due to seasonal climate fluctuations, food had to be stored in order to get the large population through bad times, and so the concept of possession arose, which in turn aroused envy and greed.

"The first lords and elites were created to control the peasants and either protect or rob them. They consolidated their rule by accumulating wealth and exploiting the fictions already mentioned that people could believe in. They invented monarchies, and gods that legitimized these monarchies.

"A single king would hardly have had anything with which to oppose the ninety percent or so of humans that were peasants at the time—except for the possibility of making them believe in a shared truth.

"Number and writing systems were developed to regulate ownership rights and make more extensive social networks controllable and manageable. In the following millennia, large communities became ever larger ones, conquering and swallowing each other. Cultures of the vanquished were incorporated into the culture of the victors.

"The first world orders were created by conquerors, merchants, and prophets—namely empires, money, and world religions. Money united humanity in the shared belief in the value of stamped coins—using precious metals worthless for everyday use—and later using painted paper.

Money made trade much more efficient and was accepted everywhere.

"Even during the Crusades, neither Christians nor Muslims cared what coins they seized. Crusaders used Islamic gold just as gratefully as the caliphs and sultans valued coins with Christian symbols. Religions invented superhuman orders and shared value systems, and united humanity through a moral foundation in which to believe.

"About five hundred years ago, the scientific revolution followed. In the region of today's Europe, Homo Sapiens recognized that, through systematic research of nature and its laws, technologies could be developed that could lead to more wealth and power. The Chinese invented gunpowder about six hundred years before the Europeans, but used it only for fireworks. The Europeans continued to explore the potential of science, and soon the first cannons rolled over the globe.

"The scientific revolution was driven by both imperialism and capitalism, the next great belief systems that sought steady growth. The first financial markets emerged, based on the confidence that the quantity of goods produced—and their consumption—would continue to grow. Both systems invested in science to become more efficient and achieve even more growth. Life expectancy increased dramatically, as did the overall efficiency of Homo Sapiens.

"However, these developments also ensured that animals, especially pigs, chickens, and cattle, were subjected to the same principle of efficiency. Industrial animal husbandry and slaughter turned living beings into industrial goods, which had to submit to humanity's considerable cooperative networks. In 2042, there are about seventy times more domesticated animals than humans on the planet. This could be measured as an evolutionary success because they are able to live in great numbers and pass on their genes, but they have achieved this not in freedom, but because humans guide their evolution.

"The alliance of capitalism and science has allowed the human population to increase from five hundred million to more than eleven billion over the last five hundred years. Like the human capacity for overarching cooperation, both capitalism and science have made a great positive contribution to human development. For the first time in history, capitalism has created a surplus of goods and has all but eliminated periods of permanent shortages. Science has ensured longer life expectancy, modern forms of communication and an understanding of nature.

"It also created a growing human community. Today, the whole world is virtually united by its shared belief in money and science. But progress and growth have also led to unprecedented destruction of the environment, which has had to give way to the needs of an ever-growing humanity.

"Strong social communities such as the family also had to cede ground. They have been superseded by invented communities of the individual such as nations, fan clubs, or faith communities. No development is good or bad in itself, neither capitalism nor science, religions nor the principle of growth.

"The question is always—what will come of it all? By discovering the energy potential in an atomic nucleus, science created the atomic bomb, but it also provided the most long-lasting and statistically significant period of global peace. Above all else is humanity's ability to unite in mass cooperation. This is your most unique quality.

"It is your strength, your capital, your chance for an even better future and, as with all talents, it is about guiding this quality along meaningful paths that are important for the survival of your species, because every talent can be abused. I simply ask you to look at the fundamental character of your species as a whole, from its creation to the present day, and to remember the one reason that has propelled it to the forefront of evolution."

Hortat uttered a rattling sound, which was something like a sigh for a Builder, as Filio knew, before he continued.

"Confronting a second consciously intelligent species on your planet has now led, for the first time, to a change in the global status quo. My species has undergone a very similar development to yours, and we share your ability to collaborate in the creation of shared beliefs and cultures. That is why I am sure that, at the end of this long history, including all the dangers it brought with it, we can say in retrospect that we can combine these skills of cooperation in order to learn from each other and not to commit the mistakes the other has already made.

"A displacement like that suffered by Neanderthals at the hands of Homo Sapiens does not have to be repeated. Let us create something in common, something new, and let us show evolution that we have understood the critical advantage that cooperation affords and will consciously implement it, together. Today, we have the chance to do so."

The hologram, which the G7 heads of state had already seen and approved, ended. The chamber fell silent. Filio had to think of Hortat and his wise cunning with a mixture of joy and sorrow. She could still clearly see herself in her mind as she'd inserted the tiny tube containing Microphage Twenty-One when she toured the incubators in the Geth Pyramid. The task had not proven to be an easy one. Although he had meticulously described the exact place to introduce the microphage, Hortat himself had never been there and only knew that an appropriate interface field had to be there somewhere.

When she returned to the lectern, she could not stop smiling. His words had been so calm and wise, and at the same time, he had made sure he conveyed his underlying message. It was precisely this principle that she and Karl-hammer would continue—starting now.

"Ladies and gentlemen," she intoned after quietly clearing her throat and letting her gaze wander over the heads of state. "We have a lot to discuss. Hortat and Xinth have not only honored us with their presence and their words, they have also left us the chance to share in their technological and social heritage. Such an opportunity, however, is subject to certain conditions..."

EPILOGUE: AGATHA

2050

Agatha sat on the terrace of the chalet in the South Tyrolean Alps and looked at the impressive panorama of the Dolomites. The setting sun bathed the unique features of the rugged mountain slopes, creating a red glow that made them look as though they were heated from the inside out.

"Hey!"

Agatha turned her head and gave Pano a warm smile as he stood by the open glass door between her and their living room with two wine glasses, one in either hand.

"Hey, yourself."

"Fancy celebrating the end of the day," he said, handing her a fruity-smelling red wine, before sitting down beside her in the sofa swing and looking at the natural spectacle in the distance.

"Are we celebrating something in particular?"

"Anything you want."

"How about the last seven years?" she asked, smiling. "Yes, I can toast to that."

"I wouldn't call that a reason for celebrating."

"Why?"

"Well, for a while I was really worried that Karlhammer would shoot you or hand you over to the authorities after... you know."

Agatha waved his objection aside and took a sip from her full-bellied glass. "He couldn't do anything. It was more important to him to protect his secrets and confront the public, only after he had arranged everything with Amorosa."

"I don't think that he is just an opportunist. He was, after all, able to recognize and understand our particular situation."

"That's why he wanted us out of the picture as soon as possible, hmm?" she asked, shaking her head.

"That's what you wanted, wasn't it?"

"Mm-hmm."

"Do you think it was right to inform only the President?" Pano asked thoughtfully. His eyes sparkled darkly, reflecting the glow from the red wine in the low evening light.

"You mean, that we informed only her of Xinth's death?" The pictures of the dead Builder appeared in her mind, and she sensed an unpleasant tug in her stomach. She was grateful that it no longer felt like being kicked by a horse.

Pano nodded.

"Yes, it was the right thing to do," she replied. "That's how we found out that the compulsion disappeared as soon as the programmed command had been executed or could no longer be executed."

"But we didn't inform all the other infected people," he said.

"We've chewed through all that enough times already. What should Harris have done? A nationwide speech in VR? 'Oh, by the way, the alien you all wanted to kill out there is now dead. You can all calm down now.' Even though the people in Washington have decided otherwise."

"They decided to use our investigative technique to have the FBI hunt down and imprison all those who were infected," Pano snorted.

"Yes, and extract Xinth's microphage from my body and study it to fabricate an antidote. Apparently, the microphage that healed me after my gunshot wound was an even more recent development than the one Karlhammer had included in his lottery in the same year. As I recently heard from the President, the first results have been promising."

Pano suddenly changed the subject. "It's beautiful here, isn't it?" It sounded like a statement of fact and a hopeful question at the same time.

"Yes. I like the quiet," she answered ambiguously.

He took her hand into his and gave it a gentle squeeze. "We won't give that up anymore," he assured her.

No, we won't, she thought. The memory of Dalam's coercive control leading to her murder of Xinth still hurt her after all these years, but she had learned to accept that control was an illusion, and perhaps fantasy was not so bad —otherwise, she might never have given up her independence for a relationship with Pano. She looked at his right leg, which ended in an old-fashioned metal prosthesis below his knee-length pants. People who were even more stubborn than she was had always fascinated her.

"The new UN government was sworn in today. Have you seen the news?" he asked quietly, taking a sip from his glass.

"Yes, I saw it in my feed. It's hard to believe that the prospect of marvelous technological advances was the one thing able to finally unify the world under one flag."

"And in just seven years!" Pano added, shaking his head.

Agatha thought of the extensive domed buildings in

Siberia that the world community had built for the descendants of Xinth and Hortat. The first batch of embryos had already grown up there and they lived under the four domes in sealed atmospheres. They were cared for and raised by both the Geth Being and the contact staff selected by the UN and Human Foundation, something she somehow could not really imagine.

It had worked so far, and the world seemed to like playing midwife to a newly established Builder civilization, notably because in return, it was constantly receiving new technologies released by the advisory board of the Human Foundation appointed by the United Nations. She did not believe that Karlhammer and Amorosa had completely relinquished the reins, but whatever their agenda was, it seemed to work, and no one was asking questions.

"Have you seen the live feed from Jupiter's moon Ganymede?" Pano asked after a long moment of pleasant silence. "The first UN flag beyond Mars and Earth was hoisted by Heinrich Marks."

Agatha nodded into the quiet whisper of the breeze that supplied them with fresh mountain air. "Yes, I've seen that too. Since there is often good news on the feeds, it is actually fun to watch." She paused and leaned her head against his shoulder. "I'm also old, so I'm constantly looking at the news, or have you already forgotten?"

"Do you think it will all work out?" he asked wistfully, swirling the wine glass in his free hand.

"I don't know," she admitted, watching the sun set behind the mountain crest. Its last rays did not appear pale or dying, but powerful and decidedly cheerful. "But I think that together we've achieved one of the best possible starts for coping with what is, in effect, the project of the century. Besides, I can't shake the feeling that this Amorosa had an amazingly precise idea of what her goals were when she returned, and which path she wanted to take. She's clearly the type who doesn't like to rely on chance, and she seems quite optimistic in all her interviews."

"Have you thought about the offer the CTD made you?"

Agatha thought of the letter from the new Governor of the United States—which was now a kind of federal state of the UN—and grimaced as she gazed into the twilight. "No— I mean, yes I've thought about it, and my answer will be, 'No.' We contributed absolutely nothing toward the solution of the most important case of our careers, except to kill the target we were supposed to protect, whether under coercion or not. I think we'd better not get involved in future problems so as not to make them any worse."

Agatha replaced her grim face with a smiling one, which she found surprisingly easy after having spent a lot of time with herself and a therapist in the last few years. "We just talked about celebrating the end of the day. I think we deserve it now, and I wouldn't be able to bear working with a partner like you anyway."

"How about if you 'bear' me inside?" he asked teasingly, and she emptied her wine in one swallow.

Thus they exchanged the onset of darkness for the warm light of their fireplace, and the warm comfort of their togetherness.

AFTERWORD

I hope you liked the story of Xinth and Hortat. Book 3 will be available by May 20. Every new story is also a journey into the unknown for me, and every journey is more fun if you can experience it with others. With this in mind, I thank you for sharing the adventure. If you liked this book, it would be great if you would take the time to leave a short review on Amazon. This is the best way to support me as an independent author.

Visit www.joshuatcalvert.com to subscribe to my newsletter, to be informed of all upcoming releases!

Did you notice any errors or plot holes? Would you like to contact me with criticism or feedback—positive or negative? I am happy to answer every single e-mail! Please write to me at joshuatree@www.joshuatcalvert.com

Yours sincerely, Joshua T. Calvert   April 2021, La Palma

CHARACTER INDEX

Alberto (Angulo Camacho): Treasure diver and engineer on the *Ocean's Bitch.*

Alhy, Romain: Captain of the *Ocean's Bitch.*

Amorosa, Filio: Member and sole survivor of the first Mars mission, *Mars One*, and crewmember on the *Ocean's Bitch.*

Bateman, Jonathan: Operator of the Human Foundation, stationed in the pyramid in Antarctica.

Bergensen, Thomas: Treasure diver aboard the *Ocean's Bitch.*

Bordotta, Marcello: Member of the *Mars Two* mission, xenobiologist.

Brewster, Hannah: Laboratory assistant in forensics at CTD.

Brown, Barbara: Wife of Bob Brown.

Brown, Bob: Republican U.S. Senator.

Brown, Fred: Captain of the security forces in the Antarctic pyramid.

Burton, Audrey: Member of the *Mars Two* mission, engineer.

Chapati, Putram: Member of the *Mars Two* mission, botanist.

Cortez, Silvia: Secretary of Homeland Security of the United States.

Dalam, Workai: legendary treasure diver, lost.

Danatouth, Andrew: U.S. Navy lieutenant, Navy SEAL member.

Danes, Roger: U.S. Senator, member of the Republican Party. A pronounced critic of the Human Foundation.

Degeunes, Liza: Secretary to Jenning Miller.

Devenworth, Agatha: Special agent at the Counter-Terrorist Directive (CTD), United States citizen.

Dong Won, Jackie: Pilot in the service of the Human Foundation.

Dornwald, Mikwart: "The man in the black suit."

(The) Enemy: Alien entity hypothesized by the Sons of Terra terrorist organization to be secretly pulling the strings of world affairs, and who has infiltrated national institutions worldwide.

Engels, Jakob: Hired bodyguard for Filio Amorosa.

Gould, Peter: Former CFO of the Human Foundation.

Greulich, Alexander: Chancellor of the Federal Republic of Germany.

Greynert, Markus: Major in the Security Forces of the Antarctic Brigade of the Human Foundation.

Harris, Elisabeth: President of the United States.

Hofer, Pano: Capitano in the Italian police, assigned to Europol. Comes from South Tyrol.

Hortat: Captain and Builder who became *The Enemy*.

Hue Tao Xing: Member of the *Mars Two* mission, medical doctor.

Jackson, Dan: Professor of Archaeology, Anthropology and Linguistics.

Javier, Dr. Camarro: Maintenance engineer on the *Mars One* mission. Presumed killed in the crash of 2040.

Johnson, Betty: Secretary to Jenning Miller.

Jones, Hugh: Director of SETEF (Space Exploration Training and Evaluation Facility) in Nevada.

Kalashnikov, Tatyana: Member of the *Mars Two* mission, chemist.

Karlhammer, Luther: South African engineer, inventor and technocrat, head of the Human Foundation.

Knowles, Timothy: Pilot of the *Mars One* mission. Presumed killed in the *Mars One* disaster of 2040.

Longchamps, Michel: Commander of the *Mars Two* mission.

Marcello (Bonimba): Receptionist at Cape House Green Hostel in Cape Town.

Marks, Heinrich: Geophysicist on the first Mars mission, *Mars One*. Presumed killed in the crash of 2040.

Matthews, Sasha: CTD agent.

Meinhard, Geronnimus, Dr.: senior physician in the Antarctic pyramid.

Miller, Jenning: Director of the Counter-Terrorist Directive (CTD).

Mombatu, Mitchu: Secretary-General of the United Nations.

Moosbech, Petr: Agent of the South African intelligence service.

Morhaine, Cassidy, Dr.: Test leader of Level T in the Antarctic pyramid, and co-pilot of the transport module. Physicist and chemist.

Morris, Laura: Assistant to Hugh Jones, Director of SETEF.

Nikitu, Mayuka: Japanese envoy to the United Nations.

Patchuvi, Mitra: Indian archaeologist and professor at the University of Delhi.

Phelps, Montgomery: President of the United States of America.

Pickert, Dana: Student at the Maximilian University of Munich.

Richter, Nicole: Former member of *Mars Two*, removed from the mission.

Rietenbach, Manfred: Director-General of ESA (the European Space Agency).

Ross, James: Doctor of Archaeology, assistant to Prof. Patchuvi.

Sarandon, Jane: Treasure diver and first officer on the *Ocean's Bitch.*

Shapiro, Warren: Deputy director of the CTD (Counter-Terrorist Directive).

Shoke, Solly: Former receptionist at Cape House Green Hostel in Cape Town.

Spärling, Regina: Secretary to ESA Director-General Manfred Rietenbach.

Strickland, Ellen, Dr.: Head of Research of the *Mars One* mission, presumed killed in the crash of 2040.

Sue Tse: Lieutenant in the Security Forces of the Antarctic Brigade of the Human Foundation.

Tombatu, Aluwi: Agent of the South African Secret Service.

Treuwald, Markus: Employee of the mercenary company B12.

Vlachenko, Dimitry: "Dima," Commander of the *Mars One* mission, *Mars One*, presumed killed in the crash of 2040.

Wayan, Cho: Assistant to Luther Karlhammer.

Wittman, James: Member of the *Mars Two* mission, geophysicist.

Xinth: Builder.

GLOSSARY

Accelerator mass spectrometry: Age determination of fossils and archaeological finds using a particle accelerator.

Adrenaline: Hormone released in response to stress, responsible for "fight or flight" response, a.k.a. epinephrine.

Analgesic: Painkiller.

Andesite: A volcanic rock

Antarctic Treaty: An international agreement that stipulates that uninhabited Antarctica between 60- and 90-degrees south latitude is reserved exclusively for peaceful use, especially for scientific research.

AR glasses: Augmented Reality Glasses.

AR harness: Exoskeleton that, in combination with Augmented Reality, can be used to perform work on an object remotely through a robot receiving the signals from the harness.

B12: Mercenary company with headquarters in Unterhaching, Germany.

Basalt: Form of igneous volcanic rock.

BCD: Buoyancy Control Device. Wearable buoyancy compensator, i.e. a vest that a diver can inflate or deflate with buoyant gas at the touch of a button.

Bio Suit: see MMSS.

Black Aces: Elite brigades of the mercenary group B12.

BND: Bundesnachrichtendienst, Federal Intelligence Service. German foreign intelligence service.

Breathing Earth One: System of algae "carpets" constructed by the Human Foundation and located in the Pacific Ocean to filter CO_2 out of the atmosphere and convert it into oxygen.

Breathing Earth Two: System of algae "carpets" constructed by the Human Foundation and located in the Atlantic Ocean to filter CO_2 out of the atmosphere and convert it into oxygen.

C-2 Moonhopper: Business helicopter of Northrop Grumman's deluxe line.

C-220 Albatross: Military turboprop transport aircraft designed for heavy cargo or moving large troop contingents.

Cape House Green: Hostel in Cape Town, South Africa.

Chin-Feng Battery: Chinese air defense missile battery.

Clean Ocean Project: Human Foundation project designed to remove plastic waste from the oceans.

Cleaning robots: Robot that independently performs cleaning work indoors and outdoors.

Cortisol: Hormone released in response to anxiety/stress, affects blood pressure, metabolism, and other body functions. Sustained high levels are harmful.

C-reactive Protein: Inflammatory blood factor; high levels indicate inflammation from infection, injury, or some types of health conditions.

CTD: Counter-Terrorist Directive. Intelligence unit falling under the authority of the United States Department of Homeland Security.

Dart rifle: Rifle that shoots stun arrows.

Data glasses: Augmented Reality glasses with audio earbuds and a completely enclosed visual area.

Desertec: Solar project in the northwestern Sahara operated in collaboration between the EU and the Maghreb states.

Perfuser: Device for transporting substances between two membranes without an injection needle. Medical use.

Drone ship: Autonomous transport craft that automatically collects algae from sweeper ships and adds them to the algae carpets in the Pacific and the Atlantic.

Earthling: Colloquial name for a supporter of the Human Foundation and participant in the lottery system.

EDI: Ship's AI on the *Mars One*.

Emergency capsule: Rescue capsule on a spaceship.

ESA: European Space Agency, the space agency of the European Union.

Evac capsule: See emergency capsule.

FHR Reactor: Fluoride-salt-cooled High-temperature Reactor. A new liquid salt reactor (nuclear) concept that combines spherical graphite fuel elements, liquid salt as a coolant, safety systems consisting of sodium-cooled fast reactors, and the Brayton circuit process.

Fission cutter: Mono-bonded blade made of a single-molecule layer, capable of cutting even the hardest materials.

Flettner Rotor: A rotating cylinder exposed to an airflow that generates propulsive force perpendicular to the airflow utilizing the Magnus effect. It is the basis of a zero-emissions propulsion system first patented and used as a ship propulsion system by Anton Flettner.

Furious Fifties: Region of the Antarctic Circumpolar Current (West Wind Drift) between 50 and 60° S latitude. Characterized by violent storms.

G-8: Gulfstream VIII, a business jet produced by Gulfstream Aerospace.

Gloucester: British-registered scrapper ship.

GMC E-Falcon: Electric SUV made by U.S. car manufacturer GMC.

Iridium: A chemical element, precious metal and a metal belonging to the platinum group. Known to be the most corrosion-resistant element.

Jet: A handheld device with a propeller system used by divers to move more quickly through the water.

Joint Chiefs of Staff: Military Chiefs of Staff for the four armed services of the United States (Army, Navy, Air Force and Marines).

Leucocytes: White blood cells, essential to the human immune system.

Maglock: Locking system that uses polarized magnets for closing and opening.

Maglocksmith: Device for used for picking maglocks.

McMurdo: Antarctic research station first operated by the United States (and later the Human Foundation).

Medical cuff: Autonomous medical device that can independently control analyses and medication infusion.

Membrane perfuser: See Perfuser.

Microphage: Immune cells that can absorb and transport foreign substances (e.g. bacteria). They can also envelop and devour foreign objects.

MMR 3: Mars Mission Reconnaissance 3. The third robotic mission to Mars sent to prepare for the human-crewed landings.

MMSS: Maximum Mobility Space Suit. Flexible spacesuit that works via contact pressure.

Muon detector: Detector system that uses cosmic rays to detect and locate subterranean cavities.

Muon tomography: A method for three-dimensional imaging of large-volume objects using muons found in cosmic rays.

Nanonic: Used to describe substances at the nano level manufactured by nanites.

NASA: National Aeronautics and Space Administration, the space agency of the United States of America.

National Intelligence Service: The South African domestic intelligence service.

Neuro T5: Liquid nerve venom that strongly sedates its victims.

Ocean's Bitch: Old scrapper ship under the command of Romain Alhy.

Okamalé: A ship belonging to the Coast Guard of the Maldive Islands.

Paleocene: Geological epoch of the Earth that began around 66 million years ago and ended about 56 million years ago.

Paleogene: A geological epoch of the Earth, lasting from approximately 66 million years ago until the start of the Neogene approximately 23.03 million years ago.

Pleistocene: Geological epoch of the Earth that began around 2.588 million years ago and ended about 12,000 years ago with the dawn of the modern era.

Polymer: Materials made of chained macromolecules.

Programmable foam: Nanonic foam, used for sealing holes (especially in spacesuits), automatically hardens but remains flexible.

Project Blue Hole: Research project exploring the mysterious "blue hole" in Antarctica, the location where the

Antarctic ice sheet exhibited the phenomenon of melting from the inside out.

Project Globe: Human Foundation project to use microwaves to transmit energy from space-based solar power systems to earth.

Project Heritage: A top-secret Human Foundation project.

Pyramid Mountain: A 2,800-meter-high mountain in Antarctica, roughly pyramid-shaped.

Radionuclide battery (also radioisotope thermoelectric generator = RTG): Converts thermal energy from the spontaneous core decay of a radionuclide into electrical energy.

Regolith: Covering layer of loose material on top of an underlying source material, which formed on rocky planets in the solar system as the result of various geological processes.

Roaring Forties: Region of the Antarctic Circumpolar Current (West Wind Drift) between 40 and 50° S latitude. Characterized by violent storms.

Roskosmos: Space Agency of the Russian Federation.

RTG: See Radionuclide battery.

Ruthenium: A silver-white, hard and brittle platinum metal.

Scrapper: Term denoting a treasure hunter searching for wreckage from *Mars One* in the Indian Ocean.

Seal patch: Self-adhesive patch for sealing cracks and tears in spacesuits. Can be used to cover wounds.

Self-driving software: Artificial intelligence responsible for the control and safety of a vehicle, and capable of autonomous action.

SETEF: Space Exploration Training and Evaluation Facility. Astronaut training center located north of Reno, Nevada, in the United States.

Sharkskin: Skintight neoprene suit worn to protect divers from minor injuries.

Solar Genesis: Human Foundation project in its planning phase to use giant solar sails in near-Earth orbit to supply the Earth with clean energy.

Sons of Terra: A terrorist organization the goals of which include warning humanity against an alien presence known as The Enemy, which they claim has taken control of the world powers.

Space Dream: Lottery operated by the Human Foundation promising the winner a place on a future Mars mission.

Space Walker Suit: Plastic spacesuit for Mars, developed by the Human Foundation.

Sweeper: Huge autonomous ship sweeping the world's oceans to collect plastic waste, which it then breaks down into carbon dioxide and hydrogen.

Thrombocytes: The smallest blood cells, responsible for blood clotting.

Traffic control system: AI-controlled road network connected to GPS satellites to control autonomous drive cars.

Transducer net: A mesh of electrodes that can be worn on the head and which measures and interprets brain waves to produce speech output through a computer system.

TSA: Transportation Security Administration. The American federal agency tasked with the security of the transportation sector.

Universal connector: The universal interface architecture that replaced the USB (Universal Serial Bus) system.

USS Barack Obama: Gerald R. Ford-class aircraft carrier of the U.S. Navy.

Volkswagen E: The best-selling electric car in the world.

VR Compartment: A distinct space with VR glasses, VR suit with feedback sensors, and a multidimensional treadmill to completely immerse a person in virtual reality.

X-ray fluorescence analysis: A method of material analysis based on X-ray fluorescence. It is one of the most commonly used methods for determining the qualitative and quantitative composition of a sample.

Builders:

Aartan butterfly: Primeval butterfly in the time of the Builders.

Antuan: Temple capital of the Builders.

Astrogator: Operator on a Builder spaceship. Responsible for the energy nodes and drive systems as well as all active external systems.

Deka: Time unit of the Builders.

Follicle: Inflammatory reaction medium for incubation processes.

Geth: Builders' Name for the pyramid in Antarctica.

Goldan: Mars.

Controller: Operator on a Builder spaceship. Responsible for the interior of the ship.

Machine Weaver: Engineer of the Builders.

Mammarian: Highly regarded caste of Builders who take care of the offspring.

Monnbat: Whale-like giant mammal that dominated the oceans in the era of the Builders.

Navigator: Ship navigator on a Builder spaceship.

Pendum: Time unit of the Builders.

Photon manipulators: Light sources of the Builders, which consist of artificial electromagnetic manipulators and do not have a physically visible source.

Plasma rod: Welding torch.

Quantum singer: Quantum researcher of the Builders.

Quantum mirror: Portal capable of transporting to an alternate reality.

Sleep coffin: Sleeping cabin of the Builders, which is equipped with all life support systems.

Tangir: Southern continent as it was 66 million BC.

Technolog: Builder researchers.

Editing: Steven and Marcia Kwiecinski

English translation: Duane March

Cover: Cakamura Designs

First edition: 2021

Joshua Tree Limited

Skoutari 25, App. 73

8560 Peyia

Cyprus

www.joshuatcalvert.com

joshua@joshuatcalvert.com

Made in the USA
Middletown, DE
13 February 2024

49675924R00274